TWO ACTION-PACKED WESTERNS BY LEWIS B. PATTEN FOR ONE LOW PRICE!

RIFLES OF REVENGE

Mart came from behind the cedars and saw the rider dismounting, gun in hand. Even at this distance, Mart could see the man's black bushy beard. He flung his rifle to his shoulder, looped his reins around the saddle horn and held the dangling end with one knee. He steadied his aim as best he could on the running horse and squeezed the trigger.

Then he saw a second man come sliding down the hill, and a third sitting his mount on a high point, unmoving and watching. By this time he was but a short hundred yards away. His frantic mind shouted, "If you never shot straight before, shoot straight now!"

There was only one thing that mattered—death! And only one man could win....

RED RUNS THE RIVER

Sessions finished the last of the meat. He already felt stronger. He was already thinking about tomorrow, about going after the man with the broken arm.

Reaching his rifle pit, he slid into it, lay back helplessly and closed his eyes. He was sweating heavily and breathing hard. His body seemed to be one continuous area of pain.

He kept thinking that tomorrow, with luck, he would find and kill the man with the broken arm. He would, at least, find out who he was. Then he would have the names of all three of his family's murderers. Afterward, all that would remain would be to kill them, one by one.

RIFLES OF REVENGE/ RED RUNS THE RIVER

LEWIS B. PATTEN

LEISURE BOOKS **L** **NEW YORK CITY**

A LEISURE BOOK®

April 1994

Published by special arrangement with Golden West Literary Agency.

Dorchester Publishing Co., Inc.
276 Fifth Avenue
New York, NY 10001

RIFLES OF REVENGE

Chapter 1

Fall came to the high country, and night's frosty breath, blowing out of the north, stained the quakie leaves bright yellow, the sarvus orange, and the scrub-oak a rusty ochre. Grass underfoot, long and dry, rustled as the beef herd moved through it, turning at the urging of two riders who had galloped around to head them, and then, still prodded from behind by the bulk of the crew, filing down the long draw toward the rim.

Twelve hundred steers, mostly triple-wintered, but with a few four-year-olds among them. There was solid satisfaction for Martin Joliffe in watching them file past, for this was what every hand on Tincup worked toward the whole year through. This was the climax of the year's sweat and toil; this was the end of the beef roundup and the start of the drive to the railroad.

Tincup's foreman, Floyd Timmons, twitched the reins of his horse and rode past Mart, saying, "I'll take a swing down on the point and make sure there ain't no more shaded up in the spruces above the rim."

Mart shook his head. Abruptly the satisfaction of

the moment was gone from his pale eyes, and there lurked instead in their depths plain shame, and guilt that did not escape Timmons' notice.

"No," he said. "I'll go with you. I've stayed off that point all summer because I didn't want to remember what was down there at the bottom of it. A man has got to face things sometime." He swung away and kicked his horse into a swift trot. Timm took off his dusty black hat and ran a reflective hand across his damp hair. Then he followed.

Mart did not look back. He was thinking how a man got to dreading some things, how when he did, it was time to start facing them. There would be no help for Mart in letting Timm ride the point alone. It was a thing he had to face himself.

All of Tincup's roundup worked toward this point, this finger of high land that marked the southernmost tip of Tincup's vast summer range. They gathered this ridge as they came, pushing the beef before them, dropping behind she-stuff, calves and steers too young to ship. But the trail dropped down through the rim a mile from the ridge's end, and this always left the long point for someone to ride at the very end of the drive.

Timm's offer to ride it had been considerate, Mart realized, even though Timm's thoughts cherished no blame for the thing that had happened here early in the spring.

Mart's own thoughts were where the blame was born. His own mind was the womb where the seed of guilt kept growing.

The trail kept to the ridge's spine, almost to its exact center. If a man looked close, he could still see evidences of the damage four thousand cloven hooves had wrought in the grass roots as they crowded and pounded toward the four-hundred foot drop at the end of the point. The point was like a funnel, narrowing inexorably, so that when you reached its end, there was nothing left, nothing save the drop into empty space.

A vagrant twist of the wind, which at this time of year came almost altogether from the north, lifted up the face of the rim, bringing still the sweet, nauseating odor of decaying flesh. Mart reined his reluctant horse close up against the edge of the drop and looked down, holding the fidgeting and frightened animal still with a ruthless hand.

Timm reined up beside him, also looking down. Sheep made a grayish mass down there, but here and there a carcass picked clean by the vultures had bleached, and now shone pure white in the afternoon sun. A gray cloud hovered over the mass, and Joliffe knew that this cloud was composed of flies. A buzzard, feeding, was but a speck at this distance. Mart's horse kicked over a rock, and after an interminable period, it hit the slide below and startled the vulture, startled an old dog coyote who ran, a lean gray shadow on the sun-washed slide.

Mart could hardly suppress a shudder. Timm, still-faced, said, "Boy, there's no damned use in blaming yourself for this. You've been brooding about it all summer, and you've got to quit it. Raoul gave the order to do it, and if you'll think about it you'll have to admit it was the only thing he could do."

"I know, Timm." He reined around, putting his

back to the ghastly sight and rode along the rim, poking, with but half his mind alert, through the tall spruces that fringed the rim-top.

Timm watched him somberly from behind, and at last wheeled his horse and headed along the rim on the opposite side of the point.

A steer got up in front of Mart and lumbered, crashing, through the timber. Another joined the first. Mart had three ahead of him when he broke from the timber and rode down the draw toward the cattle that had bunched and now awaited their turn on the narrow trail.

He let them go, and halted, fishing a sack of tobacco from his vest pocket. He shaped a cigarette absently and touched a match to its end. Timm came from the opposite side of the ridge with a single steer, pushed it into the bunch and then rode up beside Mart.

Timm asked roughly, "What would have been a better way to handle Robineau?"

Mart shrugged. He shouldn't let Robineau's sheep bother him this way. He had told himself this a thousand times, but there was a vast gulf between telling and doing. Robineau had asked for what he got. This was Tincup grass, had been so since the Ute nation had surrendered it to the whites.

"It's free range, aint't it?" Robineau had asked defiantly.

"Free?" Mart had laughed without amusement. "Hold your sheep on it and you'll find out it ain't quite free. It's Tincup grass because Tincup claimed it when no one else wanted it, because Tincup has held it since and because we'll keep on holding it."

It was some consolation to Mart to recall that he had not proceeded against Robineau at once. He had warned the man repeatedly, and had only acted when Floyd Timmons brought him word that half the sheepmen in Eastern Utah were waiting, waiting only to see if Robineau would make his grab stick.

Well, he hadn't made it stick. His sheep lay rotting at the foot of the rim. And the others had found their summer grass elsewhere. It could have been worse. Men could have been killed. Men would have been killed, but for the decisive way Mart had moved, throwing Tincup's entire crew against the sheepmen so that a fight would have been suicide.

But he couldn't forget the undulating mass of gray, woolly backs, crowding, pushing, bleating—moving like a tide to the end of the point—disappearing. He couldn't forget the mind sickness that obsessed him for a week afterward, that still obsessed him at times. He couldn't forget the way Robineau had looked—not angry, not even hating—just beaten, thoroughly beaten.

Timm said sharply, "Marty! You got to forget it. If you had refused, Raoul would have made me do it. And if it hadn't been done, you know as well as I do that it would be sheep coming off today instead of cattle."

"No. We'd still have brought cattle off."

Timm's voice rose. "In what kind of shape? Skinny. Poor. You'd be shipping Tincup she-stuff too, because you'd know there wouldn't be feed for them next summer. Tincup would be through as a ranch and you damn well know it!"

Mart shrugged. "I guess you're right." He made

9

himself grin at Timm. The cattle made a long red serpentine column that crawled slowly down the trail. Shadows lengthened. Dust lifted from the cattle's hooves and the shouts of the crew rose in the still air, sharp and clear. Dusk came on, and the last of the steers lumbered off onto the trail. Mart and Timm, and the rest of Tincup's crew, fell in behind.

John Robineau sat in his bare hotel room three hundred miles to eastward and stared out the window at the same gray dusk. His sheep were gone, the fruit of a lifetime's work—all for one mistake, all because he had guessed he could make a steal of Tincup's grass stick, and because he had been wrong.

He fondled the heavy Colt's navy revolver in his lap. Fondled it and lost his courage as he had lost it so many times before. He saw Lucille coming down the street, small and pretty and red-haired, coming from work.

Perhaps it was the droop in her shoulders that gave him the courage he needed. Perhaps it was the sudden realization that he could never be more than he was now, an old man, a tired one, a beaten one. He could never be more than a drag on his daughter, who must work twice as hard to feed two as she would to feed one.

Before he could change his mind, before he could lose his courage, he thrust the muzzle of the Colt into his mouth, thumbed back the hammer and pulled the trigger.

Lucille heard the shot as she entered the shabby lobby. At once her weariness was gone, replaced by an intensification of the fear she had been feeling for

10

weeks. With no real surprise, she saw him as she came into the room, slumped on the floor.

Now it was shock that she felt, and the empty, terrible sense of loss. Later tonight, she would grieve, but before morning she would begin to hate—hate the man, the ranch, the greed that was responsible for this. Later she would hate, and in the still, cold hours of dawn would begin to plan her vengeance, the bitter gall of vengeance.

On Thursday evening, the herd arrived outside the town of Cedar City, slow-moving, patiently plodding. There, Mart reined aside. Timm, stocky and graying, rode over beside him to say, "Go on, Mart," grinning with cheerful derision. "You can't keep a girl like Rose waiting. I'll see that the cattle get to the pens all right. I'll make the arrangements to load them in the morning. Go on."

"All right, Timm." Mart Joliffe returned the foreman's grin. Dust caked his face, turning it a peculiar, grayish hue, hiding its healthy tan. His eyes were rimmed with mud where moisture from the eyes had mingled with dust. His teeth were white, big and solid like all the rest of him.

Tincup's beef roundup had taken six hard and grueling weeks. The strain of roundup, where Joliffe would drive no man harder than he drove himself, showed in the bone-weary sag of his wide shoulders, in the oddly inert way he sat his saddle.

But anticipation danced now in his pale blue eyes, and his wide mouth stretched out and smiled.

To Mart Joliffe, life was a series of tasks, each entirely separate from the others. When one was done, he put it behind him and promptly forgot it. Roundup, the year's most satisfying task, he now relegated to the past along with other things entirely finished, and turned his glance toward the town, lying squat and ugly on the banks of the Little Snake River.

His horse broke into a trot as it entered Main's dusty length, but Joliffe reined up short before Stoddard's saloon, still grinning a little, thinking, "Hell, she can wait until I wash the dust out of my throat."

He was tall, tall and solid—big-boned. He banged open the saloon door and stood for a moment looking into the gloom, trying to accustom his eyes to this after the glare of autumn sunlight outside.

Pete Stoddard, behind the bar, said to someone patiently, "Go lead him over here to the bar. He's dazzled by all that gold on the hoof he's been driving ahead of him for the past six weeks."

Mart's grin widened. He walked, loosely relaxed, across the sawdust floor to the bar. He said, "I think I'll sleep a week." He looked at Pete for a minute, and finally finished, "Well, maybe I'll wait till tomorrow to start."

Stoddard chuckled. Mart tipped the brown bottle and poured himself half a tumbler of its amber content. He downed the first one quickly, feeling the burn of the whisky against his throat, raw from dust and shouting. Talk murmured through the saloon, working men's idle talk, talk about horses and weather, grass and hunting. Mart poured his second drink thoughtfully, letting the warmth of the first course through his body.

Pete Stoddard, tall, hollow-chested and thin, put

his elbows on the bar before Mart and said, "By golly Mart, I'll sell more whisky tonight than I have for six weeks. But I wonder if I ain't gettin' too old for that much excitement."

Mart grinned at him. "I'll buy until ten o'clock. I'll pay for the damage, too. Six weeks is a long time."

"They know you'll pay the damage. Maybe that's why there never is very much."

Mart tossed off his second. Far up the canyon to eastward, a locomotive wailed, and Stoddard automatically dragged his heavy silver watch from his pocket and looked at it to check the time.

Mart tossed a dollar on the bar and turned away. A warm glow was in him from the whisky, and a lift in his spirits, a lift that made him forget some of his aching tiredness. As he put his hand on the door handle, someone gave it a push from outside, and Mart stepped back instinctively.

Odd, this feeling—this feeling of almost physical revulsion, as Howie Frye stepped into the saloon, laid sour, mocking eyes upon him. Howie's thin, pale lips drew away from his yellowed teeth. He made a mock bow. "The cattle king. The great man. The sheepslayer."

Mart's great hands fisted, and Frye laughed softly, triumphantly. His face was seamed and sharp, his eyes as cold as the Little Snake in February. Frye muttered, "Go ahead Marty. Hit me. I'm half your size so that ought to be about right. You can lick me easy, almost as easy as you licked Robineau."

The veins in Mart's forehead bulged. Trust this one to find his only sore spot and probe it constantly with his cruel, mocking barbs. Frye stood blocking

13

the door, his spindly legs spraddled out, his thumbs hooked in his belt. Mart, fighting for control, tried to nudge past him, thus giving Frye fresh ammunition.

"The great man's in a hurry," he said, facing the bar and talking to Stoddard and to the others. Then he swung back to Mart, whining, "You don't have to shove us common folks out of your way, Marty. We'll move aside for you." He made a ceremony of stepping aside, then saying, "Going to see Rose, huh? In a hurry?" His voice rose, assuming a violence that was strangely akin to madness. "Damn you, Mart! Someday, king or not, I'm going to kill you! You hear that? I'm going to kill you! But I want to see you in the gutter first. I want to see you broke—and hungry—and down in the dirt in front of your throne!"

Mart spoke between clenched teeth, "Shut up, Frye. Shut up." His hands were fisted again, in spite of his efforts at control. He looked wildly at the sun-washed street—near, yet so damned far. Because he couldn't run, and he couldn't fight. He had to stand and take Howie Frye's abuse.

"Go on! Go on! Rose is waiting for you—with open arms. She saw the herd at the edge of town from her hotel window."

Mart looked at Howie, was astonished to see that the man was shaking. He stepped past Frye and into the street. Wildness and violence flared in his eyes. His jaw was hard-set, his teeth clenched.

If Howie had not been Rose's father, Mart would have said his trouble was jealousy. He could think of no injury Frye had suffered at the hands of either Mart or Tincup. Was it simple jealousy because of

14

Tincup, and the wealth that flowed from it? Or had Howie some secret grudge against Raoul? Mart shrugged.

He guessed that whoever had the wealth, the power, must always be subject to the violent hates of people like Howie Frye. Yet it never ceased to be a source of wonderment to him that a girl as sweet and beautiful as was Rose, could be the offspring of a man like Howie, who was bitter, vicious, sour and vindictive.

The meeting with Howie Frye, a task completed, was harder for Mart to put behind him than most. Yet if he had learned nothing else from Raoul Joliffe, he had learned this: that worry over things that cannot be changed drove more men to their graves than any other single cause.

Frye was a recurring task, an unpleasantness every time he saw the man. And Frye had somehow divined the guilt that tortured Mart over the Robineau sheep. Recalling that again now, Mart thought, "Timm is right. What else could I have done? Killed Robineau? Killed half a dozen of his herders? Would that have been any better?"

He shook his head savagely. For most of his twenty-six years he had gone with satisfaction from one task to another, finishing them and promptly forgetting them. Spring this year had changed all that. Now he seemed no longer able to forget the things that were past. It was almost as though some instinct told him the Robineau affair was not finished. It was almost as though some inner cautiousness warned him that Howie Frye's vitriolic hatred could not be lightly dismissed.

Yet what could Robineau do to hurt him? What could Howie do? Resolutely he pushed his black uneasiness to the back of his mind and stepped along the walk toward the hotel.

Chapter 2

Rose Frye stood at her hotel window, a bay window jutting conveniently into the street to give her an excellent view of both sides of Main along its entire length. She stared uneasily down into it now, and saw Howie standing between two buildings across from Stoddards'.

She saw Mart ride in from the edge of town, thinned a little perhaps from the rigors of roundup, tired, dirty, slumping slightly in his saddle. But her heart quickened at the sight of him. She did not begrudge him the lift of a drink or two, for she knew that he would not stay long.

She was turning from the window, unconsciously smoothing her hair, when she saw Howie detach himself from his place of concealment and cross the street toward the saloon.

Now the reason for her vague uneasiness became apparent to her, for it increased sharply at Howie's seemingly harmless move. Rose Frye knew Howie; she had grown up as his daughter. She knew his deviousness, knew as well that none of his actions were aimless. She knew that he hated Mart with vicious intensity, and even knew why.

17

But how could she tell Mart the reason for Howie's hatred? Even yet it seemed incomprehensible to Rose; even now it seemed like a terrible nightmare, something which had not really happened, which could not really happen.

And she was beginning to feel afraid, afraid of the man she had called "father" as long as she could remember. Mart wanted to marry her, and tonight, perhaps, would demand that she answer him one way or the other.

How would she answer? Rose did not know. She saw Mart step out of Stoddard's and knew instantly that Howie had been baiting him. Her smooth face colored with anger. Howie knew the advantage his small stature and his position as Rose's father gave him. He knew it and he never failed to take advantage of it. Mart would not fight back, being what he was. Pride stirred in Rose, pride in Mart, and all of the old yearning came back to her, the yearning that had lived in her heart since she was twelve, skinny and pig-tailed, peeking through the hedge at Mart as he passed on his way to school.

For she had loved him since she was twelve, had lived with the terrible knowledge that he did not return her love, might never return it. She had lain awake so many nights, praying, "Oh God, let me grow up faster. Keep him for me until I'm big enough for him."

Now she had him. He lifted his tired and dusty face to her window, and a smile flashed across it, a wide-mouthed, open smile that swept the weariness, the anger, the discouragement from his face as though by magic. Rose waved back, returned his smile, and

18

turned toward the door to wait for the sound of his eager pounding feet on the stairs.

She had him, and loving him, was afraid to keep him. Her answer tonight, if it must be the final one, would be no. It had to be no. For if Rose married Mart, Howie would kill him. Howie had promised her that, and the concentrated intensity of his promise had made her believe.

"Tell Mart the whole story," her heart cried out, "and if he won't believe it, tell Joe Herdic." But she knew this was only the frantic seeking of her mind for escape from an intolerable predicament. What could Mart do? Frye had done nothing but make a threat. Mart's hands would be tied until Howie made his move. Then it would be too late. Then it would be a case for Joe Herdic, the sheriff. No, there was no way out. Howie had known there would be no way out. That was why he had been so sure.

All the way down the street, Mart Joliffe nodded right and left at each man who spoke to him, although he could not muster his usual cheerful grin. The train puffed noisily into the yellow frame station and began to discharge its passengers and freight while a stream of steam idly hissed beneath it.

Mart looked up at Rose Frye's second story window in the front of the hotel, and raised a hand when he saw her standing there. He grinned at the clerk behind the desk and mounted the steps two at a time, taking the familiar turn that put him directly before Rose's door.

The door flung open, and Rose stood waiting, wearing her familiar, warm, full-lipped smile for him. He kicked the door shut behind him and wrapped his arms around her, roughly, hungrily.

The kiss was long, yet Rose's kisses never satisfied him. They only set up a consuming, flaming desire for more. It was Rose who recognized this hunger, who knew it could not forever be put off, and pushed him gently but insistently away. "You smell like a thousand white-faced steers, a dozen horses, and man-sweat. You need a bath." Her voice was shaky, and she moved against a table and leaned there so that he would not see the trembling in her knees.

"Is that any way to greet a man after he's been gone six weeks?"

His eyes mocked her and she could not help laughing. "You know I don't care. You could crawl out of a mud hole and wrap your arms around me."

"I'll try it sometime." He stared down at her, turning strangely sombre, wishing he had not run into Howie Frye at the saloon. Howie had a way of upsetting him, of spoiling his good, reckless, happy moods. He said, "Rose, it's time we did something about you and me. It's time for you to stop letting things drift and marry me."

A look of sharp unhappiness crossed Rose's face. She crossed the room and settled herself nervously on a straight-backed chair.

She was a tall girl, brown-eyed, with gleaming, midnight hair. Her skin was like flawless ivory. She was beautiful, with the glowing, satin-skinned beauty of a wild mare. She gave the same impression of wildness. She was a bird that could be caught briefly, but not held. She poised now on her straight-backed chair as though it were but a brief resting place before she again took flight. Mart felt the uneasiness crawling through his body, felt a new touch of fear. He knew in that instant what her answer would be. He knew but he could not understand.

He asked himself, postponing her answer, "What the hell's the matter with Howie? Would he feel better about us if we did get married?"

She shook her head, and her answer was sharply emphatic. "No."

Mart had a new idea, one that had not occurred to him before. "Does he think we ought to be married? Is that what's eating him?"

Her smile was wan. "No. That's not it."

"Then what is it? I'm tired of hearing him kick your name around the saloon. I'm tired of having my hands tied when he does. I can't hit him; I can't shut him up without hitting him, and he damn well knows it."

Anger raised his voice, anger he could not seem to control. Rose looked at him with her disturbing, soft eyes. "Marty, oh, Marty, let's not fight! I haven't seen you for six weeks. Don't let Howie spoil tonight for us."

"Then say you'll marry me." He was growing stubborn and could not seem to stop. "Raoul's an old man. He needs a woman around to look after him. I'm a young man, and I need a woman too."

"Marty, I don't know. I don't know!" Her voice was a cry.

He came across the room and stood behind her. His hands tipped her chin up and he kissed her, slowly, insistently. "Rose, damn it, aren't you sure?"

21

She was pale, serious, her eyes wide and still. Mart straightened, briefly cuddled her cheek with his hand. "Think about it. I'll go get cleaned up." He strode to the door, tossed her a grin that was less than light-hearted and closed it behind him.

Always before, he had been warmed by the certainty that some day Rose and he would be married. He had planned it in his own mind for this very fall, when the heavy summer work would be done, when he would be able to spend some time with her. When you have gone with a girl for more than a year you get to know her. You don't need her words to tell you how she feels or what her answer will be when you finally put the question to her bluntly and plainly. They had talked about marriage. She had never accepted his teasing proposals, but neither had she refused.

Tonight had been different. Something had changed Rose in the six weeks he had been away on roundup. Another man? Mart scowled. He didn't think so.

He was half afraid to come and say, "Rose, give me your answer," but damn it, they couldn't go on forever as they had been. A man wanted more from a woman than this. He wanted her companionship all the time. He wanted her face across his table from him. He wanted her beside him at night.

Mart tried to tell himself that he had been imagining things, that he had imagined the clear look of refusal in Rose's eyes. It was a little easier to convince himself here in the busy lobby of the hotel, yet deep within him he knew he had made no mistake.

He was in a black mood, scowling, bitter. In this

country, he was a powerful man. Yet he was not powerful enough, he told himself, to take the one thing he wanted most. He was not rich enough to buy it either—he would never be rich enough.

Born to cattle and the open range, these things had become his life. Never pretentious, never loving wealth for its own sake, he had only managed what Raoul handed him to manage. His scowl deepened. His thoughts had returned unwillingly to Robineau, and Robineau's sheep. Why couldn't a man ever forget? Why must he go on forever with this guilty feeling, this feeling that nudged him continually with its unpleasant pressure?

Viciously he kicked the hotel door open and stepped onto the veranda. The sun was down, and over the town lay October's evening haze, compounded of woodsmoke, dust and the earth's light moisture, these things held close to the ground by the weight of chilling upper air. The stores along Main were closing and the street was briefly busy with townspeople walking leisurely toward home. Mart rubbed at the stubble on his face.

A buckboard rattled along Main from the depot, bearing, beside old Sherman Dawson, the driver, a fashionably dressed, tiny red-haired woman. Another time, Mart would have given her beauty a brief, passing glance and no more. Yet tonight, feeling the dissatisfaction Rose had stirred in him, feeling too a puzzled resentment, he searched this woman's face with warm male interest.

He could not have said definitely what it was about her that impressed him the most. Perhaps it was the very obvious fright that widened her large, cool eyes.

23

Perhaps it was the determined set of her red lips. At any rate, almost without thinking, he stepped down off the hotel veranda and offered her his hand to alight upon. She stumbled and fell against him, murmuring, "Oh, I'm sorry. I . . ."

So small was she, so perfect, that he was all at once overpoweringly conscious of the dusty, dirty clothes he wore, of the stench of horse and cattle that must emanate from him. He loosed her hand as soon as he decently could and strode off across the street toward Johanson's barber shop.

He heard the reedy voice of Dawson behind him. "Ma'am, you got met in style. That there's Marty Joliffe. Him an his paw own the biggest ranch in this part of the country." He heard the woman's murmuring voice, but not her words. The voice was pleasant—warm. And Mart was surprised to discover that most of his sourness was gone.

"Wonder who she is," he thought, and then promptly forgot her in the shouting banter of Tincup's crew that surged noisily out to greet him from the open door of the barber shop.

"He's already got the prettiest girl in town. But is that enough for him? Hell no, it ain't. Marty, you leave that redhead for some of us handsome men. She deserves better than you."

Mart grinned, lounged in the door and spoke with a mocking edge to his voice. "I told Stoddard I was buying until ten. I guess you boys don't drink, or you'd be over there."

The clumsy, boisterous rush crowded him out the door, into the street. He watched them go, grinning, then stepped again into the nearly empty barbershop. Johanson, "Swede" as he was called, was a medium-sized, pale man with light, thinning hair and thick-lensed spectacles through which he habitually peered owlishly. Mart asked, "Got a tub out back that ain't in use, Swede?"

Johanson peered at him, then laid aside his razor and led the way to the back room. As backwoods tonsorial parlors went, this was a good one. The back room was partitioned into booths, with a swinging half-door on each. An oak tub and a bench furnished each booth, and in the center of the room was a huge, cast-iron stove, red-hot, upon which two wash boilers sat, filled with steaming water.

Swede pushed Mart into an empty booth and bellowed in a high bodiless voice for his helper.

Mart pulled off his boots. The room was steamy, filled with shouted laughter, ribald comment. Mart began to relax. A bull-shouldered oldster named O'Hara came in tipsily, carrying a bucket in each hand which he dumped unceremoniously into the tub. Mart tested the water with one foot. "Too cold."

O'Hara went back out, grumbling and scowling, and Mart grinned. O'Hara's breath, in these few short moments, had permeated the booth with the sour odor of whiskey. He brought the other bucket of hot water and dumped it in, then standing with fists on hips to survey Mart sourly, said, "Now I suppose it's too damned hot?"

Mart wiggled his toe in the water. "Just right." He fished a dollar from his pocket and handed it to O'Hara. "Go over to Stoddard's and buy yourself a pint." The sourness went out of O'Hara's face and he turned to go. But he halted at the door and waited expectantly. Mart grinned. "Oh, by the way. Stop in at the hotel and get my valise, will you? I had Raoul send me down a change of clothes."

Now O'Hara left. This was a sort of ritual, expected by both and never changing. He could as easily have carried the valise over here himself. He shrugged, shucked out of his clothes and lowered himself gratefully into the scalding water, letting the soreness soak out of his heavily muscled body. He closed his eyes and drowsed, yet upon his relaxed thoughts intruded the two things which always lately seemed to occupy him whenever the pressure of work eased off. Rose Frye, and the slaughter of Robineau's sheep.

Until tonight, thoughts of Rose had always been able to counter-balance the unpleasantness of that other thing. Tonight, those thoughts were as torturing as thoughts of Robineau and his sheep. And tonight, the vaguest sort of uneasiness touched Mart briefly and went away.

Chapter 3

Howie Frye watched Mart leave the saloon, a sardonic, triumphant smile creasing his thin lips. Pete Stoddard said loudly, "Never could understand why the good Lord made so many rattlesnakes. What good are they?"

Howie had heard the train whistle, and now felt a compulsion to get out of here, to get down to the station. Yet pride would not let him leave without his drink, the ostensible reason for his coming here. He strode over to the bar, skinny, his complexion sallow and unhealthy.

He rang a quarter on the bar, and Pete silently slid him glass and bottle. Howie smiled unpleasantly, his aplomb unshattered by Pete's obviously pointed remark. "Never could understand why the Lord made leeches, either. All they do is suck blood out of the common people."

Pete colored, and Howie laughed, "Oh, I don't mean you, Pete. I was thinking about the Joliffes. I read in the paper that Robineau blowed his brains out over at Denver. The Joliffes sucked him dry. So he killed himself."

He tossed off his drink, heard the train wail again

27

as it entered the town's outskirts. Stoddard scowled. "What would you have done, if it had been up to you—met Robineau with open arms? You know damned good and well that if they'd let him stay, their whole range would have been loaded with sheep before the end of the summer. I say they done right, by God. At least Marty rigged it so nobody got killed."

"You figger Robineau would have killed himself anyway?"

"Hell, that ain't Marty's fault. He had his chance to get off Tincup grass. He had more chances than I'd of given him."

Howie sneered. "I'd expect you to stick up for Tincup. You'd starve to death if it wasn't for Tincup."

Pete scowled viciously, and clenched his hands. "I wouldn't starve without you. Drink up and get out of here. I don't give a damn if you never come back."

Frye laughed, but he downed his whisky, wiped his mouth with the back of his hand and turned toward the door. A lot of men thought being small was a disadvantage. Howie had discovered just the opposite. He got away with a thousand things he could never get away with if he were larger.

With a challenging grin he crossed the saloon and stepped out on the walk.

He had been meeting every train for a week now, covering the fact with his diffident query each time he went to the station, "You got a telegraph message fer me? I been expectin' one. Reckon mebbe the booger's too cheap to wire. Guess I'll get a letter instead."

Tonight he was forced to hurry, for the train was already pulling into the station. He saw the small,

28

red-haired woman alight, and then he stepped into the musty station and turned to stare through the window across the narrow platform.

Lucille Robineau had not been the westbound train's only passenger. A man descended behind her from the coach, a man nearly as small and scrawny as Howie Frye—a man whose eyes were tawny yellow, whose mouth was thin-lipped and inclined to jerk nervously at its corners.

He wore a single gun in a holster at his right thigh, a dark broadcloth coat, and pants tucked into his miner's boots. He carried a capacious, but obviously nearly empty, carpet bag.

Joe Herdic, star gleaming silver against his vest, pushed his shoulder against the station wall and straightened up. He advanced toward the stranger, saying then in his overly smooth and courteous way, "Stayin' over, stranger? The hotel's halfway up on Main. There's a boardin' house over at the edge of town if," he eyed the frayed sleeves of the stranger's coat, "you ain't too flush."

He fished in his vest pocket for his sack of tobacco, carefully poured the flaky stuff into a wheatstraw paper and rolled a smoke, all this while watching the stranger with cool, questioning eyes. He said as he licked the cigarette, "I'm Joe Herdic. I didn't catch your name."

The sheriff was not a big man, nor did he look like a lawman. Yet about his gray eyes was a cool steadiness, an unflinching, calm consideration. He was something of a dude in his dress, wearing fawn-colored trousers, fancy tooled boots, an ivory-

29

handled Colt's in a silver mounted holster.

Wildness flared in the stranger's tawny eyes. His own gaze met Herdic's steadily. "I didn't tell you my name. Do you meet every train that comes through here? Do you question every stranger that steps down onto the platform?"

Herdic smiled with deceptive gentleness. "No, not every one. Just the ones I wonder about."

The stranger let his bag drop to the platform. His right hand seemed to tense slightly. His voice was low, hissing out through a gap in his front teeth. He said, "Do one of two things, sheriff. Put me back on the train, or let me alone."

Herdic's smooth face lost its smile. "Tough, eh? All right. But this is a peaceful town, friend. I'm here to see that it stays that way. If you so much as. . . ." He shrugged and turned away, but he flung a soft warning over his solid shoulder, "Be careful." Thick and precise, he walked across the wooden platform, his heels tapping hollowly, and stepped down into the dust of Main. Without looking back, he went uptown, turning in finally at Stoddard's saloon.

The stranger picked up his carpetbag. He stood for a moment, scowling at the little town which was so much like other little towns he had seen before.

The station door opened, and Howie Frye came out. Howie appeared to be reading a telegraph message from a yellow form he held close to his face. He wandered absently to within ten feet of the stranger, keeping his back toward the station, and then his mouth moved cautiously, "You Shanks?"

He raised his eyes and peered at the stranger, as though now seeing him for the first time. The stranger inclined his head. Howie said, very softly, "I'll see you at Stoddard's later."

He crumpled the sheet of yellow paper and stuffed it into his pocket. Then he turned and sauntered slowly up Main.

The stranger spat disgustedly onto the platform. The corners of his mouth jerked nervously. Another rabbit who was afraid to do his own killing. He scowled. At last he shrugged fatalistically as though realizing that without the rabbits there would be no employment for the wolves, turned and followed Frye up the dusty street.

He did not go as far as Stoddard's, however, for he was ravenously hungry. Instead, he turned in at the hotel, shabby and small, but exceedingly dangerous for all that.

Down in the cattle pens below town, twelve hundred Tincup steers crowded and bellowed. A long train of cattle cars labored noisily onto the siding beside the pens, and as soon as they got off the main line, the passenger train whistled and puffed out of the station.

Gray dusk dropped over the town, bringing its high-country chill. Out on the benches across the Little Snake a coyote pack yammered and quarreled. Somewhere in town, a piano tinkled the refrain, "Flow gently, sweet Afton" rather uncertainly. The racket of Tincup's celebrating punchers filled Main street with its uneven murmur.

Just another night, like a thousand that had gone before it. Yet somehow, this one was different. Joe Herdic, at Stoddard's bar, felt an odd and unaccustomed tension he could not explain.

31

Mart Joliffe, as he stabled his horse, untied the slicker behind the saddle and got out his Colt's and belt and strapped them on, wondering at the unnamed compulsion that made him do so.

Howie Frye, at a small table in a far corner of Stoddard's, could keep neither his feet nor his hands still, and drank more than was usual for him. But in spite of his nervousness, a gleam that was part triumph and part wicked anticipation shone in his eyes.

And only Shanks was calm.

Mart Joliffe, shaved and bathed and attired in clean clothes, climbed the stairs to Rose Frye's room with a certain reluctance. It was not usual for him to feel this way after a six weeks absence from Rose. Usually he was wildly exuberant, impatiently ardent.

Tonight, an odd chill possessed him whenever he thought of Rose. He told himself impatiently, "She isn't going to turn you down. What gives you that notion?" But he found it hard to believe his own assurances. He had sensed something in Rose today, knew as well as though she had told him, that something had happened to change their relationship since he had gone on roundup, something over which he had neither control nor influence.

The very fact that he was so sure something had happened, had the power to stir unwilling resentment in him, but he fought to control this as he rapped on the panel of her door.

She opened it, her eyes troubled, her mouth unsmiling. Mart put his hands on her shoulders and looked steadily into her eyes, knowing at once that this needed to be brought out into the open before it went further in either of their minds.

He said, "Rose, you know that I love you. I'm pretty sure you feel the same way about me—hell, I know you do. Will you marry me?"

"Oh Marty!" She buried her face against his chest. For a moment her shoulders trembled, and then she stood back. The faintest suggestion of moisture lingered in her eyes, yet her lovely mouth was firm with determination. She took his hands from her shoulders and stepped away from him, then giving her answer in a low, steady voice, "No, Marty. I won't. I can't."

"Why? Why? What's happened since I've been gone?"

"Nothing. Nothing at all."

He knew she was lying. He said, "You're not a very good liar."

Rose raised her eyes, looking directly at him. "Nothing has happened since you've been gone." Her lips began to tremble, and she lowered her eyes immediately.

Anger began to grow in Mart. He wanted to shake her; he wanted to shake some sense into her. He asked bitterly, "You found yourself another man?"

"Yes, Marty." She would not look at him, so it could not have been her eyes that betrayed her. Yet he was sure she was lying. His anger increased. He shrugged. Reason told him that impatience and anger were useless to him in dealing with this. Yet he could not seem to get rid of either.

"You ready to eat?" he asked.

"You're angry, Marty."

"Sure I am. What do you expect? We've been going

together for over a year. You haven't found someone else. That's a bum excuse. What's the real reason, Rose?"

"I told you." Her voice was almost soundless.

"All right." He shrugged. "Come on, we'll eat."

"You don't have to take me, Marty. I'll get something later."

"No. Come on."

She picked up a light shawl from the bed. He noticed suddenly how carefully she had dressed herself for him tonight. Why had she done that? Only to refuse him? He could feel his bitterness increasing. He guessed no man would ever understand a woman, least of all, himself.

He let her precede him through the door, and took her arm as they descended the stairs. Her smooth skin was oddly cold, and Mart could feel the chill growing between them, his own defiance at it. This was not his doing, he told himself emphatically, it was not his fault.

But it was his loss. Quiet desperation came over him as he stared at the future, a future without Rose. What was a man supposed to do, crawl?

He followed her into the hotel dining room and took a table near the far wall. He saw no one, noticed no one, so absorbed was he with his own private misery. Rose seemed unnaturally pale, and she studiously avoided his glance.

Molly Freret threaded her way through the tables and paused behind Mart's shoulder. Rose forced a weak smile. "Hello, Molly."

Molly was plump and jolly. Her smooth forehead and her upper lip were beaded with perspiration. She

34

spoke in her loud and throaty voice, "Marty, send your boys in tonight in shifts, will you? This is the damnedest night. Everybody in town must have taken a notion to eat out at the same time. It's been like this for over an hour now."

Mart glanced around, suddenly becoming aware that the place was jammed. He grunted, "Sure, Molly, if it will help."

Molly said briskly, "It will. What'll you two have, beef or pork?"

Rose murmured in her subdued voice, "Beef," and Mart grunted, "Me, too." When Molly had gone, he put his elbows on the table and stared hard at Rose. She met his glance defiantly. He grunted, "Rose, there's too damned much between us to ever give it up. Do you want to go on for a while? Do you want to pretend I didn't say anything at all tonight?" He gritted his teeth, for to say now what he had to say was the sharpest kind of torture. "What am I going to do, Rose? How am I going to go on without you?"

For the briefest instant, Rose Frye's eyes misted, and she blinked them, hard. Her eyes showed him a flash of her naked eagerness, and then even this was gone, leaving only a cold core of refusal, a core of hardness he did not know she possessed. She shrugged her beautiful shoulders and said resignedly, "We can go on if you want. But it will make no difference. I'll never marry you, Marty."

Desperately she wished she could tell him of the years she had followed him around Cedar City, hoping with quiet desperation that he would notice her. She wanted to tell him how her heart had pounded, of the sharp and bitter ecstasy she felt when

35

his eyes chanced to fall upon her.

She wanted to show him the bitter jealousy that had raged in her when she saw him with one of the town's older girls at the Saturday dances in the Odd Fellows hall.

She had loved Mart for as long as she could remember; she loved him still, but if she married him she would be killing him.

Molly Freret brought their dinner and set it before them. Molly stared penetratingly at one, then the other, then finally asked doubtfully, "You two spattin'?"

"Stop it, Molly!" Rose's voice was unnaturally sharp.

Molly Freret shrugged, raised the hem of her apron to mop her streaming forehead. She grumbled, "Well, it ain't none of my business, I guess," ducked her head and went on.

Rose bent her head to eat, but the food was tasteless, like dry cotton in her mouth. A sense of loss, of life slipping out of her fingers, obsessed her. She looked at Mart, but he would not raise his head.

Depression and hopelessness greater than she had ever felt before turned Rose's dark eyes slack and dull, turned her thoughts dull too. And over all her being was a new feeling of apprehension, of desperate uneasiness, as though tonight death waited in the streets for someone—someone she loved—for Marty.

Chapter 4

Shanks came out of the hotel and stood on the veranda, picking his yellowed teeth idly with a sharpened match. Crisp October night had settled in the streets while he was eating, and now lamps winked all along Main in the windows of the few stores which remained open this late, and in the houses at Main's upper end.

Most of the town was at supper, and the street was nearly deserted. Before Stoddard's, horses bearing Tincup's brand were racked solid. An early drunk weaved back and forth from walk to walk, singing in a low and indistinguishable voice. Uptown, a dog barked ceaselessly.

Shanks was watching for Joe Herdic, and saw him saunter at last from the saloon, cross Main and enter his office. Shortly thereafter, a lamp threw its feeble rays against the window, illuminating the painted legend, "Sheriff's office — Jail."

Shanks stepped down off the walk then and made his way upstreet toward Stoddard's. The doors of the saloon were open to the chill night air, and smoke and sour whisky fumes drifted out, visible, almost tangible in their acrid strength.

The place was packed. Shanks did not immediately see Howie Frye and so he moved gently through the crowd, diffident, careful to jostle no one. He knew the temper of these payday puncher crowds. He knew that they were usually quarrelsome, itching for a fight. He knew as well that the quarrelsome ones would always seek a stranger for their opponent, since tomorrow there would be no need for apology to a sranger, while a friend was different.

He reached the bar eventually, found it full, and waited patiently for a space to open up. Standing this way, he felt a touch against his arm, heard a murmured, cautious voice, "Get your drink and come around to the alley. I want to talk to you."

Shank's face twisted and the corners of his mouth twitched. He looked around, but Frye was gone, lost in the crowd. A careful one, this—a very careful one. Well, he had met a good many careful ones along the kind of trails his sort traveled.

Still he waited, determined to have his drink. After a few moments, a narrow space at the bar opened up, and he moved into it. Pete Stoddard slid a bottle and glass toward him, saying, "It's on Mart Joliffe, friend. He's buying until ten."

Shanks rang a quarter down on the bar. "I pay for my own," he said shortly, and ignored Stoddard's unfriendly stare. He drank the one, and poured the second. He drank that, and wiped his mouth with the back of his hand. Then he turned and again made his slow and careful way through the crowd.

On the boardwalk, in the dim glow from the saloon window, he paused and idly shaped a cigarette. He put his shoulder against the saloon wall and smoked it thoughtfully. As he moved away, he arced the stub into the street.

Almost immediately upon leaving the saloon, he entered the darkness that shrouded the rest of Main, and here he increased his gait. At the corner he turned, and again at the alley.

Those glowing, tawny eyes could apparently see in the dark, for he threaded his way along the alley silently, avoiding piles of rubbish and tin cans with no missteps until he came to the back door of the saloon.

Frye's voice whispered softly out of the shadows, "I'm over here."

"What do you want? What's the story?"

"I want a man shot. Not killed, mind you—just shot. You pretty good at hittin' whatever you shoot at?"

"Never had no complaints before," said Shanks laconically. A short warning of suspicion traveled through him. "What makes you think I'll do something like this?"

"I heard that you would." Something rabbit-like quavered in Frye's voice, and then it was gone. "What'd you come for then? You must've known what was in the wind. A man don't travel three hundred miles for . . . ."

Shanks interrupted. "All right. All right. What's his name, and what does he look like? Where do you want him shot?" He thought he knew the pattern of this now. Someone had been messing with this Frye's wife. He wanted the man disabled, so's he'd let the woman alone, but he didn't want him killed. Shanks shrugged. Damned if he blamed the woman, whoever

39

she was. for wanting something better than Frye.

"Mart Joliffe is the man. Big man. Pale blue eyes, big, solid teeth. A young man." A sort of vicious pleasure colored Frye's tone, and Shanks snickered softly. Frye said, "I want his knees shattered, both of 'em. I want him so's he'll never walk again. I want him in a wheel chair."

"He carry a gun?"

"Damn seldom."

"How much is it worth to you to cripple this Joliffe?"

"Two hundred?"

"Three. And a horse and saddle." Shanks was hard, callous. He killed for pay, with no questions asked about who was right and who was wrong. But this Frye, the apparent intensity of Frye's hatred, put an odd coldness at the base of his spine.

Frye hesitated. Finally he said reluctantly, "All right."

"How about the horse?"

"There's a sorrel stabled at the livery barn that's mine. He's a good pony and I hate to part with him. But he'll get you away if you have to run."

Shanks grunted, "All right. Write out a bill of sale for him."

"How do I know you'll do the job? How do I know you won't take the money and the horse and run?"

There was a sudden, ominous silence in the alley. Frye spoke hastily, "All right. All right. No offense. But I can't write here. It's too dark. I'll be on the hotel veranda with it in fifteen minutes."

Shanks held out his hand. Frye dropped the money into it, fifteen gold double-eagles. Shanks counted

40

them absently and dropped them into his pocket. "All right. Where's Joliffe now?"

"At Stoddard's. Getting drunk. He oughtn't to give you any trouble." Frye chuckled.

Shanks retraced his careful way down the alley, and a few moments later emerged on Main. He crossed over, and walked slowly toward the livery stable across from the depot.

Checking these small details was part of his defensive armor. He could remember one time when his employer had waited until he had done his job, and then had ambushed him at the place where his getaway horse was tied. He smiled a little. He had left two bodies behind him in that particular town.

He passed the sheriff's office, but Joe Herdic, his head buried in paperwork, did not even look up. A tow-headed kid of about fourteen sat at a desk in the tiny stable office playing solitaire. Shanks asked, "Frye have a sorrel here?"

"Sure. Why?"

"I want to see him. Frye said he'd sell."

"All right." The kid riffled through the cards in his hand, laid down two face up instead of three. He played the queen from the top, and then the seven. Shanks said, "That's cheating."

The kid looked at him self-consciously. "You wasn't supposed to notice." He laughed, got up and ran a hand through his long hair. "The horse is out here." He opened the stable door.

Shanks looked at the sorrel, a big gelding with plenty of staying power. Not a fancy horse, but one to carry a man in rough country. Shanks' opinion of Frye rose slightly. Still, Frye had as much to lose by

Shanks being caught as Shanks had himself. The gunman said, "Saddle him up. Tie him out on the street. I'll have a bill of sale when I come after him."

"Sure." The kid's face in lantern light was curious, but the stamp that was on Shanks turned him unsure and kept him silent.

Shanks went back out of the stable through the big double door, and the kid began to saddle the horse.

From here, the lights of the town were dimmed by the smoky haze that lay in the streets. He walked uptown slowly. There were times, even yet, when Shanks felt a fleeting regret at the way his life had gone. This was one of them, and he didn't know why. Unless it was the smell of fall, so sharp and clear tonight, the haze that lay in the streets, the sound of that damned piano, that stirred some unnamed memory from out of the past.

Then the corners of his mouth twitched again, and he climbed the hotel steps. Frye was a shadow in the depths of the deserted veranda. He handed a paper to Shanks and the gunman read it carefully in the dim light. More of his defensive armor. No one caught him riding a strange horse without a bill of sale to prove ownership if he could help it. Satisfied, he asked, "Still in the saloon?"

"Yeah."

"I'll wait. Give me a wave when he comes out." And Shanks slipped down off the veranda, crossed the street and lost himself in the shadows.

Lucille Robineau was somewhat too young to fully realize the power which her striking beauty gave her. She had seen some evidence of this power during the past summer, working as a waitress in Denver. She had seen further evidence of it during her trip to Cedar City on the train. But she had no concrete plan for revenge against Mart Joliffe, other than the certainty that if she put herself in the same town with him, something was bound to occur to her, some opportunity was bound to present itself.

Since her mother's name had been Roberts, and since Robineau would be a name too well known, too widely remembered, she registered at the town's hotel as Lucille Roberts.

Now she sat at a tiny table in a far corner of the large hotel dining room, unnoticed, and watched Rose Frye and Joliffe eat their dinner and quarrel.

Hatred had become an obsession with Lucille. All in the course of one short summer, her father had been robbed of the accumulation of a lifetime, she herself had been reduced to penury, and as though this were not enough, she had been cast adrift by her father's death in a world with which she was untrained to cope.

She blamed Mart Joliffe for her father's death just as much as she would had it been he who actually pulled the trigger of the Navy revolver.

With eyes that reflected this naked hatred, she studied the big man. He was tall, just over six feet, and he was solidly built, so that he must have weighed close to a hundred and eighty. His face, deeply tanned, was bony and hard-planed, with high cheekbones that made him look almost as though he had Indian blood. And perhaps he had. The Joliffes were a pioneer family of French descent, who had followed the tide of conquest westward for a hun-

43

dred years.

His hair was black, crisp and coarse, and his eyes below it were pale blue, like the sky on a hot day. His was a singularly arresting face, yet one which could stir nothing but hatred in this tiny, red-haired woman. Perhaps the powerful virility of his face stirred a greater hatred in her than it otherwise would have because it had the power to attract her against her will.

In her mind she marshalled her assets, and stacked them against the strength of the man she had to beat. Money was the least of her assets, there being but sixty-seven dollars remaining of the pittance her father had left when he died. Burial costs had been high, and there had been the train fare here, a few small additions to her wardrobe.

Her strength was nothing against that of Mart Joliffe. There remained then, only what beauty she happened to possess, only her woman's body, to be used as weapons. How could these things be used to their best advantage? "In marriage," came her mind's immediate answer to the question.

Then for the present she must make herself forget that she hated Joliffe. She must will her mind to believe she loved him. She must make him aware of her, at once, and after that she must show him only the things in her that a man can love and want.

If he so much as sensed that hate festered in her heart, then she was lost.

Though she had never tested the particular attributes which she now needed, Lucille had them in abundance. She was an actress born. She had as well a powerful will, one which could force from her

44

mind and body the obedience it desired.

She had been watching Mart Joliffe coldly, with her hate plainly mirrored in her lovely eyes. Now, as quickly as she decided upon her course of action, all the coldness left her glance, all the hate, and there remained only a woman's intense interest in a man, only the helplessness of her attraction to him.

She watched him as he coldly helped the beautiful woman who was with him to her feet, watched him as he followed her from the dining room, looking neither to right nor left. She smiled faintly, for she could tell that Joliffe was very angry, could also discern that he was hurt, desperately so.

Instinct told her instantly that if he was angry with this woman he was with, that no time could be better than the present for Lucille herself to make herself known to him. She therefore, although her dinner was not quite finished, rose immediately after the two had left, and placed herself, standing, near the wide stairway, so that when he descended, she would be unavoidable.

She had sensed that his quarrel with the dark-haired woman was an advantage to herself. She could not realize what a terrifically powerful advantage it was. She could not know that Mart Joliffe had reached a crossroads in his life and was now hesitating at the turn.

As he descended the stairs, anger blazed in his light blue eyes. For an instant those blazing eyes rested upon her, flickered with recognition. Then she was crossing in front of him, as though she had just then remembered something, so that he had to stop for her, so that for the briefest instant she had his full attention.

Appearing completely preoccupied, completely unaware of his presence, she deviated from her course the slightest bit, and felt the contact of their bodies. "Oh! Pardon me." She stepped back and looked up at him, smiling apologetically. She made the smile dazzling; she made her eyes warm, made them show him the full extent of her startled interest.

Her voice was low and throaty, "We seem to keep bumping into each other. I'm sorry. It was my fault. I was thinking of something else."

She seemed to realize suddenly that this man was a stranger, to whom she had not been properly introduced. She repeated, "I'm sorry," again, in a cooler voice, and started to step away.

He caught her arm. He was smiling as she looked up, all his anger gone. He said, "I'm not a bit sorry. It's not every day in Cedar City a man can bump into a girl as pretty as you are. I'm Mart Joliffe."

Her eyes remained soft and interested, but they showed him her quick reserve as well. She answered, "And I'm Lucille Roberts."

"I know."

"How?" She was genuinely surprised.

"I looked at the register."

Lucille gave him a long, speculative look, lips gently curving.

He asked, "You'll be staying here for a while?"

"Yes."

"Then I'll see you again." For a long moment he stared at her, his eyes turning strange as though he were seeing not her, but someone else. At last he turned and strode across the lobby.

He banged through the doors and turned upstreet toward Stoddard's saloon. Lucille watched the closed door through which he had passed for a moment, her face thoughtful and still. Then she slowly climbed the stairs.

She knew there was a long path to be traveled. Yet she could feel a certain satisfaction. She had at least met the man she was after within hours of her arrival. She had made him notice her.

In the privacy of her room, her face hardened. There would be no rules in her coming contest with him. And if she ever weakened, which was unlikely, she had only to think of her father, the back of his head blown away. She had only to think of the bones of Robineau's sheep, moldering at the foot of the rim.

Chapter 5

Mart poured drink after drink for himself, yet tonight the liquor had no power to bring him forgetfulness, no power to ease his tortured thoughts. He kept asking himself, "Why? Why? What the devil's got into her?"

He was enraged and wildly jealous as he considered her assertion that there was another man, yet he knew she had been lying about that, knew there was no one else for her. There was no subterfuge in Rose. Her love for him had been one of the steady things, the things he could count upon, like the sun rising every morning, like snow in winter and rain in summer.

Morose, sour, he scowled at the brown bottle before him, now more than half empty. When he had first come into the saloon, Tincup's punchers had been friendly and jocular with him. His responses had been sour, and now at last they let him alone, to drink in solitary misery. The hubbub and uproar in the saloon increased as the hours passed, but Mart did not notice, and finally, unable to find release from his thoughts in liquor, he walked carefully to the door and stepped out into the night.

Cold air felt good against his damp brow. Swaying slightly, he rolled a cigarette. He stared hard at the second-story window of the hotel, the room which Rose Frye occupied, his mind still wrestling futilely with the enigma of her refusal. Then he headed downstreet, toward the river, toward the livery barn where he had stabled his horse.

Darkness closed about him as soon as he left the glow that lay in the street before the saloon. He crossed the street, remaining in darkness, and there, before the sheriff's office, paused again to stare regretfully at the hotel.

A light still glowed in Rose Frye's room, but the shades were drawn, and billowed slightly into the room with evening's cool breeze. He made a high, broad shape against the light in the sheriff's window. Shadow hid the pain in his face, hid the awful indecision. If he went out of town tonight, Rose would be lost to him forever, for his earlier words, his parting words, had been harsh and uncompromising. If he could unbend, if he could go over there now and humble himself before her, then there was still a chance, a chance that he could discover the reason behind her adamant refusal, and knowing the reason, could change her decision.

He went back over, in his mind, the things that had happened in the past year and a half. For one thing, Rose had moved from her home with Howie, to the hotel. He thought he had detected a change in her then, yet it had been, and still was, a thing upon which he could not put a finger—more a feeling than a certainty.

Even then, immediately following her move to the

49

hotel, there had been little noticeable change in her attitude toward him. If anything, she had been a little more affectionate, a little more anxious for the assurance his love could give her. Why then, the abrupt about-face?

He could not help thinking that he had the ingredients for the solution of the puzzle, yet he could not fit them together. His mind was fuzzy tonight from liquor, from the strain of trying to break his puzzlement.

He shrugged lightly, glanced once more at her window. He thought he saw the shade move, but decided it must have been a vagary of the wind. He turned, and walking beneath the board awnings that stretched out over the walk, continued on toward the stable.

He had consumed a prodigious amount of whisky tonight, yet it now affected him not at all, and the only indication of its presence within him was the faint headache that throbbed above his right eye— that and the slight dulling of his senses, at all other times so very sharp.

He did not hear the faint scuff of a miner's boot on the walk behind him, nor the faint click that the hammer on Shanks' gun made as he thumbed it back.

But he heard Rose Frye's frantic scream as it crashed along the silent street, "Marty! Look out!" and whirled toward the hotel. She stood in her hotel window, the shade thrust aside, and now she screamed again, "Marty! Behind you!"

She had been watching him, even as he had watched the shade-drawn window of her room, yet he had no time for this realization now. As his eyes dropped from Rose's window, they caught a blur of movement on the hotel veranda, as Frye moved across it and took his place at the rail. A voice behind him rasped intemperately, "Damn you, stand still!"

He whirled toward it, stepping aside, still puzzled, still bemused. He did not yet realize what the danger was, nor from what quarter it threatened, yet this voice gave him something to act upon. It was a strange voice, one Mart knew he had never heard before. It had a sort of hissing quality, as though the speaker had a gap in his teeth.

He saw the flare of a revolver muzzle split seconds before the roar of the gun clapped against his ears, and his hand immediately started its swift, unerring way toward his holster. Uneasiness, upon which he cold not put a finger, had compelled him to wear his gun tonight. Now he was briefly and desperately glad that he had.

A post that supported the awning, catching a glow of light from the hotel across the street, caught Mart's eye, and he leaped to put himself behind it.

A bullet tore a shower of splinters from the post, briefly startling to Mart, because it struck so low. Another bullet struck the post, equally low, making its dull, whacking sound. Mart raised his own gun, but before he could bring it to bear, the ambusher's fourth bullet slammed against his leg with the force of a mule's hind hoof and ripped it out from under him.

He went sprawling to the walk, and rolled immediately off, raising his own gun against the shadowy form there against the wall.

Joe Herdic's door slammed open, and Joe pounded

down the walk toward him, gun in hand. The hotel across the street erupted half a dozen of the curious, and Stoddard's saloon spewed Tincup punchers from its door in a solid stream.

Mart got off his shot and heard a hoarse grunt as the bullet found its mark. Yet again, that shadowy, fisted revolver in the ambusher's hand flashed, and the last shot, fired in desperation, entered Mart Joliffe's side, brought its searing pain, its immediate lassitude, and then, unconsciousness.

Shanks' gun clicked in his hand, the hammer falling on an empty chamber. He cursed and fumbled frantically in his belt for more shells. Herdic, the sheriff, was a looming, rapidly approaching form on his right, and angling across the street behind Herdic, came a full dozen Tincup punchers, some of them carrying guns.

Downstreet, Shanks could see the railroad station agent standing on the platform peering into the street. The livery barn, across from the station, had a shadowy figure before it, probably the tow-headed kid who cheated at solitaire. Tied to the rack before the stable was the sorrel horse. If he could reach that horse . . .

But Shanks had Mart's bullet in his thigh. Holding onto the wall with his left hand, he put weight experimentally on the wounded leg. It gave out from under him and he fell against the wall.

Well, this was it. A man traveled the crooked trails for years, taking worse risks than he had tonight a dozen times every year, and he always came out of it. It was some little thing that tripped him up. Like

Frye's insistence that Joliffe be crippled. That was the thing that had tripped Shanks up tonight. He could have killed Mart with one shot. But the damned fool kept moving his legs, and Shanks had not been able to shatter them in this kind of light, moving as they were, and partially protected by the shelter of that damned unforeseen post.

Pure rage had made him put his last bullet into Joliffe's body. Pure anger, and bitter resentment. Now he knew he would have done better to save it for Herdic.

He thumbed shells into the Colt's loading gate, one, two, three. He fumbled the fourth and it ticked against the boardwalk.

Herdic's shot crashed out, slammed into his body, drove him viciously backward. He recovered, closed the gun's loading gate. Three would have to do. But he forgot one thing, so used was he to fully loading the gun. He forgot the empty chambers which would have to pass under the hammer before the gun could fire.

He lifted the gun, centered on Herdic's body, and thumbed back the hammer. The gun clicked. Desperately, Shanks tried again, and again the gun clicked. Herdic was but half a dozen paces from him now. Shanks thumbed back the hammer a third time.

It was then that Herdic's bullet took him, tearing into his shirt-pocket and his chest beneath. There was the briefest instant of shocked realization that a lethal bullet had at last struck him and then he was falling. The harsh sounds of the street faded from his consciousness. The light died. Shanks was dead.

＊　　　＊　　　＊

Joe Herdic toed the still form of Shanks viciously. The killer's body was yielding and soft. Herdic knelt and snatched the gun from the killer's hand, flinging it into the street. He came to Mart Joliffe's inert body and yelled out, "Doc! One of you run for Doc!"

A Tincup puncher raised a querulous voice, "Who the hell is it? What'd he have against Marty?"

These were the questions Herdic had been asking himself. He had recognized the killer as the seedy, sour one he had warned at the railroad station earlier this evening. He had known the breed even then, had recognized the plain stamp of viciousness the man had worn. The only thought that touched him was brief but sure: "Robineau's work."

Rose Frye came running across the street from the hotel in bare feet and nightgown, a woolen wrapper clutched about her, silent, running like a terrified doe. She shoved Joe Herdic aside, so that he staggered in the dusty street, and flung herself down beside Mart Joliffe.

Tears coursed down her cheeks, silent, terrible tears. A circle formed close about Mart's body, and Herdic bawled, "Break it up, damn you! He ain't dead yet. Who went after Doc?"

A dozen subdued Tincup voices murmured, "Timm went. Here he comes now, with Doc."

Rose Frye stood up to give Doc Saunders room beside Mart. Another woman, the one who had come in on the train this afternoon, came up beside her and Herdic heard her ask, "Is he dead?"

Rose's voice was not her own. "No. He isn't dead."

Herdic could see her lips moving in silent prayer, "Oh God, not yet, please not yet."

Herdic watched as Doc Saunders made his hasty examination by the flickering light of a lantern someone had showed the foresight to bring. He stood up, grunting, "Leg bone. Above the knee. Another one in the ribs. Dunno what it done. Pick him up carefully, boys, about six of you. Hold him level and don't move him no more'n you got to. Bring him over to the hotel."

He snapped his bag shut and waddled on his short legs toward the hotel, puffing. Herdic swiveled his glance back to the inert form of the killer, and saw Howie Frye standing over him, looking down.

Herdic could not account for the fleeting suspicion that stirred in him, but he was somehow sure that had he turned an instant sooner he would have seen Frye kneeling over the killer's body.

Floyd Timmons stood spraddle-legged before Joe Herdic now, and shoved his belligerent jaw forward, "Who the hell is that one? What's he doin' in Cedar City? What's he got against Marty?"

Herdic replied snappishly, "I don't know a damned bit more about it than you do. That little guy came in on the train this evenin'. He hadn't done nothin' then. Was I supposed to run him out because he didn't look good?"

"You're the sheriff, ain't you? Is Tincup supposed to watch your blasted railroad station?"

Joe Stoddard pushed between them. He yelled, "Hey! Hey! It ain't nobody's fault, Timm. We all like Marty, and we're all sore about this. But there ain't nothin' t' be gained by callin' names."

55

Floyd Timmons' wide shoulders sagged. He muttered "Sorry, Joe."

"Sure. Forget it. I should have put the bastard back on the train. I'd a done it, too, if I'd known he was after Marty."

He stepped up on the walk and went over to where the killer's body sprawled. He heard Cassius Riley, the fifteen-year-old, tow-headed kid who watched the stable evenings, say to Howie Frye, "Did he buy your sorrel, Mr. Frye? He was down there just a few minutes ago, big as life, lookin' at your horse."

Howie grunted irritably, "What the hell you talkin' about, Cassius? I never seen him before in my life."

Cassius looked nonplused. "Well, he said your horse was for sale and he wanted to look at him. He said to saddle him and tie him out front and he'd bring a bill of sale from you when he came after him."

Something troubled Herdic, and suddenly he knew what it was. He said, "Howie, you was at the station when the train pulled in, wasn't you?"

"Sure," perhaps a little defiantly. "Is that any crime? I been expectin' a wire from Denver."

"You get it?"

"No."

Herdic mused, "There ain't half a dozen passengers get off at Cedar City every month. Don't seem natural you wouldn't notice the ones that got off tonight, seein' as you was down at the station. You see that girl that got off tonight?"

"Sure."

"But you didn't see this one?"

"I didn't say I didn't see him. Sure I saw him. But I didn't know who he was." Herdic thought Frye was nervous. He persisted, "But just now you told Cassius you never saw this man before in your life."

The overly prominent Adam's apple below Frye's chin wobbled a couple of times as he swallowed. He began to get red. "Sheriff, damn you, what are you tryin' to say? If you've got anything on your mind, by God you get it out, but don't stand there skirtin' around it."

Herdic shrugged. "Don't get on the prod, Frye. I'm just trying to find out what this is all about."

"Well, I don't know what it's all about. So don't be pryin' around me with your damn questions."

Herdic scowled at him. He knelt beside the body and began a systematic search of the man's pockets. Tobacco and cigarette papers in the two upper vest pockets, matches and change in the two lower ones. A plug of chewing tobacco in the shirt pocket, damp with the man's blood.

Suddenly Herdic halted. If he had needed proof that Frye had rifled this man's pockets, he had it now. Proof enough for his own certainty anyway, if not proof that would hold up in court—for one of Shanks' side pants pockets was half turned inside out. The other pants pocket, on the left side, had a big hole in it and was empty.

Herdic stood up. Timmons asked, "What'd you find?"

"Not a damned thing." He pointed to the handful of small change where he had laid it on the boardwalk. "That's every dime he had. Don't look like business is very good for killers these days. One

57

thing I'm sure of, though. He didn't shoot Marty for nothing. He was paid for it. So where's the money? Maybe he didn't get it all when he agreed to do the job, but he sure as hell got part of it. I know how these guys work. And another thing. He must've been figurin' on buyin' Frye's horse. How was he goin' to pay for it?''

Howie suggested in his whining voice, "Maybe that was just a stall. Maybe he was going to steal him. I'm glad you killed him, Joe. I reckon you saved me a hundred dollars worth of horse by killin' him."

Joe grunted drily, "Glad to do you a favor anytime, Howie." He surveyed the thinning crowd. "How about a couple of you carrying him into my office for tonight? I guess we can wait till tomorrow to plant him."

He had thought that Robineau must be behind this attempt at Mart Joliffe's life. Now he was not so sure. He turned again to Howie Frye, a little uncertain, but determined for all that. He asked, "Howie, what'd you think of Mart Joliffe? You don't like him much, do you? Why?"

"It ain't no damn secret that I don't like Mart. Everybody in town knows it."

"You had a run-in with Mart down at Stoddard's this afternoon, didn't you?"

"So what if I did?"

"Pete says you threatened to kill Mart."

Howie laughed. "It ain't the first time. Pete tell you what else I told him?"

"What was that?"

"That I wanted him down on the ground in front of his damned throne. That I wanted to see him broke and hungry. That I wanted him crawling by the time I killed him."

Herdic felt contaminated by the virulence of Frye's hate. He murmured wonderingly, "What'd Mart ever do to you, Howie? What'd he do to make you hate him like that? He's been going with Rose. Everybody figures they're going to get married. That'll make you Mart's father-in-law."

Howie fairly screeched at him, "They ain't goin' to get married! By God, they ain't! Damn you, Herdic, you say that once more and I'll kill you! You hear that? Sheriff or not, I'll kill you!"

For an instant, Joe Herdic was too startled to speak. Then, at last, the nervousness and the fear that sane people feel in the presence of the insane, came over him. He grunted, "Go home, Howie. You're nuts." He backed off and repeated, "By God, I believe you are. I believe you are crazy."

Chapter 6

Rose left the bickering men behind, following the six Tincup punchers who carried Mart. She followed up the stairs, her face contorting every time they unavoidably twisted or jarred Joliffe's body. They carried him into an empty room, and placed him on his back on the bed. Doc shooed them out irritably and impatiently, and closed the door.

A moment later, he poked his head out, saying, "Get me a quart of whisky. Quick."

One of the punchers took the stairs running, and after what seemed an eternity, but could not have been more than a minute or two, came back. Again the door closed.

Rose waited. She put her hands over her face, and the tears welled out of her eyes and flowed unchecked across her cheeks. Howie Frye had not fired the shots into Mart tonight, but he had directed them. Howie's gold had hired the gunman.

"Oh God," she prayed. "Let him live. I'll go away, and then Howie will have no reason for killing him."

She was trembling, partly from cold, partly from her horror and fear. Lucille Roberts came to her and timidly touched her arm. "You're cold. It will be a while yet. Why don't you get some clothes on? I'll go downstairs and get you some coffee.''

Rose looked at her gratefully. "All right." She went down the hall to her room, and closed the door behind. She walked to her window and stared down into the steet. The body of the killer still lay where it had fallen, and before the sheriff stood a defiant Howie Frye. Rose felt a quick stab of hope. Perhaps the sheriff entertained the same suspicions about Howie that Rose did. Perhaps he would be able to prove them where Rose could not. Perhaps he would make Howie pay for his crime.

But the longer she watched, the dimmer her hope became. Howie stood defiantly, not at all as a man would stand who was unsure of himself. And at last Herdic turned away from him.

With tears standing in her eyes, Rose slipped out of her nightgown and began to dress. She was slipping on her shoes as Lucille knocked at the door. Rose raised a pleading, questioning glance, but Lucille shook her head. "He's still in there with the doctor. Here, drink this coffee. It will warm you up and make you feel better."

Rose smiled gratefullly. She gulped the scalding coffee, and then rose. "Do you mind if we go back? I'm so worried."

"Of course not."

They went out into the dimly lighted hallway. Joe Herdic had come upstairs, and now squatted with his back against the wall, waiting. Floyd Timmons was there too, and Stoddard, and a few of Tincup's older punchers, men who had known Mart as a boy.

At last the door flung open. Doc spoke instinctively to Rose. "I think he'll make it, honey. I think he will. The bone in his leg wasn't shattered—just broke. The other bullet got a couple of ribs an' shaved a lung. But he'll be here a while. He'll be here quite a while." He seemed to realize suddenly that he was holding the quart whisky bottle in his hand. He muttered, "Used this for an antiseptic. Guess I could use some inside me now." He took a long drink and then passed the bottle to Timm.

Abruptly every bit of Rose's strength went out of her. Dizziness mounted to her brain until the corridor and the people in it swam crazily before her eyes. She could feel herself falling, and then Floyd Timmons' strong arms were about her, scooping her up.

He carried her down the hall to her own room and laid her on the bed. Through a haze of half-consciousness, Rose heard the soft, sweet tones of Lucille Roberts saying, "Go on now. All of you. I'll look after her."

She heard Floyd's gruff, "Good girl. Thanks," heard the door close. Then the woman was hovering over her, helping her out of her clothes, laying a cool cloth on her forehead.

Lucille asked softly, sympathetically, "Are you and Mr. Joliffe going to be married?"

"No." Rose's voice was low, without expression. No, she could not marry Mart, could never marry him. Not while Howie Frye lived. She said, "I'm going away tomorrow. I'm going away." A sort of daze seemed to come over her, a daze in which all things were vague and unreal. Her mind contemplated the empty years. She sat up while Lucille helped her into her nightgown, but she did not seem

62

to see the girl. She simply stared at the wall.

Lucille asked worriedly, "Rose, are you all right?"

Rose nodded and lay back on the bed. Lucille pulled the covers up to her chin and turned toward the door. "Go to sleep."

Again Rose nodded. But as the door closed behind Lucille, a great shudder ran through Rose's body, and at last she began to cry.

In mid-morning, Friday, a long freight pulled out of Cedar City loaded with Tincup's steers, and commenced the long, puffing drag toward the Continental Divide. Rose Frye stood at the window of her room, looking down into the dusty street, looking eastward and watching the line of brick-red, slatted cars crawl out of sight.

She saw the gleaming, yellow-wheeled buckboard that was Raoul Joliffe's private vehicle, come rolling into town behind a team of shining bays, high-stepping, high-spirited animals that Raoul had shipped in from Kentucky for this especial purpose.

She saw Raoul's stiff, ramrod figure behind the reins, and Floyd Timmons' bulkier shape beside him, straight-sitting with nervousness over the old man's reckless driving.

Raoul pulled up with a flourish before the hotel, cursing the team in his vigorous voice, "Whoa, dammit, whoa. Get down, Timm, and take the reins. Whoa!"

Timm got down and caught the bridles of the horses. One of them reared. Both were excited, lathered and hot. Raoul climbed from the seat, only a little stiff. He made a tall, bony, but regal figure. His flowing mustaches were snowy white, accentuating, by their whiteness, his dark, ancient skin. His lips were sensitive, smooth and firm. His nose was hawklike. His was the face of an Indian chief, save for the eyes, pale blue like Mart's and fierce as an eagle's. An old scar slashed upward across his cheek from the point of his nose, giving him a certain savage look.

Rose could not help thinking, wistfully, "Mart will look like that when he gets old." Then she thought of Mart as she had seen him this morning, white and wan beneath the blankets of his bed, his face drawn and twisted with pain.

Raoul fished his cane from behind the buckboard seat and stalked up the hotel steps, tall and gaunt, muttering savagely, "Hell! They'd let the boy die afore they'd send for me! By God, next time. . . ." He went into the door, out of Rose's sight, still muttering. Rose could not help smiling fondly. She liked Raoul, and knew he liked her.

She could tell Raoul the reason for Howie's hate, could tell him that Howie was behind Mart's shooting last night. She knew very certainly what Raoul would do if she did. He'd go down in the street, find Howie and kill him, kill him as he would kill a gray wolf on Tincup's range, and with no more compunction.

Then Joe Herdic would have to arrest him. He'd lie in Cedar City's dirty jail until the District Court was in session, and after that he would go to the pen in Canyon City to spend the rest of his days like a caged lion. He'd die with his spirit broken; he'd die a senile and helpless old man.

Rose never even considered this course. She couldn't

do that to Raoul. She couldn't be the one to start him on the course that would kill his savage grandeur, humble him and break his heart.

She shrugged bitterly, got her alligator bag out of the closet and began to pack. Doc Saunders had definitely assured her this morning that Mart would live. There was nothing further, then, to keep her here.

Mart would find someone else. Perhaps Lucille .... Rose's face contorted, and tears of pure jealousy welled into her eyes. She dried them fiercely, angrily. This was no way to act.

She was finished at last. She picked up her bag, slung her coat over her arm and stepped to the door. As she put her hand on the doorknob, someone knocked. Rose opened the door.

Raoul stood in the hall, hatless, his long white hair framing his dark face. "Where you goin'?"

"Away. To Denver I guess."

"Why?" He was blunt, direct. He could make Rose feel very guilty in the way he looked at her, and she could feel defiance rising in her.

She murmured, "Because I want to."

Raoul's eyes narrowed bitterly. "He's hurt, so now you're runnin' out on him, that it? You ain't woman enough to stick around an' look after him till he's well again. Hell, ma'am, I'm glad he didn't marry you. I'm glad he didn't. He's all man. He's ..." He stopped, glaring. "He deserves a real woman when he catches one. You ain't it, so I'm glad you're goin'." His shoulders sagged suddenly. "No, I ain't glad. I'm sorry. What's got into you, Rose? There's somethin' wrong. You're runnin', but you ain't runnin' from

Mart. Whyn't you tell me?"

Rose shook her head stubbornly, making her expression cold. She said, "I don't love Mart. There's someone else." She knew that if Raoul didn't leave that she would break down. She made her voice sharp, cruel, "Go away. I'm busy. I haven't got time to talk to you."

He scowled at her fiercely for an instant, then turned and stamped back down the hall to Mart's room. For a long moment Rose stood quite still, her face drained of color, her eyes dull and still. Then she was hurrying, down the stairs, past the desk and into the street.

An hour later, when the eastbound train puffed out of town, Rose was on it, staring back at the diminishing, ugly shape of Cedar City.

Mart recovered consciousness only briefly and at widely spaced intervals during that first week. During these lucid intervals, he was intensely aware of Rose's absence, and at last, during one of them, he recalled all the events of Thursday night, the break with Rose, the brooding afterward in the saloon, the shooting. . . .

Someone laid a soft, cool hand against his brow. He opened his eyes, saw a woman's face above him, looking down. For the briefest instant, he thought it was Rose, come back, and that all his troubled thoughts were over. Then he saw that her hair was red, that her eyes, instead of being a soft, dark brown, were hazel, bordering on green.

She murmured, "Well! So you've come out of it at last? Doctor Saunders said you might today. How do

66

you feel?''

Mart made a wry, weak grin. "Terrible. What time is it?''

"Mid-afternoon." She looked at her watch. "Three o'clock to be exact. The day is Wednesday. It has been almost a week since you were shot.''

"And you've been here all that time?''

She looked away. "There wasn't anyone else. Oh, I suppose your father could have got one of the women in town to look after you, but . . . . ." She hesitated.

"But what?''

Lucille was blushing. She raised her eyes defiantly. "I wanted to do it.''

Mart stirred and grimaced with pain, "Good of you." His mind groped, rummaged around in the things he remembered. After a while he asked, "Who was it that shot me?''

"A stranger. Nobody in town knew him. He came in on the same train I did. A little man, thin and shabby. The sheriff thinks he was hired to kill you.''

Mart closed his eyes. "Robineau.''

Occupied by his own thoughts, he did not notice the long silence. Finally the girl said, her voice small, "No.''

Mart opened his eyes. "Couldn't be anyone else. What makes you think it wasn't Robineau?" He wondered at the sudden flush that stained her cheeks. He wondered at her abrupt confusion. She said hastily, "I was thinking of something else. Who is Robineau?''

Mart grunted, letting his eyes fall closed again. "Sheepman. He ran a thousand sheep onto Tincup's grass last spring. Wouldn't move off. I ran his sheep

67

off the rim." He let his thoughts wander, remembering Robineau, recalling that there had been neither hate nor anger in the man, but only the bitterness of complete defeat. It seemed strange that Robineau would let the entire summer pass without making a retaliatory move, and then when fall came, send a gunman to kill Mart.

Most of the folks in Cedar City liked Mart. There were a few who didn't—men like Howie Frye, whose hates were incomprehensible and apparently without cause. But he doubted if any of them hated him enough to spend good money trying to get rid of him. It must have been Robineau. It could be no one else. He asked, his voice weakening, "What happened after he got me?"

"The sheriff shot him."

"Kill him?"

"Yes. Mr. Herdic went through all his pockets. He didn't find anything, though, but some tobacco, and a little small change. The sheriff says he's keeping the man's gun for you. He thought you'd like to have it for a souvenir."

Mart grinned. Lucille said, rising, "You sleep now. You've tired yourself out, talking."

Mart nodded. "All right." He heard her rustling passage to the door, heard it close behind her.

His thoughts turned bitter. So Rose had not even cared enough to stay with him when he was hurt? He had wanted desperately to ask Lucille where Rose was, where she had gone. He had withheld the question only because of the shreds of pride that were left to him. Yet it was obvious to him now that she was no longer in Cedar City. He could not believe that Rose hated him. He could not believe that if she were in town that she would not have come to see him.

It left but one inevitable conclusion in his mind. Rose was gone out of his life forever. Well, other men had lost the things they loved before this. Life did not stop because of it. Life went on. Mart's life would go on, too.

Raoul was getting old, and Raoul would like to see some grandsons playing in the yard at Tincup before he died.

Mart's thoughts turned to Lucille Roberts. He thought of her for a while, wondered about her. But as he began to drowse, it was not Lucille's face that hovered in his thoughts. It was Rose's. And he went to sleep, bleakly contemplating what his life would be without her.

Chapter 7

October slipped away. Yellow leaves whirled down Cedar City's dusty streets, driven by November's icy blasts. The high country got its first coat of winter's ermine, light and powdery and soft. Tincup's last roundup brought the remaining cattle off the high plateaus. And at last, winter set in in earnest. Day after day, the frigid wind howled down Cedar City's main street, driving before it blinding, stinging clouds of drifting snow. Snow piled up, and the weather cleared. The temperature went to twenty below and stayed there, except for a brief, ten-degree climb during each afternoon.

As Martin Joliffe mended, Lucille saw all the signs of a man's interest and a man's gratitude in him, and felt a growing, satisfying contentment.

She had quickly seen, immediately following the shooting, that here was a rare opportunity, perhaps a never-to-be-repeated one. And as though fate saw fit to deal Lucille a winning hand, Rose, the only one who could have frustrated Lucille's plan, had left.

There were times when Lucille puzzled over this. She puzzled over Howie Frye, Rose's father, and wondered often what lay behind Howie's obvious hatred of Mart. She sensed in Howie an ally, and perhaps her feeling that Howie might some day be useful to her caused a great deal of curiosity about the man. It was not natural for a father to so hate the man his daughter loved, particularly when that man was as wealthy as Mart, and as well endowed with other admirable characteristics. Discreetly, Lucille inquired about Mart's relationship with Rose, feeling that if there was anything in that which would bear scrutiny, she would hear about it quickly in a town the size of Cedar City. But she heard nothing.

She was very good to Mart, very patient with him. Slowly, very slowly, she allowed the warm, personal interest to creep into her eyes, so that by the time he got up and hobbled about the hotel on his cane, her glance had become a caress.

But each night, in the privacy of her own room, she would remind herself that Mart Joliffe had driven her father's sheep off the rim, had driven him to suicide. She would nurture her hate with memory, and renew it, so that it never died, but instead became a growing cancer in her thoughts. And each day she became a more convincing actress.

She began to notice that Mart watched her more and more. The brooding, nearly continuous in him, immediately following his return to consciousness, bothered him less and less. He smiled oftener, and occasionally would laugh outright.

One afternoon in mid-December, Lucille answered a knock on her door to find Howie Frye standing there, hat in hand, a diffident smile upon his sallow, seamed face.

She was startled. He said, "Missus, could I talk to

71

you for a minute?''

She did not know the reason for Howie's visit, nor the nature of whatever it was he had to say. She did know, however, that his visit might give her an opportunity to probe his hatred of Mart, and for this she wished complete privacy. So she said, "Why, I guess you can. Will you come in?"

"Thanks." He stepped into the room, and she closed the door behind him.

"Won't you sit down?"

"Thanks." He perched on the edge of a straight-backed chair and laid his hat on the floor at his feet.

"What did you want to see me about?"

"You was with my girl some the night Joliffe was shot. She left the next mornin'. I found out from the agent at the depot that she bought her a ticket to Denver, but Denver's a sizeable place. I ain't heard nothin' from her, an' I was wonderin' if she told you just where she was going to stay or anything."

Lucille gave him a startled stare. "But she's your own daughter! Didn't she tell you where she was going?"

He ducked his head and stared at his boots. "No, ma'am. She an' I had fallin' out durin' the summer over her goin' with Mart Joliffe." Lucille thought she detected an increased color in his face, a certain guilty overtone in his voice.

She asked sympathetically, "Didn't you approve of Mr. Joliffe?" She had no information to give to Frye, but he did not know that. She intended to pump what she could out of him before she told him.

He looked up at her, his eyes angry, his stare hard. He spoke with emphasis, "No, ma'am, I didn't. Not a little bit."

Lucille's glance was soft and innocent—sympathetic. "Why?"

The look in his eyes frightened her. She could have sworn that it was jealousy, raw, murderous jealousy. Her surprised mind thought, "But she's his daughter! She's his own daughter!"

His look turned sly. He showed her his yellowed, uneven teeth. "Lots of people in this town'd like to know that. I jist hate him. I hate him good. I've told him I'd fix him, an' I'll tell you. I'll fix Mart Joliffe good one of these days."

Lucille could not afford now to confide in Frye, nor could she afford to ask his help, or even to have it known that she knew him. Yet she felt a stir of excitement that was incomprehensibly mingled with fright. She could be sure of his hatred for Mart. She could be sure of his cooperation in any scheme she might hatch to hurt Mart. The gleam of insane virulence in his eyes assured her of that, even as it frightened her by its ruthless intensity.

His hands trembled, and he clasped them together to still them. He fought for control, and when he achieved it, he looked at her. His look had the power to stir terror in her heart, for it was not the look of a man possessed of a whole and healthy mind. He said harshly, "I jist asked you a question, missus, an' you ain't answered it. You know where my girl Rose is?"

"What would you do if you found her?"

"Why I'd go bring her back, that's what. I'd bring her back."

"Perhaps she had a reason for not telling you where she was going. Perhaps she didn't want you

73

to know." Lucille, frightened as she was of Howie, knowing she was treading on dangerous ground, still could not resist the urge to draw Howie out. His hate puzzled her, and unlike herself, he went to no trouble to conceal it.

He jumped to his feet. His gnarled hands fisted at his sides, dirty, long-nailed. His shirt was stained, black around the collar and sleeves. He needed a shave, and he had a rank, sour odor. He screeched, "Don't you say that, missus! Don't you say that no more! She's my girl, and I reckon she'll come back if I say so. You tell me, do you know where she is? That's all I came here for. Do you know?"

"I'm afraid I don't, Mr. Frye." Lucille conquered her fear of him, the crawling uneasiness that was sending chill after chill along her spine. She showed him a cold, haughty stare. "I'm afraid I'll have to ask you to leave. I have done nothing to make you shout at me. There is no reason why I should stand for it."

Now his look turned sly, his voice wheedling. She could see that he did not believe her. He whined, "Now see here, missus, I ain't goin' to hurt Rose when I find her. I reckon you know, but you jist ain't tellin'."

"I'm sorry. I don't know." Lucille's voice was cold, intentionally so. "She left town the day after I arrived. I could hardly have gotten very well acquainted with her. If she would not tell her own father where she had gone, why do you think she might have told me?"

She saw that she had made her denial convincing. But she could see lingering doubt in the man. He stooped and picked up his hat, turning it around and around in his hands. He said, "All right. All right. But I'll find her afore I'm finished."

"I'm sure you will, Mr. Frye." Lucille gave him a warm smile.

He walked to the door and yanked it open. She could see with what an effort he mastered his frustration. At last he asked, "Will you let me know if you hear from her? Will you do that?"

"Of course I will, Mr. Frye."

He grunted, "Thanks," and closed the door behind him.

For an instant, Howie stood in the hallway, his back to Lucille's door. He scowled and his eyes were deeply puzzled. Lucille Roberts appeared to be just what she professed to be, yet there was that about her which stirred Howie's uneasiness.

He strove to put his finger on this feeling, to pin it down. And failed. Perhaps it was that she seemed too poised and confident. Perhaps it was the fact that he sensed her insincerity. "She knows," he thought. "She knows where Rose is at."

He shrugged and went down the hall. On the stairs, he passed Mart Joliffe, hobbling upward with the help of his cane. Mart was terribly thin, a gaunt skeleton of what he had been before Shanks had shot him. His face was drawn and white, showing little trace of its previous healthy tan. Howie could not conceal his triumphant grin. He stopped, for this was the first time he had seen Mart face-to-face since the night of the shooting.

Mart's first obvious reaction was anger, and a desire to go on past without speaking. Yet he did not do this. He stopped, gave Howie a lopsided grin, saying, "Satisfied, Howie?"

For the barest fraction of time, Howie admired him. But then he thought of Rose, and all the old hatred returned. Howie grunted sourly, "No. You're on the way down, but you ain't at the bottom yet. That's where I want you, and that's where I'll see you before I'm through."

Mart shrugged fatalistically. "What's eating you, Howie? Rose is gone, so she can't have anything to do with it. Neither Raoul nor I have ever had any dealings with you."

Howie was silent, thinking his thoughts, letting himself sink into the pool of violence that churned in his brain. His eyes must have reflected his thoughts, for Mart's face quickly sobered. He stared at Howie for a moment more, as though gauging him, evaluating the danger he presented. A new thought brought a flicker to Mart's eyes. "Howie, you didn't hire that gunman, did you?"

In spite of himself, Howie started, yet by no sign or change of expression did Mart show that he noticed. Howie grumbled sourly, "Wish I had. Wish I'd thought of it. By God, you've given me an idea."

He clumped on down the stairs, and behind him he could hear the awkward slow tapping of Mart's cane as he ascended. Howie went on out the door, and paused for an instant in the street to gather his old sheepskin about him and button the single button that dangled from its greasy front. He reached up and pulled down the ear-flaps on his cap, and then turned east off Main toward home.

The sun, sterile and without warmth, laid its

slanting rays in the street. The wind, ever cold these days, whipped at Howie and quickly chilled him. Hunched over, miserable, he thought of Rose; then he thought of Lucille. Again he was troubled by the incomprehensible feeling that had stirred in him as he talked to her. He went back, in his mind, over their conversation, recalling it word for word, mumbling it to himself as a dialogue in a play.

He frowned. With his thoughts gradually assuming an orderly form, he recognized that a part of his puzzlement over Lucille was caused by the fact that he sensed an insincerity in her, sensed as well that she had a direct and undeviating mind a good deal like his own.

Her attraction to Mart was obvious to all the people of the town, who already were speculating about the date of the wedding. Howie had heard the talk, had thought, "Why shouldn't she be attracted to him? Why shouldn't she want him? He's the richest man in the county."

But suddenly, following this line of thought, the thing that had bothered him so during and after his talk with her came to him. It had the force of a blow. He grunted aloud, "She's been takin' care of him for two months. She'll likely marry him. But she listened to me threaten him and didn't turn a hair!"

Even Howie's hate-twisted mind could recognize the unnaturalness of this. By all her actions she indicated that she had, if not love, then at least a genuine liking for Mart Joliffe, enough feeling to make the townspeople wink knowingly at each other when the two appeared together in public. Even if there were nothing between them but the natural and necessary tie to nurse and patient, there should still have been enough loyalty in Lucille to make her refuse to listen to Howie's threats.

He kicked this around in his mind for the rest of the distance home, coming to the eventual conclusion as he stepped inside, "There's more to that heifer than meets the eye. She's got her own axe to grind, by golly; I'll bet my neck on it."

Who, besides himself, could hate the Joliffes, could want revenge against them? Only one that Howie could think of. John Robineau. And John Robineau was dead, a suicide months past, the week Mart had brought his steers off the mountain, the week Shanks had arrived on the train with Lucille. . . .

Howie thought, aghast, "Now why didn't I think o' that before?" He murmured her name to himself, "Lucille Roberts," and then, "Lucille Robineau." His eyes lighted up and he began to laugh.

The house was cold, and Howie got up, shivering slightly, and began to build up the fire in the pot-bellied stove that sat in the center of the room. Howie felt as a man must feel when he is suddenly notified that he has inherited a vast fortune. He chuckled and grinned. "What's her game?" he wondered, but he had the answer to that before his question was fully phrased in his mind. "Revenge. She wants to see Mart Joliffe in the gutter, just like I do, and she's willin' to marry him to do it."

As though reaching a sudden decision, he went to the untidy, roll-top desk, and fished a sheet of paper from a cubby-hole. He opened a bottle of ink, dipped a pen in it and began to write, "Chief of Police.

Denver, Colorado. Dear Sir:" He hesitated a moment, grinning. Then he went on. "In settling the residue of the estate of one John Robineau, late of your city, we have occasion to distribute certain personal property, and are seeking his next of kin. Since he was a suicide, we believe you may have some information concerning the names, ages, general description and present whereabouts of such next of kin. Will appreciate whatever information you are able to furnish." Frye signed the missive, "Howard Frye, Cedar City, Colorado." He did not add, "Attorney at Law." He did not need to. That would be assumed from the tone of the letter.

He sealed it, stamped it, and then shrugged again into his sheepskin coat. Chuckling, he went out the door and into the blustery, wintry wind.

As he walked to the post office, his thoughts raced wildly. For months, in the back of his mind, had slept a plan, a plan that waited only upon the appearance of some crack or weakness in the Joliffe armor. Howie Frye knew how desperately Utah's sheepmen needed summer grass. He knew that their covetous eyes were upon Tincup's range. So long as Tincup, personified by the Joliffes, remained strong and unassailable, the task of persuading the sheepmen to move in would be difficult, if not impossible in view of what had happened to Robineau. But with Mart Joliffe wounded, a virtual cripple, with a Robineau woman in the Joliffe household, weakening it with the fungus of her hatred, betraying Tincup's plans and weaknesses to its enemies . . .

Damn it, the thing was possible! And Howie could enforce her complete cooperation, in the very unlikely event that she refused to cooperate, simply by threatening exposure.

He slipped the envelope into the slot at the post office, flushed and feeling his excitement rise. On the return walk home, he did not even feel the cold. He was envisioning spring, the relentless tide of sheep moving onto Tincup grass. He was envisioning a tight core of hard-eyed gunmen riding in the vanguard, itching for battle with Tincup's forces. He was envisioning Mart Joliffe, weak from his wounds, embittered and broken by the acid of Lucille Robineau's hatred, too uncaring to put up any real fight. He was watching with satisfaction the inevitable disintegration of Tincup, the eventual utter ruin of the Joliffes. He did not even consider the possibility that he might be wrong about Lucille. Everything he had seen in her, everything he had felt, bore out his conclusion. He couldn't be wrong. He couldn't!

Chapter 8

The days passed slowly for Mart. He was used to action, to movement, to hard work. He was thoroughly amazed at his own weakness, at his own lack of desire to get back into harness.

He mentioned this to Doc Saunders, and Doc scoffed, "Hell, what do you expect from a rum-soaked old sawbones? Miracles? You damn near died, boy. You got to give your body a chance to come back." He chuckled lewdly, "Marry that pretty nurse of yours. Any fool could see she's in love with you. And by God, there ain't nothin'll make a man remember he's a man quicker than a pretty woman in his bed."

He stared hard at Mart with his wise old eyes. "Think about that. You might find out there's blood runnin' in your veins after all."

Mart did think about it. Lucille was not Rose, but she was a lovely, desirable woman. She had been kind to him, had been completely unselfish all these months, taking care of him. He could never repay what he owed her, but if Doc were right about her wanting him, he could repay a part of what he owed.

A week before Christmas, Doc stood up from his

examination of Mart and growled, "Go on home, Marty. You'll mend as fast there as you will here. And there ain't a damned thing more I can do for you."

Mart thought of the big house at Tincup, of the comfortable, leather-covered furniture, of hot, crackling fires in the stone fireplaces. He thought of the beds at Tincup, soft and warm. He thought of Christmas, of merrymaking and feasting. He did not love Lucille, but Doc had said she loved him. He would make her a good husband, would never let her know that Rose was in his heart, and would always be in it. In time, perhaps a man could forget. In time, he would grow to love Lucille.

That night as they sat alone in the hotel lobby, watching the dancing play of flame in the fireplace, he said, "A woman and man do not live as close as we have without something growing up between them. Marry me, Lucy. Come home with me to Tincup."

He interpreted the look she gave him, the soft cry she made, as joy. "Oh Mart! I've been hoping you'd ask me." She came to his arms, warm and soft and desirable, and Mart felt a flush of desire. He grinned inwardly, thinking of Doc's words. Then he laughed aloud. "I'll get ahold of Timm. He can go up to the ranch after Raoul and any of the boys that want to come. How about tomorrow, Lucy? Too soon for you? I want us to be back at Tincup for Christmas."

At ten the next morning, Raoul galloped his hot-blooded bay team into town, and behind him rode a score of howling Tincup hands. They swarmed into the white clapboard church at the town's edge, subdued and embarrassed as soon as they crossed its threshold, and Cris Lebsack, the town's part-time preacher, intoned the marriage ceremony.

They drove home in Raoul's buckboard with a sour and brooding Floyd Timmons at the reins. For Timm, perhaps less confused and unhappy than Mart, had recognized Lucille's elation for what it was, triumph. Timm had sensed, as had Frye, the insincerity of the girl, had known without doubt that her meticulous care of Mart during the long months of his convalescence had been part of her careful planning.

Yet even Timm's suspicions of the girl could not encompass the full extent of her bitter plans for Mart. Timm suspected she was merely interested in money and in being Tincup's mistress. He could not know that her interest lay, as did Howie Frye's, in complete ruin for Martin Joliffe.

Raoul remained in town that first night, getting drunk, celebrating, thought Mart. Yet he was puzzled at the way Raoul had acted after the ceremony. Sour. Sore about something. Grumpy.

"Thinks he ought to have been consulted," Mart growled to himself. Yet if he had stopped to admit it, he would have known this was not Raoul's trouble. Raoul's trouble was the same as Mart's. Raoul had loved Rose, had wanted it to be her Mart married, not Lucille.

He jumped down from the buckboard as it whirled into Tincup's yard and drew up before the house. Weakness was momentarily gone in the excitement of the moment. He tossed Lucille up, caught her in his arms while she squealed with pleasure, and carried her up the steps. The massive front door flung open and Fu Ling, the Chinese cook and houseboy, stood framed in it, grinning his wide, toothy grin. His black eyes sparkled with merriment and approval. "You better, boss. Fu Ling glad. Everything ready. 'Allo, missy. Come in out of cold afore you freeze."

Mart was surprised to realize that Fu Ling was the only one who seemed to heartily approve this marriage. Smiling down, he carried Lucille into the house and over to the roaring big fireplace, where he set her down. But he did not take his arms from around her. He held her quietly for a moment, while his blood began to heat from her nearness, while excitement soared to his brain. He whispered softly, "Welcome to Tincup, Mrs. Joliffe."

Her eyes were very soft, and there was a cryptic half-smile on her mouth, a teasing smile. She wet her lips with her tongue. Fu Ling's slippered steps receded toward the kitchen.

Suddenly, hungrily, Mart's arms tightened. Roughly he drew her close. She raised her mouth to him, lips parted slightly, moist and trembling. He kissed her, bruisingly, fiercely, and there was no retreat in her. Fire roared through his body like a holocaust. Her tongue was a darting, searing flame, seeking, searching. Her body arched against him with a passionate intensity that surpassed his wildest dreams. New strength, new blood pounded through his body. She drew away, her eyes clinging to his, hot, pleading, naked and unashamed. Her hands went up, behind his neck, tightened and drew his head down. Again her moist, sweet lips sent their scalding waves of desire through him.

Her voice was a soft caress: "Oh, darling, do you know how I have dreamed of this moment?"

Behind them, Fu Ling cleared his throat and coughed self-consciously. Mart grinned. "Fu Ling would like to tell us that there will be time for that later. Meanwhile, he has prepared an excellent dinner for us, and has raided Raoul's wine cellar."

"Fine. I'm starved." Her voice was low, filled with tense excitement.

Fu Ling touched a match to the tall candles on the table. Mart held Lucille's chair for her, then went around and sat down facing her. Fu Ling carried in the food. Roast duck, stuffed with apples. Golden baked potatoes. Preserves and delicacies. Steaming, fragrant rolls. Pies and cakes. A dinner only Fu Ling could prepare for this very special occasion.

Afterward he brought a bottle of Raoul's fine, light wine. And then he noisily left the house, singing. Mart heard the bunkhouse door slam louder than necessary. He looked across the table at Lucille, found her smiling that odd, provocative, teasing smile. Her lips were parted, full, moist.

He was a lucky man, and Lucille was a wonderful woman. He looked at the years ahead, and found them good. There would be children on Tincup, laughing and shrilly yelling in the yard. Blood began to pound hard in Mart's veins. He rose, carried his glass in to the sofa before the fire. Lucille curled up in the opposite corner.

Mart laughed at himself. There had been a time when he could drink straight whisky all night and still handle himself. Not tonight. Sickness had done its damage. He was feeling even these few glasses of wine, feeling them in a heady sense of well-being. He whispered, "Lucille, you're beautiful. I love you. I'll always love you."

Her smile as he said, "I love you," was triumphant. The fire flamed and died, and the coals dwindled to a pile of gray ashes. Talk with Lucille was good, but so was silence. At last she rose, catlike, conscious of his eyes upon her. She waited, tense, while he rose to his feet. For an instant he stood before her, looking down, breathing fast.

Then gently, as though lifting a child, he took her into his arms, lifted and carried her up the wide stairway. He put her down at the door of the room that had been Raoul's and his mother's so long ago.

"The lamps are lighted," he told her. "The room is ready for us. Go on in. I'll come later." He opened the door for her, and watched her move into the delicately furnished, softly lighted room. Then he went down the hall to his own room.

Half an hour later, filled with a bridegroom's nervous apprehension, he entered the room. The lamps had been blown out. A crescent moon, setting in the west, laid its cold glow across the bed, lighting Lucille's beautiful body. Trembling, Mart settled himself beside her.

With a little cry, she flung herself against him, hot, demanding, urgent. She was all he had dreamed a woman could be. She was life; she was love; she was fragile and delicate; she was earthy and strong. She was the fire that burns the dross from a man's body and replaces it with newer, stronger tissue. Time was endless, non-existent in this sharp, sweet ecstasy.

* * *

Mart must have slept. He thought he had, for the thing he heard must have been a dream. It was laughter—shrill, high, insane and mocking laughter.

But when he came awake, he could sill hear the laughter. His blood turned cold, and the hair on his neck stirred and stiffened. Frantically he turned to her. "Lucille! What's the matter?" His arms went out to gather her in.

Her nails were like claws. They raked his shoulder, his neck, his face. Her laughter died, and he heard her voice, unbelievably harsh, the bitter, vicious voice of a harridan. She sprang out of bed and stood in the middle of the floor, half crouched, entirely naked, but seemingly unaware of it. She screeched at him, "You fool! You stupid, clumsy, bumbling fool! Do you know who I am? Do you know what you've married?"

So hideously startling had been this sudden change in her that Mart, chilled and horrified, simply stared at her uncomprehendingly.

"Lucille Roberts?" She laughed again, harshly, wildly. "That was my mother's maiden name. I'm Lucille Robineau, do you hear? I'm your wife!"

Mart sprang up, unbelieving, utterly shocked. He caught her arms and his fingers were like claws. She did not struggle. She made no effort to break free. She simply stood and stared up into his glaring, maddened eyes. She said in a still, cold voice, "Do you want me now? Take me. Take me if you want. I'm your wife."

87

He did not move, did not speak, but still he held her in his two great hands. Her eyes turned wild, and her voice gained a touch of wild hysteria. "Take me!" she screamed, "so that you will know what you are missing! It will never be like it was tonight! It will never be like that again. Take me, and see how cold a woman can be, how unmoving, how dead!"

Her skin was smoth, warm-toned from anger. The eyes she turned up toward him were—hell, he'd never noticed before—hazel usually, green when anger stirred her. Green now. Her body was perfection, smoothly rounded, full breasted. Long, smooth thighs. He looked at her eyes again.

Suddenly he flung her from him, and his action was a reflex, like that of a man whose hand was closed upon something and suddenly realizes that it has touched a snake. Unprepared, she staggered back across the half-darkened room, slammed against the wall and slumped to the floor. Mart snatched his robe from the bed, shrugged into it. He found a match in the pocket and lighted the lamp. Lucille still lay where she had fallen, staring up at him, unmoving, cold and hard as ice. He snatched a blanket from the bed and flung it at her. "Cover yourself!" he said harshly.

She got up, staring at him unwinkingly, and draped the blanket about her shoulders. Mart shuddered. Lucille went to the mirror, picked up a brush, and began to brush her hair.

Shock gave way to anger in Mart, and anger gave way to puzzlement. He asked, "Why did you marry me? What do you want?"

In the mirror he could see the thoughts that

flickered across the screen of her eyes. Defiance, and hate—consuming, corrosive hatred that turned the beauty of her face to ugliness. Mart didn't really need an answer to his question. The fact that she had married him was answer enough. She wanted revenge. She wanted to see him unhappy. Well, she should have been pleased enough all winter. She had seen in him the pain of his wounds, the emaciation they had caused in his normally healthy body. She had seen in him the bitterness Rose's desertion had caused. She had seen him brood and scowl. She had hardly seen him smile. Then she had given his life back to him, tonight, in this very room, only to snatch it away, to laugh like a harridan and say that it was all a lie, only another torture for one already damned.

He repeated, "What do you want?"

She smiled at him,—the familiar, teasing smile. "I'm Lucille Robineau. That ought to be answer enough." Her eyes flamed emerald green. "Do you know what my father did after you slaughtered his sheep? He killed himself. He put a gun into his mouth and pulled the trigger."

Mart had not known. He seldom bothered to read newspapers, never read them at all in summer when the work was so heavy. He'd had no time to read them in Cedar City the night he was shot. And if Raoul or Timm had read of it, they had not told him. Her words came as an almost physical blow to him. He muttered, "No, I didn't know."

"He didn't really kill himself. You killed him!"

Mart said resignedly, softly, "I suppose it's no good trying to explain it to you. You have lived with your hate too long. Your father brought his sheep onto Tincup grass after I had warned him not to. I warned him repeatedly after that first time—four more times to be exact. I told him that we couldn't allow him to stay. It was not that your father's sheep were hurting us particularly. We could have stood that all right. But Utah is full of sheep and they're all short on summer grass. If I had allowed your father to stay, there would have been thirty thousand sheep on Tincup's range within a month and Tincup would have been out of business."

"So you butchered them. You ran them off the rim. You broke my father's spirit and he killed himself!"

Mart saw no point in telling her that driving the sheep off the rim had been Raoul's idea, had in fact been Raoul's orders. He would not now shift blame to Raoul's shoulders. It had been Mart, himself, who had carried out the orders. Listlessly he repeated his question, "What do you want?"

His patient tone seemed to infuriate her. She whirled on him, tiny, filled with the uncleanliness of her hatred. He was watching her face, totally amazed at the realization that this was the same girl he had carried up here not an hour past.

She screeched, "Money, to begin with! Lots of money. Murdered sheep come high."

Mart said, "All right. What then?"

Lucille laughed scornfully. "Don't think you're going to get off that easy! I'm your wife. I'll stay your wife. I'll live here at Tincup. And when you die, I'll be there by your side, laughing. Do you hear? Taunting you!" Her laughter grew bitter—and wild. It grew to hysteria, and she made no attempt to halt it.

Mart put his hand on the door. He looked at her for a moment more. There was a feeling in him that this was not real—could not be real. He tried to convince himself that it was a fever-induced nightmare, and that in a moment he would awake.

Then he shook his head. It was real enough.

He went into the darkened hall and closed the door behind him, trying to deafen his ears to her hysterical shrieking. He felt degraded and unclean. Life, once so good, had become a farce—an ugly, bitter farce. Mart went into his own bedroom and crawled beneath the blankets. But he did not sleep. He wondered if he would ever sleep again.

Chapter 9

Christmas passed, its merriment strained, and New Years came and went. January wind whistled and sighed against the stout house at Tincup. It snowed and it cleared, and snowed again. In February, the wind came, piling drifts to the eaves, clogging the roads, making even the cattle feeding a nightmare of icy, chilling work.

In the bunkhouse, Tincup's crew sat before the potbellied stove and played poker, pitch and solitaire, or they sprawled on their bunks and speculated about what went on between Mart Joliffe and his wife up at the big house.

Raoul Joliffe lost weight, turned haggard, and his pithy humor disappeared. His eyes sunk deeper into his head. The corners of his mouth turned downward and stayed that way. And Mart gained no weight, no strength.

Only Lucille Joliffe seemed happy, and even her happiness had a brooding, unhealthy aspect about it. March came, bringing a howling, zero wind out of the north. For days it beat against the house, until it seemed that its force would beat out the windows, would tear off the roof, would collapse the walls.

Mart watched Lucille surreptitiously, and finally during mid-March, sure at last of the thing he suspected, he went one night to her room. She sat before the huge mirror that had been his mother's, brushing that red hair, brushing with steady, even strokes. She counted the strokes, he knew. A hundred in the morning, a hundred at night.

Her skin was flawless, white as milk. The eyes she turned toward him flickered green. "Don't come bursting in here without knocking, Mart."

"Be damned to that. You're my wife." His tone failed utterly to conceal the repugnance he felt for her.

Her eyes turned greener. The hazel was gone entirely from them now. She wore a thin, gauzy nightgown, as transparent almost as glass, but the sight of her beautifully shaped body stirred no feeling at all in Mart. He was watching her face, marveling at the transformation that hate could cause.

She stood up, facing him, and in a gesture he knew to be automatic, ran a slim hand over her abdomen, absently smoothing. Mart's eyes turned cold. This completed her hold over him. He said, "You're pregnant."

She stared at him for a moment, and at last broke into harsh, mocking laughter. She screeched, "You know, then? You know that I am carrying your child?" She controlled herself with an effort, and when she spoke again, it was calmly, yet she could not keep triumph out of her voice. "You know this is what I've prayed for. Now I have really got you where I want you. Do you realize how many accidents can happen to a baby? Do you know how many of them smother in their cribs?"

The veins in Mart's temples throbbed, yet his face turned white. Thin he was, and weak, but there was no weakness in the hands that clutched her shoulders and bit deep, deeper, until she cried out with pain and struggled to be free.

He said harshly, "You won't do that." He stared at her hard. He was thinking how easily he could break her tiny body, how terribly easy it would be for him. Lucille took a backward step, her eyes widening. Mart growled again, "You won't do that, and do you know why you won't? For one reason: if you do, I'll kill you—with my hands. I'll give you another reason why you won't. Money. I'll give you thirty thousand dollars the day you turn him over to me, sound and healthy. If anything happens to him, I'll chase you clear across the world until I find you. And when I do. . . ." His great hands clenched and unclenched.

He began to tremble with the effort he made to control himself. Finally he said, "Pack your things. Tomorrow morning you're going to Cedar City. Raoul owns a couple of houses there. Take your pick of them and stay until the baby's born. I'll pay your bills at the store and give you a couple of hundred a month for yourself. But I don't want to see you again until the baby is born, do you hear?"

Lucille opened her mouth to speak, but Mart interrupted her, "Thirty thousand is a lot of money, a lot of money to pay for revenge. Thirty thousand and your life is too big a price. And I promise you, Lucille, that's the price you'll pay. If anything happens to that child, that's the price you'll pay!"

His icy rage chilled her and for once she was silent.

Mart turned his back and went out of the room, slamming the door behind.

The face he had showed her had been brutally, coldly sure. The face he wore as he stepped back into his own room was full of quiet terror and uncertainty. Indecision tortured him and he wondered, "Did I do right? Does she think more of money than she does of the child? Does she think I could kill her? Or will she kill the child?"

These were questions that had no immediate answers. Yet to have showed her any sign of weakness would have, he knew, doomed the child instantly. This way, at least, he had a chance.

He stripped off his clothes and stood looking at himself in the mirror on the massive oak dresser. He was skinny yet, almost emaciated. Muscle and bone was all he had left. There was no flesh on his body. His skin was white, and on one side was the ragged, red scar where Shanks' bullet had entered, and another farther back and larger, where it had come out. On his leg the scars were larger—Doc's knife scars where he had cut the bullet out, the cross marks of stitches.

Mart raised the leg, flexed it. It was stiff, stiff and sore. He walked with a noticeable limp, and when he was tired, the pain spread from the wound, up and down his leg until it permeated his whole body, robbed his brain almost of other consciousness.

Doc had said the leg would heal. He had promised that it would be good as new. Yet it did not seem to be healing.

Mart crawled into bed and blew out the lamp. Perhaps sending Lucille to town was a mistake. People would talk, would inevitably discover the reason she was there, would discover her true identity. But until they did, Mart would lose their respect. He shrugged fatalistically. He admitted that anything was preferable to living in the same house with her, reminded every time he saw her, every time he heard her step, of who she was, why she was here.

Too, he felt he owed it to Raoul to get her away from Tincup. He had not missed the weight loss from Raoul's lanky frame, nor the dourness that had lately come over his father. He had not missed the way Raoul picked at his food, and he had heard Raoul pacing the floor of his room in the small hours of the morning.

He stared tonight with mounting horror at his life, lying in wreckage, in ruin. Rose Frye, the only woman he could ever love, was gone. Lucille's threat would bring Tincup to the verge of bankruptcy. Mart himself felt only half a man. . . .

Yet within all the Joliffes ran a streak of stubbornness, a streak of cold, raw courage. Mart, lying still in bed, clenched and unclenched his fists, and his anger began to grow. It was not sudden, spectacular anger. It was slow growing, steady anger that would mount and mount with the months until it either broke the binding chain of circumstances that shackled Mart, or destroyed Mart himself.

At seven the next morning, Mart heaved Lucille's trunk into the back of the Tincup buckboard. He stood motionless while she laid her smaller alligator bag beside it, and then climbed to the seat unassisted. There were no goodbyes, only cold, unfriendly stares between the two. Floyd Timmons, scowling, took up the reins and slapped the backs of the team.

Timm was foreman, and it was hardly his job to drive the buckboard. Yet Timm was Tincup, as much a fixture on Tincup as the great, old house. Tincup's troubles were Timm's troubles, the Joliffes' responsibility, Timm's. Mart wanted Lucille delivered safely in Cedar City, settled in one of Raoul's houses. Timm would see that Mart's wishes became realities.

Great clouds of steam rolled from the horses' nostrils. As they stepped away on the packed and frozen snow, their hooves and the wheels of the buckboard squeaked against its smooth, frosty surface.

There was little need for words between Mart and his wife. They understood each other perfectly. What remained between them now was as cold as the still, sub-zero air this morning, sterile as the frozen ground underfoot. Mart shrugged as the buckboard whirled out of the gate onto the road, and then turned back toward the house.

He was sweating from the exertion of carrying out Lucille's heavy trunk. He could feel himself shaking, perhaps partly from the cold, partly from weakness.

As he opened the great, wide door, the friendly heat of the roaring fireplace struck him, and he saw Raoul, tall, white-haired, standing before it, waiting.

Raoul's hands were held behind him, fingers spread to catch the heat of the fire. They were thin, bony, blue-veined. Mart was struck suddenly, unpleasantly, with the way Raoul had aged in the past three months. He made himself grin. He had hoped to get Lucille away before Raoul was up. Raoul had taken lately to lying in bed until about seven-thirty. This morning, he must have sensed something amiss and arisen early.

Mart said lamely, "She's going to stay in town for a while. Says it's too cold up here."

Never yet had the trouble between Mart and Lucille been discussed between these two. Raoul had respected the reticence of his son. Mart himself had not wished to burden Raoul with the additional worry concerning Lucille's desire for vengeance, and Lucille, probably realizing that Raoul's action, if he knew, would be direct and sudden, had refrained from telling him until such time when he might be powerless to intervene and when the blow would have its most telling effect.

Now Raoul's eyes were frosted beneath his bushy white brows. "Don't lie to me, son. You quarreled with her. A long time ago. The first night you brought her home."

Never in his life had Mart been able to deceive Raoul. He nodded reluctantly.

"What about? There's more to this than one quarrel. People make up, unless it's something they can't make up. She's got her room, and you got yours. That ain't no way for a man and wife to live." From Raoul, this was an accusation, an accusation in this case tempered with tolerance only because Mart had been hurt and was still weak. Raoul asked, staring directly at him, "Ain't you man enough for her?"

Mart grinned. "You old stud-horse, you think that's the only thing that could cause trouble between a man and a young wife, don't you? I wish to God it was as simple as that."

Raoul breathed a sigh of relief, and the stern rigidness of his bony old face relaxed. He grunted, "Boy, you had me worried," as though all problems were simple and solvable except for this one.

Mart laughed aloud, and was surprised that he did. For so long had he brooded, first over Robineau's sheep, then over Rose's desertion, finally over Lucille and her continued presence, that he had almost forgotten how to laugh. Perhaps just the awareness that Lucille was no longer in the house had its lightening effect. Perhaps the torture of the last months with her had erased his feeling of guilt over Robineau's sheep and his subsequent death. Perhaps with Lucille gone, he would be able to work something out.

Raoul waited for his explanation, but Mart remained silent. Raoul was old, weaker than he himself would admit. Mart saw no reason for burdening him further. Yet would it not be better for Raoul to get it now, here, than to wait until some later date and get it cruelly, tauntingly from strangers?

Raoul himself did not seem inclined to let it go this way. He muttered, "I've been quiet about it all winter. But when a Joliffe sends his wife away from him then it's not a thing to be kept secret forever. You tell me, boy, or by Jupiter I'll saddle up and ride to town. I'll get it from you right here, or I'll get it from her in town. Take your pick, boy."

Mart peered at him in the flickering light from the crackling fire, in the cold, dim light that filtered through the window. He knew that determined look in Raoul's pale old eyes. He knew that set in Raoul's jaw. He shrugged, "I was only trying to spare you."

He hesitated, trying to think how he could put this

99

so that it would be less of a shock to his father. Finally he said, "It all seemed innocent enough when it started. Lucille came to Cedar City the night I was shot. . . ."

Raoul interrupted, "You ain't trying to tell me she had any connection with that killer?"

"No, I don't think that. But I'd been after Rose that day to marry me. I'd thought all along that it was kind of settled. I even counted on it. When she turned me down it was kind of a shock."

"She say why she turned you down?"

"She seemed scared of something. I wouldn't let it drop, and finally she said she had another man. But I knew she was lying about that. She was scared, and come to think of it, it wasn't for herself she was afraid. It must have been for me."

"Mebbe she knew that killer was comin'. Mebbe she knew you was goin' to get it."

"No. Rose would have warned me. No, Raoul, I'm damned sure that the killer surprised her as much as he did me. It was Rose that yelled out her window, and saved my life. When I came to, a week later, she was gone."

"I talked to her the mornin' she pulled out," Raoul said. "I was pretty rough on her. She stood an' took it like a lady, but it didn't stop her from leavin'." His high forehead creased with puzzlement, but then he semed to return to his original question. "What's all this got to do with Lucille?"

"I don't know. But I've got a feeling that whatever is happening is all tied up together. Lucille made herself pleasant. She nursed me and took care of me. Maybe she knew how men are with their nurses. Anyway, I asked her to marry me and she accepted."

Memory of their wedding night was still a pain in his chest when he thought of it. But he kept on grimly. "She was all a man could want in a wife that first night. I went to sleep I guess, and when I woke up . . ."

Raoul was grinning maliciously. "Man oughtn't to be a hog on the first night. Specially when his wife's little, an' a virgin too."

Mart waved his hand impatiently. He growled, "Damn it, when a man gets to your age, they ought to take him out and shoot him." He hesitated. "It was awful. I woke up with that screaming laughter in my ears. She screeched at me—clawed me, acted like she'd gone plumb crazy. Finally she told me who she was."

Raoul asked patiently, sarcastically, "Who was she?"

"Robineau's daughter. Now, you damned old fool, do you see what's been happening? Do you see why I've been sleeping in another room?"

Raoul sat down on the sagging, leather sofa. He leaned forward and stared into the flames. His face was gray, colorless. When he spoke, it was as though he spoke to something in the fire. "She hates us then, and married you to get even." He looked up at Mart. "There's more you ain't told me. Why'd you send her to town?"

Mart sat down beside him and buried his face in his hands. Suddenly it felt good to have someone to share this with, even though he knew the burden was too heavy for Raoul. "Because I was afraid I'd. . . ." He rubbed his forehead, and although it was cold, it was beaded with sweat. "She's going to have a baby, and she has threatened to kill it."

He saw the anger come to Raoul's face, the wildness; then he saw it leave, and Raoul sank back helplessly. Raoul asked lifelessly, "What you goin' to do?"

"What can I do? I sent her off to town to live. I told her I'd pay her bills until the baby was born, and then afterwards, when she brought it to me, I'd give her thirty thousand dollars."

Raoul had gone white, and his gnarled old hands shook as they rested upon his bony knees. Mart stared at him. "I told her that if she hurt the child, I'd break her in two—that I'd kill her with my hands."

Raoul released a long, pent-up sigh. "She believed you?"

"I think so. But I couldn't do it. No matter what she did, I don't think I could touch her." He fished a sack of tobacco from his shirt pocket and began to shape a smoke. "I'm sorry, Raoul. Your whole life has gone into Tincup. Now I've let a woman wreck it. But I had to make it big enough so that she couldn't turn it down. I couldn't let her do what she threatened to do."

Raoul's voice was like a curse. "The bitch!"

Mart repeated, "Raoul, I'm sorry."

"Sorry? Why, you damned young pup, Tincup is yours anyway. You think I'll live forever? I ain't worried about Tincup." He aged years in the next few moments, and Mart was shocked at the aging process. Finally, Raoul stood up. He gripped his son by the elbow and steered him toward the kitchen. He even managed a sour smile. "I been wondering why you didn't get well. Now I know. Come on. Let's eat."

The anger that had been born last night in Martin Joliffe now began to grow anew. But it was helpless anger—terrible, helpless anger. There was nothing he could do—nothing. Lucille had laid her plans too well, and luck had been on her side, the luck that made her pregnant and hardened her iron grip on Mart. There was nothing he could do now. But later . . . He scowled. "Raoul, I'm going to work this morning. It's time I started getting well."

Chapter 10

Above Tincup, the valley narrowed, slowly, imperceptibly, and the walls of the mesa on either side rose ever steeper, providing shelter from the howling wind of winter—providing too, a well which caught the daytime sunlight and stored its heat against the bitter night.

This was Tincup's winter range, where the snow thawed days after it fell, where the grass was long and dry. It was Tincup's winter range, but it was not enough. So the weak and the old were brought regularly to the ranch in winter, and fed from the rich green haystacks there. And when spring came, a third of the herd would be clustered about the fenced stockyards, and the other two-thirds, above in the valley, would have stripped the ground bare of feed.

Mart started out riding. A crew of three rode the upper valley every day, and Mart rode with them.

It was not a hard task, or an exacting one. They rode and they talked. They spent the day in the saddle. Perhaps at night they would drive slowly before them a half-dozen they had culled out during the day. Perhaps they would drive none.

But it was a winter job, and winter jobs are scarce

in cattle country. Most ranches laid off their extra hands after the final roundup. Tincup never did. And Tincup earned the loyalty of the crew by this simple gesture.

The first day exhausted Mart utterly. But he stayed with it. He came in at night, spent, beaten, his face twisted from the cruel pain of his leg wound. The second day, he was up as usual at daylight, and at sunup, rode out again. If it were possible, the second day was worse than the first. The second day he did not even eat, but clumped up the stairs and fell onto his bed, fully dressed.

Raoul watched him silently. He did not urge him to quit, nor to take the easier course, breaking himself in gently. Raoul knew that in bodily punishment lay a cure for the ills of the mind. Mart was taking this cure, a far better one than the one Raoul had once employed—that of drowning all thought in liquor.

Raoul himself one day saddled one of the bays, and rode into Cedar City. He was weary by the time he reached the town. Weary and filled with the melancholia of age. But determinedly, he dismounted before Doc Saunders' door, and clumped through the snow to the porch. Doc seldom used the front door. The stable, where he kept his horse and buggy, was out back. Only scattered callers ever used Doc's front door.

Doc was a bachelor, and his house looked it. Once a week, a town woman came in to clean, but between-times the litter collected, and Doc simply kicked it aside and ignored it.

Today, Raoul was lucky. Doc answered the door, only a little surprise showing in his face.

"Well, by God! Howdy, Raoul. How's Mart gettin' along?"

"He's workin'. How's his wife?"

"Fine. Comin' along fine. You gettin' anxious?"

"Anxious for you to know what you're up against." He sat down on Doc's sofa after first pushing aside an accumulation of old papers, Doc's clothes, and Doc's bag. Then he briefed Doc quickly and brutally on the happenings at Tincup, on the identity of Mart's wife, on her intentions toward her baby.

"I want you to watch that girl. I want you to be prepared to tell me, if anything happens, whether or not she had anything to do with it."

"That's a hard thing to ask a man to do. And it won't stand up in court. If she's what you say she is, there won't be a damned thing you can prove."

"All right. But I want to know anyway. I ain't thinking of taking her to court." And he turned and stalked to the door. Doc stood watching him reflectively as he swung stiffly to his saddle. Raoul put spurs to the hot-blood, and his long, lanky body whipped back in the saddle as the startled horse leaped. He took the icy turn and headed toward Tincup at a hard gallop, the hooves of his horse scattering gobs of snow and mud behind.

Howie Frye, whose eyes missed nothing, saw him go from his vantage point on the hotel veranda. Howie had, a couple of months before, received a reply from Denver, confirming his suspicion that Lucille was Robineau's daughter.

He had kept his silence, feeling that to reveal

Lucille's identity would be to forewarn Mart as to whatever her plans might be. Now, however, since it was obvious that Mart knew she was a Robineau, it occurred to Howie that he could drum up a pretty good case against the Joliffes in Cedar City if the town knew who Lucille was.

The Joliffes stood high in the community. Yet always there is an element in any town that, while benefiting from the business of the big ranches, nevertheless feel a certain disgruntled envy and are always ready to seize upon a story that will bring discredit to their owners.

Howie stood up, stretched, and headed for the saloon. Mid-March had brought a cessation of storm to the country, and the sun beat down warmly in Cedar City's main street. A chinook blew in from the south, thawing the snow, turning the street into a sea of mud. Howie could hear the ice in the Little Snake cracking and grinding, as the pressure of water broke it up and started it moving.

He toed open the saloon door and shuffled across the sawdust floor to the bar. Pete Stoddard grunted, "What'll it be, Howie?" Howie jerked a thumb toward a bottle halfway down the bar, and Pete slid it to him along with a glass. "Swede" Johanson, the barbershop proprietor, stood five feet away from him on his left, and Joe Herdic perhaps ten feet on his right. Howie poured his drink and downed it.

"Kinda feel sorry fer that little woman of Mart's," he said.

Herdic eyed him suspiciously. Pete Stoddard grunted, "Why? Looks to me like she's doing all right."

"Guess she is if bein' run off is doin' all right."

Stoddard placed both hands on the bar before Howie. He said unpleasantly, "You sure you know what you're talkin' about?"

Howie felt like grinning, but he did not. He mustered an angry expression. "You're damned right I do. It's a shame, that's what it is. Just because she's a Robineau, he booted her out. Mart hates sheep, he hates sheepmen, he hates a sheepman's daughter, even if she happens to be his wife."

He had the full interest of everyone in the saloon now. Herdic said unbelievingly, "You mean to stand there and tell us that Mart's wife is Robineau's daughter?"

"That's what I said, ain't it? I said it was a damned shame, too. She come in here last fall, an' all she wanted was to try an' make Mart pay fer them sheep. Her daddy shot hisself over in Denver, and didn't leave her a dime. But before she had a chance to say anything about it, Mart got shot."

Howie liked to be the center of attention. He liked this feel of all eyes being upon him.

He went on, "She didn't have no money. Mart needed someone to look after him, so she took the job."

Herdic grunted, "Looks to me like she'd have hated Mart."

"Sure. She should have. But she didn't. Lookit the way she took care of him. Doc says she was as good a nurse as he ever seen. There ain't no figgerin' women. She was around Mart all day, every day, an' she fell in love with him. He asked her to marry him, an' she took him up on it. But I reckon she was scairt to tell him who she was. She knew how he hated Robineau. She knew how he hated sheep. So she kept quiet, an' used her mother's maiden name when she got married."

Herdic whistled, "Well I'll be damned."

But Pete Stoddard would not give up. He would not accept this damnation for Mart from Howie Frye's lips. He said, "I don't believe it."

Howie shrugged. "Hell, I don't care whether you believe it or not. Looks to me like the facts speak for themselves. Someway or another Mart found out who she was. Mebbe she let it slip. Anyhow, did it make any difference to Mart that she was expectin'? Hell no! He booted her out, sent her to town. An' I'll tell you somethin' else. You know what's goin' to happen when she has the baby? Mart's goin' to take it an' run her clear off." He shrugged eloquently, spread his hands before him. "Hell, mebbe he'll give her a couple of thousand dollars to get rid of her. But he'll do it. Wait an' see."

He had not gone this far before, even in his thoughts. He did not know that Mart intended to run Lucille off. But it seemed the logical thing for Mart to do. He would not continue to live with a woman who hated him as Lucille did. He couldn't.

Pete Stoddard grumbled, "I don't believe it. Mart ain't that kind."

Howie only shrugged. Pete would come around. He poured himself another drink, fully aware of the dead silence in the saloon, the silence that was as condemning of Mart as a flood of angry words. The people of Cedar City, like people in all small cowtowns, were a warmly sympathetic bunch, particularly toward women. Howie could feel sure that his story would be common knowledge in town by nightfall, and would be embellished and enlarged until every woman in Cedar City would be highly indignant. Tomorrow Lucille would have callers—dozens of them.

Then if he wanted to see Lucille himself, he had better do it today. He tossed off his drink and rang a quarter on the bar. Pete Stoddard scowled at him helplessly, and Howie grinned maliciously. He went outside, pausing a moment to roll a cigarette, hold it to his thin lips and light it.

Then he put his head down and scurried across Main and up the side street that led to Lucille Joliffe's house. As he walked, he considered with satisfaction what he had already accomplished. He had sown the seeds that would completely discredit the Joliffes in a matter of days. Now he had only to lay the groundwork for the complete defeat of the Joliffes this coming spring. The Joliffes could do a lot of things that ordinary people couldn't so long as they had the solid good will of the community. But with the people against them?

Howie grinned. With the people against them, the Joliffes would also find that the sheriff was against them. The Joliffes were a power in the community, but they did not elect the sheriff. The people did that.

Howie knocked sharply on Lucille's door, and after a few moments she answered it, gazing at him suspiciously.

He was amazed at the change the months had wrought in her. She was thinner. Her face had grown older and now showed an unwonted sharpness, almost a harshness. Hate had wrought these changes in her, even as it had made the perpetual sourness in Howie Frye. She asked sharply, "What do you want?"

Howie grinned ingratiatingly. "I want to help you Missus, if you'll ask me in. You remember, I hate Mart Joliffe too."

"Why?"

"It's a long story, but I ain't goin' to tell it to you standin' here on the porch."

"How can you help me?"

Frye's face grew hard. His eyes glittered. He shrugged and started to turn away. He muttered, "I thought you hated him. I thought mebbe you'd like to see him fixed. I guess I was wrong. Good bye, Missus."

"Wait!" Her hesitation finally vanished. "Come in."

Howie Frye grinned his sour grin, but there was triumph in his narrow-set eyes. He was like a turkey buzzard alighting on carrion, savoring, relishing, full of ghoulish anticipation.

He stepped into the dim and dingy parlor, which was not enough, and sat down on the sofa.

Lucille took a straight-backed chair across from him. She said irritably, "I don't know why I let you in. I'm doing all right without you. Mart Joliffe has been miserable since the day I met him, since the night that man shot him in the street."

Howie grinned. "You owe me something for that. You might never have married Mart if he hadn't been shot." He leered at her. "I put that gunman on Mart, only I told him to shatter Mart's knees so's he'd never

111

walk again." His face twisted. "The fool bungled it."

Lucille's eyes widened. Howie said, "I've helped you other ways, too," and he told her the story he had just related down at Stoddard's.

She began to smile, but it was a cold and humorless smile. She asked, "How can you help me?"

"We can help each other. We can wreck Tincup for him. There's half a hundred sheepman in Utah that are itchin' to move in on Tincup grass. All they need is a little encouragement. All they need is someone to organize them so they'll move all at once. And they need half a dozen gunslingers to head them up and give them courage. I can do the organizing. I can hire the gunslingers. You can furnish the money to hire them."

Her eyes had turned suspicious at the mention of money. But he gave her no time to further consider her suspicions. "I've turned the town against him today. The sheriff does what the townspeople tell him to. Mart won't get away with the things this spring that he did last spring. If he kills anybody, he'll hang. If he destroys any sheep, he'll go to jail. And if he don't fight, he'll lose Tincup."

Still Lucille showed hesitation. Frye cackled, "By golly, when it's all over, you let him know that it was his own money that whipped him."

That turned the trick. Lucille asked, "How much do you need?"

"Mebbe a thousand to begin with. Another thousand later. I don't know. Gunslingers come high."

Lucille stared at him, but he could see her mind churning, could see wicked pleasure growing behind her eyes. She stood up finally and went into the kitchen. She came back in a moment, carrying a glass fruit jar that contained a jumble of gold and silver coins, a wad of paper bills. She dumped it out on the table. "He gives me two hundred a month and pays my bills at the store. But most of this I got from him while I was living up there."

She counted the money rapidly, then said, "There is almost eight hundred here. Is that enough?"

"I'll make it do." Howie could hardly keep the elation out of his voice. He could make the sheepmen themselves put up enough money for the hire of the gunmen. This eight hundred was Howie's own, to pay his expenses while he traveled around in Utah.

"How do I know I can trust you?"

He shrugged and looked at her with his cold, expressionless eyes. "You don't. But you'll take the chance. It's an eight hundred-dollar gamble for you, and you don't really give a damn about the money. You want what I want, and that's to see Mart Joliffe in the gutter, broke, beaten and crippled. Maybe even dead." He stood up. "Make up your mind. If I'm going to do this, I've got to get started. The sheepmen will want to move by the first of May."

"All right." She shrugged almost imperceptibly. She shoved the pile of money at him. "Take it."

Frye stuffed it into his pockets. He was grinning. "You won't regret it, missus." He picked up his hat and sidled to the door.

He heard the wail of the train as it sat in the station awaiting the time of departure, and he started to run. When it pulled away from the station, he was on it, looking back at the squat and ugly shape of Cedar City, smiling his evil, triumphant smile.

Chapter 11

Howie Frye, hunched and sour, sat in the worn velour seat of the train coach heading westward into Utah and stared out at the flat desert landscape. He thought of Mart Joliffe. He thought of Rose. He thought of the years that were gone and wondered at length what changes he could have made in the way he'd lived them, changes that might have altered the way things ended.

His hate for Mart went back a long way. Contrary to Mart's belief, his hatred was born of jealousy, pure and simple, the kind of jealousy that had rankled and grown until it had motivated his entire life.

Rose had been but a small child when Howie Frye came to Cedar City, newly married to her quiet, sweet-faced mother. She was not his own, but he had seen no reason then to make the fact known. That was mistake number one. If Rose had but known all along, things could conceivably have been different.

Seven or eight years later, her mother had sickened and died, and Howie had been left alone with the girl, then twelve.

He could remember Rose, growing up, growing

lovelier every day. He could recall the way his own interest in her had increased after she had begun to fill out and look like a woman. Howie had been a lonely man, one to whom women did not take readily. He had been long without a woman, and Rose was really not his own daughter. So, he told himself emphatically, there was nothing really wrong in his attraction to her.

Yet because of the people of Cedar City, who did not know that he was not her father, he controlled his feeling toward Rose, even managed to hide it for a time.

He watched her grow. He watched her grow so breathtakingly beautiful that it wrenched a man's heart just to see her coming up the walk from school.

He listened to her confidences, listened as she bared her young love for Mart Joliffe, and it was then that the seed of hatred was planted in his heart. Hatred born of enraged futility because his hands were tied, because he was old and she was young, because he could never have her so long as she thought of him as her father, so long as Mart unwittingly held her love and her loyalty.

And Mart Joliffe was young, young and heedless, not even noticing Rose because she was a couple of years younger than he. Lord! Howie would have traded the world to be but two years older than Rose, five years, even ten.

He lived with this for five long years. Alternately, he hated Rose and loved her. He hated himself for the feelings he could not control. Often as not, he was surly toward her, cross and angry without justification save that overpowering, denied hunger.

115

She was bitterly unhappy during those years, terribly in love with Mart, crushed because the only interest he showed her was the polite, passing interest he showed to all the town's girls younger than himself.

And Rose's unhappiness served to increase Howie's hatred of Mart, until it became an obsession with him, greater even than his love for Rose. These two rankling things he lived with for five long years—an unrequited, hopeless love and a hatred that festered and grew. Both things became more intense because of the fact that Howie must daily live in Rose's presence.

A dozen times he swore to himself that he would go away, or that he would send her away. But he had not the strength to do it. He could not bear to deprive himself of her, of the exquisite torture of her nearness.

Things had drifted on. Howie traded in livestock, horses, land, town lots, anything that would earn him a dollar, as he had always done. Rose had seemed uninterested in men at all, but Howie had noticed that her face would light up wonderfully whenever Mart Joliffe came near.

Mart must have seen it at last. He must have seen the fire that burned in Rose for him, for he took to seeing her, taking her to the town's dances at the Odd Fellows hall on Saturday nights.

Perhaps it was her association with Mart that brought it on. But at last there came a time, as Howie had known it inevitably would, when he lost his stern control, when he took Rose hungrily and clumsily into his arms and told her he was not her father.

Even now, more than a year later, his face would color and grow hot as he remembered her biting scorn, her utter terror. But even for this, he could not hate Rose. So he hated Mart the more.

Rose moved to the hotel after that and lived on the small legacy her mother had left her, which Howie had preserved more or less intact.

Howie had seen her less. Mart had seen her more. In late summer, last year, maddened by the knowledge that she would marry Mart when he returned from roundup, he went to her one night, told her plainly that if she married Mart, he would kill him.

He knew she had believed him. He knew as well that he had severed finally the last tie that bound Rose to him. Knowing this, in utter bitterness, he had sent to Denver for Shanks.

Now Rose was gone, gone out of his life forever. But Mart Joliffe remained, and Howie's hatred of Mart remained.

The train puffed westward, and night came down over the broad, flat desert. Tomorrow, at last, Howie's hatred could translate itself into action, and he could begin to build the chain of circumstances which would utterly destroy the Joliffes.

Snow was almost gone on the desert. It lay yet, dirty and gray in the shady draws, but in the open the ground, with its sparse cover of grass, was bare, sere and brown for as far as the eye could see.

In the far distance, to eastward, Howie could see the high, rocky escarpment of the Tincup Plateau, making a thin, indistinct line along the horizon. Sun beat down into the single street of the town of Tillman as Howie stepped onto the sagging hotel veranda.

The entire town was no more than a quarter mile long. At one end of it was the tiny railroad station, across from this the livery stable, gray and weather-blasted from nearly continuous desert wind. Hunched against the stable was a saloon, closed and locked at this hour of morning, and a vacant lot's width from the saloon was a tiny restaurant before which a couple of horses drowsed, hip-shot, soaking in the warmth of the early morning sun.

The hotel before which Howie stood was a two-story affair, sadly in need of paint, which looked as though it might collapse, and whose sign bore the unimaginative and obvious legend, "Tillman Hotel."

A bare town. A drab one. Howie swung his glance uptown with complete disinterest. His eyes touched the windmill, slowly turning in the exact center of Main, feeding a tank which squatted in a foot-deep wallow of mud. Beyond the windmill were the town's business establishments, a general store, a hardware store, and, surprisingly, a dressmaker's shop.

A band of loose horses strayed through the residential district at the town's upper end and gathered about the water tank in the center of town to drink, laying their ears back at each other, biting and kicking, crowding for a place at the tank.

Howie shrugged, stepped down off the veranda and walked toward the restaurant. Its window was dirty, almost opaque with grease and fly specks: At the counter sat two men, apparently the owners of the horses out front. Howie took a seat one stool removed from them.

A Chinese, his face shining with sweat, shuffled from the kitchen and Howie said, "A couple of eggs and bacon. Some coffee while I'm waitin'."

He stirred cream into the coffee and studied the man nearest him at the counter. He judged the man was about thirty. He asked, "This is sheep country, ain't it? Who's the biggest sheepman hereabouts?"

"Huh? Oh. I'm damn near a stranger myself. But I can tell you that. It's Anthony Poulos. Why? You huntin' a job?"

Howie found his appraisal of the man bogging down. He looked like neither cowman nor sheepman, yet there was the stamp of outdoors on his dark-tanned face, in the fine lines that framed his eyes. His eyes were ice-green, and utterly without warmth of expression. Howie felt a quickening of his interest and dropped his glance to the man's side, saw then what the eyes had told him would be there, a low-swung, cleanly oiled, holstered Colt's .45.

Howie grinned inwardly. He grunted, "No. But I might be hirin'. Hirin' guns."

"For what?" The man showed no open interest, but Howie could see that he felt it.

Howie said, "Sheep an' cattle ruckus."

The Chinese brought his eggs. Howie directed his attention to them, now ignoring the man beside him. But he could feel the man's eyes upon him, studying him. From the corner of his eye, he saw the other one lean forward and stare at him. The second wore a beard, black and ragged, but his eyes had the same

119

cold stamp that characterized the first.

The bearded one asked, "What you payin'?"

Howie shrugged. "Depends on who I hire."

"You a cattleman?"

Howie shook his head, but did not explain. He finished his eggs in silence and wiped his mouth with the back of his hand. Winter was long and jobs scarce. He would have bet a hundred dollars that these two did not have more than a couple of dollars between them. But they looked like what Howie wanted.

He gulped the last of his coffee and fished a sack of tobacco from his pocket. He knew it would help his argument when he faced Poulos if he had a couple of hardcases like these two with him. But he had made his bid. Now it was up to them.

He touched a match to the end of his cigarette, inhaled deeply and stood up. He fished the tight roll of bills Lucille had given him from his pocket and peeled off a one which he laid on the counter. As the Chinese made change, the first one, the smooth-shaven one, said, "I'd like to hear more about what you got in mind. Hank and me ain't busy just now." Howie sat down again.

"Sheep are goin' to move in on Tincup over in Colorado this spring. Tincup ain't going to like it. I want maybe a dozen men that can make Tincup like it. Tincup is tough. The men I hire have got to be tougher."

The man grinned mirthlessly. His teeth were even, white. His face was thin-lipped, flat-planed, bony. His nose was long and sharp. He shoved his battered Stetson back to reveal reddish, thinning hair, and stuck out a hand. "My name's Ben Corbin. This here's Hank Moya." He grinned suddenly, showing Howie the faintest bit of warmth. "Mister, we been broke so long, we ain't even going to ask you which side is the right side in this ruckus you're talkin' about. But when we fight, we aim to get fightin' wages."

Howie took the hand. "You'll get 'em. I'm Frye. Howie Frye. You want to take a ride? We'll talk about it, an' you can show me where Poulos' place is."

Corbin shrugged and looked at Moya. Moya nodded slightly, his eyes hooded and blank. Corbin made a thinlipped grin. "All right. Let's go."

Now, at seven-thirty, a few solitary souls stirred about in the streets of Tillman. A graying, stooped man who looked as if he had neither washed nor combed his hair since rolling out of bed swung open the wide, squeaking doors of the livery barn and went in. Howie turned around and headed that way. Behind him, Corbin and Moya untied their mounts and swung easily to their saddles.

They waited outside while he hired a horse, while the old man saddled him up. Then Howie mounted, and the three rode out of town, crossing the tracks and taking the north road.

Silence, the utter silence of the desert, lay over the land. In a few moments, the town was behind them. Howie dropped to the rear of the column, and instinctively his hand went to his inside coat pocket where a tiny Colt's .41 rested. Treacherous himself, Howie expected no less than treachery from those he dealt with.

The miles dropped behind. Once, Corbin's horse

halted at an arroyo for a drink, and when he started up, he was behind Howie. Howie turned, his eyes cold. "Move ahead. You're broke. I ain't. And I don't know you yet. But I'll tell you one thing. You try for me and you'll not only miss out on my money. You'll miss out on wakin' up alive tomorrow mornin'." He lifted out the derringer and fondled it lightly in his hand.

Corbin laughed. "Reckon I might have been thinkin' about it. But you'll do. You can quit worryin' now."

Howie thrust the gun back into his pocket. "I wasn't worryin'. You was doin' that."

He knew then, very suddenly, that the next three months would be the most dangerous of his life. But he recognized, as well, that the first few days of organization would be the worst. After that, he would have the weight of the sheepmen behind him.

At eleven, they sighted a string of low buildings ahead, and Corbin swung in his saddle to say, "Anthony Poulos' outfit. He runs damned near ten thousand sheep."

Howie grunted. He was studying the layout as they drew nearer. Plainly, Poulos was almost as big a man as Mart Joliffe. As they rode into the bare yard, Howie spoke to Corbin, "Hang back. I want to talk to Poulos alone."

A man came out onto the wide veranda of the house, a thick-set, grizzled, dark-skinned man. He looked questioningly at Howie, and did not miss Corbin and Moya, nor did he miss the efficient guns they carried. Howie asked, "You Anthony Poulos?"

Poulos nodded. Howie asked, "Lookin' for summer range?"

Interest flickered in Poulos' eyes. He nodded guardedly.

Howie jerked a thumb toward the east. "Plenty over there if you know how to get it."

Poulos shook his head. "Robineau tried that. He didn't do so good." He spoke with a heavy accent.

"The Joliffes are done. Feller shot Mart Joliffe last fall, and he ain't recovered from it. Robineau's girl rigged him into marryin' her, an' you can imagine what she's doin' to him. The old man's aged ten years this winter. You been wantin' Tincup's grass. You'll never see a better time to take it than this spring."

"Where do you come in?"

Howie laughed. "I knew you'd ask me that. I want to see the Joliffes broke and beaten. I want to see Tincup split up and sold off in little chunks." The old intensity of hatred was in his voice and in his eyes.

"You want more than that."

Howie nodded, "Five thousand for myself after Tincup's grass is yours. Wages for half a dozen gunslingers while we're taking it. Your backing and the backing of all the others you take in with you."

"That all?" Poulos' dark eyes were sardonic.

Howie felt a stir of anger. "No, by God. I want to run the show. I want Mart Joliffe to know when it's over that I did it."

"How you plan to do it?"

"Easy enough. I know Mart Joliffe, which is something you don't. Mart's got a soft streak in him. He feels guilty about Robineau's sheep. The woman will be workin' on him." He swung down from his horse because he could talk better with his two feet on the ground. "Move up in small bunches, but all at once. Scatter 'em all over Tincup grass. Make him think each outfit is separate. He'll hesitate long enough for you to get all the sheep you want to on Tincup grass. By the time he sees you're organized, it'll be too damned late."

Poulos drew a cigar from a vest pocket and bit off its end. He said, "He'll fight then."

"Yeah. But his heart won't be in it. He's paid too much for that Robineau deal." Howie jerked his head at the two hardcases, Corbin and Moya. "I'll hire half a dozen more like them. We'll bring Mart Joliffe to his knees, and you'll have Tincup's grass."

Poulos, stocky, squat, puffed furiously at his cigar for a moment. Finally he said, "I ain't going to say yes or no to a proposition like that on the spur of the moment. You give me a week to think it over. I got to see some of the other boys."

Howie's face hardened. He said sarcastically, "You hand a man a fistful of gold and he don't want to take it. He thinks there's something wrong. If you don't want this deal, there's plenty of others that do. You're the biggest around here, but you ain't the only one."

Poulos' eyes turned hard. Howie said, "Two days. It's damn near the first of April now. If you're goin' to take this, sombody's got to get a move on. I can't pick up gunslingers just anywhere. It all takes time." He stared at Poulos, his eyes slitted and angry.

Finally Anthony Poulos shrugged. "I need the grass. I been figurin' I'd have to sell some sheep. With Tincup grass, I could buy more." He made a cold smile. "Two days. I'll drive around and see the others today and tomorrow. Come back tomorrow night."

But Howie shook his head. He knew when he had won. He said, "No, you drive into Tillman. I'll be at the hotel."

He wheeled his horse, and at a gallop went out of the yard, his two hired guns falling naturally in behind him.

Chapter 12

Rose Frye usually rose at six-thirty. From habit, she washed and dressed at once, then built up the fire in the tiny stove in her living quarters behind the dressmaking shop. Then she prepared her breakfast. Usually she had two cups of coffee, and this morning was no exception. Afterward she went into the shop and began her day by sweeping the floor and dusting.

Often she would pause and stand before the window to stare out across the barren desert floor eastward toward the visible thin line that marked Tincup boundaries. Yet for so many weeks had she stared at it each morning that now she could do so without feeling the pangs she had known at first without having her eyes mist over with tears.

The Tillman Hotel was on the same side of the street as the dressmaker's shop, so she did not see Howie Frye until he crossed toward the restaurant. Even then she could hardly believe her eyes. How could he have found her here? Howie thought she had gone to Denver.

And she had. But she had not stayed. The big city was too much for her. She missed the open vastness of the range country; she missed the feeling it gave her that Mart was not entirely lost to her.

There was really no excuse for a dressmaking shop in Tillman. Tillman was too small. Rose scarcely made her groceries out of it even though she was good and got all the business that was to be had. But while she still had a good part of her mother's legacy, the dressmaking shop reduced the drain on it besides keeping her busy, keeping her from thinking too much.

She began to tremble as she watched Howie's scrawny figure cross toward the restaurant. She could not tear herself away from the window after he went in, and so, later, saw him come out, apparently on friendly terms with the two strangers who had been in Tillman less than two weeks themselves.

Rose immediately thought with quiet terror, "He knows that I am here. What does he want? Why won't he let me alone?"

It puzzled her when Howie headed downstreet toward the livery stable, when he mounted and with his two companions took the north road out of town. "Perhaps he is not after me," she thought, "or he would have come directly here."

Then what was in Howie's devious, unhealthy mind? Not an innocent, aimless ride on the desert. Howie hated riding, hated horses. No, whatever brought Howie to Tillman was important, but if it was not concerned with her, then what could it be?

Rose shook her head. She went about her work,

preoccupied, troubled. She hung the capacious folds of Mrs. Poulos' dress from the dummy and knelt beside it, her mouth crammed with pins. But she could not keep her mind on the dress. Time after time she wandered to the window and stared out into the street. The town began to fill with men from the outlying ranches, and at last Rose was forced to stay away from it.

She did not dislike the dozens of men who paid her such persistent court. She was even a little flattered. There were three or four she liked who would, she knew, have been glad to have her on any terms. They had said as much. But Rose was too honest to give the man she married such a small part of her as she had to give. Most of her—all of her heart—belonged to Mart Joliffe and perhaps would always belong to him.

So, whenever possible, Rose avoided her suitors and today stayed back from the window whenever one passed. She had not yet relinquished all hope. Some day, something might happen to Howie, or he might go away. Then, if Mart still wanted her, she would return to him.

Mrs. Poulos was to have been in this afternoon for a fitting, but she did not come. Watching for Mrs. Poulos, Rose, at two, saw Howie ride back into town, saw him stable his horse and walk toward the hotel. She studied the two he was with as they left him and headed into the saloon.

Even to Rose, the way their guns hung advertised their calling. Saddletramps. Drifters. Gunmen, men who hired their murderous talents and who were always to be found in a country where trouble was shaping up. What did Howie want of them? Was he planning more trouble for Tincup?

With a sigh of relief, Rose saw Howie turn out of sight into the hotel with never a glance upstreet toward the dressmaking shop. He was not after her, then, perhaps was not even aware that she was in Tillman. And indeed, how could he hurt her if he did know? She was of age, dependent only upon herself. Howie was not even her father.

Mrs. Poulos did not come in, although Rose lingered in the shop all afternoon waiting for her. She ate her dinner in solitary, brooding silence, and then went to bed early. For endless hours she lay awake, worrying about Howie, about his errand in Tillman. And a dark suspicion began to form in her mind.

Tillman was the heart of eastern Utah's sheep country, lying close to the edge of Tincup domain. Conceivably, Howie was trying to stir up the sheepmen, trying to persuade them to take over Tincup's range as soon as the grass turned green.

Eventually, though she despaired of so doing, she dropped off to sleep only to dream of Mart, standing with his back to a wall, with Howie and his two Tillman acquaintances closing in on him from three sides. In the dream, Howie's face was a mask of snarling rage, and the other two were coldly sure. Rose screamed, "Mart! Look out!" and woke up.

She was on her feet beside the bed, shivering, and she realized with wonderful relief that her cry had been the only real part of the dream. She was perspiring, but she was also cold. She got up and made herself a cup of tea, sat sipping its scalding warmth gratefully.

But the hideous reality of the dream would not fade from her mind. She thought, "Mart is in danger—in terrible danger." Desperately she wondered what she could do to help, and finally, finding no ready answer to this, crawled back into bed, and in the small hours of morning, slept.

On the following afternoon, late, Mrs. Poulos drove into town with her husband, and came at once to Rose's tiny shop, her broad face smiling apologetically. "That Tony! I plan to come in yesterday as I told you I would, but no! These men, they have always got something else to do."

Rose smiled wanly. "That's all right, Mrs. Poulos. It didn't matter."

Mrs. Poulos put a thick arm around Rose, and squeezed her affectionately. "You are a sweet girl. It was not Tony's fault, I think. Some stranger come out yesterday morning—something about grass—and then Tony had to hitch up the buckboard and go see his neighbors about it. Today, Tony has to come to Tillman to see this stranger again. . . . Don't you feel well, Rose?"

"I'm all right, Mrs. Poulos. I didn't sleep very well last night." Rose helped her slip into the unfinished dress, frowning worriedly. She knelt, tugging at the dress, and spoke finally around the pins in her mouth. "There are several strangers in Tillman. What did he look like?"

Mrs. Poulos laughed, made a mock shiver. "I did not like him. He was small and skinny, like an elderly bantam rooster. He had two others with him."

Rose's heart sank. She did not feel that she should exhibit more curiosity, yet she felt that she had to be sure. When she saw Howie step across the street toward the saloon, accompanied by Poulos, she was sure enough in her own mind, and yet the question came from her lips, "Is that the one?"

Mrs. Poulos nodded violently. "That is the one." She seemed to lose interest in Howie. "When will the dress be ready? Could you have it by Saturday?"

"I'll try, Mrs. Poulos. I'll surely try." Rose had to force her smile as the woman left. Then she sat down and buried her face in her hands. First Shanks. Now this. Howie would, she realized at last, never be satisfied until Mart were dead, perhaps would not be satisfied even then. It apparently made no difference to Howie that Rose had given Mart up. Rose thought with desperation, "Oh, I've been such a fool! Why didn't I tell Mart? Why didn't I tell the sheriff? Why didn't I stay?"

Suddenly, determinedly, she stood up. "I can tell him now. I can go back and tell him now."

She did not know that Mart had married Lucille. In her excitement at the thought of going back, Lucille did not even occur to her. And perhaps it was just as well, for if she had known, she might not have caught the night train for Cedar City.

Anthony Poulos sat across the table from Howie and poured himself a drink. He said, "We think we will go along with you. But one thing we do not like. You say Mart Joliffe has a soft streak. Perhaps this is so. You should know Mart better than I. But I know old Raoul. There is no soft streak in Raoul."

Howie laughed unpleasantly. "Hell, he's an old man. Mart runs Tincup, Mart and Floyd Timmons, an' Timm does what Mart says."

Poulos shrugged. "Perhaps. But I know Raoul from the old days and a man does not change. Raoul is hard as nails. There is no weakness or pity in Raoul. There is no regret in Raoul over Robineau's sheep."

"Damn it, he's an old man. He can hardly get around."

Poulos shrugged expressively. "He can speak, can he not? He can give orders. And he can plan a fight."

"Well, I guess he could. But like I told you, . . ."

Poulos' expression was stubborn. "I have put my life into my sheep. My friends, the ones who wish to go with me in this, have done the same. We will take a chance, but we will not be fools. Get rid of Raoul, or we make no deal."

Howie stared at him. He saw the implacability of final decision in the old sheepman. He asked viciously, tauntingly, "You mean kill him?"

Poulos smiled. "I did not say that. The methods you use are your own. I am only interested in results. Get rid of him."

"That'll cost money."

Poulos shrugged. He fished a small leather bag from his pocket. "I have some money here." He flopped it onto the table and struck a blow like a sledge against the table top. "There is a thousand dollars here. There will be more when you need it."

Howie studied the old man's broad face. It showed him ruggedness, implacability, the firmness of decision. The man, Howie knew, was like all these big ranchers. To them, the ranch was all important, and the methods they used in building it were not particularly important. He felt a touch of contempt. In their minds they could justify anything, even murder. Yet in Poulos' own way, he was scrupulously honest. He had a certain code and he lived by it.

He was not Howie's sort of man, but suddenly Howie knew that there would be no quibbling from Poulos in the weeks to come about how he handled the invasion. Poulos had chosen his course, and he would travel it to the bitter end, no matter who got hurt, no matter what the cost.

He grinned. "Get your sheep ready, and stop worrying about Raoul. I'll take care of him."

Poulos stood up, but did not offer his hand, an omission Howie did not fail to notice. Poulos said, "I'll be ready to move the last week of April. But I want to know about Raoul before I move. I want to know that Raoul will not be planning Tincup's defense."

It had just occurred to Howie that this was one way of striking at Mart that had not previously occurred to him. He grinned viciously. What other blow could he strike Mart short of killing him which would cause him so much pain?

He said shortly, "You go ahead. Raoul will be dead in three days."

* * *

Later, he sat at the same table and stared across it at the flat, hooded eyes of Corbin. "I've got work for you. Your regular pay is a hundred a month, for each of you. There's a two hundred and fifty-dollar bonus for this particular job, and you split that. All right?"

"What's the job?" Howie noticed Moya, really noticed him suddenly for the first time. There was an odd sort of excitement in the man's eyes, a wildness Howie had not noticed before. Beneath the black beard, the man's lips twitched.

Howie glanced around the saloon, and lowered his voice. "A killing." Something flared like a grass fire in Moya's eyes. He grinned and licked his lips. Howie noticed that Corbin's expression as he looked at Moya mirrored Howie's own feelings.

Corbin jerked his head at Moya. "He's your man," he muttered disgustedly. "Hard times and an empty belly makes a man run with some queer ones. He likes killin'."

Howie felt cold. He said, "We all go together. I point him out and the two of you take care of him. When we get back, I want to take a ride down into Arizona. I want eight or ten more men, men that can shoot and ain't afraid to. I'll give you money enough for expenses, and fifty dollars apiece for each one you bring back."

"When do we leave?" This was Moya, but his eyes were hooded again and showed Howie no expression.

"Tonight. Go on down to the stable and hire me

a saddle horse. Hire a pack horse too. I'll go down to the store and buy some provisions and I'll meet you there." He hesitated a minute, and then rose. "We'll go into Tincup by the back door. That way, when the job's done, there'll be no one to know who did it."

He watched them file out the saloon door. A buckboard passed at that moment, and the thin, distant wail of a locomotive whistled across the desert. A woman sat in the buckboard beside its driver, and for an instant, in the brief glimpse he caught of her, a sense of familiarity was strong in Howie.

But the anticipation of this new blow he was about to strike Mart was too great in him for further consideration of the woman. Just someone he had seen in Tillman, he surmised, and promptly forgot her. But he did not forget Mart, nor did he cease to think of what he would do to Mart. He began to grin, and this way went out of the saloon and moved uptown toward the general store.

Chapter 13

Spring came to this high country always with a rush. Mart felt the soft breeze blowing out of the south, and reined in his horse, just to smell the goodness of it, the fragrance of thawing, fertile earth soaking in sunshine so very hungrily. Willows along the creek bank were brilliant red-brown as the sap rose in them, and budded with velvet gray pussy-willows. A light patina of green lay over the fields, spring green, and cattle roamed the valley, gaunt from winter, but bright-eyed with hope of a new, lush year.

He gazed across the yard at the sun-washed porch, at Raoul sitting there in his creaking rocker. Raoul was thinner than he had been last spring. Mart thought back over the past year, realizing how many things had happened, how many unpleasant things. Robineau had tried his grab for Tincup graze, and had killed himself because he failed. Rose had run away. Mart had been shot, he had married Lucille . . .

Still, on these cold, damp spring mornings, Mart could feel the stiffness and pain in his leg, the sharp bite of agony as he drew frosty breath into his lungs. But he had stopped limping, mostly by vowing fiercely to himself that he would not limp. He had gained weight. He felt better, almost as good as he had felt before being shot. Almost as good in his body. Not in his mind.

The guilt over Robineau's sheep had been washed away largely by Lucille and by the bitter things she had done to him. Now, considering it carefully, he realized that he did not hate Lucille, perhaps would never hate her even if she carried out her awful threat. Pity was what he felt for her. She had thoroughly ruined her own life. Women were so much more vulnerable than men, guessed Mart. They should never try to fight men in a man's world. They only got hurt. Mart himself would recover much more quickly from Lucille than Lucille would from Mart, and even this would be cause for more bitterness. It would hurt her to realize that in exacting vengeance from Mart, she had hurt herself worse than she hurt him.

Shrugging lightly, he crossed the yard and swung down before the corral. He unbuckled the cinch and slung the saddle to the top corral pole. He turned the horse into the corral, and then hung his bridle from the saddle horn, hung the blanket beside the saddle to dry.

Avoiding the deeper mud in the yard, he crossed, and clumped up the steps to the porch. Raoul gave him an idle smile. Mart squatted, removed his spurs, and fashioned a cigarette. He said, "Took a ride up on top this morning. Grass is coming. Another two weeks. . . ." Some prompting in the back of his mind reminded him of what he had seen on the plateau. He mused, "Funny. I cut the trail of three riders an' a pack mule. Who in the hell would be up there this time of year?"

Raoul shrugged. Mart felt saddened at the lack of fire in Raoul's eyes. He had done that to his father. He had done it by letting Rose go, by marrying Lucille.

Raoul asked, "When you going to put cattle up there?"

"I thought I'd put Timm to gathering some of the younger steers next week. They'll make out all right up there, even if there ain't much feed. Calf branding will take a couple of weeks more and we'll push them all up." He watched Raoul as he spoke. He was thinking, "Hell, I've never seen him before when a warm spring wind wouldn't heat his blood. Usually he's in the saddle from the first thaw on."

He said, on sudden impulse, "It's Saturday. Why the hell don't we saddle up and go to town? We'll get drunk together like we used to do."

Raoul showed him the frosty blue of his fierce old eyes, the ghost of a smile on his grayish lips. "What would your mother say?"

It was an old jest between them. Mart played his part seriously. "I'm a man, damn it. I can drink by myself, so why can't I drink with you?"

He was pleased to see Raoul's smile widen. Raoul stirred in his chair. "All right. Saddle me a horse."

Mart stooped to buckle on his spurs. He wondered why he kept thinking of the trail he had cut this morning. It was somewhat unusual for riders to be crossing Tincup plateau at this time of year, but it had happened before. He thought, "They ought to have come off one of the trails. It would be easier going in the valley."

He straightened, saying, "You better get your sheepskin. It could get cold," and went down the steps and across the yard. He hesitated for only an instant over his choice of a horse for Raoul, finally selecting one of the hot-blooded, shining bays. The horse would put Raoul on his mettle, and besides, Mart knew the old man would be highly insulted if he were expected to ride a horse gentler than one of the bays. He'd grumble sourly, "Reckon you're an old man for sure when they start saddling gentle old horses for you. Saddle me somethin' that can run, dammit."

Grinning a little, Mart rode to the house, leading the bay for Raoul. Floyd Timmons came out of the bunkhouse. He asked, "How's the grass on top, Mart? Good enough to move cattle up?"

"Not yet. But we'll put some steers up there pretty soon, next week maybe. Then we can get busy and brand the calves." He thought again of the trail he had found this morning, and asked, "You seen any strangers around lately? I cut a trail up on top of three men and a pack animal that wasn't over a day and a half old."

Timm shook his head. Raoul yelled from the porch and Mart grinned.

He rode over to the porch and handed Raoul's reins down to him. Suddenly, so very suddenly, he had an odd, gray feeling of depression. So strong was the feeling, so incomprehensible, that for a moment he sat utterly still, frowning. It was almost a premonition, almost a foresight of disaster. It was as though gray clouds had suddenly drifted in from the north, bringing cold fog, obscuring the sun.

Yet the sun shone warmly, through a thin, light overcoat. Timm, fists on hips, watched Raoul from the bunkhouse, grinned as Raoul howled and spurred up the lane. Then Mart's feeling of depression lessened. There was rich goodness in seeing Raoul act this way. His father was already halfway up the lane.

Mart's legs twitched and his spurs turned inward toward the horse's ribs. But he stopped them, reined in the horse that had already started to move. His rifle nested close to his hand in the saddle boot. But his hip had not the comforting weight of his holstered Colt's against it. Mart had not worn the thing for months. Somehow, today, he thought of it again as he had so long ago, that night in town when he had been shot.

His hunch had paid off then. He could not ignore it today.

Timm had approached questioningly, and now he murmured, "Mart, you better take after Raoul. You know how he is on a fast horse. And the road's still slick."

"Yeah." But Mart swung down, his indecision gone, and handed the reins to Timm. He sprinted for the house, took the steps two at a time. There seemed to be such an odd sense of urgency in him. He slammed open the door and went directly to the mantel, where his gun hung from a set of elk antlers, and snatched it down.

Raoul had never had a bad fall from a horse, he told himself fiercely. Why all this damned worry about him? Why this feeling of nakedness without the Colt's, when he had ridden without it all winter?

He snatched his reins from Timm's hand and leaped into the saddle. His spurs raked furrows along the animal's ribs, and the horse plunged away. Behind him, Mart heard Timm's startled cry, "What the hell? You see Raoul fall? Why the gun?"

Mart did not answer. He was beginning to feel like a fool. Hell, Raoul was all right. Raoul always rode at a run, in mud, in snow, in deep dust. It made no difference to Raoul what the footing was. He had often said, "The footing's the horse's concern. Not mine."

Almost, Mart slackened his pace. But then the strange feeling of depression returned, and suddenly he remembered the trail of three men and a led mule. He recalled the attack upon him last fall in Cedar City, recalled that Joe Herdic had never succeeded in figuring out a reason for it. Herdic had the firm belief that someone had hired the killer, and if that were so, that someone, whoever he was, could have hired again.

He thundered into the turn where Tincup's lane met the road. His horse floundered in the soft mud, faltered and almost went to his knees. Automatically, Mart loosened his feet in the stirrups, tensed himself to spring from the saddle as the horse fell. But he recovered, and did not fall.

Again Mart's spurs sank deep. The prints of Raoul's horse were deep in the soft mud, and gobs of the sticky stuff lay about on the road where the bay's pounding hooves had flung them.

Damn the old man anyway! How far would he run? Would he release all of the winter's stored up energy in these first few minutes? Would he run the bay until the horse could run no more? Mart admitted that it was possible. Raoul had been lately subject to dark and brooding moods. He might be finding release from them in the frantic motion of his spirited horse.

And Mart admitted this as well: if Raoul kept his spurs in the bay's ribs, Mart would never catch him, would never see him until Raoul decided to stop. For no horse on Tincup could catch that bay except the other one.

The minutes ran on, and the miles fell behind. Mart's horse dragged his breath with great labored heaves now, and his glossy coat gleamed with sweat and was flecked with foam. And still Raoul's tracks stretched on ahead.

Mart began to curse, softly, slowly, steadily. The feeling of depression, of premonition, had crystallized now. He knew suddenly that out of today could come nothing good. Some terrible thing must happen today. Someone would die.

He tossed a glance over his shoulder, and saw a single rider pounding after him nearly a mile behind. "Timm," was the brief thought that flashed across his mind.

And then he heard the shot. Flat, wicked, it rolled across the valley and bounced off the high rim on the southern side of it. Premonition was reality now. Mart scolded himself bitterly, "You're a fool! That trail you cut—why didn't you have sense enough to know what it was? Why didn't you ride with Raoul? Why . . .?"

Seconds were eternities. Mart's cruel spurs drew blood from his horse's sides. He yanked the quirt off the saddle horn and belabored the animal's rump. But he had the horse's whole effort and the weary animal could give no more.

He caught a glimpse of a rider sliding his horse down the steep and muddy slope a half mile ahead. Immediately his view of the man was obscured by a heavy clump of cedars. Mart dragged his rifle from the boot and levered a shell into the chamber.

He came out from behind the cedars, saw the rider dismounting, gun in hand. Even at this distance, Mart could see the man's black and bushy beard. He thought, "I'll know that one. I'll know that one." He flung his rifle to his shoulder, looped his reins around the saddle horn, holding the dangling end with one knee. He steadied his aim as best he could on the running horse, and squeezed down on the trigger.

He saw a second man come sliding down the hill out of the cedar jungle that covered it. And he saw a third, sitting his mount on a high point, unmoving, watching.

Distance was too great for recognition, but Mart thought with fleeting contempt, "The boss of them. Too good to kill, but not too good to hire it done."

His rifle bucked hard against his shoulder.

The bullet kicked up a shower of mud that flung over the bearded man, made him jump back, made him come around, gun held high and ready. Mart fired again, but this one was high and to the right.

Smoke rolled from the man's revolver, and seconds later the report shattered the valley's quiet, flat and wicked, but without the force or power of the first shot Mart had heard.

Mart raised his rifle for a third shot, but as the muzzle came over his horse's head, the animal shied violently, almost unseating his rider, making Mart lower the rifle and grab for the saddle horn.

Mart topped a shallow rise, and suddenly the whole, level expanse of the valley lay before him. He saw the bay, shining with sweat, standing a hundred yards from the still body of Raoul Joliffe. The horse was trembling so violently that his shaking was visible even at this distance of nearly three hundred yards.

A shout echoed down from the high knoll where the single watcher sat, and both men ahead of Mart swung around to look upward. Mart could catch no words, but the tone of the voice was frantic and hurried.

The bearded man ignored the shouted command, whatever it was. He turned back toward Raoul Joliffe, stepping carefully, raising his revolver for another shot. Hope shot through Mart instantly at this, and the racing thought cleared through his mind, "Raoul isn't dead! Raoul isn't dead!"

The other, the one with the bearded man, yanked his horse around and spurred him uphill into the sheltering cedars. Mart's mind instantly warned him, "Remember that one. He's standing in the cedars drawing a bead on you."

The bearded one shot a glance around at Mart's rapidly approaching figure. He hesitated for the barest instant between his horse and his fallen quarry. Then he turned again toward Raoul and his gun came up for the second time.

Mart was but a short hundred yards away. His frantic mind shouted, "If you never shot straight before, shoot straight now!" He dropped his rifle and snatched out the Colt's .45. Hammer came back in a swift, automatic movement as the gun cleared its holster.

Eighty yards—sixty, fifty-five. The gun bucked against his palm, and almost as an echo, the bearded man fired, not at Mart, who thundered down upon him, but at Raoul, still and gaunt in the mud, oddly twisted, looking pitiful and small.

Mart's thoughts screamed, "Too late! Too late!"

The bearded man grunted audibly, and now swung around, his left hand going automatically to his side, low on his abdomen. It took the barest part of a second for Mart's brain to register the import of the tiny shower of mud that spattered over Raoul's still face. But then he knew, and fierce gladness surged through him. The bearded killer had missed his carefully placed shot. He had deviated from his aim but a couple of short inches, and it was enough.

In a single swift movement, without checking the animal, Mart flung himself from his horse. He landed, boots digging in, sliding. His gun came away as his arms flung wide for balance. The killer, wicked yellow fire flaring in his eyes, steadied his own gun on Mart's body.

A rifle roared from the cedars. The bullet struck a rock at the side of the road, and whined eerily across the valley. Mart thought, "God! This is it!" because he could not bring in his outflung arms soon enough, could not gain balance quickly enough to match the bearded killer's deadly speed.

Neither could he stop trying. He teetered there, still in motion, still fighting for balance, and then he saw the glaze begin to cover the killer's evil pair of eyes. It was a dimming of the killing lust, a dying of life's leaping flame. The gun in the killer's hand lowered and the muzzle dropped. Only then did reflex tighten the killer's trigger finger, and the gun roared, harsh and deafening.

The bullet made a solid, flat sound as it struck the soft mud—like a beaver's tail on the muddy bank of a pond. Powder smoke, acrid and blinding, whirled into Mart's face.

He fell, rolled, brought his gun before him and trained it upward toward the green-black cedars. He saw nothing. But he heard the crash of brush as the second ambusher's horse scrambled upward.

Timm's horse slid to a stop beside him, showering him with mud. But Timm did not dismount. Instead, he yanked the animal around and started up through the cedars. Mart yelled, "Timm! Damn you, come back here!"

146

Timm hesitated. Mart said sharply, "Raoul's the main thing now. We'll get them later."

And Timm came back.

Chapter 14

Mart went at once to Raoul, and knelt in the mud by his father's side. Timm stood awkwardly over him, muttering bitter curses under his breath, and the almost frantic plea, "Mart, lemme go after the bastards! Don't let 'em get away with this!"

"They won't. They won't." Mart was almost afraid to touch Raoul. The old man had been knocked from his horse by a bullet, had tumbled onto the muddy road. He probably had some broken bones. And he had that bullet in him.

Apparently, Raoul's head had struck the road first, had plowed a furrow in the mud, for his face was unrecognizable because of the heavy mud coating it carried. Mart stripped the bandanna from his throat and wiped gently at Raoul's face. Blood welled from beneath the mud. Mart spoke sharply over his shoulder. "We're closer to town than we are to Tincup. Take Raoul's bay and ride to town. Get Doc and a buckboard and come on back. Kill the bay if you have to, but hurry!"

Raoul groaned, and stirred ever so slightly. Mart unbuttoned his father's sheepskin, flung it back, and searched with his eyes for the tell-tale welling of blood that would reveal the wound. He heard the pound of the bay's hooves on the road.

Afraid to do much to Raoul for fear of aggravating his injuries, Mart nevertheless straightened his legs and arms, so as to make him more comfortable. He knew the left leg was broken, for it had an odd limpness to it, a limberness that was unnatural.

Blood kept welling through the coating of mud at the side of Raoul's head, just above the ear. With gentle, careful fingers, Mart probed at this place, smoothing away the mud, until at last he uncovered the wound, a deep furrow that the bullet had plowed.

Mart knew that two shots had been fired at Raoul, knew one had missed. "Grazed his head," he muttered. "But there'll be concussion—maybe a fractured skull."

He closed Raoul's coat and stood up.

If only Raoul were not so old! If only he were not so weak. But in spite of Raoul's age and weakness, hope began to grow in Mart. Raoul had never given up without a fight. He never would.

With the borning of hope, a lot of Mart's grief and shock left him. Anger, slowly growing in him all through the winter, now began to stir anew. He walked to where his rifle lay and picked it up, wiped the receiver with the bandanna, peered into the barrel to see if it was stopped with mud. He walked over and toed the dead form of the killer viciously. He peered up at the screen of cedars, and his mouth made whispered words, "Ride fast and far, boys. Because we'll be coming after you."

Raoul made a low groan, and Mart's head jerked

around. The old man's eyes were open, but they were dull, and glazed with pain. His words were weak. "What the hell happened? That damn bay horse take a fall?"

"You were dry-gulched. Bullet grazed your head. You damn fool, you left me pretty near a mile behind you. It's just lucky. . . ." Mart's tone was sharp, angry, as his worry found expression in his voice. But he was instantly contrite. "Sorry. I guess if you hadn't been traveling so fast, they'd have got you dead center."

"You run 'em off?"

"Two of them. The third is still here. He's dead."

"Them was the tracks you saw then?"

"Uh huh. You shut up. Talking ain't good for you. Timm went after Doc and a buckboard. He ought to be back pretty soon."

He hunkered down on the ground beside Raoul. His hand found the old man's, felt its feeble pressure. Anger grew in him like a flame in a pile of kindling. He said, "Raoul, I'm getting damn sick and tired of being a duck in somebody's shooting gallery. Last time we had no chance of finding who was behind it, because the guy was dead. This time is different. I'm going to take that trail and stay on it till I find them."

Raoul grinned at him feebly. Mart said, "Herdic won't get them, either. They're mine!"

Raoul grunted, "All right. There's plenty of rope layin' around in the barn. Take some of it with you." He closed his eyes, smiling faintly. His hand relaxed. Mart asked anxiously, "Raoul. You all right?"

He heard a distant shout, swiveled his head around and looked downcountry. He could see a buckboard rocking along behind a running team; he could see a horseman pounding along beside it. The seat of the buckboard carried two figures, one the unmistakable, short, bulky figure of Doc Saunders, the other slimmer, somewhat taller.

Mart turned back to Raoul. His father's face was ashen beneath its coating of mud. The eyes were closed. Mart slid a hand beneath Raoul's coat, felt his chest where the heart was.

A long sigh ran out of him. The beat of Raoul's heart was weak, but steady and unfaltering, "Passed out," thought Mart. He got up and walked to his horse. The animal was soaked, chilled and shivering. There would be no trailing until fresh horses could be caught, and that meant a trip back to Tincup. The dead man's horse had wandered off, now stood a quarter-mile away, head down, giving Mart an accurate estimate of the condition of the ambushers' horses.

He thought, "I could give them half a day and still catch them."

The buckboard rounded a turn, and suddenly Mart's heart almost stopped. That figure beside Doc, that white, terrified face—the way she sat the buckboard seat, tense, beautiful, wild. Mart's lips formed her name, "Rose!"

Timm, ahead of the buckboard now, plunged to a halt. He had left the bay in town, now was riding a fresh stable horse. Mart gave him no chance to dismount. "Get on up the road. Bring a half-dozen of the boys, and that other bay of Raoul's for me.

151

Make it fast going up, but save your horses coming back."

Timm galloped away, and Mart turned toward the buckboard. Doc was climbing clumsily and stiffly down, but Rose had dropped the reins, had flung herself to the ground beside Raoul. She had no thought for the inch-deep mud she knelt in. Her head went down and her soft, fragrant cheek laid itself against Raoul's. Her midnight hair cascaded around his head. Her shoulders shook with her sobbing.

Doc said gruffly, "Get her up. How the hell is a man supposed to get a look at Raoul?" But his voice was hoarse.

Mart caught Rose beneath her arms, stood her up, turned her around. Her eyes were wide, frightened. He had the feeling that if he released her, she would run. Mart said gently, "Raoul's leg is broken. He's got a bullet burn on the side of his head. But he was awake a minute ago. I talked to him. He'll be all right."

There was mud on Rose's face—mud and Raoul's blood. She asked, her face utterly without color, "Do you know who did this?"

Mart gestured with his head at the dead gunman on his back in the mud, staring sightlessly at the sky. Rose looked at the man and shuddered. "Howie did it, Mart. Howie did it. Two days ago, Howie was with that man in Tillman, Utah."

Mart wondered why he did not feel more surprise. Perhaps he had unconsciously suspected Howie. Perhaps he had known all along, but had been unwilling to admit his suspicions even to himself.

Doc stood up, snapped his black bag shut and

wiped his hands on his pants. He grunted, "I thought Raoul was a crazy driver. But did you ever ride with Rose?"

Rose asked, "How is he? Will he. . . ?"

"Dunno why the hell he shouldn't. Help me lift him into the buckboard. You diagnosed him as good as I could, Mart. Broken left leg. Concussion from that bullet wound. Barring pneumonia or some damn thing, he'll be up in a week or so."

Mart and Doc lifted Raoul and deposited him on a pile of blankets in the back of the buckboard. Rose covered him tenderly. Doc climbed to the seat and took up the reins. "I'll drive back." He clucked to the team, drove ahead. Then he backed, turning the buckboard around in the road.

Mart looked down at Rose. White and still she stood, almost cold. He thought, "She knows about Lucille." He asked, "Are you back for good?"

She shook her head, and would not meet his eyes. Conscious that Doc was waiting, that Raoul needed to get into Cedar City at once, Mart nevertheless took a couple of minutes for Rose. He took her shoulders in his hands, waited until her eyes rose to meet his. He said, "When will you quit running away from me?"

"Mart, you're married. I can't. . . ."

He cut her off. "I'm married but I've not got a wife. We've slept in separate rooms since the night we were married."

"She's carrying your child, Mart."

His tone grew vicious, "And has threatened to kill it as soon as it's born. Rose, quit it! I don't know why you ran the last time, but I know why you're running

153

now. Give me a little time, Rose. Give me a little time to work things out."

She was hesitating, and he pressed his advantage. Roughly he pulled her to him, crushed his mouth against hers. He wanted to be brutal with her, to force his need upon her, but he found he could not. Tenderness crept into the kiss, and when Mart held her away, her eyes were wet with tears. He said, "Stay until I can get to town and talk to you. Will you promise me that?"

After a small hesitation she nodded, her misted eyes devouring his face. Then she whirled and swung up to the buckboard seat. Doc clucked to the team and drove slowly and carefully toward town. When the rig was a hundred feet away, Mart called, "Send Herdic out, Doc," and Doc raised a hand.

Rose turned on the seat, and watched Mart until the buckboard went out of sight at the bend.

Mart had told her he didn't know why she had run before. Suddenly he did know. He thought he could put it together in his mind. In some way, Howie's hatred of him was concerned with Rose. Howie had threatened to kill him in the saloon the night he was shot. He had probably threatened Rose with Mart's death, had told her he would kill Mart if she married him.

So Rose had gone away. "Why didn't she tell me?" Mart wondered, but he had the answer to that readily enough. Howie's threat from her lips would have been nothing new. And you cannot kill a man for a threat. You cannot even jail him. Besides, Rose had undoubtedly realized at what a disadvantage Mart would be against Howie. He could make no hostile move against Rose's father.

Mart was excited at Rose's return, yet he was also vaguely uneasy. Nothing was settled between them. He'd had experience with the implacability of her decisions. But he would at least have another chance at persuading her to stay. She had promised him that.

He walked to the horse he had ridden from Tincup, and offsaddled, then gave the chilled animal a brisk rubdown with the soggy saddle blanket. He took the bridle off and turned the horse loose. It shook vigorously, walked away a few steps and lay down to roll. Thoroughly muddy, but apparently satisfied, it got to its feet and trotted away. Mart caught Timm's horse, rubbed him down and turned him loose to trot after the first.

Now Mart turned his attention to the dead gunman's horse. He led it over to the road, dropped the reins, and with some difficulty, hoisted the body to the saddle. With the man's own rope, he tied him down, and when that was finished, led the horse up the hill a few feet and tied it to a tree. Herdic would be up after a while, and would lead the horse and its gruesome burden back to Cedar City, where an attempt would be made at identification, and then the body buried.

A high yell lifted distantly in the valley above him, and Timm came over a slight rise of ground, five men behind him, all trotting briskly. When they rode up, Mart took the bay's reins from Timm, saddled, and led out along the plain and muddy trail that led upward through the cedars. At the top of the rise, where he had seen the lone horseman sitting, he drew rein and examined the ground for a few moments.

There was evidence here that the ambush had been patient. Cigarette stubs littered the ground. Tracks overlaid one another until nothing was clearly distinguishable. But the running trail of the two leaving was plain enough.

So hurried had been their departure that they had not even bothered with the pack mule, which stood patiently tied to a tree. Beside him were the remains of an old fire, and a few cans of beans, unopened. Bedrolls lay on the ground, and a blackened coffee pot was overturned near the remains of the fire.

Mart said, "It's Howie Frye and a hired gunman we're after. Kill the gunman if you want, but I've got to have Howie alive."

Howie deserved to die, he knew, but he did not want the man's blood on his hands. Already there were too many barriers between him and Rose. He would not add another.

Timm rode up beside him at a spot where the ground leveled slightly and cocked an eye at the sky. "You see what I see, Mart? I think we'd better kick these horses in the ribs a little."

Mart had felt the indefinable change in the air himself. All day a thin film of cloud had lain across the sky. The air was utterly still, and its very stillness was ominous. Mart knew at once what he could expect—one of the sudden, blinding snowstorms so common to this high country in April. It would whirl and rage for half the night perhaps, and would stop in the early morning. But it would cover the ground with six inches of white, virgin flakes, and by the time it thawed enough to again pick up the fugitives' trail, it would be useless to follow.

But he calculated that they had all of the remaining daylight today and, in a quick decision, came to the hopeful conclusion that if they pressed their horses, they could come up with their quarry before night and the snow hid their trail.

He touched spurs to the bay's gleaming sides, and the animal surged ahead powerfully. The trail led upward inexorably, and it soon became apparent to Mart that Howie Frye and his companion, also aware of the coming storm, were pressing their mounts to the utmost, a killing pace, a pace that could not long endure, in the hope of staying ahead of pursuit until the snow or the night came down to hide their tracks.

Up across the slide they went, through the rimrock, and out onto the rolling top of the plateau. Now, no longer was it necessary to rest their horses every few hundred yards. It was gallop and walk, trot and gallop—and walk again.

There was little talk among Tincup's grim punchers. Timm had briefed them upon the day's happenings, and they were out to avenge old Raoul.

The hours passed, and the horses sweated and began to lag. And still the trail stretched ahead. A flake of snow struck Mart's face, and at once he realized that the sky was heavy gray, solid. The wind turned colder, and Mart rolled up the collar of his sheepskin. Timm rode up beside him, asking, "How fresh do you think these tracks are now?"

Mart grinned at him, a tight grin without mirth.

Timm knew as well, perhaps better than he, how old these tracks were. Timm could gauge them almost to a minute, particularly in mud that is soft and loses its sharp shapes quickly.

But this was a part of Timm's deference. He never told either Mart or Raoul what he thought. He asked their opinion, and then either concurred or gently amended it. Mart said, "Damned near thirty minutes."

Timm nodded. "We're licked then. You know it, and so do I. It's taken us this long to catch up an hour on them. The snow will cover their tracks before we make that other half-hour up."

"Unless one of their horses dies. God knows they've been crowding them hard enough. We might catch them over the next ridge."

Timm grinned his approval. He grunted, "What I was thinking. Their horses warn't in too good a shape to begin with. And they've poured it on today. From the looks of their tracks, they've been pourin' it on harder than we have." He pointed to the ground. "One of them ponies is groggy now."

But the minutes pounded away into hours. The snow thickened, and the creeping gray of dusk rolled over the land. Somewhere ahead rode Howie Frye and his hired killer, perhaps but a mile, a half-mile away. Yet at last snow and darkness hid the trail to where not even Timm could make it out, and Mart reined in with futile anger.

"We could flounder around in the dark all night," he said, "and probably pass them ten feet away and never know it." He shaped a cigarette and touched a match to its end.

"We'll go back," he murmured softly, "but we know who we're looking for now. We know it's Howie Frye."

Chapter 15

Timm wanted to take the boys and get on the train. He wanted to be in Tillman when Howie and his killer arrived. But Mart shook his head. "No. We got the man that shot Raoul. We know that Howie was behind him. We've got nothing particularly against the other man. Let it go. We'll pick Howie up one of these days. Besides that, I want to start gathering steers Monday. By the time they're gathered, the snow will be gone on top. Then we've got to get busy branding."

In early morning, he swung down before Joe Herdic's office, more solid than he had been for months. He could not quite understand the excitement that stirred in him, for none of his problems were solved. He was still married to Lucille, and although Rose was back, he could not see how it could come to anything. Howie still lived, and Howie would try again.

Perhaps his knowledge that spring had come was partly responsible for his lightened spirits. Perhaps it reassured him to have Raoul safely incarcerated in a room at the hotel, out of danger at least until he could get out of his room.

Joe Herdic took his spurred boots off the desk as Mart came in. He said, "Tough about Raoul, Mart. You catch the others?" His eyes were oddly cold as he stared at Mart.

Mart shook his head. "Trail snowed in. But I know who one of them was, Joe. It was Howie Frye. If he comes back to Cedar City, you throw him in the jug. I'll stand back of the charges."

"You got proof?"

"No." Mart could not understand Herdic's hostile attitude. Neither could he tell Herdic of Rose's accusation. He looked at Herdic hard. "What's eatin' you Joe? If I wasn't damned sure it was Howie I wouldn't tell you to jug him. He was back of that gunman that shot me last fall. He was back of this jigger that shot Raoul. Do I have to go get him myself?"

"Better not, Mart. People are getting kind of tired of Tincup's high-handed methods. People are commencin' to think that the Robineau deal last spring was pretty raw, but not half as raw as the deal you gave your wife."

Mart could feel his anger rising, could feel the heightened color in his face. Herdic's expression suddenly mirrored outright dislike.

Mart made a wry, tight grin. "You've changed your tune, Joe. Why? Tincup's never been a grab-all outfit. We've lived and let live, at least in the past ten years. You used to think Tincup was all right, especially around election time. What changed you?"

"Like I said. That Robineau deal. The way you're treatin' your wife. She was willing to let the past

161

die. But not you. You hate sheep and everything connected with sheep, don't you Mart? Now you hate Howie Frye, maybe because you want Rose even if you have got a wife, and Howie don't like it."

Herdic had come to his feet as he spoke, stood spraddle-legged and defiant. Mart's big fist smashed his lips against his even, white teeth. Herdic went backward, fell over his swivel chair, and tumbled against a file case. He pushed his hands against the floor and came to his knees. Blood trickled down his chin from his smashed mouth. He turned his head and spat. His eyes were venomous.

Mart's action had been reflex. He stood now in still fury, waiting for Herdic to get up so he could hit him again. Mart's light blue eyes flashed their cold fire. Mart said softly, too softly, "Joe, if I ever hear Rose's name on your filthy tongue again, I'll finish what I started this morning. I'll ram every God-damned tooth you've got down your throat."

Herdic's eyes blazed. But he did not get up. Mart whirled and went to the door. He said intemperately, his hand on the knob, "You remember this, Joe. I gave you a chance to do your job. You wouldn't do it. From here on, I'm taking over. Tincup will handle its own affairs in the future. If you can't do the sheriff's job, by God I'll do it for you."

Herdic crawled to his feet. He fished a clean white handkerchief from his pocket and wiped his mouth. He threatened, "Watch your step, Mart. Watch your step. The laws were made for Tincup, same as for everybody else. You break them, and I'll come after you."

Mart felt like laughing, felt like snorting. "The way you're coming after me now?" yet he knew that would have been unfair. Herdic was something of a dude, but no one had ever questioned his courage and Mart did not do so now. He knew that Herdic's remark about Rose had been ill-considered, that the sheriff was ashamed of it and had not fought back because he was ashamed.

The knowledge did not seem to lessen his anger. He whirled out the door and slammed it behind him. For a moment he fumed, but gradually, his calm returned. He wondered what had gotten into Herdic. It puzzled him. Herdic had always been friendly toward Tincup. Mart knew that whatever the cause of Herdic's hostility, he had not lessened it this morning with his hasty blow. Yet at the slur Herdic had offered Rose, his temper, so long repressed, had flared violently. His actions afterward had been uncontrolled and instinctive.

Scowling, he headed across the street toward the hotel, leaving his horse tied before the sheriff's office. At the desk he asked, "Which room is Raoul's?" and when the man gave him the number, turned toward the stairs. In the clerk, as in Herdic, he sensed a concealed animosity. Herdic had mentioned his treatment of Lucille. Could it be that Lucille had managed to gain the friendship and sympathy of the townspeople, and had told a story of their trouble favorable to herself and unfavorable to Mart? He admitted that it was possible, even likely. She was an accomplished actress, so much so that she had easily fooled Mart. It would not be hard for her to play the part of a wronged wife.

A woman could put a man in a damned difficult position. Because he could not betray the fact that Rose had told him, he had this morning been obliged to conceal how he knew that Howie Frye was behind the attack on Raoul.

Now, he was obliged to accept the town's bitter judgment of him because decency would not allow him to air his quarrel with Lucille in public.

He shrugged and climbed the stairs. Raoul's door was open, and Mart could hear the old man's deep tones, and in reply, Rose's throaty, sweet ones. He barged in, hat in hand.

Rose's color was high, and Raoul's old eyes had a wicked gleam in them. Mart grinned, asked, "What's he been telling you to make you blush like that?"

Rose's color deepened, and she kept her eyes on her shoes after that first, glad glance at Mart.

Raoul grunted, "Tellin' her there's a room ready for you and her at Tincup, and to hell with the country's sharp-tongued gossips."

Mart murmured, "You're getting well all right, you old stud-horse. Can you get along without your nurse for a while?"

Raoul's head was swathed in bandages. His splinted leg lay stiff and rigid beneath the thin blanket. He nodded. "Don't you let her go again, boy, or by Jupiter I'll bring her back for myself. I ain't so damned old but what I could put more sparkle in her eyes than you do."

Rose glanced at him appealingly. His bony hand came over and squeezed her arm. He said, "Go on. Remember what I told you."

Mart followed Rose from the room. He said, "I want to talk to you, but there's no place here. I'll hire a buggy."

She nodded wordlessly. She walked with him down the stairs and out into the muddy street. The only snow remaining in Cedar City was that which lay on the north side of the roofs. Rose's light hand on Mart's arm burned through his heavy sheepskin, seeming to leave its brand on the corded muscles of his forearm. Its heat spread through his body, and his excitement grew.

Trying to keep this emotion out of his voice, he asked, "What was it Raoul told you that he wanted you to remember?"

Rose was looking straight ahead. Her voice was scarcely audible. "He said there had never been a divorce in the Joliffe family. But he said there would be now. He told me to hold on to you and make you happy until things could get straightened out."

Mart's voice was hoarse. "And what did you tell him?"

She looked up. Mart's blood ran scalding hot in his veins. She said, "I told him that you would have to ask me."

Mart realized suddenly that they were at the livery barn, stopped before it. Old Sherman Dawson came down the dim, reeking alley between the stalls, glared at Mart and asked shortly, "What you want, Mr. Joliffe?"

"A buggy, Sherm." Again that hostility. Sherm had never called him Mr. Joliffe in his life. It was disturbing to Mart, who was friendly by nature, who liked to be liked. He frowned. The town's hostility had given him the answer to the question Rose had raised in his mind. But he did not speak until he had helped her into the buggy, until they had cleared the limits of the town.

Then he said, "I can't ask you that, Rose." He gripped the reins with his right hand, his knee with his left, and both hands were white from the strain. Suddenly he said harshly, "Damn Raoul for a meddling old fool! I want you, Rose. God! I want you more than anything on earth. But I won't have you that way. I won't have the country blaming you for what's happened and will happen between Lucille and me. I won't have them kicking your name around in the saloon like that of a dancehall girl!"

Her chin came up. "And if I won't stay for less?"

Mart did not know why he should not feel wildly, gloriously happy. But he didn't. He said, "Make your own terms. But stay. I can't let you go again, Rose."

She was smiling, showing him confidence that was heartening. "All right. I'll stay—at the hotel—on your terms."

He hauled the buggy horse to a stop. The horse looked around at him inquiringly. Mart did not see him. He had Rose in his arms and his lips were hard against hers.

Lucille had been able to stir him, but never like this. This was wild, sweet; this made the savage, age-old hungers stir in the depths of his body; this would go on and on and never stop.

Almost sobbing, Rose broke free of his arms, her hands pushing fiercely against his chest. Her voice was the merest whisper, "Stop it! Stop it! How can I stay at the hotel, how can I wait to be your wife when you do that to me?"

The buggy horse tossed his head and tugged at the reins. Mart turned him around, not trusting himself to speak. Then Rose's voice spoke, and he marveled at its matter-of-factness. She had herself under control, but the memory of her passion lingered in Mart, stirred him tremendously. She was matter-of-fact, but her eyes were not. They burned hotly into his.

"There is more about Howie that I haven't told you, Mart."

"What is that?"

"He has stirred the sheepmen near Tillman up. They're going to move in on Tincup grass this spring."

Mart's face hardened. "Don't they know what happened to Robineau?"

"I don't know. I don't know anything about it but what I heard and what I saw," Swiftly she told him of seeing Howie in Tillman with the two gunmen, one of whom Mart had killed the day before. She told him of Mrs. Poulos, of Howie's trip to the Poulos ranch with his promise of grass.

Finally, she told him the other thing, the thing he had to know, "Howie isn't my father at all, Mart." Tears of horror welled into her eyes as she thought of that awful night, that night when Howie, old, scrawny, lustful and clumsy, had taken her into his arms. She said, "While you were on roundup, Howie

167

told me he wasn't my father. He put his arms around me. He kissed me. He ran his hands over me." She began to cry, shuddering, shivering.

"Oh, Mart, it was awful! I thought of him as my father. I told him—he knew that I loved you." Her shoulders shook and she sobbed almost uncontrollably. "I fought away. I picked up a chair and told him I'd hit him with it."

Her sobbing quieted. Mart sat cold-faced at the reins, staring straight ahead. Anger ridged his jaw muscles, narrowed his eyes.

Rose went on, "Then he started cursing me, calling me names. He said I was a slut. He said I'd been sleeping with you. He said he was going to kill you. I told him we were going to be married, and he said if I married you, he'd kill you before nightfall."

Mart halted the horse, looped the reins about his wrist and drew Rose close. Her face was wet with her tears, and her body trembled. Mart asked softly, "Why didn't you tell me?"

"What could you have done? Howie's threatened you before. You can't kill a man or put him in jail for making a threat. And I knew how Howie would have done it, Mart. From behind. From a dark alley. From ambush like he did with Raoul.

"Mart, I know Howie. I ought to know him. I grew up in the same house with him. He never does anything openly. He slinks and sneaks around. Like this sheep business, getting Poulos to do his dirty work for him. Like with Raoul, getting a gunman to do it for him. He won't give up, Mart. As long as he lives you'll be watching, watching every stranger and wondering if Howie sent him. You'll be afraid of the dark, afraid to ride alone." She began to sob anew, "And it's all over me—it's all my fault."

Her voice ran on, hysterical, filled with her terror. "Even the bad feeling in town against you is Howie's doing. Pete Stoddard told me about it last night. Howie made it sound so logical that even Pete was doubtful."

Mart hauled the buggy horse to a halt. The buggy stood directly before the hotel. He said, "Dry your tears, Rose. Go on back to Raoul. And stop worrying about me. There's only one way to lick Howie now, and that's by beating Poulos and his sheepmen. When that's done, we'll find Howie and. . . ."

And what? Kill him? Try to force an antagonistic Herdic to put him in jail and charge him with attempted murder?

Perhaps the same questions were running through Rose's mind, but she left them unuttered. She was white, drawn. She got down from the buggy seat listlessly and tried to smile up at Mart. She murmured, "Be careful, Mart?" and then she was gone, running lightly up the steps to the wide hotel veranda.

Mart clucked to the horse, swung him around in midstreet. He turned at the next corner, drew up before a small yellow frame house whose yard was beginning already to turn green. The air was damp and cold, the sun sterile and without much warmth, shining through an overcast of moisture evaporated from the drenched earth.

He tied the horse to the cast-iron hitching post and climbed the steps to the porch. Lucille answered the door, surprised, but instantly hating. "What do you want?"

"Just to tell you something." He felt ill at ease with her, but he could not hate her. His glance dropped to her swelling abdomen. "I'm going to divorce you. There will be a settlement, but you had better not contest it. And nothing had better happen to the child, or you'll leave Cedar City without a cent. Is that clear enough?"

"It's clear enough." Her eyes were green, cold as winter ice on the Little Snake. She spoke almost thoughtfully, "Have you ever thought that a woman can hold a gun? Have you ever considered how little strength it takes to pull a trigger? I am still your wife. If you were dead, I'd inherit Tincup."

Mart laughed harshly, "No, you wouldn't. Because Raoul is still alive, and Tincup is Raoul's until he dies. Was that what Howie had in mind the other day? Are you and Howie working this together?"

For an instant her eyes betrayed her. Mart was not sure, but he felt at that moment that his random shot had scored. Then the door slammed in his face and he turned back toward the street.

Lucille had lived with her hate long enough that she was capable of anything, even killing Mart, even killing Raoul. Raoul was helpless in his room at the hotel, and Lucille would always have admittance to his room since she was his daughter-in-law.

"She wouldn't dare," said Mart's thoughts, but he could not believe them. Lucille would dare anything, and now, Mart knew, the consequences of her actions would have little deterring effect on her. She wanted to see Raoul, Mart, and Tincup in ruins. She would sacrifice her own life, if necessary, to accomplish it.

He slapped the back of the buggy horse and moved

through the deep street mud toward the stable. He handed down the reins to Sherm Dawson at the stable, and gave him a silver dollar. Then he walked back toward the sheriff's office where his horse was tied.

Chapter 16

As he walked, Mart considered the odds in this battle for Tincup's survival which loomed ahead of him. He knew what a concentrated array of power the sheepmen could assemble, knew their wealth and their determination. He guessed that Howie's part would be active to the extent of providing a spearhead of gunslingers.

He could expect no support either from Herdic or from the townspeople—could on the contrary expect only opposition. His own cash resources were going to be very limited, for he had to anticipate the large cash payments he had promised Lucille, and prepare for them. The would take all Tincup had, all they could reasonably expect to scrape together. It might be easier if he could keep the grass, for if Tincup was solvent and in possession of their range, any one of the country's banks would loan him money. But if he lost the grass . . .

He paused near his horse, and then on impulse, swung over across the street, leaving his horse tied. He banged open the doors of Stoddard's saloon. The place was nearly empty, but there were a couple of Tincup's punchers at one table, idly playing two-handed poker, a bottle between them. Mart paused by their table. "Go over to the hotel and stay outside Raoul's door. Somebody wants him dead awful bad. It's up to you to see they don't get to him."

The two stood up. Mart hesitated a moment, wondering about what he had to tell them next. Finally he said reluctantly, "Keep Mrs. Joliffe out, too. Rose Frye and Doc are the only ones you're to let in. I'll send a couple of others down in the morning to relieve you."

He watched them go out. He wandered over to the bar, watching Pete Stoddard's expression carefully as Pete slid him a bottle and glass. Pete had always been a good friend of Tincup. Now he clearly was not. He was not condemning as Herdic had been, but there was a cool, detached air about him that told Mart as plainly as words could have done that he was reserving judgment.

Mart tossed off his drink, and without a word swung around and headed for the door. There was an odd, wild tingling in the back of his head, a stirring of the old, slow anger he had been feeling lately.

"Damn them! Damn them all! Damn Poulos and his greed, Howie and his acid hatred. Damn Lucille!" He swung to his saddle and yanked the horse around. Scowling, he went up the road toward home.

He stopped fighting the threat of violence in his mind. He had been a man who disliked violence, who preferred to live in peace. Now he would try another kind of living. They had pushed him far enough. He would learn the feel of a spitting Colt's in his hand, would learn the sound that a rifle bullet can make when it strikes solid human flesh.

They wanted Tincup, did they? Well, they might take it in the end. But he'd damn well see that it cost them—cost them in sheep and human blood. He would see to it that Tincup grass was the most expensive Poulos had ever bought.

Morning found Tincup's entire crew, except for the two Mart had dispatched as Raoul's guards in town, riding in the upper valley, on Tincup's winter range.

The sun was bright and clear, the snow atop the plateau now only a light thin covering which would be gone by noon. The air was still and warm.

They rode to the very end of the canyon, where it climbed in steep stages to the final barrier of rimrock, and began the slow ride down-country, gathering as they went. On each side of the canyon, half a dozen men rode the steep slopes, the shady draws, pushing cattle ahead of them. When a pair of riders would gather a dozen or more, they would push them onto the valley floor, into the bunch that was slowly growing there, held by three of Tincup's older hands.

It was hard work on horses, for the cattle were wild, filled with spring's fresh energy. Mart changed horses four times that day, roping a fresh mount each time out of the remuda that was loosely herded along behind the cattle. At nightfall they had, he judged, a thousand head.

These were driven in to the ranch, and shoved into the big holding corral there. One of the hands drove a hayrack out to one of the haystacks, loaded it and brought it in to feed them.

The crew trooped to the bunkhouse, cheerful and boisterous. Mart halted Timm just outside, realizing that it was the first chance he'd had to talk to the foreman since he'd last talked to Rose.

Timm asked, "How was Raoul?"

"All right. Timm, the crew has got to know what we're up against. I guess they've got to know the trouble between Lucille and me as well, or they might form some opinions of their own like the people in town have. It don't seem decent for me to tell them. It don't seem right for a husband to talk against his wife. But you could tell them."

"All right."

Mart told Timm then why Lucille had married him. In embarrassment he glossed over the scene on the night of their wedding. He told Timm that Lucille had threatened to kill her child, had threatened to kill Raoul. He told him of Howie's agreement with Poulos, and what Tincup had to face as soon as the grass got green.

He was pleased at the hardening of Timm's jaw muscles, at the gleam of pure anticipation in the foreman's eyes. Timm said softly, "Boss, don't worry about the crew. When we get through with those sheep outfits they'll know enough to stay off Tincup grass."

Timm was sure, but Mart was not. He said, "Timm, Poulos' outfit is big—big as Tincup. He'll have half a dozen smaller outfits to help him. And I'm sure Howie will be in it too, probably with a dozen hired hardcases. But tell the boys they're drawing fighting wages—double wages, starting the first of May."

He headed for the house, headed for the lonely and solitary supper which Fu Ling would have ready. But before he reached it, he heard the howl of the crew from the bunkhouse, a howl of pure anticipation, a howl of gleeful approval.

He wondered how they would feel toward him a month from now, with very probably a third of their number dead. He wondered if there are any wages which will pay a man for risking and perhaps losing his life. And he wondered if he himself would survive, wondered if he did, how he would settle with Lucille, how he could free himself to marry Rose.

In morning's early darkness, the crew rolled out and ate. A wrangler brought in the remuda and each man roped himself a mount from the bunch. By the time the first gray of frosty spring dawn lay over Tincup, the crew and Mart were in the saddle.

They turned the herd out into the open brush beyond the gate, and the cutting began. Springing cows, cows and calves, bulls, the weaker animals of all descriptions were cut out and headed back up the valley. Steers and heifers were held in a bunch. By nine o'clock, the job was finished and Timm detailed a couple of men to drive this bunch to the top of the plateau.

They rode back up the valley and took up yesterday's job where they had left off last night.

The day passed. The roundup went on. At week's end they had cut through the herd and put everything on top of the plateau that was strong enough to stand the temporary shortage of grass.

There were no holidays, no Sundays during round-up. The work continued from dawn to dark, seven days a week. The calf branding commenced. The days turned hot and it seemed to Mart that the grass grew visibly every day. They would gather a bunch of two or three hundred, hold them in a tight group while riders roped out calves, dragged them to the fire, put Tincup's brand on their hips, earmarked them, castrated and vaccinated.

The air filled with the stench of burning hair and flesh, of acrid woodsmoke—with the reek of sweat, the raucous bawling of calves and cows, the shouted curses of men. And now, at each day's end, the herd handled that day was brought to the ranch, corralled, and on the following morning driven up the steep trail to the top of the plateau. Spring and fall were the hard-working times, and this was spring.

But as mid-April came, Mart began to feel uneasy about Poulos. One morning, he approached Timm as the foreman was washing in the icy water from the pump. "I've been stewing about Poulos. It's early for sheep on top, but he might risk the loss of a few lambs to get the jump on us."

Timm dried his face briskly and ran a piece of comb through his stiff, graying hair. He said, "Want to take a look today?"

Mart nodded. "You and me. That won't stop the branding, and if we find anything, we can come back for the crew before we jump into it."

After breakfast, Mart strapped on his Colt's, emptied a box of shells for his rifle into his pocket and took the gun from its place behind the kitchen door. He found Timm waiting, similarly armed, and the two turned the cow and calf herd out of the corral and started it toward the trail.

By taking up this herd as they went out on top, they would save a morning's work for two men, so that their scouting ride would deprive the branding crew of but two men for only half a day.

At nine, they pushed the last of the slow-moving herd up through the rim and rode out on top in warm April sunlight.

Already the grass was two inches high. In the shady draws, quakies were leafing out, their young new leaves the palest green. An occasional wild flower bloomed against the ground. Sage chickens, invisible in the low brush, started out from under their horses' feet, never failing to make the animals shy violently.

Foreboding, a strange feeling to come over a man in warm, bright sunlight, began to stir in Mart. Timm, riding behind, asked, "How you figure they'll hit us? You think they'll come up in one big bunch with all their guards on it, or in small bunches, scattered out?"

Mart frowned. He had been considering the same problem himself. He spoke his thoughts aloud, musing, "Howie doesn't know that Rose spilled his plans. He knows how Robineau's sheep bothered me last spring. I think he's counting on me hesitating because of that."

"Then he'd put small bunches up, try to make us think each one was independent of the other."

Mart nodded. Timm, looking out ahead toward

the horizon, asked, "What are you goin' to do? You paid pretty high for what we did to Robineau's sheep. You going to let that stringhalt you?"

Mart scowled. He had been wondering himself how he would handle this crisis when it arose. He had told himself a hundred times that utter firmness was all that could conceivably achieve his purpose. He thought of Robineau, brazenly moving in on grass that did not belong to him. He considered the man's cowardice in killing himself after he had been defeated, and the subsequent vengeance which Lucille had wrought against Mart because of it. He thought of Howie, of the pain he had suffered all winter because of the bullets of Howie's hired killer. He thought of Raoul, even now crippled, also because of Howie. He said, "No," but there was no real conviction in the word.

He wondered if it were in him to ride into a camp of sheep herders, guns spitting, cutting them down. He wondered, and his foreboding increased.

Timm looked at him doubtfully. He growled, "There ain't but one way to handle this, Mart, and you know it. You drive them off or they drive you. You kill them, or they kill you. You ain't worrying about Herdic?"

Mart could be no less than honest. "He's hostile to Tincup because of Lucille and the stories she's told around town. I can't do any fighting from a cell in Herdic's jail."

"Let the sheep outfits fire the first shot. Then you're in the clear."

The morning passed. Steadily riding, they came at noon to the squat, sod-roofed cabin that was Tincup's line camp. Mart corralled the horses, and Timm built a fire in the tiny stove. They boiled coffee, opened a can of beans. There was evidence of previous occupancy here, dirty plates, a dirty skillet. Timm grunted, "We'd better ride careful this afternoon."

Mart gulped his beans, drank his scalding coffee. He wished he could rid himself of his hesitancy. He wondered what he would do when he rode up to one of Poulos' sheep camps today. He was hoping that they would make the first, overt move, and thus release him from the reluctance that was torturing him.

And for the first time, the deep-seated question that had unconsciously bothered him for a month came to the surface. "What will it do to me? I stewed for months over killing Robineau's sheep. What will I feel when I look at the bodies of men I've killed?"

His squirming mind argued, "What did you feel when you killed the man who shot Raoul? Nothing. Why, then, should you feel more guilt over these?"

He knew the answer to that. The great majority of the men Tincup had to fight were guilty of nothing but taking their pay for doing their jobs. Howie's gunmen would bother him little, he knew. But how about the little men, the sheep-herders?

He wondered how Raoul would be if faced with the same decision, and knew the answer to that without hesitation. There was no softness in Raoul.

Timm finished washing the dishes, carried his wash water to the door and dumped it out. Mart shaped a cigarette, touched a match to its end and went out the door. Timm picked up his rifle and followed.

Up on the hillside, in a patch of dark spruce timber, Ben Corbin, lying prone, raised his rifle, rested the barrel against the trunk of a tree, and drew a bead on Mart's chest. The range was long—three hundred yards. Corbin stilled his breathing, and felt the muzzle of the gun steady in his hands. Mart was moving toward the corral now, presenting the narrower target of his side to Corbin's eyes.

The muzzle of the gun followed inexorably. Mart caught his horse, and led him out of the corral. Corbin softly cursed. Mart stood behind the horse and threw up the saddle, stooped slightly to cinch it down.

Timm rose to his saddle, his horse dancing, and then Mart followed suit.

Mart headed uphill toward the ambush, Timm riding beside him. And Corbin waited. He could hear the rustle that Howie Frye and the others made, coming up behind him. His finger tightened down on the trigger. He spoke to Howie behind him, "Two shots, and we make an end to this scrap. Raoul's dead. There's Mart and his foreman. I've got Mart in my sights. You take the foreman, and the war is over. Tincup can't fight without a leader."

He stopped his breathing and squeezed. A flurry of motion beside him made little impression upon his consciousness until Howie's boot struck his rifle barrel just as it discharged. The bullet tore up dust a foot to one side of Mart, and his horse jumped.

Corbin rolled, coming to his feet, his face a mask of rage. But before he could speak, Howie fairly screamed, "Who's giving the orders around here, you or me?"

Poulos' heavy voice cut in, "Neither of you. I'm the one that gets the grass, and I'm giving the orders. Cut 'em down, boys." His gun muzzle poked into Howie's back.

Mart and Timm were down off their horses. They were hidden in the low brush of the hillside. One of their rifles barked, and a bullet thudded into the trunk of a tree, three feet from Corbin's head. He ducked.

Howie's voice was taut and sharp. "I told you I was going to run this show. I don't want Joliffe dead. I want to see him squirm. I want to see him broke, and then I want to kill him myself."

Corbin snapped a shot down at a brush clump on the hillside, and raised an angry shout, an answering shot that ricocheted off a rock at his feet and whined away. Poulos said, "Corbin, take three men and circle around. Get them in a crossfire."

Corbin crept away, three of his hardfaced companions following. Poulos' voice was dry, without emotion, as he spoke to the others. "Keep firing. Keep them pinned down there until Corbin can get around."

Howie Frye was white, trembling with rage. Corbin heard a shot that was oddly muffled as he moved away, and turned his head in puzzlement. Howie was clutching a bloody, spreading stain on his dirty shirtfront, and Poulos, behind him, was smiling strangely, his eyes bright with some inner satisfaction. As Howie fell, Poulos shoved his gun back into his holster, backed away and followed Corbin through the heavy screen of timber.

Chapter 17

Down on the hillside, Mart hugged the ground, white with sudden, murderous rage. All his doubts were gone, and he wondered now why he had ever entertained doubt in the first place. He was not fighting ordinary men. He was fighting thieves—grass thieves—and killers. He was fighting Howie Frye. He was fighting chill-eyed hired gunmen who would stop at nothing—neither at murdering an old man from ambush, nor at murdering himself and Timm the same way.

Timm lay behind a clump of sarvus a dozen feet away. Two weeks earlier in the season, this brush would have afforded little or no protection. Now, however, with its new green covering of young leaves, the brush made an impenetrable screen. Impenetrable to the eye—not to a bullet.

As Mart had come off his horse, he'd shown the presence of mind to snatch his rifle from the boot. Timm had not. Now, Mart fumbled in his pocket for a handful of rifle shells and shoved them into the magazine of the carbine. With the rifle loaded, he holstered his Colt's.

Timm called softly, "Hit, Mart?"

"No. How about you?"

"I'm all right. But we're in a bad spot. They'll circle after a bit and put us in a crossfire."

For an instant the impulse was strong in Mart to leap up and run, but he controlled it with an effort. He had often wondered what it would be like to face certain death, had wondered if he would feel fear. He admitted now that he would probably have been afraid if he were not so damned mad. He was not ready to die. Perhaps he would never be ready. Life was a sweet and precious thing to any man, even when his life was messed up as Mart's was.

No, he felt no fear—only raging, futile anger because he knew that they would kill him, because they would take Tincup's grass, because they would win and he would lose.

The horses had halted uncertainly a hundred feet away. Gunfire had disturbed them, had made them nervous, but with some distance between them and the guns, they calmed and began to munch grass.

Beyond the horses was a shallow ravine, a dry watercourse which in rainy weather carried away the runoff. Mart thought, "If we could reach that. . . ." He shook his head. It would only postpone the inevitable, for without horses, they could not hope to escape. He gave some consideration to a dash for the ravine, a grab at the horses as they went, but again shook his head. The horses were skittish from the shooting. They would not be too easily caught. They would fidget and move away trailing their reins if a man approached them.

He shrugged. A bullet probed through the brush

behind which he hid, and a twig, but by its passage, dropped into his upturned face. Rolling, he poked his rifle ahead of him, snapped a shot at Corbin above him in the trees. He heard the ricochet of the bullet into space, a dim, receding whine. "Missed."

A rain of bullets kicked up dust beside and before him. He ducked back hastily. Timm called, "Got any ideas?"

"I was thinking about that ravine, but it's a hundred and fifty feet away. Even if we did reach it, it wouldn't do any good. It would just postpone things a little."

He heard the muffled pistol shot from above, was puzzled at this. They had rifles up there, and this range was nearly two hundred yards, hardly the range for a revolver.

He swung his glance to the right, and knew instantly from what direction the next shots would come. The timber in which the ambushers hid ran along the crest of this ridge for a couple hundred yards, then petered out on a high point which looked directly down upon the two hidden men. If they switched their position enough to conceal themselves from that vantage point, they would then become exposed to the other.

He peered around the brush clump and stared at the timber above. He thought he saw a man crawling, but the target was too uncertain, too fleeting. The man appeared to be crawling out of the timber and into the brush, traveling at a slight downhill tangent. Mart was puzzled. Surely none of them would try an open, creeping attack through the brush when the other method was so sure.

He watched the place where the man had disappeared, following his apparent course through the brush by the faintly waving tops of the bushes. He frowned.

The man was not even heading toward Mart and Timm. He was, instead, following a course which would put him between Mart and the flanking party.

Mart muttered to Timm, pointing, "What the hell's he doing?"

"I dunno. Cut down on him."

"Can't see him long enough at a time."

The minutes ran on, each one a sweating, tortured eternity. At last Mart saw a stir in the timber where it petered out on the point. He tried to edge around so as to cover himself partially from both places. He called to Timm, "Here it comes."

From directly above, bullets poured into their position. Mart rolled to escape, his eyes covering the ground to his left as he did so. Something strange about that glimpse disturbed him, but he could not for a moment tell what it was. But suddenly he knew. He whispered, "Timm, the horses are gone. You see where they went?"

Timm looked. His eyes were puzzled as he turned back toward Mart. "They sure got away fast."

Sudden hope shot through Mart. He said excitedly, "Timm, they didn't run away! They just went into that shallow ravine!"

A crackle of rifle fire burst from the point off to the right. The moment they had dreaded arrived at last, with a wicked, murderous crossfire pouring into their position.

Timm grunted as a bullet grazed his arm. He said sharply, "Mart, we ain't going to lay here an' let 'em cut us to bits. We've got to get out of here. I'd as soon be shot runnin', tryin' to get away, as shot layin' here on my belly like a snake."

"Hell, you won't make it, Timm, but try it if you want to. I can't cover both places at once, but I'll do the best I can for you. Wait till I load up this rifle. If I can keep the lead flying fast enough, you could make it, I suppose. If you get there, you catch the horses first, and cover me while I make a dash for it."

It wouldn't work. If there were only two or three men shooting at them, it might be different. But a man had little chance when eight to a dozen guns were spitting at him. Timm would run perhaps a third of the distance before they cut him down. After that Mart would have to lie and listen to bullets thud into Timm's inert body, knowing that all chance was gone, that death was but split seconds away.

If only the horses had wandered into the ravine at the very beginning! They they might have had a chance, for Mart believed he could have kept the ambushers harassed enough in their single position so that accurate shooting at Timm would have been impossible.

He knew too, that he could never pour enough lead into both widely separated positions to keep them from getting Timm.

He-had forgotten the lone man crawling through the brush, but suddenly he remembered. He felt a sudden chill in his body. What if the man had changed directions? What if he were now but short yards away, drawing a bead on Mart's head?

He raised his head the barest fraction, and peered into the screen of low brush. But he saw nothing.

He raised himself as far as he could without exposing his head and body too recklessly, and breathed to Timm, "I'm ready when you are."

He could sense the slight movement as Timm gathered his feet under him, as he crouched ready to run. A hundred and fifty feet to run, a hundred and fifty rough, exposed feet.

He turned his head, and the words started from his lips, "Timm! Don't do it! You'll never. . . ." But Timm was up. It was as though a hundred rifles had opened up all at once. Mart stood up, feeling that at least he could draw a part of their fire away from Timm. Bullets showered around him, glancing off the ground and whining eerily away. And then his rifle was at his shoulder, and he was pouring a murderous, concentrated fire into the position above him.

For a seemingly endless moment, Howie Frye's mind was stunned, too occupied with the horror of the thing that had happened to him to fully understand its consequences. He felt as though some terrible force had smashed him from behind. Then the pain struck, excruciating, greater than any Howie had ever felt before.

The front of him was suddenly soaked and hot. Automatically, he clutched himself with both hands, felt the slickness of fresh, warm blood, felt too the bulging of his entrails at the gaping hole. He knotted his hands and pressed them back. Then he was falling. Consciousness slipped away from him. His brain reeled, and the earth whirled before his eyes.

He hardly felt the impact as he hit the ground. His brain was fighting, was feebly clutching at consciousness while it shouted, "This is wrong! You're being cheated. They're going to kill Mart, and that will be too easy for him. You've been double-crossed!"

It seemed an eternity before his body responded to the frantic urging of his brain. But at last, sharp, clear consciousness returned. In the first instant of it, he knew one thing surely. He was going to die. He then thought of Mart and Timm, pinned down on the slope. He thought of Anthony Poulos, grizzled, thick-set, dark-skinned. He knew that he had underestimated Poulos' ruthlessness and determination. He had made a fatal mistake.

Too late to strike back at Poulos. But perhaps not too late to thwart him. He tried to raise his head, but it fell back.

He concentrated all the force and virulence of his hatred for Mart on the task. He felt the quickened beat of his heart, a faint surge of strength to his muscles. He raised his head again and peered down the slope. He turned his head and looked behind him.

Poulos was gone. So was Corbin, and so were a couple of the others. Those who remained had their attention fixed on the slope below, and did not notice Howie, half-hidden in the screen of low brush that covered the ground here in the timber.

Fuzziness clutched at Howie. It would have been so

easy to lie back, to let the delicious languor seize him, to let the drug of pain overcome him. But there was Mart, down on the hillside. There was Howie's acid hatred of him. Howie wanted him to die—but not yet. Howie wanted him to suffer first.

No longer could he remember why he hated Mart. He only knew that he did. He hated Mart more than he loved life. And if he could prevent Poulos from killing Mart, he might yet satisfy that hatred, could feel as he died that Mart would suffer the loss of his grass, of Tincup, before he himself was killed.

Howie's hand still clutched his rifle. Carefully, he eased himself down the slope, carefully so that none of those left above him could see.

And as he crawled, the life ran out of him in a scarlet stream and left its trail on the ground behind him.

He had started at first, with no plan, straight down the slope toward Mart. He had hardly gone a dozen feet when he realized that this was wrong. He could be of no help to Mart by crawling to him. Mart would shoot him and that would be that.

He struggled with the nausea and faintness that strove to overcome him. Poulos—Corbin—the others. Where had they gone? Then from out of his subconscious came the half-remembered words of Poulos to Corbin, "Corbin, take three men and circle around. Get them in your crossfire."

That was the most dangerous threat to Mart at the moment—that crossfire. Howie did not know how a single, mortally wounded man could stop that crossfire, but he could try. There was most certainly nothing else he could do.

His eyes scanned the timber above him, noted the place where it petered out on a high point and recognized that spot as the only logical vantage point for the flanking party.

He crawled for an endless time, and at last, reaching a fairly clear spot, raised his head and peered around. He could see Mart from here, prone on the ground, could see one of Timm's feet beyond Mart. He looked past Timm, and saw the shallow ravine. He thought, "Why the hell don't they break and run for that?"

Then he saw Timm gather his feet under him, saw him crouch and get ready to run. He saw Mart, looking around, his face wild and raging.

He knew then that they were going to do it. Poulos and Corbin opened up from the point, and the bullets sang softly over Howie's head. They had not seen him.

He saw Timm leap to his feet and begin his run. He saw Mart levering shells into his rifle, firing, levering again, shooting into the fringe of timber above him.

Suddenly Howie knew what he could do, knew what he had to do if he were to succeed in thwarting Poulos. Mart could not cover both parties of attackers at once. He could cover only the one above him. But Howie could cover the flanking party, could pin them down so that their fire would be ineffective.

He could see Mart's strategy. Somehow the horses had wandered into that gully. If Timm reached it, he would then cover Mart until Mart could reach it too.

Howie pulled himself around, rolled and came to a

sitting position. Now he had to take his one hand away from the torn and gaping wound in his belly. The hand was slick and slippery against the rifle stock. He levered the rifle and raised it to his shoulder. Pain shot through him, and he could feel his entrails pouring out of the wound.

Poulos and Corbin stood exposed, firing down over him. If they saw him, they gave no sign. Howie aimed at Poulos, and pulled the trigger. Poulos howled, slapped his thigh as though a bee had stung him there, and then jumped down to crouch behind a boulder. Howie fired at Corbin, missed. But Corbin joined Poulos behind the rock.

For the barest fraction of a minute, there was no fire at all from that quarter. Then Corbin poked his rifle around the boulder and fired. The bullet tore through the brush beside Howie's head.

He jerked his head aside, threw up his rifle and shot at Corbin's head. He knocked a shower of rock splinters into Corbin's face, heard the man's shouted curse.

Firing suddenly halted behind him, and he risked a glance over his shoulder. Mart was crouched again, grinning out of a sweaty, dusty face.

Howie felt a stir of satisfaction. Timm had made it, then, for Mart would not be grinning if he had not.

It did not seem strange now to Howie that he, who hated Mart more than anything else in life, should be helping him. His twisted mind had convinced itself that in this way his revenge against Mart could be greater, could be more satisfying.

And he entertained no doubt that Poulos would kill Mart in the end. That was inevitable, particularly now, now that he knew how ruthless and cold Poulos could be. So let Mart live to suffer the loss of Tincup, and then let Poulos have him if he would.

A shot banged out from the ravine. Mart jumped up and began to run, weaving and twisting, leaping brush, ducking low. A crackle of fire broke out from above, and the rifle in the ravine stepped up its tempo. A howl came from the high fringe of timber, and a hasty glance showed Howie a man, cut in the open, staggering downhill, his eyes glazed and dull with pain.

Howie jerked himself around and threw his own rifle to his shoulder. He had automatically loaded the weapon during the lull while Timm got set in the ravine. Now he peppered the boulder behind which Poulos and Corbin crouched. And he kept feeding fresh shells into the magazine.

Desperation was in Poulos now. He leaped into the open, Corbin behind him, and drew a bead on the running Mart. Howie slammed a hasty shot at him just as he fired. Howie fired again, and Corbin's legs went out from under him. Poulos howled at the others who were cautiously shooting from behind the screen of timber, and they reluctantly stepped into the open and raised their rifles. Howie levered and shot, levered and shot.

Suddenly the gun in the ravine was silent. Dismay touched Howie, but then he heard the thunder of frantic hooves, and the two horses, bearing Mart and Timm, thundered down the ravine, out into the open valley floor where Tincup's line camp squatted, and at last disappeared into the timber behind it.

Howie saw Poulos running down toward him. He

sought to raise his rifle, to bring the man down.

But his life lay as a stain on the ground between here and the timber fringe. His life had run out slowly through the hole in his belly, and when Poulos reached him he was dead.

Chapter 18

There was a time, during the supper hour at the hotel in Cedar City, when the lobby was almost deserted. The clerk got himself a plate from the kitchen and retired into his office cubbyhole to eat it. From past observation, Lucille knew that nothing short of a riot would bring him out until he had finished.

Raoul and Rose, like most people, were creatures of habit. At exactly seven every night, they came down the wide staircase and went into the dining room, Raoul hobbling along on his crutches, Rose walking slightly behind him.

Therefore, when Lucille came into the hotel tonight, she was wholly unobserved. She hurried to the stairs and ran panting up to the second floor.

She was now quite plainly pregnant, and had taken to wearing voluminous dresses, full at the waist, to partially conceal her condition. Without hesitation, she went directly to Raoul's room, opened the door and slipped inside.

Rose had opened the window for the purpose of airing out the room while she and Raoul were at dinner. Soft light filtered in from outside, making the outlines of furniture barely discernible. Lucille did not light the lamp.

She walked to the window and stared down. The window opened onto a vacant lot next to the hotel, but there was a narrow ledge of shingled roof, perhaps two feet wide, just below the window.

Now that she had irrevocably embarked upon this course, she felt a nervous fear in the pit of her stomach. She felt a rising nausea, but she had become accustomed to nausea in the past months. From her bodice, she withdrew the small pistol she had bought, the one she had practiced so assiduously with these last two weeks.

It was a Colt's derringer, a .41 caliber Cloverleaf model, holding four bullets. It nestled in her hand, cold and compact and very deadly. Lucille smiled shakily. Fear churned in her stomach.

Many times in the past year she had wished she could kill. Tonight was the first time she had actually come to the point of attempting it.

But she was aware that by now, Anthony Poulos and Howie Frye must surely be moving sheep onto Tincup's grass. She knew that when they did, Mart would fight, and when he fought, would very likely be killed. But if Mart were to die before Raoul died, then Lucille would be out in the could so far as Tincup ranch was concerned. And she was determined that this should not happen to her.

She was Mart Joliffe's wife. She felt that she had suffered enormously at his hands. When he died, Tincup should go to her, and she knew that only this way could she ensure it.

The room seemed excessively cold to her. She

began to tremble violently. She exerted all the power of her will to still her shaking body, for she knew she could not hold the pistol steadily if her hands were trembling.

Seconds were hours, minutes eternities. She sat down and tried to relax. She stood up and paced the floor. She went to the window a dozen times. She looked at the door longingly, and once crossed to it and almost opened it. Fear told her to leave. Hate and her need for revenge made her stay.

At last she heard steps in the hall, voices approaching. They halted just outside the door. Rose said, her voice a soft murmur through the door's thickness, "Good night, Raoul. You'll be going home soon."

"Not without you. Damn it, Rose, I've told you he was going to get a divorce from her. Why won't you come home to Tincup when I go?"

"You know the reason," Rose replied wearily. "We've been over it all a dozen times."

"Well, come in a while anyway. There's nothin' on earth so damned lonely as a hotel room."

Raw panic stirred in Lucille while Rose hesitated. If Rose came in, she was lost. She knew she could not kill them both, for she was a match for neither of them physically. Besides that, while she felt that no jury would convict her for killing Raoul in view of the sympathy Howie had stirred up in town for her, she was fully aware that killing Rose would be quite another matter.

Rose asked, "Will you promise not to try to change my mind?"

And suddenly Lucille knew that Rose would agree. She knew she was lost. Her eyes drifted frantically around the room, seeking a place to hide. The closet would not do, for they would undoubtedly hang up their coats as soon as they came in. The bed. . . ? Suddenly Lucille recalled the small roof ledge below the window.

With no further hesitation, she ran to it, lifted her skirts and put her leg through. When she felt the firmness of the shingled roof beneath her foot she put her weight on it, drew her body through, and then pulled her other leg after it. She moved aside just as the door opened, just as the room was lighted from the dim lamps in the hall.

Lucille saw the flare as Rose struck a match, and a moment later the soft light of the lamp filled the room, cast its glow on the roof outside.

Lucille drew herself back against the hotel wall. She still clutched the derringer in her hand. She heard Rose's shivering exclamation of chill, and Rose came over to close the window. Lucille was no more than three feet from her, and it seemed impossible that Rose would not see her. But apparently Rose did not, for she closed the window and moved back into the room.

Panic raced through Lucille. The window was closed, and she did not know whether she could open it from the outside or not. She had no way of knowing how long Rose would stay with Raoul. She had successfully eluded Raoul's guards, had placed herself in his room, but all her careful planning had been upset simply because he was lonely and wanted Rose to come in and talk.

Lucille looked down at the ground, perhaps fifteen feet below the level of her eyes, and shuddered violently. It took all her determination to raise her glance, to overcome the dizziness that whirled in her brain.

She looked to right and left, seeking an escape elsewhere. Raoul's room was located in a gable, and from both sides of the gable the roof rose steeply to its peak. Farther back toward the alley, the hotel was, however, a full two stories, and there the windows of the rooms made a solid line. But there was no roof ledge beneath them for Lucille to walk upon.

Even in April there was a chill in the air at nightfall, perhaps more penetrating because of the closeness of the Little Snake River. And there is something about fear and nervous tension that has its chilling effect upon the human body.

Lucille suddenly realized that she was icy cold, all through her body. Her teeth chattered with her shivering. Her knees wobbled and threatened to betray her, to give out beneath her.

And suddenly she knew that she had to get back into Raoul's room or fall to the ground below. She was becoming weaker, and she could feel the waves of dizziness rising in her head. She knew the bitterness of defeat. She hated men suddenly—not just Mart and Raoul, but all men—because physically they were strong, and she was weak.

A man would have no trouble waiting out here on this roof ledge until Rose and Raoul finished their talk and Rose returned to her own room. For a man this would have been easy.

And then, in that instant, a new ray of hope filtered into Lucille's mind. She still clutched the derringer in her hand. It was of steel, hard and solid. She could, if she were careful, break out the window with it, fire and kill Raoul before Rose could interfere. Afterward, she knew, the tension of today and tonight would burst the dam of control in her. She would be tearful, hysterical, repentant.

Pregnant women sometimes did strange things, had strange emotional upheavals. She did not believe that a person in Cedar City would fail to understand and forgive her action. Except perhaps Rose.

Carefully she eased herself around, until instead of facing the brink, she faced the wall. Then she began her side-stepping movement along the ledge toward the window. Unfortunately, she stood to the left of the window, and that meant that she would have to ease along in front of the window to its right side, so that her right hand, the hand which held the gun, would be in a position to break the window and fire at Raoul.

She peered in. Raoul sat not four feet from the window, his back to her. Rose sat across the room, lightly poised on a straight-backed chair. Lucille smiled faintly with satisfaction. Had she directed their seating herself, she could not have done it more perfectly. She knew that her aim with this small gun might be faulty. At the range of the room's full width, she might very probably have missed. Yet at a distance of four feet. . . .

Still smiling lightly, she crouched, and began to inch her way past the window. A shingle, old and cracked, loosened from the roof, slipped beneath her feet.

Panic touched her, but her left hand went down to the ledge, and she steadied herself. Slowly, with her heart pounding madly, she continued, until at last she could stand again, could look into the window again.

The soft murmur of their talk reached her ears. She hesitated for a moment more, waiting for the fright of her near fall to wear off, for her shivering knees to steady.

Then, tense and hardly breathing, she raised the derringer. Its barrel came against the glass of the window, and it shattered with a loud crash, followed by a light tinkling as the pieces of broken pane clattered inside the room.

Rose sprang from her chair, utter shock and amazement mirrored in her features. Raoul started to turn, but he could not rise from his chair without the crutches which lay now on the bed.

Gaunt and old, thought Lucille. Ready to die. She leveled the derringer, pointed it at the middle of his back and thumbed back the hammer. Her finger tightened on the spur trigger.

But the force of her feet, straining as she smashed the window, had loosened a shingle beneath her feet. She felt it slip, and clutched at the window for support. The gun wavered, and discharged. Lucille's hand encountered the broken glass of the window, and the sharp edges bit deep. The shingle slipped again, and suddenly Lucille screamed. Then she was falling back, out into thin air—falling toward the ground a dozen feet away.

It seemed an eternity before she struck. Then there was pain, awful, excruciating pain in her abdomen, a terrible shortage of air in her lungs. Wildly she thought, "The child! I've killed the child!" It was then that she knew the full force of defeat, for she knew she had missed Raoul, she knew as well that her hold over Mart Joliffe was gone. She tried to get up, but could do nothing but moan and gasp, and at last, mercifully, she fainted.

The first thing Rose did was to run to Raoul, to throw herself at his feet and question anxiously, "Are you all right?"

He nodded, somewhat dazedly. Rose gasped then, "Lucille will need the doctor." She started for the door, saw Raoul's crutches on the bed, snatched them and gave them to him. Then she fled out of the room and down the stairs.

The clerk was standing at the staircase, looking up. He asked, "What's the matter? Was it you that screamed? Where'd that shot come from?"

Close behind Rose came the two Tincup punchers who were Raoul's guards. Rose commanded, "Go back and help Raoul."

To the clerk she said, "Get the doctor at once. Mrs. Joliffe fell from the window of Raoul's room."

The clerk looked his plain disbelief, but Rose had no time for further explanations. She said sharply, "The doctor, you fool, the doctor!" Then she was out the door, running around the corner of the hotel.

Lucille lay sprawled in the weeds below Raoul's window. Rose knelt beside her, and picked up her left hand to chafe the wrist. The hand was covered with blood, sticky with it, where Lucille had cut herself on the broken window. The gun lay three feet from her outstretched right hand.

For an instant Rose was tempted to conceal the

gun. Then she thought of the suffering the woman had caused Mart, of the thing she had just now tried to do. She considered that without the motive of murder, Lucille's fall would be very hard to explain, and in the town's present temper, highly embarrassing to both Raoul and herself. People would ask, "How come she fell? Somebody push her? Were you three fightin' up there?"

No. The truth would serve everyone concerned best. Joe Herdic, who seemed to sense it whenever there was trouble in Cedar City, who could hear a gunshot from farther away than anyone else, came around the corner, his revolver in his fist. He holstered it at once, and hurried to where Rose knelt beside Lucille. His glance took in the gun instantly, then lifted to the broken window. He said, "She didn't fall out that window. The hole ain't big enough. What happened?"

Rose murmured, "She must have been outside on that ledge. The window broke and there she was, with that gun in her hand. She fired once at Raoul, but she must have slipped because she screamed and fell."

She stood up as she saw Doc Saunders approaching. Doc saw who it was, and immediately grumbled, "Only cases of violence I've had in a year have been the Joliffes. She fall out of that window?"

Herdic mumbled, "Off the ledge." He picked up the tiny derrringer, looked at it, smelled the bore, then dropped it into his pocket. There was a fair-sized crowd gathered now, their faces white and shocked. Doc got to his feet, saying, "Couple of you go fetch a door. Hurry it up." He turned to Rose.

"This ain't good. She's about four months along. Ain't much chance of savin' the child."

He fished his pipe from his pocket, stuck it in his mouth and sucked noisily on the stem. The he put it away. Two men came running with a door from the hotel, and laid it down beside Lucille. Doc moved her gently onto it, first her head, then her feet. He said, "All right. Pick it up and bring it into the hotel."

The two men lifted the door, one in front, one behind, and carried it up the steps to the hotel veranda. Doc walked beside them, steadying Lucille. Lucille moaned and stirred as they carried her through the door. Herdic faced the crowd. He said, "Mart ain't said a word in his own defense. He ain't likely to, I guess. I think I'll say one for him.

"I ain't going to talk against his wife. She's hurt, and if she ain't paid for what she's done before, she's payin' now. But tonight she tried to kill Raoul. Looks to me now like we might have been a mite hard on Mart."

Rose looked at the sheepish faces of the crowd. Herdic stumped down the steps and crossed toward his office, and Rose went inside. Raoul was in the lobby. He was hard and fierce, as always, yet tonight Rose thought she detected a bit of puzzled regret in him. He muttered, "I'll be damned if it don't beat the Dutch how much can come out of some simple little thing. Robineau runs his sheep in on us, trying to make a little steal stick. We only do what we might reasonably be expected to do, an' look what happens."

Rose was thinking, "Howie's to blame for a lot of this trouble," but she said nothing. Raoul sat down

205

and propped his crutches against the wall beside him. Rose murmured, "I ought to go up and see her. She is in for a bad time. Another woman might help."

Raoul grunted, unsmiling, "You're like Mart. You've got a soft streak in you." His severity lightened, and he gave her a small smile. "It becomes a woman. Maybe it becomes a man sometimes, too. Mart felt pretty bad about those sheep. I didn't let on, but I could see it. He felt guilty about Robineau." He stared at Rose, but for once he did not seem to see her. "Maybe Mart's the one that's right. Maybe I'm the one that's wrong. This is the first time I've realized it, I guess, but there ought to be a way to settle an argument short of shootin' it out or drivin' another man's stock off a rim."

Rose stood up and squeezed his hand, smiling. "We're what we are. The Lord made us that way."

She ran lightly up the stairs, but she slowed as she approached Lucille's room. This was foolish and useless, perhaps. Lucille could feel nothing but hate for Rose. She would be bitter, perhaps even vindictive.

Still, she was all alone, except for gruff Doc Saunders. Rose tapped lightly at the door, and Doc rumbled, "Come in."

Lucille was conscious, but her face was twisted with agony. Doc turned, saw Rose, and seemed relieved. He said, "Labor pains. She's having a miscarriage." His voice held a certain resentment. "She's weak. She ain't et all winter like I've told her to. She's been livin' on hate, and so she's weak."

Rose pulled a chair to the bedside opposite Doc,

and sat down. She found Lucille's knotted fist, straightened it out and took it in her own. She looked at Lucille, saw the ravages that bitterness and hate had left. She knew this woman had all but ruined Mart. She knew Lucille had tried to shoot crippled old Raoul in the back. But she could not hate Lucille. She could only pity her; she could only feel unbearably sad.

Lucille's fingers clenched tight against Rose's, until Rose thought her hand would be crushed. Sweat beaded the red-haired woman's face. A groan escaped through her pale lips, her clenched teeth.

Time went on—time and the tiny woman's agony. But it was over at last. It was over when Doc drew the sheet up over Lucille's thin and ravaged face. And then Rose wept.

Chapter 19

When they gained the shelter of the trees and the rifle slugs stopped whining about his head, Mart turned and shouted at Timm, a dozen feet behind, "Somebody in that bunch switched sides. Why the hell do you suppose he did that?"

Timm did not bother to answer. He simply shrugged. The way Timm rode in his saddle, light and easy on the horse, told Mart what he already knew—that this was not yet finished. Poulos was no fool. He would be fully aware that if he could kill Mart and Timm now, the war for Tincup range would be over.

Poulos probably believed that Raoul was dead— had probably been so informed by Howie Frye. Therefore, by his reasoning, if he could now eliminate Mart and Timm, there would be one left capable of waging a winning fight for Tincup. Only Lucille Robineau, and it was doubtful if Tincup's crew would fight at all for her. Besides, by the time Lucille found out what was going on, Poulos would be in the saddle on Tincup's grass.

Carefully Mart considered the condition of their horses. They had not exactly spared the horses this morning, and the animals were bound to be tiring. Mart had no way of knowing how fresh were the mounts of Poulos and his men.

Perhaps Poulos had only today ridden up from the desert. If he had, his horses would undoubtedly be worse off than Mart's and Timm's. On the other hand, if Poulos already had camps established on the plateau, his horses would be reasonably fresh.

They dropped into a gulch, scrambled out, and entered a heavy pocket of aspens—huge old trees with trunks a foot thick. Mart kept his horse at a steady run now, even though the grade was slightly uphill, for he knew that these first two or three miles were the most important. It would have taken Poulos and his men some time to return to where their horses were tied, to mount and give chase. If Mart and his foreman could gain a substantial enough lead, they would at least be able to set their own pace, and not worry about bullets singing around their heads.

They broke out of the timber and onto an open trail through the brush. They reached the summit of the grade they were on and plunged down into a wide, shallow draw. Timm yelled, "We could set an ambush."

But Mart shook his head. Poulos had too many men for that. Down into this draw they went and up its far side. Another just like it lay ahead, perhaps half a mile wide, and they crossed it as well. At the high point on the far side of it, Mart flung a hasty glance over his shoulder. He saw them, a ragged line of galloping riders at the crest of the ridge, the width of the two draws behind.

A mile! It would not be enough. He projected his mind ahead, recalling the switchback trail that led off the plateau and dropped downward into Tincup's valley. A mile lead on that trail would be nothing short of suicide. Poulos could dismount his men at the head of it and pick Mart and Timm off with rifles, like ducks in a shooting gallery.

He looked around. Timm was frowning. Now they angled off to the right slightly, entering a dark pocket of spruce timber. The hooves of their horses fell almost soundlessly on the thick carpet of needles. A clearing opened up ahead, and in it sat a roofless log cabin, a relic of the time when prospectors had roamed this country. The cabin stirred memory in Mart. He could recall the times, when he was a boy, that he'd brought a blanket and a gunnysack of grub and walked out on top to spend the night at this lonely cabin.

They swept past it, and suddenly Mart saw a way out of this. He slowed his horse ever so little, gazing behind at the almost complete lack of tracks behind them on the needle carpet of the little-used trail. He kept slowing the horse, and when he had the animal at a walk, swung off the trail and entered the deep timber, heading straight downhill toward the rim.

Timm grunted, "What the hell?"

Mart said, "We'll never ride off the trail without getting killed. Not with the lead we've got. But I used to walk up to that old prospector's cabin when I was a kid. There's a way down through the rim that a man can make afoot. We'll ride as far as the rim, turn the horses loose, and go off afoot. By the time Poulos backtracks, picks up the place we turned off and follows, we'll be clear down in the valley."

Timm was skeptical. "Depends on who's trackin' for Poulos."

Mart said, "It's the only chance we got." They had ridden out from the line camp at about one or one-thirty. It was now almost four. Mart was amazed at the swift passage of time. He urged his horse to a trot, and faintly heard the drum of hooves behind him. His ears were tuned to the sound, as he waited for the pause in their rapid cadence, the pause which would tell him his plan had failed, that they had missed his tracks and turned back. But the rapid beat of hooves did not halt or diminish, and Mart breathed a sigh of relief.

Instantly Timm's expression lightened. He asked, grinning, "You ever try to draw to an inside straight?"

Mart nodded. "I've done it, too."

"I can believe it, after today."

Mart kept angling slightly to the right, until he came to the bottom of a steep draw. He followed this for perhaps half a mile, and at last swung down off his horse. He snatched the rifle from the boot, leaned it against a tree. He flung off saddle and blanket, unbuckled the throat latch on his bridle. He slapped the horse on the rump and sent him trotting up through the timber.

Then he picked up his rifle and slid down off the rim, which at this spot was no more than a dozen feet high. He struck, sliding, still on his feet, and with rapid, running strides, went downward across the steep and brushy slope, with Timm a short ten feet behind.

211

* * *

By the time Mart reached the ranchhouse, he was footsore and irritable. He was in no mood to simply sit and wait for Poulos to attack, which Mart felt he would surely do. At this hour, the place was deserted, save for Fu Ling, and Schwartz, the punchers' cook. All of the crew was in the valley above the ranch. The day's branding was undoubtedly finished, and very probably they were no more than four or five miles away, driving their day's herd before them.

Timm went at once to the corral, roped out a horse and saddled. Mart said, "Make it quick, Timm. Poulos will be here as soon as he can get off that trail," and Timm rode out at a dead run, spurring viciously. Timm's temper was aroused too. Mart figured it would be no more than thirty minutes before Poulos and his riders would arrive. Horseback, they'd had a much greater distance to travel than had Mart and Timm. Too, they might have wasted as much as fifteen or twenty minutes trailing their quarry to the rim.

Poulos would be raging, of that Mart was sure. He had failed to kill them twice today, once when he had them pinned down on the slope above the line camp, and again during the chase, when Mart and Timm had slipped away and crawled off the rim afoot. He would be further enraged by the treachery of one of his own men which had caused his first failure.

And in his raging, thwarted mood, Poulos would most certainly attack Tincup as soon as he could get here.

Mart went into the house and gathered up a couple

of rifles. He gave one to a scared Fu Ling and stationed the little Chinaman at one of the smaller windows at the front of the house. He had Schwartz take up a vantage point in the barn loft. He himself went into the bunkhouse. And then he waited, his eyes fixed upon the break in the cedars beyond the gate, on the place where Poulos and his men would break off the trail.

The sun sank behind the rim west of the house, and its afterglow stained the thin, horizontal layer of clouds above it a bright, iridescent orange. Then they came, pouring out of the cedars at a brisk trot. They spread as they hit the road, and for an instant bunched there while a thick-set man Mart instantly recognized from Rose's description as Poulos gave his brisk orders. They came in, fanned out across the road in three ranks, twelve or fourteen in all.

Mart raised his rifle, drew a bead on a rider in the front rank. His rifle cracked, and the man pitched to the ground.

As though his shot had been a signal, now a high chorus of yells floated down the valley from Tincup's rapidly approaching punchers. Mart began to grin, and then he saw them sweep around a bend. Poulos' men turned to face them. They were not armed for a war, a fact which probably was not at once apparent to Poulos and his men. What Tincup's punchers lacked in guns, they made up with their yelling. Mart doubted if there were five guns between the whole twenty of them. But those who had guns were firing them as fast as they would shoot.

The ranks of Poulos' riders split, broke backward toward the ranch. Mart howled, "Ling! Schwartz!

Pour it on!"

He levered and fired, levered and fired. Two more of Poulos' riders pitched from their saddles. Poulos stood in his stirrups, waved a thick fist and bellowed, "Dismount! Take cover!"

Mart ran into the open, beckoned toward the barn, and a moment later, Schwartz came running. Mart hung a dozen sixshooters and belts on him, taking them from their nails on the bunkhouse wall.

Firing in the lane had slowed to an occasional shot as both sides sought cover and dug in. Mart said, "Go up the creek a ways. Circle behind our boys and give them these. With no more guns than they've got, they're licked, only Poulos don't know it yet."

He watched Schwartz disappear into the willows along the creek, and then ran across the yard to the house. A bullet plowed a furrow in the ground before him, and he dived into the back door, yelling at once, "Ling! Come here." He gathered half a dozen rifles from various corners of the living room, then tossed several boxes of cartridges into his hat. He handed the weapons and the hat to Ling, and repeated the instructions he had given Schwartz. He watched Ling go out the back door and disappear.

Now he ran to the front window of the house, broke the glass with the barrel of his rifle and poked it through. The yard before him was bare, but the brush began perhaps seventy-five yards from the house. Sagebrush, high as a man's shoulders. Poulos' horses milled in the lane, caught between Tincup's fire, Poulos' and Mart's, but as the firing slacked off, they began to drift into the yard, passed the house, and headed for the creek.

214

Mart was hoping that Poulos had not noticed how poorly Tincup's bunch had been armed. If he had, if he made a rush before Schwartz and Ling got to them. . . . Mart shivered. It would be slaughter.

To try and distract Poulos, he began a steady fire from the window. He had nothing at which to shoot, nothing but an impenetrable screen of brush, but he fired into it anyway, and after perhaps half a dozen shots began to draw their answering fire. Bullets slogged into the log walls of the house. One shattered the rest of the window above Mart and showered him with razor-sharp pieces of broken glass.

Light had faded from the sky, from the yard before him. In the gray of dusk, an uncertain figure ran across the yard and dived into the barn. Mart fired at him twice, missed both times because of the poor light, and the man's deliberately ragged way of running.

Concern touched him. If Poulos and his hardcases took the buildings, it would be an all-night job to dislodge them, and an expensive job, expensive in terms of Tincup blood.

Mart dropped the next man that ran across the yard, but he did not kill him. The man crawled until he reached the shelter of the bunkhouse wall.

They came in a rush then, four or five of them. Mart shot twice, and then his rifle clicked emptily. By the time he had yanked out his Colt's, the men had reached cover.

From the rear of the house, outside, he heard a hoarse shout, "Get the horses!"

The back door creaked. Swiftly, Mart stooped and pulled off his boots. He ran noiselessly across the

215

huge living room, dropped the stout bar across the front door. He turned. Suddenly he knew how this was to be. Poulos had dropped a man off at the barn, another at the bunkhouse. In a moment, Mart knew he would see the glare of fire against the windows of the house, the glare of fires starting in dry hay stored in the barn loft. He knew that the rest of them were in the house. He tried to remember exactly how many men had run across the yard, and felt a little unsure. Six or seven. He'd shot one. He didn't think that one could do much. One in the barn, one in the bunkhouse. That left four, probably, maybe five, depending on how badly Mart had hurt the one he shot.

Poulos had known, then, how poorly armed were Tincup's riders. But he had chosen to try and fire the buildings, leaving but three or four men to hold Tincup's crew pinned to the ground so that they could not interfere. Poulos wanted Mart, not the men of Tincup's crew.

The house was almost totally dark now, except for the faint red glow from the burning barn, a red glow that filtered through the windows and flung its indistinct pattern on the wall. Less than fifteen minutes had elapsed since Mart had sent off Schwartz and Ling.

Keeping his eyes on the kitchen door, Mart twirled the cylinder of the Colt's, feeling the blunt-nosed bullets in the cylinder. He ejected an empty and pushed in a fresh shell. He filled the sixth chamber, the one that was always empty for safety's sake.

Then he began to advance across the floor, silent and deadly in his stocking feet.

Suddenly the door flung open, and men spilled into the room. Mart's gun bucked in his hand—twice. Then he raced across the room, dived behind the leather-covered sofa. He had seen a man fall. He knew where that man was hit, knew he would not stir.

Bullets tore through the sofa. A shower of splinters stung Mart's face. He poked his head around, fired at a dim shape against the wall. The man groaned, sagged against the wall and slid down toward the floor. His gun clattered noisily as it fell.

Two left. Maybe a third in the kitchen. Mart was positive of his count this time. Four men had come through the door, and none of them had been Poulos.

He ejected the three empties, poked fresh shells into the gun's loading gate. He eased back the hammer, and spoke into the darkness, "Who's next, boys?"

He did not know Corbin, but it was Corbin who spoke. "Would you let a man ride out? This is a damn fool play. If we kill you they'll hunt us down."

Mart asked, "Poulos in the kitchen?"

"Uh huh."

"Who's with him?"

"He's alone."

Mart laughed softly. "Don't blame you for wanting out. All right. Toss your guns against the wall, one at a time, so I can count them."

"Man, we can't get out of here without guns."

"Then you don't get out."

The man sighed. "All right." A gun thumped against the wall. Another. Mart knew that Poulos, in the kitchen, had heard all this. He tried to figure when the man would make his play. Not now. He had been betrayed by these two. He would not trust them again. He would figure them as being against him.

Mart was down behind the sofa. He was covered. He knew he ought to wait there. Tincup punchers would be spilling through the kitchen door any minute now. Corbin muttered, "How do we get out of here now?"

"Walk past me one at a time. Your hands over your head. Be careful, boys. I'm pretty nervous."

A man's shape loomed at the end of the sofa, another right behind him. Mart lifted his gun. He knew suddenly when Poulos would strike. He knew it would be when these men drew abreast of him, when his attention was distracted. Suddenly it occurred to Mart that he had let himself fall into as nice a trap as had ever been devised. He knew he could thank Howie for it. He could almost hear Howie's words as he said, "Mart's got a soft streak in him."

Poulos had counted on that soft streak. Now it was going to cost Mart his life.

Chapter 20

He was raging. Fury, greater than any he had ever known before, pounded through his body, raised its smoky fumes to his brain. He knew there was only one thing to do. He knew what it was and he raised his gun. But he could not do it, and instantly realized why he could not. It was not in him to guess when human life was at stake.

He had made a bargain with these two, had agreed to let them leave. He was now sure they did not intend to leave, instead would jump him as Poulos came through the kitchen door. They had rid themselves of two guns, but they were not unarmed. Each would have a holdout gun. They would break their part of the bargain, but until they did, Mart was chained to his.

All this in the racing fraction of a second. Mart's muscles tensed. Raw fury turned him reckless, made him swift and sure. He bounded to his feet, eyes on the kitchen door, not on the two approaching him. They would be slowed by surprise. Their hands were over their heads.

He saw at once that he had been right. Poulos was there in the doorway, faintly lighted by the red glow of fire that filtered through the windows. Poulos, squat and sure, gun in hand.

Poulos' gun centered itself on Mart, followed his movements unwaveringly. Mart flung himself against the wall with a resounding crash, and then, with the steadiness of the wall against him, centered his gun on Poulos and tightened his finger on the trigger. He was steady enough to shoot; he was also for an instant still enough for Poulos to shoot at. The roar of Poulos' gun was ear-shattering in the enclosed room.

Mart had the racing, exultant thought, "Missed!" The hammer fell on his own gun, and flame laced from its muzzle. The feel of the gun as it fired told him instantly that he was all right. He shoved his shoulder against the wall and came violently away from it, falling and not trying to stop. The two stood across the room, beyond the long sofa. One of them held a long-barreled Colt's, the other a small and deadly derringer. Its noise was a crack compared to the roar of the Colt's. But just as deadly. Two bullets thudded into the wall where Mart had been an instant before.

His own gun bucked again in his hand, and the bullet tore a leg out from under the gunman who held the Colt's. But Mart was rolling then, off balance, and could not bring his gun to bear. He saw the gaping muzzle of the derringer, saw it steady on his prone body. And Mart knew at once that he would never stop that shot, that this was the one which no one could stop.

And then a gun crashed in the kitchen doorway. Confusion stirred in Mart. He would have sworn he had killed Poulos. His gun had felt so right when it fired.

Not until he saw the gunman driven back by the force of a bullet did the realization come to him that it was a rifle, not a revolver, which had fired from the door.

Timm's hoarse voice, frantic, came bellowing into the room. "Mart! Mart, you hurt?"

Mart scrambled to his feet, still edgy enough to cover the crippled gunman. His voice sounded hoarse and cracked, not his own. "No. But I sure as hell would have been in a minute."

Tincup punchers crowded in around him. A couple of them yanked the wounded gunman to his feet and hustled him out into the kitchen. Others began at once the task of dragging bodies from the room. A man stooped and began to gather up bits of broken glass from a shattered lamp.

Timm's words rushed out like a flood. "Mart, we couldn't do a damned thing. The boys kind of quit packing guns during calf-branding. There was only four guns amongst us. We were pinned down and we damned well knew it. Ling got there first, and Schwartz was right behind him. We moved right along after that."

Mart fished in his pocket and found a match. He raised a lamp chimney and touched the flame to the wick. He asked, "Poulos dead?"

"Uh huh. Dead center." Timm was staring at him, concern and a certain doubt in his expression. Mart could almost read his thoughts. He was wondering what this would do to Mart. He was thinking what the slaughter of a bunch of sheep had done to him. . . .

Reaction set in with Mart. He shivered violently. He tossed his gun at the sofa and walked to the front door. He raised the heavy bar and went out onto the porch.

Cold air was good in his nostrils, against his heated, sweating face. But he could not stop his shivering. He sat down on the step and dropped his face into his hands. He heard Timm come onto the porch behind him. Timm sat down beside him, not touching him, not speaking for a long while.

Finally Timm said, "They tried to burn Tincup. They tried to kill you and they tried to kill me. It's like shooting wolves, Mart."

Mart looked at the blazing barn, at the bunkhouse fire, now coming under control from the bucket line that stretched to the pump. At last he stood up. He was steady now, not shaking anymore. He looked at Timm and shrugged. A hint of his old grin spread across his face.

He had thought it out, there on the steps. There were times when a man had no choice. He killed, or he was killed himself. It was a satisfaction to him now that he had played this out his own way to the very end. It would help him in the months to come. He could have downed those two gunman from the comparative safety of concealment behind the old sofa, and then turned to Poulos. But he had not. He had given his word, and only their treachery had broken it.

Wearily he stumped down the steps and went across the yard. It would be morning before Tincup was entirely safe. But in work, in hard, physical work, was to be found release from the intolerable tension of the last hour.

Near midnight, one of the guards who had been with Raoul galloped into the yard and halted his horse to gaze with awe-stricken eyes at the wreckage, at the line of bodies laid out evenly before the porch.

Subdued, he sought out Mart. "Your wife's dead, Boss. She fell from a ledge outside Raoul's window whilst she was trying to kill him. Raoul's all right. So's Rose."

What were the things Mart felt? Regret? Pity? Yes, all of these. Yet he only nodded shortly in thanks, and then went back to work. When finally the last ember was extinguished, when the last of the wounded had been loaded into wagons for the trip to Cedar City, he stumped wearily into the house. Then, and only then, was he able to sleep.

Howie Frye was dead. A detachment of heavily armed Tincup riders had found his body on the slope above the old line camp where it had fallen. It now lay inside a new pine coffin on Tincup's long veranda.

Sheep, a steady, bleating stream, moved rapidly toward the trail that would take them off Tincup grass. Their herders, subdued, kept glancing back over their shoulders, as though completely terrified.

And a long line of packhorses, each bearing a grim reminder for the future to the desert sheepmen, filed down off the steep trail and onto the broad, flat reaches of desert.

Joe Herdic's jail was jammed with survivors. Doc Saunders was busy among the wounded.

Mart Joliffe had not left Tincup. Somehow he felt that all the bad things had left it untouched. And if good things were to come in the future, they must begin here.

Out of Cedar City rolled the yellow-wheeled buckboard, crowded, bearing three on its narrow seat. Raoul sat at the reins, gaunt and fierce, an odd glow lighting his eyes. He popped the whip savagely to urge the hot-blooded bay team to even greater speed.

Cris Lebsack, Cedar City's part-time preacher, sat beside him, white-faced, nervously exhorting him to slow down.

But Tincup lay ahead. Tincup lay ahead, and Raoul only laughed.

Rose Frye, the third person on the buckboard seat, smiled. In her eyes was the wild, fierce joy of a woman coming home to her man.

RED RUNS THE RIVER

ONE

He hurried over the last few miles, thinking of his snug house in the valley of Brush Creek, thinking of Sally and and of his two young sons. He was hungry and wondered now what she might be preparing for supper tonight. The wagon, loaded with supplies, creaked along behind the fast-walking team. The horses knew they were getting close to home.

This part of Kansas was still cattle country, having not yet yielded to the plow. John Sessions had driven a herd of cattle up from Texas three years ago, in 1865, and had settled here. This summer, with his neighbors, he had trailed his increase to market in Abilene. He thought now of the three thousand dollars he had made from the sale buried beneath the seed potatoes in the root cellar behind the house. Life had been good to him. He knew it and was grateful.

This was a rolling country, of ridges and ravines, of grassy expanses broken at intervals by areas of heavy brush. The road was only a two-track trail, made by John Sessions' wagon on its infrequent trips to town. He crested a rise and looked down into the valley of Brush Creek. The shock of what he saw stunned him, froze him momentarily where he sat.

The barn still stood but the house was gone, its remains a smoldering rubble pile. Sessions narrowed his eyes and fear struck through him as he saw a spot of bright blue between what was left of the house and the undamaged barn.

He snatched the whip from its socket and laid it savagely across the backs of the startled team. There was a sudden coldness in his chest. There was a shortness of breath in his lungs and his hands trembled uncontrollaby.

The horse broke into a trot, then into a ponderous lope as he continued to flay their backs with the whip. The wagon groaned as it careened down the road. A sack of oats fell off the back and burst, but Sessions didn't notice and wouldn't have stopped even if he had. It seemed forever before he reached the bottom of the hill. It seemed another eternity between the time he did and the time he drove the wagon into the yard.

He was down off the wagon before it came completely to a stop. He held his breath as he ran toward his wife. He dropped to his knees at her side, horror running through him in awful waves, because her face was not Sally's face at all. Her scalp had been taken, leaving a bloody horror where her hair had been. The skin of her face, loosened by the scalp's removal, had sagged downward, changing her expression so much that he would not have recognized her if he had not known that this was her.

He touched her arm and found it cold. Tears now blurred his vision. He brushed them dazedly away. He got stiffly to his feet and looked around, terrified of what he might see next.

The body of Joe Harris caught his eye, lying so close to the ruins of the house that the skin and clothes were scorched. Harris' body was bloated because of the heat, his belly bulging tight against his restraining overalls. He also had been scalped.

Joe had been John Sessions' hired man, an oldster he had brought from Texas to do the chores. Sessions had known the Cheyennes were on a rampage but they'd done no damage closer than a hundred miles away. He had warned Joe to keep a sharp lookout, though, just in case.

The boys. Oh good God, where were the boys? He ran behind the barn and stopped as suddenly as if he had run into a wall. The bodies of the two boys lay no more than ten feet apart. He looked, and closed his eyes and gripped his hands into fists where they hung so helplessly at his sides.

Young John, the oldest, had been eight. Frankie had been six. Neither had been scalped, but their faces were frozen into masks of terror and were streaked from tears. They had been tortured by the Indians before they died.

A blind, terrible hatred was born in John Sessions. He'd never hated Indians until now. But he would find those who had done this if it took him the rest of his life.

He looked once more at his sons, one after the other, tears streaming silently across his tortured face. He returned and looked at Sally. Numbly he went into the barn and got a shovel. Fifty yards from the rubble of the house he began to dig. It was after noon when he started. He drove himself without mercy because the hard work helped to ease the pain. He finished just at dark.

He found a lantern in the barn and lighted it with fingers that trembled both from shock and from fatigue. By its light, he carried Sally to her grave. There was nothing to wrap her in. Everything had been burned up with the house. He put her gently into the bottom of her grave and climbed back out.

Next he carried John, and after that, young Frank. Joe Harris was last. When all four bodies had been laid carefully in their graves, he stood at the graveside, sweating, exhausted, drained of everything but his new-found hate. He knew a prayer and said it now. "The Lord is my shepherd, I shall not want. He maketh me to lie down in green pastures . . ."

When he had finished the prayer, he picked up the shovel. He had to force himself to throw earth into the graves, but once he had begun he worked with frantic haste, not stopping until all four graves were filled and mounded carefully.

He was breathing hard and soaked with sweat. Carrying lantern and shovel, he walked slowly back to the ruins of the house. He had to have food and he had to have sleep if he was going to take the Indians' trail tomorrow.

He built a fire and unloaded the supplies from the wagon. He stacked them neatly in the barn even though he knew he might never see this place again. He fried pieces of bacon on a stick, ate crackers with them and washed the food down with water from his canteen.

He unhitched the horses and led them into the barn. He removed their harness, hanging it carefully from habit even though he knew it might hang here until it rotted away from age. He put the horses into their stalls and gave them oats.

He climbed into the barn loft and lay down on a pile of hay. He shivered violently for half an hour, but at last exhaustion and shock robbed him of consciousness. He slept, a tortured, dream-wracked sleep that kept his body twitching intermittently until dawn grayed the eastern sky.

He awoke chilled to the bone and shivering. With an almost physical pain he remembered the way Sally's face had looked. He remembered the terror and pain in the faces of the boys. He climbed down out of the loft and began a circle of the yard.

He picked up the tracks of the Indians' horses almost immediately. He followed them long enough to ascertain that there had been three of them, and that they had headed south.

He returned at a jogging trot. He saddled one of the wagon horses and rode downstream until he found his saddle horse. He caught the animal, changed the saddle from the wagon horse and rode back to the barn. He packed a gunnysack with grub from the load of supplies he'd brought home yesterday. He shoved his rifle into the saddle boot.

He walked to the four graves and took off his hat. With his head bowed, he stood there silently for several moments. Then he returned to where he had left his saddle horse.

He realized suddenly that he had completely forgotten the money buried in the root cellar. It had no special importance to him now but it would be useful to him while he searched. He could hire men with it, men to help him find and kill the red-skinned animals who had butchered his family.

He hurried to the root cellar. It was half buried in the ground and roofed with two feet of earth and sod. He opened the outer door and descended the earthen steps. At the bottom he opened a second door and went inside.

It was dark and musty smelling here. But it was not too dark for him to see the hole that had been dug in the floor. The money was gone. It had been taken by . . .

His thoughts stopped cold. Taken by Indians? Indians didn't care about money. They had no use for it.

He was running when he burst out of the root cellar. He ran until he reached the trail of the three horses that he had found earlier. He knelt, frowning, studying each hoofprint meticulously.

The horses had not been shod, but it was obvious upon close examination that their hoofs had been trimmed and filed. They were too regular, too even for natural wear.

Stunned by his discovery, John Sessions got slowly to his feet. The men who had attacked and burned his home, those who had scalped his wife and Joe and tortured his boys had not been Indians at all.

They had been white. It explained the torture of the boys. They had done that to make Sally tell where the money was. Having found it, they had killed and scalped her and Joe to make it look like the work of Indians. The money had not bought her life, or Joe's, or the lives of the two little boys.

Hurrying, he turned the remaining wagon horse out of the barn. The milch cows were already gone. Chickens were scratching in the yard. Coyotes and wolves would get them but it could not be helped.

He mounted and rode out toward the south, following the trail left by the three murderers. His hatred had been terrible before but it had been nothing then compared to what it was now.

South, the nearest ranch was that of Silas Hawks, one of the men with whom he had made the drive to Abilene. He wondered if Silas' place had also been attacked and he began to wonder how the three killers had known there was money hidden at the Sessions ranch.

He kept his horse at a steady trot. The miles dropped behind. Apparently, the three had made no attempt to hide their tracks.

Riding south, John Sessions made a tall, broad-shouldered shape that seemed outsized for the horse he rode. His hair, graying and curly at the temples, grew long over his thick, bronzed neck. His chin was a jutting crag with a deep cleft in the center of it. His cheekbones were almost as high and prominent as those of an Indian and his nose was like the beak of a hawk, though less sharply hooked.

Blue eyes looked out beneath bushy, graying brows. John Sessions was forty. Sally, his wife, had been a mere twenty-eight, a girl when he married her, hardly more than a girl the day she died.

It was almost noon when he reached Hawks' place. He

rode in, after noting from their tracks the way the three men he was following had paused on a hill overlooking the place before going on.

Hawks came out the kitchen door, shading his eyes against the blazing sun. "John! What brings you over here?"

Sessions did not dismount. There was no friendliness in his voice. "Three men killed and scalped my family. They burned my house and dug up the cattle money that I'd buried in the root cellar after we got back from Abilene." He pointed toward the little rise. "They stopped up there and watched your place."

"My God, John! That's awful! Indians?"

Sessions shook his head. "White men. Why didn't they stop here?"

"Why? Hell, I don't know why. You don't think . . . ?"

"I think somebody got drunk and blabbed in Abilene. And I think there was a reason why they didn't attack this place."

"There's been some buffalo hunters here. They only left this morning." Silas Hawks couldn't meet John Sessions' glance. He stared guiltily at the ground between his feet.

Sessions asked coldly, "It *was* you, wasn't it? You had to brag about the money we got paid for the cattle in Abilene. You probably said we didn't trust those flimsy-looking banks, too, didn't you?"

Hawks looked up. He was a scrawny man past fifty with a prominent Adam's apple that bobbed noticeably when he talked. "I suppose I did, John, but my God, I didn't know . . ."

Sessions turned his horse and rode out of the yard. He didn't trust himself to stay. He knew if he didn't get away he'd be down off his horse with his hands closing off the air from Silas Hawks' scrawny throat. If Silas had only kept his damned mouth shut . . .

But he hadn't. John Sessions reached the trail of the three killers and turned into it. It veered east now, heading straight toward the ranch of Dow Perrault.

Even before he reached Dow's ranch, John knew what he would find. Dow lived alone, except for his elderly mother. He had no hired hands.

He found what he had expected when he reached the place at dusk. The scalped bodies of Dow Perrault and his mother lay in the yard not far from the small sod house. John didn't look for the money. Dow's mother had been tortured the way his own boys had been. Dow had told where the money was. He couldn't have done otherwise.

He dug two graves and buried Dow and his mother side by side. He filled the graves, built a fire and ate for the first time that day. He lay down near the fire and covered himself with the blanket he always carried on the back of his saddle.

His hatred was no less. But nothing, no emotion can sustain itself at fever pitch for long. John's hatred had subsided the way a fire does, to a glowing bed of coals. Only the blood of the three murderers could completely extinguish it. Before he slept he promised himself one thing. The killers would not die quickly or easily. They would suffer as they had made their victims suffer. He owed that much to Sally, to John and Frankie, to Joe and to himself.

TWO

As soon as it was light enough he was trailing again. He had risen well before dawn and cooked himself some food. The trail headed southeast but before he had gone a dozen miles it split and became three trails, one continuing southeast, one going south, one southwest. This, then, was why the three had not bothered to hide their trail. They had planned to split. Maybe they would meet again later on; maybe they would not.

Sessions sat his horse for several minutes, frowning. If the three did not intend to meet again, he would lose two of them because by the time he caught the one he chose to follow and came back, the other two trails would be gone.

But he had no choice. He could only follow one. He'd just have to hope the three intended to meet up later on.

He chose to follow the middle trail, that which headed south. At a place where the ground was fairly soft, he dismounted and studied it carefully. It was at least two days old. He'd been a day behind the three when he got home from town. He'd lost time burying his family. He'd lost time burying Dow Perrault and his mother. Besides that, the killers had been able to travel at night while he had not.

Fort Hays was south and a lot of travelers went in and out of Fort Hays every day. The three might be thinking that it would be a good place to lose themselves.

He kept his horse at a steady trot throughout most of the day and brought the fort into sight half an hour before sundown. A quarter mile out, he turned and began to circle the place, studying the ground carefully.

He had gone a full half circle before he picked up the trail of the second man and he had returned almost to his starting point before he found that of the third. He dismounted and knelt to unmistakably identify each trail. He returned to his starting point, satisfied that the three he was following had entered Fort Hays, also satisfied that none of them had left the fort. At least they had not left riding the horses upon which they had arrived. It was always possible, of course, that they had sold their horses and had departed by wagon or by stage.

There was tension in him as he approached the buildings of the fort. Once he loosened his revolver in its holster. Before he slept tonight he might know who the three men were. But it was possible that he would never know. There must be dozens of civilians at Fort Hays. He had no way of knowing his men by sight. He only knew what the hoofprints of their horses looked like.

There was a lot of activity at the fort. The sutler's store was packed with boisterous men, both soldiers and civilians. Horses were tied out front, five in all. He dismounted and tied his horse, then picked up the hoofs of the five horses one by one to study them.

Disappointed, he left the sutler's and walked toward the stable. From more than a hundred yards away he could hear the ring of the blacksmiths' hammers. The acrid smelling smoke from the forge drifted toward him on the breeze.

The corral behind the blacksmith shop was jammed with horses. He stopped at the fence and stared at them. All appeared to be newly shod. He went into the blacksmith shop and stood for a moment just inside the door. There was a sinking feeling in his stomach. The men he had pursued here might have had their horses shod. What better way to hide themselves forever from pursuit?

Three blacksmiths were working busily. Sessions stood there until one of them looked up. The man, red of face and bearded, asked, "Want that horse shod, mister? I can get to him just as soon as I finish this one here."

He'd had to yell over the noise of hammer against anvil, over the noise of the bellows at the forge. John Sessions yelled back, "What's going on? How come those horses in the corral are freshly shod?"

The man put the horseshoe he had been shaping back

into the fire. He laid down his tongs and hammer and approached. "You just ride in?"

Sessions nodded.

"Then I reckon you ain't heard. They're enlistin' scouts to ride against the Cheyenne."

"Who is?"

"Colonel Forsyth. He arrived three days ago from Fort Harker farther east. He got thirty men there. He's trying to get another twenty here."

"How many has he already got?"

"Last I heard eighteen. You want to go? Pay's good. Fifty a month if you ain't got a horse. Seventy-five if you have."

"Who do I see?"

"Colonel Forsyth I guess. Or Lieutenant Beecher. Ask over at Regimental Headquarters. They'll tell you where they are."

Sessions nodded. He was so disappointed the hurt was almost physical. He asked, "Where do civilians keep their horses while they're staying here?"

"Tied in front of the sutler's store I guess. Or in that corral out there."

"Any unshod horses in that corral?"

"Not now there ain't. We've shoed 'em all."

Sessions nodded. He walked back toward the sutler's store. The three men he was pursuing had arrived here at least two days ago. If they hadn't left by wagon or by stage they could have had their horses shod and ridden out. Or they might still be here.

A burly sergeant reeled out of the sutler's store and stopped in front to pack his pipe. John Sessions nodded agreeably. "Howdy, Sergeant. Can I buy you a drink?"

The man peered at him, feeling his liquor but a long ways from being drunk. He nodded. "You can, mister. You can."

John followed him into the sutler's store. There was sawdust on the floor. He followed the sergeant through the crowd of shouting men to the bar. The sergeant bawled at the bartender who brought two glasses and a bottle. Sessions laid a dollar on the bar.

He had to shout to be heard over the hubbub of the crowd. "Busy place!"

The sergeant nodded. "Be quieter tomorrow. Most of

these civilians is leavin' here at dawn, headin' west into Indian country."

"I'm looking for some friends of mine. Three of 'em. They'd have reached here yesterday morning, I figure, but I doubt if they'd have signed on to fight Indians. Most likely they'd have left by stage, or by wagon if there were any freight wagons leaving here."

"Ain't been but one stage left in the last three days. Nobody but some women and kids and soldiers on it though. No freight wagons leavin' goin' east. They all been comin' in."

Sessions drank his whisky and poured another both for the sergeant and himself. "Maybe they left by horseback. Maybe they got their horses shod and left the way they came in."

The sergeant studied him suspiciously. "You don't sound like you was talkin' about no friends."

Sessions decided the truth would serve him better than a lie. He said, "No. I'm talking about three white men who burned my house and killed my wife and two sons and my hired man for some money I had buried in the root cellar. I trailed them here."

"You sure it wasn't Indians? Them Cheyennes been kickin' up a hell of a fuss over west a ways."

"It wasn't Indians."

The sergeant studied Sessions closely for a moment. Then, without touching his second drink, he said, "You let me ask around. I can find out whether they've left or not. What you goin' to do if they've up and enlisted with Forsyth's scouts?"

Sessions said, "I'll enlist too."

The sergeant left the sutler's. John Sessions downed his drink and poured another one. He stared moodily at the glass, seeing Sally's face in his mind, seeing her shining black hair tumbling to her shoulders when she let it down at night. He could almost imagine he heard the shrill voices of the boys as they played in the yard outside the kitchen door.

The whisky was beginning to go to his head and he knew he couldn't afford less than full possession of his faculties. Accordingly, he ordered dinner and sat down at a table from which he could watch the door in case the sergeant returned.

The food was plain but filling. Tough roast beef. Boiled

potatoes. Boiled beans and stewed dried apples for dessert. By the time he had finished, his lightheaded feeling was gone.

He studied the faces of the civilians milling around at the bar. About half of them were bearded. Nearly all had the faces of men used to coping with the hardships of the frontier. Some were talking animatedly with the soldiers and he guessed that these were men who had served in the Union Army during the war. He saw one wearing a gray Confederate cavalry hat from which the insignia had been removed. The man wore the hat defiantly, like a chip on his shoulder, as if daring anyone to knock it off.

The sergeant came in the door, still a bit unsteady on his feet. John Sessions poured the sergeant's glass full and waved him over. The man sat down across from him, picked up the glass and emptied it. He said, "Nine men rode in here yesterday. I guess they'd heard about Forsyth wantin' volunteers to go after the Indians."

"Any of them leave again?"

The sergeant shook his head. "Not as near as I can find out. They all enlisted with Forsyth's scouts. You want a list of names? I can get it from the corporal at Regimental Headquarters."

Sessions said, "Sergeant, you get me that list and I'll buy you the biggest damn hangover you've ever had."

The sergeant grinned. "You've got it, mister. I'll be right back." He poured himself another drink, downed it, then got unsteadily to his feet.

Sessions got up too. He said, "Where will I find Colonel Forsyth, Sergeant? I want to enlist with his scouts before he gets all the men he needs."

The sergeant went outside with him. He pointed to a house across the parade ground, one with lamplight shining in the window. "Over there. I'll see you back here at the sutler's store in half an hour."

"All right." Sessions hurried across the parade ground. He climbed to the little porch of the house that had been pointed out to him and knocked.

The door opened. A man stood in the door, a dark-haired man with a full mustache. He wore a blue Army tunic with tarnished gold leaves on his epaulettes. Sessions said, "Colonel Forsyth? I'm John Sessions. I understand you're enlisting scouts to ride against the Indians."

Forsyth nodded. "I am. Come in, Mr. Sessions."

Sessions went inside and Forsyth closed the door. He offered Sessions a drink, which he refused. Forsyth said, "Pay is fifty a month if you don't have a horse, seventy-five if you do. We'll be leaving tomorrow."

"All right."

"Mind telling me why you're signing up?"

Sessions said, "No sir. Three men burned my house and murdered my family. Scalped 'em to make it look like the work of Indians. I trailed them here, and I've found out that they haven't left the fort. Those three are with your bunch of scouts, Colonel, and I mean to find out who they are."

Forsyth frowned. "I'm not so sure I want you along," he said doubtfully. "We'll have trouble enough without you adding more to it."

Sessions stared straight into Forsyth's eyes. He said, "Colonel, I could have lied to you. I didn't. I won't endanger your mission but I want those men."

"You intend to turn them over to the law?"

Sessions frowned. "I don't know, Colonel. I had two little boys, eight and six. They tortured the boys to make my wife tell where the money was."

"I can't believe any of the men I've enlisted could do a thing like that."

"They did, Colonel. Three of them did."

Forsyth nodded reluctantly. "All right, Mr. Sessions. You can go. But if you cause me trouble, I'll send you back no matter where we are."

Sessions took his hand. "All right, Colonel. That's fair enough." He signed the colonel's list, thereby agreeing to the conditions of the enlistment. Forsyth said, "I'll talk to you again tomorrow."

Sessions went out into the darkness and crossed the parade ground toward the sutler's store.

THREE

The sergeant was waiting in front of the sutler's store when Sessions returned. He was swaying slightly, but he had a piece of paper in his hand. The two entered and found a table against the wall. Sessions walked to the bar and got a bottle and two glasses. He returned to the table and poured both glasses full.

The sergeant gave him the list. The light from a hanging lamp a dozen feet away was scarcely adequate, but Sessions found that by holding the paper close to his face he could read the names. He read them twice, but none meant anything to him. He folded the paper and put it into the pocket of his shirt.

He stared moodily at the drink in front of him. He kept seeing Sally as a spot of bright blue against the dusty ground. He saw her face, so horribly changed because the scalp had been removed. He shuddered involuntarily, then lifted the glass and gulped it down. He poured another with hands that shook and gulped that too.

The sergeant was watching him. "I wish I was goin' with you. I'd like to be there when you find out who they are."

Sessions finished his drink. His head was whirling now and he stared at the bottle gloomily. He wanted nothing more than to drink himself into insensibility. He wanted to drug his senses so that he could forget the way Sally's face had looked, so that he could forget the terror that had been in the faces of the two dead boys.

He got up suddenly. He crossed to the bar and bought

another bottle. He brought it back to the sergeant, put it on the table, then extended his hand. "I'm obliged."

The sergeant took his hand and gripped it briefly. "Good luck."

Sessions went outside. His horse was still tied to the rail in front of the sutler's store. He untied, mounted and rode to the blacksmith shop. Though it was dark, he could still hear the clang of a blacksmith's hammer as the smith shaped a red-hot horseshoe on his anvil. He dismounted and tied his horse next to the one the blacksmith was shoeing. He yelled above the noise, "Shoe him. Put him in the corral afterward."

The man nodded. Sessions unsaddled. Hoisting the saddle to his shoulder he headed back across the parade ground toward the sutler's store.

He was assigned a bed in a long, barracks-like room where more than a score of other civilians were already asleep. A dimly burning lantern near the door was the only light. Sessions removed his boots and pants. He hung his hat on a nail over his holster and gunbelt. He put his gun beneath the blanket close to his hand. He didn't know the names of the men he was hunting but they must have known his in order to follow him from Abilene and find his ranch.

The room was noisy with snores but the whisky he had consumed soon put John Sessions to sleep. He did not awake until someone shouted from the door, "Roll out, boys! This is the day we ride against them Indians."

For an hour, Fort Hays was a very busy place. Newly shod horses were caught out of the corral and saddled. Each man was issued a Spencer repeating rifle and 140 rounds of ammunition, plus a Colt's Army revolver and thirty rounds for it. A blanket, a lariat and picket pin, canteen, haversack, butcher knife, tin plate and cup were also handed out to each civilian scout.

Half an hour after sunup, the command rode out, with Major Forsyth, commissioned Brevet Colonel for this expedition, Lieutenant Beecher, and Surgeon Mooers riding at its head.

Following were the fifty scouts, in a column of twos. Bringing up the rear were the four mules of the pack train carrying camp kettles, picks and shovels, 4000 rounds of extra ammunition, medical supplies and extra rations of

salt and coffee. Each man had seven days' cooked rations
in his haversack.

Sessions rode next to a man named Krebs. He had
shaken hands earlier when Krebs introduced himself. He
had watched the man carefully as he gave his own name
but he had been unable to detect any sudden start or
unusual interest in his name. At the first stop he looked at
the list the sergeant had given him and discovered that
Krebs' name was on it near the top.

Out of Fort Hays, the command headed west-north-
west toward the headwaters of the Solomon. It was
August 29, and the early morning air was clear and cool.
Meadowlarks trilled and the long grass waved in a gentle
breeze.

There was a growing feeling of urgency in John Sessions
as he rode. Not until now had he considered what might lie
ahead. He had joined Forsyth's scouts to put himself close
to the men he sought. Now he realized that almost certain
trouble with the marauding Cheyennes was in prospect for
the command. The men he sought might be killed before
he ever found out who they were.

He turned his head. "Where'd you hear about Forsyth
wanting men?" he asked.

Krebs glanced at him. "I heard about it in Abilene.
Everybody was talking about it in the saloons. I guess
it came over the wire."

"What made you sign up?"

Krebs was a gaunt, tall man of forty. His eyes were an
unusual shade of gray. He did not appear to have shaved
for more than a week. He frowned slightly as if he resented
the questions but he answered, "Money. Seventy-five a
month is a hell of a lot more'n a man makes trailin' cows.
Besides, winter's comin' on an' jobs is gettin' hard to find."

Sessions let the conversation die, putting his attention
on the two men ahead, and on the surrounding country-
side. He spotted a lone buck antelope on a distant hill,
watching the column curiously. Farther on, he spotted
several dark shapes a mile away and recognized them for
buffalo.

The hours slowly passed. At noon, they were more than
twenty miles from the fort. They halted, and rested the
horses half an hour. They built small fires for coffee, and
afterward went on.

In the middle of the afternoon, Sessions turned to Krebs again. "Know any of these other men?"

Krebs shook his head. He was silent a moment, then turned and looked at Sessions. "You ain't said how you happened to join up."

Sessions said, "Indians are why I joined up. I got a ranch a ways north of Hays. They raided my place while I was in town for supplies. Killed my family and burned the house."

"That's awful! When did it happen?"

"Week ago."

"I don't blame you for wantin' to go after them murderin' Indians. Couldn't you trail the ones that attacked your place?"

Studying Krebs to see what his reaction would be, Sessions shook his head. Krebs asked, "Why not?"

"They went into the stream. I rode upstream and down for more'n ten miles but I never found where they came out." It was a deliberate lie that drew a startled look from Krebs.

Sessions felt a surge of triumph. A look wasn't enough to base an accusation on, but it was a start. He avoided looking at Krebs but he felt the man watching him.

The column wound across the brown, rolling hills, not yet with flankers out because they had not yet crossed an Indian trail and knew themselves to be a long ways from any Indians.

That night they camped on the Saline River about forty miles from the fort. Sessions watched Krebs closely while fires were being built, and coffee brewed. He was disappointed that Krebs seemed acquainted with none of the others even though he acted friendly enough toward whoever he encountered in his normal movement about the camp.

Sessions listened for other names that he had memorized from the list until he heard them all. Farley. Donovan. Oakes. Jouett. Zeigler. Vega. Chalmers. McGrath. Before he retired for the night he had matched the names of four with the men themselves. He knew Louis Farley, Manuel Vega, Jack Donovan, and George Oakes. Besides, of course, Floyd Krebs, with whom he had ridden today.

The next day he rode with Jack Donovan. He found the man taciturn and untalkative, frankly disbelieving of his story that he had ridden ten miles up and ten miles down Brush Creek without finding the tracks of the Indians leaving it. Donovan was also skeptical of his story that it had been Indians who attacked his ranch. He said he doubted if there were any Indians that far east.

That night they camped on the bank of the south fork of the Solomon River and again took time only to brew coffee and eat cooked rations before turning in. Guards were posted and the camp fell silent for the night.

John Sessions lay awake, staring at the sky, listening to the snores of the sleeping men, the stirring of the horses where they were picketed and the yammering of coyotes on the surrounding hills.

He thought back to Texas, and to the war. He had ridden home defeated in the spring of 1865, to a wife and sons he had left three years earlier to join the Confederates. The boys had been babies when he left. They were hardly more than babies when he returned. Almost immediately afterward they had all started north to Kansas behind a herd of longhorned Texas cattle. Sally had cooked for the trail crew and the two boys had helped. Now she was dead, murdered for $3000 buried in the root cellar and scalped to throw blame on the Indians.

He got up and paced nervously back and forth. Once a guard challenged him and he went to sit with the man and talk, and smoke the blackened pipe that he always carried but seldom smoked.

He slept at last, near dawn, and awakened red-eyed and tired to mount and ride on again, today through rain that intermittently drenched the column winding through the drab hills toward Cheyenne country along the Republican and Arickaree. They had orders to turn south and report at Fort Wallace for further orders. They were expected to arrive there five days after leaving Hays.

On the third night they camped on Sappa Creek and on the fourth day reached Beaver Creek where Short Nose Creek emptied into it. Here they found the remains of an Indian camp abandoned less than two weeks before. Here they also found a Sun Dance pole still standing, the earth pounded by many feet in a circle around the pole. Some of the men said the Sun Dance had been in preparation for making war upon the whites, but Donovan said the Sun Dance had nothing to do with making war. It was a dance to prove the courage of the young men who drove skewers through the flesh of their chests, then attached the skewers by thong to the Sun Dance pole. They then danced until, in a moment of courage and frenzy, they lunged away from the pole, literally tearing the skewers out when they did.

The command followed the Indian trail for a time, but it thinned and finally disappeared. Thereafter Colonel Forsyth traveled a direct route to Fort Wallace, arriving on the night of the fifth day out.

Upon arrival, Forsyth was handed a message from the Governor of Kansas urging him to move forthwith to Bison Basin and protect settlers there. Preparing to leave on the following morning, the plan was changed when a rider pounded into the fort from the town of Sheridan, thirteen miles east. The rider said Indians had attacked a freighter's wagons, killing two teamsters and run off several of the teams.

Two hours later, the command reached the scene of the attack. The wagons were burned, the two murdered teamsters scalped. John Sessions looked at the scalped teamsters, remembering against his will the way his wife and Joe Harris had looked lying near the ruins of the house.

Forsyth, Donovan, and a few of the other scouts milled around in the marshy ground where the attack had taken place. Grover and Donovan agreed that no less than twenty nor more than twenty-five Indians had participated in the attack. They further agreed that the trail was no more than twelve hours old. Immediately Forsyth called the men in and spoke to them.

"We have determined that twenty or twenty-five Indians attacked these wagons and killed these men. We are going after them."

The men cheered raggedly. John Sessions turned his head and caught Floyd Krebs watching him.

Colonel Forsyth said, "Lead out, Lieutenant. Take Grover along with you. The two of you are the best men with a trail I have."

Once more the column moved across the drab brown plain. But with a difference. Now they had a trail. At last they were following hostile Indians.

FOUR

The trail headed northwest and they followed it steadily until dark. At this night's camp, there was unconcealed excitement among the scouts. The talk was that tomorrow they might overtake the Indians. They might come upon an Indian village and see some action at last.

The scouts were becoming acquainted with each other now. There was a card game going. The other men gathered in small groups to talk.

Sessions moved from group to group, his particular attention on the men whose names were on his list. Tonight, he wanted to become acquainted with the remaining seven if he could.

Krebs and Donovan he had ridden with and already knew. So tonight he talked with Louis Farley, George Oakes, Vin Jouett, Manuel Vega, Chalmers, McGrath, and Eli Zeigler. He was able to eliminate Louis Farley as a suspect because Farley had his son with him. Hudson Farley had arrived at Fort Hays at the same time his father had. That cut the list of suspects to eight. He had almost decided Donovan should be eliminated as well and that left seven.

He asked no questions of anyone tonight. But once he caught Colonel Forsyth watching him, a worried frown upon his face.

In the morning they rode on, but as the day progressed, the trail became dimmer and dimmer until at last it completely disappeared. Forsyth told the men, "The Indians have been leaving the trail one by one every time it crossed hard ground. The fact that they have tells us one important thing. They know we are following. They also know we are too strong for them."

Donovan asked, "What do you intend to do?"

"They have been heading northwest, toward the Republican. I think we shall continue in the same general direction in the hope that we may cross another trail, one that will lead us to their main encampment on the Republican."

Someone asked, "And what if we should run into a couple of thousand Indians?"

Forsyth stared at the man. "This expedition was formed to hunt and engage Indians and that is what I intend to do. We have Spencer repeating rifles and revolvers. That much firepower makes us equal of several hundred Indians. We may not be able to defeat a large band, but neither can they beat us."

There was no more discussion after that, though a few of the men grumbled uneasily. The command continued in a northwesterly direction as before except that now Colonel Forsyth put out flankers on both sides of the column so as to cover a wider area in his search for Indian trails.

In midafternoon, John Sessions, flanking in company with Floyd Krebs, spotted a faint trail leading toward the creek. Leaving Krebs he followed it, and in an extremely thick growth of willows near the creek, discovered a Cheyenne wickiup, a temporary shelter made by traveling braves. He also found where two horses had been picketed. He mounted and yelled for Colonel Forsyth, then about a hundred yards downstream.

Forsyth and Beecher, along with Grover and McCall, forced their horses through the nearly impenetrable willow growth. Forsyth said, "Good work, Sessions. How'd you happen to find it?"

"I spotted a trail heading toward the creek. Looks like there were two of them, Colonel. I make their trail to be less'n twenty-four hours old. They probably left this spot at dawn today but we can tell better after we've followed them a ways."

Leading his horse, he pushed through the willows, following the trail left by the two Indians. Where it came up out of the creek bottom, the prints were plain and distinct. He studied them, then straightened. "These were made this morning before the dew was off the grass."

Forsyth said, "All right. Follow them." Standing in his stirrups, he waved the column on.

Sessions rode out, his eyes fixed steadily on the ground. Lieutenant Beecher rode beside him and Grover and McCall came along behind. Colonel Forsyth rode with Surgeon Mooers. The flankers had been ordered in.

Sessions kept his mind on the trail, which now was fairly plain. The two Indians had apparently made no attempt to hide their tracks.

A couple of miles beyond the creek, Sessions came to a place where three other Indians had camped less than twenty-four hours before. Afterward, the trail of the two he was following overlaid that of the three, and a little farther on, these two trails were joined by a third, apparently that of a small war or hunting party. With the three trails joined into a single one a man could follow without difficulty at a hard gallop if he wished.

Forsyth and Beecher were jubilant. Some of the scouts were equally so but some looked glum as if they feared Forsyth was going to bite off more than he could chew. There was a little grumbling but it soon died out.

Sessions caught Krebs watching him. He pretended not to notice. The command was traveling at a steady trot, urged on by Forsyth who had an excited gleam in his dark eyes and a half smile of anticipation on his mouth. Once he said to Beecher, "We've got 'em, Lieutenant. By the Lord they're not going to get away this time!"

Forsyth did not halt the command until dusk. He ordered that no fires be built. He also ordered that there be no unnecessary noise. The men unsaddled and picketed their horses. Lieutenant Beecher posted sentries around the camp and particularly where the horses were picketed. Sessions drew sentry watch until midnight on the west side of the camp.

Walking his post, he stared through the darkness toward the camp, wishing that he could see the men. He wondered what Krebs was doing and who he was talking to.

Pacing back and forth, occasionally stopping to stare into the darkness and listen for unfamiliar sounds, his mind went over the men whose names were on his list.

Krebs was his best suspect, and he had, by now, all but eliminated Farley and Donovan. Of those remaining, which were capable of the kind of cold-blooded murder that had been committed against his family?

When he was relieved at midnight, he rolled himself in his blanket and went to sleep, thinking only that he expected too much if he thought he was going to identify the guilty men in a day or two. It would take longer. He would have to be patient, however hard being patient was.

On the following morning, he was again ordered to ride at the column's head along with Lieutenant Beecher even though the most inexperienced of the scouts could have followed the trail today. And as the miles dropped behind it kept getting wider and wider. Whole villages were apparently following it now. The ground was furrowed by dozens of travois. Here and there lay a discarded piece of clothing, or some bones or a broken arrow or a piece of dried buffalo meat.

Nearly all the command's rations now were gone. Only a little salt and coffee remained, that which had been carried on the mules. Furthermore, no game had been spotted for two days, testifying to the fact that the country had been thoroughly hunted by the Indians who had made this broad and easily followed trail.

In the midmorning Forsyth called a halt. Sessions dismounted and removed the saddle from his horse. He rubbed the animal down with the saddle blanket, then fanned his sweaty back with it. Holding the horse's reins, he squatted and packed his pipe. His tobacco was almost gone.

Forsyth talked with Lieutenant Beecher nearby. The two were approached by a group of half a dozen men. One was Krebs. Another was Vin Jouett. A third was Manuel Vega. None of the others were on Sessions' list.

Krebs had apparently been appointed spokesman for the group. He said, "Colonel, there's more Indians up ahead than we can handle with fifty men. We figure we're followin' more'n five hundred Indians. God knows how many are camped on the Republican. We been talkin' an' we figure we ought to go on back."

Forsyth frowned. "Is that the way all of you feel?"

The other five nodded their heads.

Forsyth's voice turned cold. "Well, we're not going back. I'll ask no man to take risks I won't take myself, but we came out here to find Indians and it looks to me like we've found some. We're going on and we're going to engage these Indians, and maybe when we're through with them they won't be so anxious to attack white settlers."

Krebs said, "Colonel, we got too much to lose . . ."

"All of us are risking the same thing, Mr. Krebs. Our lives. What makes you think you've more to lose than anybody else?"

Krebs turned his head and looked at the five men with him. Jouett, a tall, beefy, yellow-haired man turning bald, grunted, "We've had our say, Krebs. I reckon that's about all that we can do."

Forsyth glanced at him. "You're right, Mr. Jouett. It's all that you can do." He looked beyond Jouett at the lounging, resting men. "Mount up! Let's go!"

Sessions threw his soggy saddle blanket on his horse's back. He followed it with the saddle and cinched it down. He mounted.

The fact that Krebs, Vega, and Jouett had been the only three on his list to speak to Forsyth interested him. He stared back along the column. Krebs was riding with a man named Ranahan. Vega and Jouett rode side by side.

Frowning he led out with Lieutenant Beecher at his side. Beecher was plainly excited now. His eyes shone and there was a half smile on his face. Sessions turned his head and grinned. He realized it was the first time he had smiled since finding his family killed. He said, "Getting anxious, Lieutenant?"

Beecher nodded. "We've been out two weeks. It's time we saw some Indians."

"From the looks of this trail, we'll be seeing plenty of them soon."

Sessions couldn't help thinking about the three who had protested to Forsyth a while ago. Krebs had said something about having too much to lose. What had he meant? Did he have the $3000 that had been buried in the root cellar at Sessions' ranch? Did he have Dow Perrault's cattle money too?

The afternoon slowly wore away. Horse manure found in the trail was so fresh it seemed to steam. Sessions could feel his nerves tightening.

They reached a stream that Forsyth believed to be Delaware Creek and followed its course through wild plum thickets and swamp willows until at last, in late afternoon, they came through a narrow gorge and then out into a broad valley two miles long and two miles wide.

Here, opposite a small island in the middle of the stream, Forsyth halted his command. Though several hours of daylight yet remained, they made camp. Sessions was unfamiliar with the country, never having been very far west of Hays. But both Grover and McCall claimed this was not Delaware Creek at all, but the north fork of the Republican, called the Arickaree.

The men stared uneasily at the bluffs on the north, bluffs that hid the plain beyond. They stared uneasily up and down the stream and at the broad trail they had been following. Every one of them knew that thousands of Indians were in the vicinity, perhaps less than half a dozen miles away.

FIVE

The movements of the troop of civilian scouts were not as orderly as those of cavalry, but they were as efficient. Horses were quickly watered, then unsaddled and picketed to graze in the long grass beside the stream. In the center of the sandy streambed, sixty yards from the bank, water ran fifteen feet wide, divided by the island and flowing on both sides of it. Sessions doubted if the water was more than five or six inches deep. The island itself was, perhaps, three feet higher than the bed of the stream. Grass covered it. In the center was a thicket of willows and alder shoots and at the lower tip was a young cottonwood twenty feet in height.

Guards were stationed immediately around the picketed horses. Sentries were detailed to begin standing their watches as soon as it got dark. Tonight Sessions drew no watch since he had stood sentry duty the night before. As dusk fell, Forsyth issued the order that each man was to personally hobble his own mount, see to the picket pin and check the knot in the picket rope to be sure all was secure.

Forsyth was jumpy about the freshness of the trail. He knew the Indians could not be far away, and he intended to be prepared if they attacked at dawn.

Sessions spread his blankets near the picket pin of his horse. If Forsyth was right and the Cheyennes did attack at dawn, he wanted to be near his horse. The worst thing that could happen to a man in Indian country was to lose his mount.

Though it was early September, the air turned chill as soon as the sun went down, and as the night progressed, it grew colder still. Sessions shivered in his blankets and slept fitfully. Several times he heard Forsyth pacing uneasily back and forth. He heard the soft voices of the sentries as they were changed sometime during the night.

Wakeful, unable to keep from thinking of the past, John Sessions tonight stared into his future and found it bleak. If he survived this campaign and his showdown with the men who had murdered his family, he would undoubtedly go back to his ranch on Brush Creek. There was nothing else for him to do. But it would be an empty place, an empty life. Not yet could he think of starting another family. All he could think of now was the moment when he would face the three murderers, knowing at last for certain who they were.

Dawn began as a thin line above the horizon in the east. Sessions, who had slept but little during the night, was up immediately, striding back and forth in an attempt to bring circulation and warmth to his chilled body.

Forsyth was also up. So was Lieutenant Beecher. So were scouts Grover and McCall. Sessions joined them and the five peered anxiously into the darkness both upstream and down, waiting until objects would become visible.

John Sessions could see his breath. He packed his blackened and stubby pipe and put it into his mouth. Cupping the match with his hands, he lighted it.

He couldn't help thinking of the men's empty haversacks. The last of the cooked rations obtained at Fort Wallace had been eaten yesterday. All that remained was a quantity of coffee and salt carried on the pack animals. Unless they could kill some game, they were going to get damned hungry in the next few days.

And if they should happen to be attacked . . . With no food, their situation could quickly become desperate.

Still, Sessions understood Forsyth's anxiety to find and engage the Indians. That was what he had been sent out here to do. It was believed the Cheyennes were massing and making medicine for an organized attack upon all the white settlements west of Hays. If Forsyth now withdrew, his retreat might cost the lives of dozens, even hundreds of settlers. And in the end, some other military force would have to do what he had failed to do.

The five stood near one of the sentries, all but holding their breaths. A bird chirped out in the graying darkness. Suddenly Forsyth stiffened and raised an arm to point.

Sessions caught the same movement Forsyth had. It was not an identifiable movement, but it had to have been that of a man or horse dimly seen against the slowly graying sky.

The sentry raised his rifle. The hammer clicked, coming back. Forsyth whispered, "Wait."

John Sessions heard the new sound and felt it simultaneously. It was a dull thunder in the ground and air, distant, faint, almost something a man might think he was imagining. But Sessions had heard that sound before, during the war. It was the sound of horses' hoofs, galloping. It was the sound of hundreds, perhaps thousands of mounted Indians. They had already begun their dawn charge, knowing that by the time they reached their prey it would be light enough to shoot.

Sessions said softly, "That sound, Colonel . . . they're coming, sir."

But there was a closer sound, also in both the ground and air. This came from a smaller group, riding in advance of the others, probably to try and stampede the picketed horses and leave the hated whites afoot.

Sessions shouted, "There, Colonel! Three of them!" Simultaneously he raised his rifle. He fired and instantly the sound of his shot was was echoed and re-echoed by the others' guns. Forsyth yelled at his sleeping scouts, "Indians! Turn out! Indians."

One of the mounted Indians fell from his saddle and was immediately lost to sight in the darkness near the ground. Others came galloping out of the grayness, beating Indian drums, rattling dry hides, yelling crazily as they tried to stampede the picketed mounts of Forsyth's scouts. Two pack mules broke away along with two horses that had not been securely picketed. The remaining horses were now held by their owners, most of whom were coiling picket ropes and retreating back toward the riverbank.

Forsyth roared, "Saddle up! Saddle up!" and once more there was that moment of orderly confusion out of which in an amazingly short span of time came the disciplined readiness of a troop of mounted cavalry albeit they were civilians instead of soldiers.

Grover, in the act of mounting, suddenly said in an awed voice, "Holy Christ. Look at the Indians!"

Out of the light that gradually drove darkness from the surrounding land, there now came hundreds of feathered, mounted Indians, brandishing rifles, lances, tomahawks and bows.

Galloping, they came toward the scouts from up the stream, from the side and from across the stream. This was the rumble Sessions had heard. And behind the horsemen came other Indians, these on foot but also armed.

The command was all but surrounded and about to be overwhelmed. Sessions suddenly became aware of Floyd Krebs, standing near to him, standing next to Jouett and saying angrily, "You and your goddamn bright ideas. We'll never live to spend a dime . . ."

Jouett said savagely, "Shut your mouth!" as he caught Sessions looking at him. Then the Indians were in range and every man of the command was firing as fast as he could. Horses were rearing and snorting, pulling to be free but held by the scouts' inflexible grip.

Sessions saw one Indian fall before his gun. Then his horse moved in front of him, preventing him from firing again immediately.

A gun discharged almost in his ear and the bullet burned along the side of his neck. Swinging his head, he saw Krebs not six feet away, rifle leveled, aimed straight at his head.

Sessions released his horse. He lunged toward Krebs, at the same time swinging his rifle like a club. Its barrel connected solidly with the side of Krebs' head and the man went down like a pine that has been undercut by a woodsman's ax. Sessions looked quickly around for Jouett but in the confusion he failed to locate him. Turning back, he ran to recover his horse and having done so, swung to the saddle and galloped toward the riverbank.

Krebs lay where he had fallen, his horse standing nearby, fidgeting, pulling against the picket rope held only by the man's body lying on it.

Jouett appeared, galloping toward Krebs. Two other men, afoot, were running upstream toward the horses and mules stampeded by the Indians. The Indians charging down upon the trapped command were now less than a hundred yards away.

Jouett dismounted, running. He reached Krebs as the man stirred and groggily raised his head. Jouett seized the picket rope of Krebs' horse and tried to pull it out from under his body. Krebs rolled and came to his knees. . . .

Sessions watched, savagely elated, knowing he had

identified two of his family's murderers. Krebs was one, Jouett another. Jouett had showed more interest in Krebs' horse than in Krebs himself. That meant the money, or Krebs' share of it, was in the saddlebags.

Commands from Forsyth and Beecher were unnecessary. Most of the scouts had fought in the war. Some had fought with the Army previously against Indians. They had Spencer repeating rifles and they stood fast beside their nervously fidgeting horses and laid a cool and deadly fire into the ranks of the advancing braves.

Indian ponies fell, throwing their riders into the long prairie grass. Braves, struck, toppled from their mounts.

Glancing around, Sessions saw that the Indians had left the way open to the east, downstream. They obviously expected the beleaguered scouts to mount and retreat that way, but Sessions was willing to bet that around the first bend in the stream an ambush awaited them.

Forsyth apparently came to the same conclusion for he stood in his stirrups, waved his revolver toward the island and roared, "Retreat to the island. Form a circle and tie your horses outside the circle! Dig in as fast as you can!"

So far, nobody had been hit, though a number of dead and wounded Indians lay in the grass just beyond where the horses had been picketed. Sessions had lost sight of Jouett and Krebs.

Slowly, firing as they went, the scouts backed out across the dry, sandy riverbed toward the island in its center. For an instant the Indian attack slackened as the Cheyennes apparently tried to decide what the scouts were going to do. They had expected the white men to retreat downstream toward the east. When the scouts did not, it confused and puzzled them.

Beecher, Grover and McCall knelt in the grass on the west flank of the retreating command. Sessions joined them in laying down a deadly fusillade that kept the Indians back long enough for the command to reach the dubious safety of the island. It did not take long. Quickly the scouts tied their horses to alder and willow shoots and retreated behind them to dig in.

Beecher got to his feet. He yelled, "Let's go," and the four-man rear guard raced across the sand toward the island, dragging their mounts behind. Reaching it, they climbed through the willows, tied their horses and dived to the safety of the high grass and brush.

Sessions was breathing hard. His arms and legs were trembling. He grinned shakily at Lieutenant Beecher, lying next to him, and Beecher returned the grin. Both knew they had reached only temporary safety here. Both knew how many Indians were out there, knew as well that there was no chance of defeating them or even of escaping annihilation at their hands. Beecher grunted practically, "At least we'll have water here."

Sessions nodded. He heard Forsyth exhorting the men to dig in and leaped to his feet and ran for his horse. He unsaddled with shaking hands, keeping the horse's body between him and the Indians. He was pulling the saddle off when he heard the unmistakable sound of a bullet striking flesh. His horse went to his knees, tried to get up, failed, then collapsed onto his side. Dragging the saddle, Sessions crawled back to where he had left Beecher only moments before.

The lieutenant was gone, having left to join Forsyth. From the riverbank, Indians concealed in the high grass poured a withering fire into the defenders on the long, narrow island. A man, hit in the belly, screamed with pain as he died. Several more were badly wounded and their cries for the surgeon added to the noise.

Sessions temporarily gave up trying to dig in. He rested his rifle barrel on his saddle and fired at puffs of smoke on the riverbank. Twice he was rewarded by seeing hidden Indians straighten and fall dead on the bare sand of the dry riverbed.

Bullets cut through the willows viciously. Horses died and collapsed quietly, or bucked, or pulled loose and ran. A panic-stricken voice shouted, "Don't let's stay here and be shot down like dogs! Who'll try for the opposite bank with me?"

Half a dozen voices agreed to try. Sessions hadn't identified the man who had shouted. Nor could he identify any who had agreed to go with him.

Forsyth's voice rose above the tumult. "Stay where you are! It's our only chance. I'll shoot any man who attempts to leave the island!"

McCall's voice bawled, "And so will I."

Beecher, firing as coolly as if he were on a rifle range,

stopped long enough to shout, "Addleheaded fools! Have you no sense?"

Sessions returned his attention to the Indians on the riverbank. No one else mentioned leaving the island, because now the Indians had occupied the riverbank on the other side. The island was completely surrounded by the Cheyennes. Sessions hadn't tried counting them, but he knew there must be between five hundred and a thousand. It was only a matter of time until Forsyth's scouts would be overwhelmed. The men who had murdered his family would die here at the hands of the Indians. And he would die with them.

SIX

Seventy yards of bare sand and water separated the island from the nearest bank. The few mounted Indians who dared try traversing it promptly died for their pains. Two horses lay kicking on the sand. One Indian lay dead, staring at the sky. Another had managed to crawl to the safety of the long grass growing on the bank, despite the concerted efforts of half a dozen men to kill him before he could.

Forsyth, pacing up and down the island, completely oblivious of the danger, exhorted the men repeatedly, "Don't shoot unless you've got a chance of hitting something! Save your ammunition! Our lives depend on how well we make it last!"

Badly hurt and confused by Forsyth's unexpected tactic in occupying the island, the Indians now drew back. Snipers hidden in the grass and brush on the riverbank continued to harass the scouts, but since they were invisible, the men refused to waste ammunition shooting at them. Using their butcher knives to cut the sod and then their tin plates to scoop out the sand beneath, they began to dig rifle pits, first throwing up sand between themselves and the riverbank, then lengthening their pits so that they could lie prone comfortably, resting their rifles upon the bulwark of sand thrown up in front.

Sessions, after glancing around at the men nearest him searching for Jouett and Krebs, began digging a rifle pit for himself. He knew that while the Indians had withdrawn they had not given up. They were having a pow-wow to decide what they should do and they were making medicine.

Two years ago they had wiped out eighty-one troopers at Fort Phil Kearny in forty minutes. They weren't likely to give up easily on fifty men they knew were out of food, alone in the heart of their own country without hope of reinforcement or support.

Satisfied that the command was in fairly good shape under the circumstances, Forsyth finally yielded to the repeated exhortations of the men that he stop exposing himself so recklessly. He lay down in the high grass even though he had no rifle pit in which to conceal himself.

Scarcely had he done so when he uttered a sharp grunt of pain. Sessions, fifty feet away, raised his head and saw the colonel double up, staring at a bloody wound in his thigh. Sessions started to crawl out of his rifle pit but Forsyth said sharply, "Stay there, Mr. Sessions! There's nothing you can do and there's no use in you getting hit too."

Surgeon Mooers, considerably closer to Forsyth than Sessions, raised up and said, "I'll enlarge this pit enough so that it will hold both of us, Colonel. Hold on a few minutes and I'll come after you." The surgeon began to throw sand out almost frantically. Sessions got up and ran to the pit. He jumped in and began helping the surgeon to enlarge it. Occasionally he glanced at Forsyth worriedly, wondering how badly he was hurt, wondering if the bullet had shattered the bone in his leg.

Ten minutes of hard work resulted in a rifle pit big enough for both Mooers and Colonel Forsyth. The surgeon and Sessions climbed out and crawled to the wounded man. One on each side, they dragged him as carefully as possible to the pit and into it. Forsyth, white and sweating, said weakly, "Back to your rifle pit, Mr. Sessions."

Sessions crawled back to his own rifle pit, belly against the ground, pulling himself along with his elbows. The surgeon had already started cutting Forsyth's trousers away from the bloody wound in his thigh.

Sessions reached his rifle pit and rolled into it. It was maddening for him to know the identity of two of the killers of his family and be unable to do anything. He didn't even know where Krebs and Jouett were. It infuriated him to think they might be dead, or that they might be killed before he had a chance at them.

Brave men and decent men were dying here on this island in the middle of the Arickaree. He thought angrily that this kind of honorable death was too good for Jouett and Krebs and for their unknown confederate.

Two snipers had managed to crawl up onto the lower end of the island and were exacting a heavy toll of the dug-in scouts. One had shot Forsyth. Every time a man would expose himself a bullet would come flashing from the bush behind which the two had concealed themselves.

Farley, Harrington, Gantt, and Burke crawled as close as they could, then waited anxiously for the next muzzle flash. When it came, all four fired into the bush. They were rewarded by seeing an Indian straighten up, a bloody hole in his head. Though they watched for a long time afterward, the other Indian did not fire and they were forced to assume he was either dead or afraid to risk revealing his location to the waiting scouts.

Sessions glanced toward the pit occupied by Surgeon Mooers and the colonel. "How is he, Doc? That bullet didn't break his leg, did it?"

It was a moment before Mooers replied. "That one didn't," he finally said. "The first one went into his right thigh. But the second broke his left leg between the ankle and the knee."

Sessions hadn't known the colonel had been wounded twice, and the colonel had made no sound to indicate when he'd received his second wound.

With two wounds, both painful and one very serious, it was doubtful if Forsyth would be able to command for long. Sessions glanced toward the upper end of the island, wondering where Lieutenant Beecher was. He didn't see him but that wasn't strange. He didn't see anyone. Only dead and wounded horses and sand bulwarks thrown up by the men when they dug their pits.

With practically all the horses either dead or wounded, leaving here was now impossible. Surrounded by from five hundred to a thousand Indians, survival also was impossible. Both Forsyth and Beecher must realize the hopelessness of their predicament. Only by exacting a terrible toll of the Indians could the doomed scouts hope to make their deaths meaningful. Only by decimating the ranks of the hostiles could they hope to wring victory from defeat.

Sessions stared over the sand bulwark in front of him and across the dry riverbed toward the bank. The sun was now well up in the sky. He judged it must be close to eight o'clock.

No Indians were visible within rifle range. Beyond it, hundreds milled around, riding aimlessly back and forth. Many rode spotted ponies, a color favored by Indians. Others rode what appeared to be captured cavalry remounts. Squinting, Sessions tried to see how well the Indians were armed. He was startled to observe that many carried repeating Henrys, Spencers, and Remingtons. Others had breech-loading Springfields, probably captured at Fort Phil Kearny two years ago.

Riding up and down in front of them, gesticulating and shouting, was a tall, magnificently muscled Indian, naked to the waist. Sessions heard Forsyth, who had pulled himself up to a sitting position at the side of the rifle pit, yell at Grover nearby, "Who is that one, Mr. Grover? Roman Nose?"

"That's him, Colonel. You won't see another like him anywhere on the plains."

"Then these must be the Northern Cheyenne."

"Yes sir. And some Oglala and Brûlé Sioux. I figure there's five hundred Northern Cheyenne under Roman Nose. There must be a couple of hundred from the other tribes."

The last of the horses went down, kicking, and after a moment lay completely still. From across the river came a shout in English, "There goes the last damn horse, anyhow."

Forsyth spoke to Grover again. "One of them seems to know English pretty well."

"Maybe it's that half breed renegade whelp of Bent's."

Sessions supposed he was talking about young Charles Bent, who, then living with the Indians, had seen his family slaughtered by Chivington's volunteers in 1864. In fact, Sessions knew that most of the current troubles with the Cheyennes were directly traceable to that bloody massacre.

About twenty feet separated Sessions' rifle pit from that occupied by Forsyth and Surgeon Mooers. Forsyth, peering over the sand bulwark, was suddenly struck in the head by a bullet. He disappeared.

Sessions angrily returned his attention to the snipers on the bank less than a hundred yards away. He watched for puffs of smoke or a muzzle flash, and each time he saw one, fired instantly, aiming carefully at the smoke or muzzle flash.

He saw one Indian fall sideways away from the bush

that had concealed him previously. He waited several moments, then called to Mooers, "Is the colonel dead?"

Mooers called back, "No. Just knocked down. The bullet grazed the top of his head. If it hadn't been for his hat . . ."

Suddenly, beyond the riverbank, the Indians began to shriek. Urging their horses to gallop, they came toward the island. Short of it by seventy-five yards, they turned and began to circle it.

Sessions held his fire, waiting until they would be close enough to make each shot a certainty. Some of them had concealed themselves, except for an arm and one foot, behind their horses' necks and were firing from underneath. Sessions paid little attention to these, knowing it was a practical impossibility to hit anything from such a position. It was difficult enough to shoot from a normal position on the back of a running horse.

They were now galloping in a line between the island and the bank. Their horses' hoofs kicked up showers of dry sand. Sessions took careful aim at a yelling brave, then led him a few inches the way a man might lead a duck. He fired and saw the Indian straighten, drop his rifle, and tumble limply off the rump of his running horse.

Mooers, in the next rifle pit, was also firing, slowly and carefully. When one of his shots brought down a second brave, he shouted, "There's one that won't bother us again."

Almost immediately afterward Sessions heard his shocked voice say, "I'm hit." He glanced toward the pit where Mooers and Forsyth were, but could see neither. He called, "Colonel? Is he hurt bad?"

"He's shot in the head. He's unconscious but he isn't dead."

Sessions had an empty feeling in his stomach. If the surgeon was hit in the head, then the wounded would have no one to care for them. Not that it would matter very long, he thought. By nightfall they would all be dead.

He glanced toward the head of the island, wondering where Krebs and Jouett were, and who the third man was. If he lived through the day, he promised himself that he would use the night to search them out. He wanted to kill them before the Indians did. Just the thought of the three escaping his vengeance made him furious.

If he survived until dark. He stared over the sand bulwark, frowning now. The Indians had stopped circling the beleaguered island. They were trotting their horses away, without even looking back.

Could it be possible, Sessions wondered, that they were withdrawing, that they were giving up? He shook his head. No. The Indians' losses hadn't been heavy enough to make them withdraw. And besides, they wouldn't withdraw from fifty men, who had no food, whose horses were dead and who could not escape.

It made more sense that they were massing for a final charge against the embattled island. The clear notes of a bugle floated from a gorge downstream to the west. All the Indians seemed to be headed that way except for several hundred squaws and children gathered on a bluff overlooking the valley of the Arickaree to watch.

Forsyth raised his voice. "Lieutenant Beecher?"

From the upper end of the island Beecher answered him. "Yes sir?"

"I believe they're forming for a charge!"

Sessions was relieved to know that Beecher was alive. With three wounds, it was surprising that Forsyth was still alive, but at any moment he might lapse into unconsciousness.

Beecher answered, "It sure looks that way, sir!"

"Then let the men get ready! Have them reload their rifles, six shots in the magazine, one in the barrel. Load and make ready the guns of the wounded and dead. Load revolvers and place them close at hand."

Sessions reloaded his rifle and placed his revolver on the sand in front of him. Forsyth tossed the rifle Mooers had been using toward him. He crawled out and retrieved it, then loaded it and placed it beside the revolver.

Once more Forsyth raised his voice. "Wait for the mounted charge. Don't waste bullets on Indians on foot and don't fire until I give the word. Make every shot count, men. It's our only chance of stopping them."

Beecher repeated each of his orders for the benefit of the men at the upper end of the island, who might not have heard. There was no firing now from the dug-in men. There was only an ominous silence as they waited for the charge of Roman Nose's Northern Cheyennes.

Sessions admitted to himself that they had little chance of stopping such a charge. It would roll over the island, obliterating everything in its path.

He made himself think of his burned ranchhouse, of Sally and Joe and the boys. He made himself think of Jouette and Krebs and their confederate, whoever he was.

He refused to admit the possibility that he might be killed. He *had* to live until darkness fell. As he stared down the valley toward the invisible 'warriors massing for the charge, his eyes were determined and he was thinking fiercely what it would feel like to have Floyd Krebs' skinny neck between his hands.

SEVEN

Suddenly across the sun-washed valley came the clear notes
of the bugle sounded either by some renegade white or
half breed or by an Indian who had learned its use. Immediately following, the first of the mounted warriors
moved into view from beyond the river's bend.

Emerging from the same gorge through which the fifty
scouts had ridden yesterday, they came at a slow, deliberate
trot, halting with only a part of their number visible to the
island's defenders and waiting, motionless.

Firing from the riverbank had now ceased altogether
and a few of the snipers were retreating, crouched low
or crawling through the grass until they would be out
of rifle range.

None of the island's defenders paid them any attention.
Their rifles and revolvers were loaded in anticipation of
the charge of Indian cavalry and each man knew how
valuable every cartridge might be before the Indian charge
could be repulsed.

Along the length of the island rose the men's awed
whispers as they viewed the body of Indian horsemen.
And then, from the ranks of the savages came Roman
Nose.

Forsyth said, "Just look at him." His voice was charged
with reluctant admiration.

Roman Nose was a sight worth remembering as he
turned his horse, raised his arms for silence and began
talking to his warriors. He was mounted on a large, clean-
limbed chestnut horse and sat well forward close to the
horse's withers. His knees were tucked beneath a horsehair
lariat that twice encircled the horse's body.

266

His left hand held the bridle reins, the trigger guard of his rifle and the horse's flowing mane. His right hand was free to direct his men.

He was completely naked except for a red sash around his waist. Even at this distance, Sessions could see that his face was painted for war even though he could not distinguish the colors or patterns in which the war paint had been applied. He could also see the magnificent headdress worn by the Cheyenne chief.

Two short, black buffalo horns adorned the front of it, seeming to grow out of the Indian's head just as they do from that of a buffalo. Behind the horns were eagle feathers and heron's plums, trailing down his back to below his waist.

Turning and waving on his men, Roman Nose now urged his horse into a full gallop. Behind him came his warriors, appearing from the river's bend by tens, by hundreds until at last all were visible.

It was a magnificent sight, filled with savage splendor that, even though he knew the peril he was in, Sessions could not help admiring. Dust rose in clouds behind the galloping Indians. They spread slightly as they came on, and headed straight toward the island's lower tip.

Feathered headdresses bannered out in the wind. Lances and rifles waved in the air. Suddenly, throwing back his head and striking his mouth with the palm of his hand, Roman Nose issued a war cry that Sessions could clearly hear even though the distance was several hundred yards.

Raising an arm, Roman Nose shook his fist at the island under siege. And then, as though echoing his cry, a blood-curdling shriek came from every warrior's throat, rolling across the valley with enough intensity to make chills run down the white men's spines in spite of the heat of the morning sun.

As if in answer to the war whoop came a cry from the thousands of squaws and children watching from the bluff. It was a cry of encouragement and it seemed to lend speed to the already galloping horses of the Indians.

Nearing the island, the fast-moving horde of savages took a more clearly defined form. They now were sixty abreast in front, riding in a line that was very nearly straight. Behind the first line of braves were other lines, six or seven in all. The whole formed a solid square of galloping, massed might that seemed certain to overwhelm both island and defenders by literally pounding them into the sand.

At a distance of two to three hundred yards, Sessions could now clearly see Roman Nose's face, painted with alternate lines of red and black that gave it an appearance both hideous and terrifying.

The chief brandished his Springfield above his head. He rode five paces in front of the center of the line. To his left, and also slightly in advance of the line, rode a medicine man, much older than Roman Nose.

Sessions turned his head from the fascinating sight and looked toward the upper end of the island. He could see the heads of the scouts now raised above their bulwarks of sand. He could see their rifle muzzles, all pointing toward the charging Indians. He caught a glimpse of Krebs and ducked his head and afterward wondered if Krebs would shoot him in the back when the colonel gave the order to open fire on the Indians.

Suddenly, from both banks of the stream came a withering hail of bullets. Sessions had thought most of the snipers had gone, but he had been wrong. The Indians had only wanted the white men to believe that they had gone. Into the exposed scouts they poured their deadly hail of bullets, wounding several in the first few seconds before the scouts had time to duck their heads.

But the scouts could not long keep their heads down because the charge was coming toward them at frightening speed. At any instant Forsyth would shout the command to open fire. At any instant . . .

John Sessions stared at the oncoming Indians with numb fascination. He had heard a lot of stories of Indian warfare but never had he heard of anything even faintly resembling this. The scouts were doomed. They had no chance against such a charge. The Indians would ride over the island and when they were gone nothing would be left alive.

Suddenly he heard Colonel Forsyth's hoarse voice, "Now!" and as though echoing Forsyth's command came Beecher's from the island's upper end. "Now!"

The first line of Indians was less than a hundred yards away. Sessions drew a bead on the chest of the warrior on the right and squeezed off his shot. He saw the brave stiffen and throw his arms wide, throw his head back to utter a shriek of pain. The Indian tumbled off his horse and the animal veered to one side, riderless.

The volley from the scouts had come almost as a single shot and it exacted a terrible toll among the Indians. Horses reared and fell, to tangle the feet of the horses coming on behind. Indians tumbled from their saddles, but those remaining answered the destructive volley with a shrill, defiant cry.

The scouts' second volley followed close on the heels of the first, crashing out across the valley and echoing back from the bluffs as a ragged roar. More warriors fell, bloodied and writhing, to be trampled by the close-riding phalanx of screaming savages who could neither stop nor would.

More than half the front rank of riders was by now either dead or wounded. The third volley slammed into them, further decimating their numbers but neither slowing them nor turning them aside. Roman Nose still rode at their head, his rifle waved over his head to urge them on. Men from behind filled in the ranks for those that had gone down.

The fourth volley crackled from the rifle pits. A cloud of bluish powdersmoke now lay heavy in the island's brush. It drifted downwind on the sluggish breeze. Some of the hard-riding Indians now were firing, though their accuracy could scarcely be expected to depend on anything but luck. Behind Sessions a scout rose to his feet clutching his streaming throat, trying to stop the flow of blood from his jugular with his hands. There was no help for him. Every man was firing as rapidly as he could at the advancing horde of Indians.

The medicine man went down, dead before he hit the ground, but Roman Nose came on, as if charmed, as if unkillable. Sessions took deliberate aim at Roman Nose's chest, half ashamed to kill such a magnificent figure yet knowing that Roman Nose's death was the only thing that could stop the Indians' charge.

Even as he squeezed his trigger, he thought of Krebs and Jouett behind him and wondered if they would stop shooting Indians long enough to kill him if they got the chance. He doubted it. Even Jouett and Krebs knew their own survival depended on halting the Indians' charge. They would wait until this danger from the Indians had passed.

Roman Nose stiffened on his horse, arching his body, throwing back his head, riddled by half a dozen bullets that struck him almost simultaneously. Blood streamed from several wounds. He clung to the back of his horse by means of his fingers tangled in the horse's mane for a distance of perhaps twenty or thirty yards. He went down a short handful of yards from the grassy lower tip of the island. His horse, riddled as thoroughly as his rider, fell almost simultaneously. Neither horse nor Indian chief moved again.

Crash! The seventh volley tore into the advancing ranks of the charging Indians at point-blank range. And now each scout flung his rifle aside and grabbed for his revolver, lying on the sand barricade in front of him.

But Roman Nose was dead, unmoving on the dry sand of the riverbed. The ranks of charging Indians hesitated for the barest instant and in that instant Sessions saw hope for himself and for the other scouts. He knew how superstitious the Indians were. He knew that the death of a chief was regarded as a bad omen, an omen of defeat and death.

He fired his revolver at them, the range less than fifty feet. He heard the ragged crackle of revolvers behind him and he suddenly saw the doubt on the painted faces of the Indians.

Without a leader, the savage, unstoppable charge of Indians suddenly broke around the lower tip of the island like a wave breaking around the prow of a sailing ship. A few rode up over the island itself but these few were killed before they could penetrate more than a dozen yards. The main body of Indians broke to right and left and streamed on past, heading for the safety of the riverbanks.

Passing, they drew the rapid, concentrated fire from the revolvers of the scouts and, to protect themselves, hid behind the bodies of their galloping horses, holding on with a hand tangled in the horse's mane, with a moccasined foot clinging to the horse's back.

As the charge broke past the island, Forsyth's voice raised in a hoarse bellow, to be echoed and re-echoed by Beecher and McCall and Grover, "Down! Down! Lie down in your rifle pits!"

Sessions had turned his head to follow the Indians' charge as it split on both sides of the island. Something caught his eye on the island itself and he glanced quickly away from the retreating Indians.

He was looking straight into the muzzle of a revolver and the face behind it was that of Krebs.

He flung himself frantically into his rifle pit just as the revolver roared, just as it belched blue powdersmoke straight toward him.

He felt something burn along his ribs, something that felt like a red-hot iron. He hit the sand and rolled into his rifle pit as a second bullet showered him with sand. He lay still in the pit, feeling the quick rush of warm blood from the gouged wound in his side, and shaking almost uncontrollably.

Above him bullets from snipers who had re-occupied the riverbanks during the charge by Roman Nose cut through the grass and willow brush like hail. He waited several moments until the worst of the volley had spent itself, then cautiously raised his head and stared back toward the place he had last seen Krebs.

The man was gone. But beyond Kreb's rifle pit, Sessions suddenly saw Lieutenant Beecher get to his feet and come staggering out of his rifle pit.

His face was a ghastly shade of greenish gray. His eyes were narrowed with excruciating pain. Both hands clutched a wound in his side from which, despite his tunic and both his hands, blood leaked and dripped onto the sand.

He staggered toward the lower end of the island, coming on with disregard for the bullets cutting the air ahead, behind and above him. He didn't even see John Sessions as he passed Sessions' rifle pit. He went on past to the pit occupied by Colonel Forsyth and collapsed into it.

His voice was harsh and hoarse as he said, "I'm dying, General. I'm shot in the side and dying."

Forsyth's voice was filled with shock and dismay. "Oh no, Beecher! It can't be as bad as that!"

"Yes." After that single word, Beecher groaned. A few moments later he began to shout deliriously about the charge that had just been deflected by the resolute resistance of the scouts.

Sessions was still shaking, from reaction at finding himself alive when death had seemed so inevitable—from the shock of the wound in his side—from surprise at finding Krebs taking aim at him.

He pulled his shirt tail out and unbuttoned his underwear to look at the wound. It was a bullet gouge less than a quarter of an inch deep. Even so it had bared the bone of three of his ribs. They gleamed white where the bullet had scoured the flesh from them.

The wound was bleeding slowly. It was painful and would remain so for a long, long time. But it would not incapacitate him, even if all three of the exposed ribs were cracked.

Suddenly a wild kind of exhilaration came over him. The scouts had broken the Indians' charge. They might live through the day after all. He would get his chance at Jouett and Krebs.

EIGHT

━━━━━━━━━━━

Sessions lay motionless in the bottom of his rifle pit for several minutes, until the intensity of firing from snipers on the bank decreased. Raising his head, he saw Forsyth pulling himself up the side of his rifle pit. His voice tight with pain, Forsyth called, "Grover?"

"Yes sir."

"Can they do better than that?"

Grover shook his head. He said, "I've been on these plains for more than thirty years, General, and I never saw anything like that before. I think they have done their level best."

Sessions grinned at Grover shakily. "I thought we were goners for sure."

"So did I. That ain't the way Injuns ordinarily fight. And I don't reckon they'll fight that way again."

From the bluff, the wailing of women and children was a continuous, minor-key, mournful sound. Roman Nose lay dead on the baking sand, and not far away lay the medicine man. Warriors were scattered everywhere along with the bodies of their horses. A few still lived, both among the horses and the men. Two wounded braves crawled laboriously to the bank and disappeared into the high grass and brush.

Once more, Sessions looked back to where he had last seen Krebs. He wanted to get up and go charging up the island to Krebs' rifle pit. He wanted to challenge and kill the man.

But he knew such an action would only result in his being placed under arrest by Colonel Forsyth, and perhaps disarmed. He would defeat his own purpose by attacking Krebs now. He wanted all three of the murderers, not just one. When darkness came he might then be able to do something about Krebs. In darkness, he could move freely around the island. Indians never attack at night.

In the meantime, he had better keep his head down unless he was actually firing at the Indians and when he was, keep checking behind him to make sure one of the three didn't shoot him in the back.

The several hundred mounted warriors who had participated in the abortive charge now waited uncertainly on both banks of the river just out of rifle range. Snipers in the grass and brush along the bank still fired occasionally when one of the scouts exposed himself.

After milling around aimlessly for ten or fifteen minutes, the mounted Indians began to withdraw to the little gorge from which they had begun their charge a short time ago. Within a matter of minutes they had all disappeared. Up on the bluff the women and children still were visible, and their wails and chants were audible.

Forsyth shouted, "Reload your rifles and, if it is necessary, deepen your rifle pits! Rest when you can because they surely are not finished with us yet!"

Sessions had already reloaded his Spencer carbine and that of Mooers. Now he carefully reloaded his revolver, an Army Colt's percussion piece. He was both hungry and thirsty but he had neither food nor water. Moving to the foot of his rifle pit, he began to dig, lengthening the pit, digging deeper in the area lengthened thus.

He went down nearly three feet before water began to seep into the hole. He kept digging until he had a pool of water six inches deep. He drank, filled his canteen, then yelled at Forsyth, "Colonel, I've got water in my rifle pit. If anybody wants to throw me his canteen, I'll fill it up for him." Forsyth tossed his canteen into Sessions' rifle pit. Grover and McCall followed with theirs. Sessions filled the three and a dozen others that were thrown to him. Raising up, he began to toss them back. He saw Krebs' face briefly as the man lifted his head. He snatched for his revolver but the face quickly disappeared.

He was tired from the exertion and he was soaked with sweat. He lay on his back in his rifle pit, trying to sleep. He knew that sooner or later the Indians would attack again. It must be maddening to them to have been defeated by only fifty men. Over four hundred must have been involved in that charge a while ago.

Grover yelled suddenly, "Here they come again!"

Sessions raised up. From the position of the sun he could tell that it was well past noon. He wondered where the time had gone.

The Indians came galloping out of the little gorge, spreading this time and not staying in close order as they had before.

In a long wavering line they came galloping toward the island, bending and surrounding it, but without the fierce war cries, without the certainty this time of victory. Sessions began firing upon Forsyth's command, occasionally looking back over his shoulder toward Krebs' rifle pit.

Six or eight of the Indians fell, some dead, some only wounded. The charge broke before it got closer than a hundred yards to the island and once more the mounted Cheyennes drew back, to mill uncertainly while trying to decide what next to do.

John Sessions began to believe there was a good chance he and some of the others might leave this place alive. The toll taken of the attacking Cheyennes had been terrible and while Forsyth's scouts had not come off unscathed, well over half of them had received no wounds at all. The Indians must have sustained a hundred dead, perhaps twice that many with wounds.

Again the snipers on the bank began firing, with more persistence than before as if they were determined to do what the charge had failed to do. Sessions ducked his head and tried to relax and rest. The sun beat down against him mercilessly. The air in the rifle pit was still. It was September, but the day was hot as if it had been midsummer. He saw a few puffy clouds and wished one would cover up the sun, if only for a little while.

Flies, drawn by blood and the dead horses, buzzed around his head. They crawled on his bloody shirt where it had been soaked by the bullet gouge along his ribs. The wound was more painful now but he tried not to think of it.

He began to think ahead, to plan what he would do when darkness fell. The first thing he would do would be to find Floyd Krebs. Krebs would tell him who the third man was. When Krebs faced death he'd spill his guts.

The hours dragged. Once Sessions dozed off and when

he awoke he realized he was feverish and that fever had made him sleep. He could tell from the position of the sun that it was close to six o'clock. The day was almost finished. They had lived through the first day, or at least most of them had. When darkness came they could cut meat off the dead horses and eat.

In the slanting light of the dying sun, the Cheyennes came charging out of their little gorge again, yelling and firing.

But they seemed to know this charge was doomed even before it had begun. The scouts were battle tested now. They had faced a charge several times worse than this. They held their fire without being told until the Indians were close enough so that they could scarcely miss.

The first volley took a terrible toll of the charging Indians. And that first volley broke the charge before the nearest of the galloping warriors had reached the foot of the island. They spilled off to both sides, once more like a wave breaking around the prow of a ship, and galloped out of rifle range on both riverbanks.

On the bluff, the wails of the women and children redoubled in intensity. Sessions knew that while the scouts weren't out of the woods, this would be the last charge by mounted Indians made against the embattled island. From now on, the Cheyennes would rely on snipers to decimate Forsyth's scouts. They would wait, knowing they could starve the white men out.

Slowly the sun sank toward the horizon in the west. Clouds piling up high in the western sky flamed brilliant orange and gold. A wind stirred in the west, growing gusty and stronger as the light faded. Lightning snaked downward out of those high-piled clouds and distant thunder reached the ears of the weary scouts.

There was a flurry of firing from both riverbanks just before it got too dark to shoot. And then came a silence almost as terrible in its own way as the racket of battle had been all through the endless day.

Men stood up in their rifle pits and stretched. Some cursed. A couple laughed. Some shouted defiance at the Indians.

From his rifle pit, Forsyth called, "Mr. Grover. Mr. Sessions."

Sessions, already standing beside his rifle pit, walked

to where the colonel lay half in and half out of his rifle pit. Forsyth said, "Lieutenant Beecher is dead."

Neither Grover nor Sessions spoke. Forsyth said, "Surgeon Mooers is still alive, but he hasn't regained consciousness. I doubt if he ever will." He paused a moment, then went on, "And I'm shot in both legs and cannot get around. So I'll have to depend on you gentlemen. Mr. Sessions, will you get a casualty report for me? I want to know how many are dead, how many too seriously wounded to fight, and how many slightly wounded and able to continue fighting."

Sessions said, "Yes sir."

"You will find a notebook and paper in my saddlebags."

"Yes sir." Sessions walked to where Forsyth's saddle lay. He found the notebook, which had a bullet hole in it, and a stub of pencil.

Forsyth spoke to Grover. "Tell the men to dig a pit in the middle of the island where it will be hidden somewhat by brush. They may build a fire in the pit and cook meat from the horses over it. I want you to direct some other men to dig another pit large enough to hold all the men who are wounded seriously."

"Yes sir." Grover started to move away, but stopped when Forsyth said, "Grover?"

"Yes sir?"

"There must be some men among us with experience dressing wounds. Find out who they are and put them to work. You will find medical supplies in one of the mule packs."

"Yes, Colonel."

Sessions moved away in the darkness, the pencil and notebook in his hand. Every nerve, every muscle in him was tight as a fiddlestring. Moving around the island in the dark would be one of the most perilous things he had ever done. His voice would identify him as he called out to the men to let him know who the dead and wounded were. He wouldn't know who he was talking to until it was too late.

He had slung the carbine across his back. Now he loosened his revolver in its holster. And he headed through the high grass toward the island's upper end.

NINE

Grover's voice, yelling at the men to dig pits in the center of the island for cooking and for the wounded, followed Sessions as he moved through the dry grass and willows toward the island's upper end. The only light was that from the stars, filtering through a thin overcast. Twice in the first dozen yards he stumbled and nearly fell. Both times he wrenched his side and the second time his wound began to bleed again.

Men crawled out of their rifle pits in obedience to Forsyth's relayed orders. Sessions collided with a couple of them and muttered an apology, his hand on his revolver in case they should turn out to be the men he was hunting and who now were also hunting him.

Picking his way carefully along, it took him nearly ten minutes to reach the island's upper end. He could feel the warmth of blood flowing from the wound in his side. He stood there a moment, the cool evening breeze in his face, hearing the murmur of the river as it divided and flowed past on both sides of the island. He looked toward the riverbank and beyond, toward the fires of the Indians, seeing the Indian women moving about the fires as they prepared the evening meal.

He edged to the first rifle pit. "Anybody hurt in here?"

A voice spoke out of the darkness. "Yeah, but not bad."

"Name?"

"Harrington."

"Can you keep fighting or do you want to come to the pit being dug for the wounded in the center of the island?"

"I'll stay here. I ain't hurt that bad."

Sessions moved on carefully to the next rifle pit. "Any wounded here?"

"Yeah. And a dead man too."

"Names?"

"Tucker, wounded. Wilson, dead."

"Can you keep fighting, Tucker, or do you want to come . . . ?"

He didn't get to finish. Tucker said, "I'll stay here."

It was difficult to write names in the dark and Sessions didn't know how readable they would be, but he had no light and didn't dare strike a match. There still might be Indian snipers on the riverbank and there were three men on the island who would kill him instantly if they got the chance.

He picked his way to the next rifle pit. He now held the notebook in his left hand, marking the place where he had last written with his thumb. He carried the pencil in his right.

He was tense and uneasy. Sooner or later he was going to encounter Krebs and Jouett and the third man, as yet unknown to him. When he did, he could expect either an immediate attack or he would be followed stealthily until they had a chance to plunge a knife into his back as he knelt to write. Still in a way he welcomed the chance to come to grips with the men. Forsyth couldn't condemn him for defending himself against attack.

There were no wounded in the next two rifle pits. In the third, a weak voice moaned and Sessions called back to the two unwounded men to help this one to the shelter being dug. He stood aside while the two crawled into the rifle pit and lifted out the wounded man. The man groaned once and then was still. The two carried him past Sessions and he knelt and scrawled, "Unknown. Badly wounded," in the notebook.

He moved to the next rifle pit. A voice called in answer to his query, "McLaughlin. Slight wound. Thayer. No wounds."

He wrote the name of McLaughlin in his book. Going on, he found yet another man so seriously wounded that he couldn't speak. Thayer crawled out of his pit and helped the man down the island toward the pit being dug for the wounded men.

From the next pit, no one answered him. Sessions crawled into it, his foot encountering a body. He risked striking a match and recognized the face of Chalmers Smith. Blowing out the match, he wrote Smith's name in his book.

It was now necessary to turn the page. Straightening, he did so and climbed out of the rifle pit. Right here willows were very thick and he made considerable noise pushing through. He stopped at the side of the next rifle pit and said, "Wounded? Names?"

He received no reply from the pit. It yawned blackly in front of him. He opened his mouth to speak again, at the same time heard a rustling in the willows through which he just had come.

There was something stealthy about the sounds . . . He dropped both pencil and notebook and started to whirl around . . .

Before he could complete his turn, he was struck violently from behind. Bowled forward, he was knocked into the rifle pit from which he had just come.

Pains stabbed from his wounded side, which had been wrenched violently by the fall. Blood began to flow more freely from it, but he had no time to think about his wound. His assailant had a knife. It ripped through his shirt and raked a deep, foot-long gash across his back. Trying to get his hand on the man's knife wrist, he encountered the blade instead and felt it cut deeply into his hand. The man's body was on top of him, holding him down. The knife was raised to strike again.

Sessions' unwounded hand, clawing, encountered only sand. He seized a handful of it and flung it into his assailant's face. The man cursed savagely. The poised knife hesitated for an instant before plunging down . . .

There was suddenly an almost superhuman strength in Sessions. He arched his body violently, pitching his attacker up and slightly to one side. The knife came down, but Sessions had twisted his body out of the way and it buried itself harmlessly in the sand.

Before the man could yank it out again, Sessions managed to fight from beneath him, to claw part of the way up the steep side of the rifle pit. Pacing the shadowy figure of the man across the width of the pit, he grabbed for the revolver at his side.

His hand encountered only the empty holster. The gun was gone, lost during the struggle in the bottom of the rifle pit. He began to feel for it with his foot as he waited tensely for the attacker to lunge at him with the knife. He had to catch the man's wrist before the knife buried itself in him. There was no place to which he could retreat.

It was impossible even to circle in an effort to stay out of the way.

Both he and the other man were breathing hard. The man hesitated, rubbing his eyes with his left hand, knuckling sand out of them. Sessions leaped forward, taking the offensive unexpectedly. He had suddenly seen in his mind the charred ruins of his house, the scalped body of his wife, his two dead sons. Here before him was one of the men who had murdered them . . .

Both hands, groping for the hand that held the knife, closed instead on the man's forearm. He held on, trying unsuccessfully to wrench the knife away.

The man's struggles became frantic. The sand in his eyes was forgotten. Sessions could feel blood running down his back. The palm of one hand was slick with blood from the knife wound it had sustained. That hand, on the man's wrist, began to slip . . .

Suddenly he gave up trying to wrench the knife away. He wasn't going to succeed in doing it. He could feel the man's wrist slipping from his grasp.

Turning slightly away from the man, whose face he still was unable to see clearly enough to identify him, he brought up his leg, at the same time bringing down the arm he held in both his hands. He put all the strength and force of which he was capable into doing so and felt the arm strike his rising leg.

Bones snapped with a sound that, once heard, can never be forgotten. The knife fell soundlessly into the sand in the bottom of the pit. The man opened his mouth and yelled wordlessly with pain.

Disarmed, his arm broken, he now wanted nothing but to get away. He struck out blindly at Sessions and knocked him back. Sessions lost his balance and fell helplessly against the side of the pit. As he did, his hand belatedly encountered the revolver. Lifting it, he thumbed the hammer back and fired just as the shadowy figure of his attacker disappeared over the lip of the rifle pit.

The sound was deafening in the silence. But the man was gone, lost before he could be identified. Cursing, Sessions suddenly remembered that he had broken the man's right arm. He had marked him indelibly. Tomorrow he could identify him easily.

A voice said, "Who the hell is that? What's going on?"

Sessions struggled to his feet. He said, "Damn redskinned son-of-a-bitch! He must've sneaked on the island to see how bad we were hurt. He liked to have killed me with that damn knife!"

A man climbed down into the rifle pit. Sessions remembered his notebook and struck a match. He recovered it and the pencil, then let the man help him out of the pit.

He handed the notebook to another man. "The colonel wants a tally of the dead and wounded. I don't think I can finish it. My damn hand's bleeding so bad I'll get it all over the paper."

The other man asked, "You want any help?"

Sessions grunted, "Huh uh. I'll be all right." He dragged his bandanna out of his pocket and wrapped it around his bleeding hand. He couldn't do anything about his back or about the wound in his side. But maybe if he could get bandaged, he could stop the bleeding before loss of blood weakened him too much.

Behind him, he heard the man to whom he had given the notebook calling out, asking for the names of the wounded and the dead. He picked his careful way toward the middle of the island.

He saw the cooking fire in the pit that had been dug for it. Men were squatted around it, cooking chunks of raw horsemeat on sticks. The aroma of cooking meat made Sessions' mouth water, made his belly cramp. He hadn't eaten since noon yesterday and he felt hungry enough to eat that horsemeat raw.

Beyond, a pit dug for the wounded was still being enlarged. Sessions stopped at the edge of it. "Any chance of getting bandaged up? I'm losing a lot of blood."

One of the scouts, evidently filling in for the mortally wounded surgeon, Mooers, crawled up out of the pit. "I'll do the best I can, but we haven't got bandages or medical supplies. The mule packing that stuff got stampeded by the Indians."

Sessions slid into the pit, where there was a small fire burning so that the men working with the wounded would have light. The scout said, "Take off your shirt. I'll have to use it to bandage you."

Sessions carefully took off his shirt. The man knelt by the fire and began tearing it into strips. Finished, he helped Sessions to drop the upper half of his bloody, knife-cut underwear and began to bandage both the deep knife wound on his back and the bullet wound along his ribs.

He grumbled as he worked. "This is a hell of a filthy way to do anything. Them wounds are bound to fester but there ain't nothin' I can do about it. We ain't even got whisky to pour over 'em."

Sessions said, "Just stop the bleeding. Don't worry about anything else."

"Oh I can do that all right. But you've already lost a heap of blood. I expect you feel pretty weak."

Sessions nodded. He did feel weak. He felt that if he stood up he would faint. The man finished bandaging him, then helped him put the top of his underwear back on and button it. He said, "Lie back and rest a while. I'll get you some water and some meat."

He left and Sessions dozed. The world whirled crazily. He thought about how helpless he would be if Krebs, Jouett, or the man with the broken arm came looking for him now.

After a while the man who had bandaged him came back with a cup of water and a chunk of half-cooked meat. Sessions thanked him. He sat up and began to wolf it down. It was tough and stringy and only half cooked but it was the most delicious meat he had ever eaten. He chewed patiently, washing each mouthful down with water from the cup.

The man left to help others among the wounded. Sessions finished the meat, finished the last of the water. He already felt stronger. He was already thinking about tomorrow, about going after the man with the broken arm.

Tonight he would have to rest. If he wanted to be strong enough tomorrow, he would have to rest tonight.

But he didn't want to stay here. There was light here and he would be vulnerable to attack. He got up and crawled out of the pit. He walked unsteadily toward the lower end of the island, toward his own rifle pit.

Reaching it, he slid into it, laid back helplessly and closed his eyes. He was sweating heavily and breathing hard. His body seemed to be one continuous area of pain. His hand throbbed and ached.

He kept thinking that tomorrow he might, with luck, find and kill the man with the broken arm. He would, at least, find out who he was. Then he would have the names of all three of his family's murderers. Afterward all that would remain would be to kill them, one by one.

TEN

Sessions had scarcely stopped breathing hard before he heard Colonel Forsyth shout, "Pass the word to connect all rifle pits! I want four men to cut meat off the horses and bury it so that it will keep. Get busy now. We can rest when it is done!"

He couldn't help marveling at Forsyth's stamina. The man was shot in one thigh. His other leg was broken by a bullet between the ankle and the knee. He had been hit a grazing blow on the head. Yet he had remained conscious all through the day. He was still in charge, still able to plan for the survival of his men.

Sessions was weak and weary but if Forsyth could keep functioning, so could he. He fumbled around until he found his tin plate and with it he began to scoop sand out, working toward Forsyth's rifle pit.

He worked slowly and deliberately, favoring his wounds because he did not want to start them bleeding again. The air was cool but in spite of that he began to sweat. There were sounds of activity all up and down the island.

He had been working about an hour when he finally dug through into Colonel Forsyth's rifle pit. He stopped to rest, saying, "Are you all right, sir?"

"I'm all right, Mr. Sessions. I've been thinking. I've got to send someone to Fort Wallace to bring a force to our relief. You're wounded, aren't you?"

"Yes sir." Sessions didn't want to go. He didn't want to leave the island, to leave the men behind who had murdered his family. He might be killed and thus cheated of his vengeance. Or he might return to find the three men dead.

Forsyth said, "Get some men to help carry Surgeon Mooers to the pit that has been dug for the wounded."

"How is he, sir?"

"He hasn't regained consciousness."

Sessions crawled out of the pit and walked across the island. When he found some men digging he said, "The colonel wants two men to help get Surgeon Mooers into the pit where the other wounded are."

A couple of men got up and headed toward the colonel's rifle pit. Sessions stood at the edge of the water, staring out across the seventy yards or so of dry sand between the island and the riverbank. It must have been providence that caused the colonel to camp right here. This island was the only refuge for miles. It was all that had saved their lives. Without it they would all have been killed early in the day.

He suddenly realized that Colonel Forsyth hadn't had anything to eat and that he was hungry again himself. He cut a couple of chunks of meat from the nearest horse, and then cut himself a couple of willow sticks. He walked to the pit where the fire was and joined the circle of men around it. He cut the meat into steaks, impaled them on the sticks and held them close to the coals to broil. Juice soon began to drip into the fire.

They had plenty of meat tonight, he thought, but by tomorrow night the horses would have begun to spoil. Buried meat would remain fresh no more than a couple of days at most.

By day after tomorrow, the stench of dead horses here on this island would become almost unbearable. The prospect wasn't pleasant. Nor were the chances of their being relieved very promising. Even if two men left for Fort Wallace tonight, they could not possibly reach it afoot in less than four to five days. It was a hundred and ten miles away. No man could walk more than thirty miles a day.

Sessions didn't particularly care whether they were relieved or not. Everything that had made his life worthwhile was gone. Sally was dead and so were his sons. His home was burned. But if he could live long enough to revenge himself on Jouett, Krebs, and the unknown man with the broken arm . . .

He heard someone in Forsyth's rifle pit giving the colonel the casualty report that he himself had begun compiling earlier. Lieutenant Beecher, Surgeon Mooers, Chalmers Smith, and Wilson were either dead or dying. Louis Farley and Bernard Day were mortally wounded. O'Donnell, Davis, Tucker, Gantt, Clarke, Armstrong, Morton, and Violett were severely wounded. Harrington, Davenport, Halley, McLaughlin, Hudson, Farley, McCall, and two others slightly wounded.

Only twenty-eight men out of fifty-three were unhurt. But there was plenty of ammunition and water was available for the digging. Tonight there was meat and tomorrow there would be meat again.

The meat on his sticks was done. Sessions climbed out of the pit and carried it to where Forsyth was. "I brought you some meat, Colonel. If you don't mind eating horse."

Forsyth took it and ate ravenously, taking sips of water at frequent intervals from his canteen. Sessions ate a piece of the meat himself, then gave Forsyth the rest.

Finished, Forsyth said, "I want volunteers to go to Fort Wallace, but don't call out for them because there's at least one Indian over there that understands English very well."

Sessions nodded. Once more he moved up the island, calling out softly for volunteers. He was wondering what he would do if Forsyth selected either Krebs or Jouett to try making it to the fort.

There was no need for him to go very far. Eight or ten men had already climbed out of their rifle pits and headed down the island. Sessions returned to his own rifle pit. McCall had almost finished connecting it with his own. He had halted work to volunteer for the trip back to Fort Wallace. All those who had volunteered now stood in front of the Colonel's rifle pit. Forsyth said, "It's too dark to see who you are, gentlemen, so give me your names."

Starting from the left, they gave their names. Forsyth was silent a moment. Sessions had listened carefully, relieved when he heard neither Jouett's name nor Krebs'.

At last Forsyth said, "Trudeau. Stillwell. Cook enough meat to last you several days and take it along with you. Take water and whatever else you think you will need, but don't try to carry too much weight. Fort Wallace is a hundred and ten miles away."

The men who had not been selected began to leave. Each of them shook both Stillwell's and Trudeau's hand and wished them luck. Sessions knew Trudeau had been a trapper and mountain man. Stillwell was only nineteen, but he had been raised on the frontier. He was both smart and strong.

Forsyth said, "Tell Colonel Bankhead our situation. Tell him there are between five hundred and a thousand Indians besieging us and that we have many wounded and no medical supplies. Tell him that Surgeon Mooers is mortally wounded and that he should send a surgeon along with our relief."

"Yes sir." Both men spoke in unison. Forsyth said, "Get ready then. And report back to me before you go."

The two moved away into the darkness. Over on the riverbank well out of rifle range, some Indians were doing a war dance. Their shrill cries echoed from the bluffs.

Sessions' hand throbbed mercilessly. He still had the bandanna wrapped around it to try and stop the bleeding but the bandanna was now soggy with blood.

He went back to the pit that had been dug for the wounded. Men lay in a circle around the fire. Two of the scouts who had volunteered to help were bandaging wounded men with strips torn from shirts. Sessions slid down into the pit. "Think you could do something about my hand?"

"Just a minute. I'll try."

Sessions sat down and waited patiently. The whole night stretched ahead. He had plenty of time but if he was to be a match for Krebs and Jouett, who were both unhurt, he had better get his hand properly bandaged at the very least.

One of the men finished what he was doing and came to him. The man knelt and carefully unwound the soggy rags from Sessions' hand. The hand continued to throb mercilessly.

Blood drenched the palm of his hand as soon as the bandage was removed. The scout began ripping strips from a dirty shirt. He said, "You ought to close your hand into a fist. That's the only way you're going to stop the bleeding. It's a deep cut. How the hell did you get it anyhow?"

Sessions grunted. "No fist. I need the use of the hand."

The man shrugged. "It's your hand." He began to bandage it. When he was finished, Sessions got up, thanked him and climbed out of the pit. Trudeau and Stillwell passed him, heading for Forsyth's rifle pit. Sessions followed, since his own rifle pit was next to Forsyth's.

Trudeau said, "Colonel Forsyth?"

"Yes?" The colonel's voice was filled with pain and was considerably weaker than it had been earlier. For an instant, Sessions wondered what this command would do if it lost its commanding officer. So far, Forsyth had conducted the defense brilliantly. He had exacted a heavy toll of the Indians. Roman Nose was dead and the morale of the Indians shattered by their defeat at the hands of such a small body of men. This might end in a defeat for the scouts, but no matter what happened, it was also a victory. Their heavy losses and the loss of their chief might just prevent the Indians from launching their planned attacks upon the white settlements.

Trudeau said, "We're ready, Colonel."

"Do you have any plan?"

There was a brief silence. "Not really, Colonel, except that we're going to try and get through the Indians without leaving a trail for them."

"How do you think you're going to accomplish that?"

Trudeau chuckled. "By taking off our boots and walking in our stocking feet. Backwards at least as far as the riverbank. If the Indians see the tracks they'll probably think they were made by moccasins."

Forsyth grunted approval. "Good luck to both of you."

"Good-by, sir. If we don't see you again . . ." Trudeau hesitated. "Well, I mean to say it's been a pleasure to serve with you."

"Thank you, Mr. Trudeau."

Trudeau and Stillwell walked to the edge of the island, where they sat down to pull off their boots. Carrying boots in their left hands, rifles in their right, they stepped down onto the sand, waded through the water, then walked, backwards, toward the riverbank. In the darkness, they were almost instantly lost to sight.

Sessions crouched, rifle ready, straining his eyes in the direction they had gone. If they were caught, he would hear a commotion soon. He didn't know if he'd be able to shoot but he intended to give them all the support he could.

Up and down the island, he could still hear the clanking of tin plates as the men finished connecting their rifle pits. Now and then a man cursed angrily. Someone was groaning steadily in the pit where the wounded were. Other men were cooking meat. A breeze carried the smell of it to Sessions' nose.

Trudeau and Stillwell had been gone what he judged must be ten minutes now. And he had heard no sound of any kind from the riverbank. Give them another twenty minutes, he thought, and they ought to be in the clear. If there was no commotion by then, they should be through the Indian lines.

All but holding his breath, he waited, while the seconds and minutes ticked deliberately away.

ELEVEN

The unnatural silence on the besieged island lasted half an hour. At the end of that time, the men suddenly began talking excitedly among themselves. Some laughed. Some sighed with relief. All knew that Trudeau and Stillwell must have gotten away. If they hadn't, there would have been a commotion over on the riverbank. Neither Stillwell nor Trudeau would have given up without a fight. And it was doubtful if both could have been taken by surprise.

Sessions thought of the four hard days that lay ahead of the pair. After that it would probably take a day for the relief force to be organized, and a couple of days to come from Fort Wallace here. That added up to at least seven days. Seven days of lying in these rifle pits, smelling the putrifying flesh of fifty horses, of several dead men, of wounded men. There was no medicine; there were no bandages. There was no surgeon to make the lot of the wounded bearable. There was no morphine to kill their pain.

Feeling weak from loss of blood, Sessions lay back in his rifle pit and closed his eyes. The Spencer carbine lay across his chest. His head whirled. He knew he needed rest. He wanted to go after Jouett and Krebs right now but he had to admit he was too weak.

He dozed fitfully for a couple hours. Still no shots had been heard from the riverbank. On the island, men finished connecting their rifle pits, cut meat off the horses and either cooked or buried it. Others deepened their pits so that they would have water close at hand.

Out in the darkness, sounds began to be audible. Sessions heard Forsyth call, "Grover, what are they doing out there?"

290

"Carrying their dead and wounded away, Colonel."

"Do you think they will attack?"

"No sir, Colonel, they ain't going to attack. Injuns never fight at night. They got a superstition that if a warrior is killed at night his spirit wanders forever somewhere between the earth and sky and never gets to the happy hunting ground."

"Then pass the word that the men are not to fire unless the Indians do."

"Yes sir." Grover called the order to Sessions, who relayed it to McCall. He heard McCall pass it along, softly so that the Indian among the Cheyennes who spoke English wouldn't hear. Not that it mattered much whether he heard this particular order or not.

Several minutes passed. Then Sessions heard Forsyth's voice. "Mr. Sessions. Will you come here a minute?"

Sessions crawled out of his rifle pit. He walked to the colonel's pit and sat down on the edge of it. "Yes sir?"

"Have you discovered the identities of the men who killed your family?"

"Two of them, sir."

"Who are they?"

"Jouett and Krebs."

"How do you know?"

"Krebs shot me."

"Did you see him do it? Or are you just guessing that he did?"

"I saw him, sir."

"And how do you know Jouett is one of them?"

"He and Krebs were talking about spending the money."

"Any idea who the third man is?"

"I'll know tomorrow."

"How?"

"He jumped me with a knife while I was making a count of the wounded and the dead. He cut a hell of a gash across my back and I got a bad cut in the palm of my hand while we were fighting for the knife."

"But how are you going to know who he is?"

"I broke his arm."

Forsyth was silent a moment. At last he asked, "What are your plans, Mr. Sessions? You know, of course, that we need every able-bodied man we've got."

"Yes sir. I know. But if I don't get them, they're going

to get me. I've got a bullet wound in my ribs. I've got two bad knife cuts that won't stop bleeding no matter what I do. I'm going to get weaker as time passes and they aren't. They'll kill me first chance they get."

"And you want to try and kill them first."

"Yes sir."

"Well, I can't give my blessing to anything like that."

"No sir. But I don't reckon I need anybody's blessing for what I've got to do."

Again Forsyth was silent, as though trying to decide what he should do. He said finally, "Well, I'm not going to put a wounded man under arrest, particularly since you haven't yet done anything. Nor am I going to put two able-bodied men under arrest on your say so. I guess all I can say is that I'm not in any shape to stop you from doing anything you think you have to do. But I warn you, Sessions. You'll be called to account."

"Yes sir. I know that."

"All right. You can go."

Sessions went back to his rifle pit. He stood there uncertainly for several moments. If he didn't go after Jouett and Krebs tonight, they might succeed in killing him tomorrow. They would be shooting at him all day every time he showed himself, instead of shooting at the Indians. He wouldn't dare stick his head out of his rifle pit.

That prospect didn't appeal to him. He got up suddenly, moving carefully so as not to start his wounds bleeding again. They were temporarily scabbed and bleeding only sluggishly.

He stood for a moment in the bottom of his rifle pit, waiting for his head to stop whirling. There was only one possible way for him to manage this. He couldn't see and he didn't dare make any light. He'd have to move from pit to pit, asking the men in each pit what the names of the men in the next pit were. Fortunately all the pits were connected now. Every one of the men would know who his neighbors were.

He started with McCall. "Who's in the next pit, Bill?"

"Groves. Him and Bill Reilly are together. Why?"

"Nothing." Sessions went on and a moment later asked softly, "Groves? Who's in the rifle pit next to you?"

"Ketterer and DuPont. Why?"

"I'm looking for someone."

"Who?"

"Jouett and Krebs."

"Is Forsyth going to send them to Fort Wallace too?"

"Not that I know of."

"That's good because that pair wouldn't go. They'd save their own skins and to hell with the rest of us."

"Know them, do you?"

"I knew them in Abilene."

"But you don't know where they are?"

"Huh uh. They're somewheres toward the upper end of the island."

Sessions went on. At the next pit he said softly, "Ketterer?"

"Yeah?"

"Who's in the next pit?"

"Nichols."

"Seen Jouett and Krebs?"

"They're in the pit next to Nichols."

Sessions felt weak and dizzy. He asked, "Got any water?"

"Sure. Here." Ketterer handed him his canteen.

Sessions sat down wearily on the side of Ketterer's rifle pit. He wished his head would stop whirling. He took a drink of water and felt himself swaying. Ketterer said, "You all right?"

"Yeah. I've lost some blood. I guess I'm a little dizzy from it."

"Why are you looking for Jouett and Krebs?"

Sessions didn't answer the question at once. Instead he asked, "You got a family?"

"Yeah."

"I had one. Wife. Two boys. They were murdered for some money I had buried in the root cellar. Wife was scalped. The boys were tortured to make her tell where the money was."

"You know who did it?"

"I know. It was Jouett and Krebs. And another man."

"How do you know?"

"I trailed 'em to Hays."

"Why didn't you turn 'em over to the law?"

"I didn't know who they were until Krebs took a shot at me. And until I heard them talking about spending the money."

"What does Forsyth say about it?"

"He won't put me under arrest because I'm wounded.

And he won't put them under arrest because he needs 'em."

"So what are you going to do?"

Sessions grinned weakly in the darkness. "I was going to kill them. That's why I came up here looking for them. But it doesn't look like I've got what it takes right now. I guess I've lost too much blood."

"Lie down and get some sleep. You'll feel better when you wake up."

"It'll be daylight then."

Ketterer said, "I don't figure there's any hurry, Sessions. We ain't goin' any place. Not just yet anyhow. You can go after 'em tomorrow just as well as you can tonight."

"Yeah. I suppose I can." Sessions got wearily to his feet. "I'll go back to my own rifle pit."

"Don't worry. I won't let them go sneaking past here."

"Thanks." Sessions staggered toward the lower end of the island. In the pit which had been dug especially for them, the wounded groaned, or thrashed around, or cried out with their agony, or lay unconscious and near to death. Not much farther on, men squatted around a blazing fire cooking horsemeat steaks on sticks.

Sessions considered sourly what he had managed to accomplish so far. Not much. He knew who two of the killers were and he had broken the arm of the other one. But at what cost? He was bleeding from three wounds, all of them serious. He felt feverish and, in the coolness of the night, was beginning to have chills.

He reached his rifle pit and slid weakly into it. He groped around until he found his blankets. He wrapped them around him, now shivering violently. He sat down, hunched, miserable, weak and getting weaker all the time.

He had the feeling that he was running out of time. Ketterer had said there was no hurry, that tomorrow was as good a time for going after Jouett and Krebs as was tonight.

But it wasn't true. Time was against him now. Without medical aid, without proper bandaging and medicines, he was going to get progressively weaker as the hours passed. If he didn't get Jouett, Krebs, and the other man within the next twenty-four hours, he wasn't going to get them at all. They were going to get him instead.

TWELVE

Sessions dozed fitfully throughout the remainder of the night. The Cheyennes, who had spent the earlier part of it carrying off their wounded and their dead, were now silent, their task complete. The Indian fires had died down and disappeared. The fire in the pit where the men had cooked meat for themselves had also died as had the fire in the pit where the wounded were.

The only sounds now were the snores of the sleeping men and the groans of the wounded. At last, a line of gray appeared along the eastern horizon and birds in the grass along the riverbank began to sing.

Sessions awoke and lay for a moment staring up at the graying sky. He moved slightly and realized that his underwear and shirt were stuck to his back and ribs by blood that had dried during the night. His hand had swelled and now pained terribly. He unwrapped the bandage and rewrapped it more loosely than before. The cloth was stiff with dried blood but it was all he had.

Carefully, so as not to start his wounds bleeding again, he raised his head above the sand bulwark of his rifle pit. From the pit next to him came Forsyth's cautious voice. "Keep down, Sessions. The Indians are approaching. They think we've gone and they're trying to pick up our trail. If we wait until they are close we may be able to give them a surprise."

Sessions pulled his head down. He reloaded his rifle and checked the loads in his revolver. He wriggled into a more comfortable position, and afterward lay still, waiting for Forsyth's command.

He could now hear the Indians calling back and forth

to each other. From the sound he judged they still must be a couple of hundred yards away.

Forsyth said softly, "Pass along the word to hold fire until they're close enough."

Sessions called to McCall. "The colonel says to hold fire until the Indians are close. He says to pass the word along."

He heard McCall speak softly to the men in the pit next to him. Faintly he heard one of them pass along the word. After that he heard nothing. The birds along the riverbank, frightened by the approaching Indians, stopped singing. The only sounds were the rustling of the breeze in the grass and willows on the island and the soft moans of the wounded men.

Closer and closer the Indians came, about thirty in all, questing like dogs on a rabbit's scent. They were now no more than a hundred yards away, within rifle range. Apparently Forsyth wanted them closer still because he issued no command.

It would be slaughter, Sessions thought as he peered cautiously over the sand bulwark in front of him. The scouts should be able to kill half the Indians with their first volley.

He felt no compunction about doing it. They were fighting for their lives. The heavier the casualties they were able to inflict upon the Indians, the better their chances of survival were going to be. And the more they hurt the Indians the less likely the Indians were to mount their planned offensive against the settlements. In defeat, Forsyth might still accomplish the purpose for which he had been sent west out of Fort Hays two weeks ago.

Sessions held his breath, waiting for Forsyth's command. Suddenly from the upper end of the island a rifle shot broke the silence unexpectedly. In the pit next to him, Sessions heard Forsyth curse. Instantly the colonel shouted, "Commence firing! Commence firing!"

A volley roared raggedly from the rifle pits. But the scouts had been startled by that apparently accidental shot. It threw off their aim. Only two of the Indians were hit. One limped away, blood streaming from a wound in his leg, to throw himself flat in the grass along the riverbank. The other fell, dead before he hit the ground. Those remaining scattered like quail toward the cover of grass and brush along the riverbank and as quickly disappeared.

The second volley rang out just as the last of them were disappearing in the grass. None of these bullets hit anything. Next to Sessions, McCall cursed sourly, muttering something about a "stupid, trigger-happy son-of-a-bitch."

What might have been a serious blow to the Indians had resulted in only two casualties. But it was the sort of thing that might easily happen, particularly where an order had to be passed along from one man to another as this one had.

Sessions wriggled into a position from which he could see Forsyth. It seemed as if every small movement only opened one or another of his wounds. He could feel blood running from the knife cut across his back.

Forsyth was lying against the sloping wall of his rifle pit. His head was exposed, high enough to see both riverbanks. His face was pale and strained with pain, but his eyes were alert and bright. He felt Sessions looking at him and briefly turned his head. Sessions said, "I don't know how you keep going. That bullet is still in your leg and you haven't been able to bandage it."

"Maybe it's better if it stays open. The bleeding carries away the infection."

Sessions grinned. "Then there can't be much infection left in me."

"You look pale. Why don't you try and get some sleep? Nothing is going to happen for a while and I doubt if they'll try rushing the island again. The last time cost them too many casualties."

"How many of them do you think we've killed?"

"I've counted over thirty. But I know they've lost more than that. And a good many of the wounded are eventually going to die."

Sessions said, "You get some sleep, Colonel. I'll watch and call you if anything happens."

Forsyth shook his head. "I slept some last night. I don't think I could sleep any more just yet. Maybe later, Sessions, if you still feel up to it."

Sessions nodded. He crawled deeper into his rifle pit and tried to get as comfortable as possible. The sun came up and several green-bodied flies began to buzz around in the rifle pit. He cursed them silently. They'd find every open wound on the island and wherever it was moist, they'd lay their eggs. Before many days had passed, the eggs would hatch, and then the men would find maggots in their wounds.

He made sure that his own wounds were covered, then closed his eyes and tried to close his ears to the monotonously buzzing flies. Sally's face was there in his thoughts, smiling at him as she so often had while she was alive. He opened his eyes, his face twisting involuntarily with pain. He stared at the sky for a long, long time before he closed his eyes again.

Eventually he slept, while the sun climbed inexorably across the sky. It was the sun's direct heat that eventually woke him. From its position he knew it was close to noon.

He could hear the wounded groaning, moaning, occasionally shouting with pain in their protective pit. He could hear a couple of men talking somewhere nearby.

The flies still buzzed endlessly. He sat up and looked toward Forsyth's rifle pit. The colonel was in the same position he had occupied when Sessions went to sleep. Again he marveled at the colonel's stamina, at his stubborn will. Forsyth asked, "Feel any better, Mr. Sessions?"

Sessions nodded. "I think so. I think I'd feel even better if I could move around."

"I could use an up-to-date casualty report if you feel up to it."

Sessions glanced sharply at Forsyth's face. He wondered if the colonel was deliberately giving him a chance at Jouett and Krebs. Then, imperceptibly, he shook his head. Forsyth knew he wouldn't shoot either one in broad daylight unless he was attacked. Then maybe Forsyth was giving him a chance to discover who the third man was. It was possible that Ketterer had talked to Forsyth while he was asleep.

Forsyth tossed him the notebook and pencil. "Go ahead, Mr. Sessions, if you feel strong enough."

"Thank you, Colonel." Sessions moved at a crouch along the trench connecting the rifle pits. He stopped frequently to write names in the notebook, to make a note of their wounds or lack of them after the names. He reached Ketterer's pit, and went on to that of Nichols. Moments later he was looking down at Jouett and Krebs.

Neither was wounded. Both appeared to have been asleep. They were sweating and haggard and unshaven. When they saw him, the eyes of both gleamed with triumph. They could see how weak he was, he thought. They could see that they had little to fear from him. All they had to do was wait.

Sessions stared straight at Krebs, hating him, his hands tightly clutching his rifle. He said softly, "You son-of-a-bitch, you'll have to shoot straighter if you're going to get rid of me."

For an instant he thought Krebs was going to deny having shot at him. Then Krebs apparently changed his mind. He said, "Looks like I shot pretty near straight enough. But I'll do better next time. Don't worry about that."

Sessions looked at Jouett. He asked, "Which of you killed her? I want to know who to save for last."

Neither man answered him. Neither could continue to meet his eyes. Jouett's hand inched toward the revolver at his side. Sessions said, "Go ahead. Give it a try. I'll let you have it right in the belly where it will hurt."

Jouett's hand stopped. Sessions felt a savage satisfaction because he could see that he had shaken them. He might be weak and his weakness might show, but something else showed too and whatever it was, it had frightened them.

Sessions went on cautiously, looking back over his shoulder until he passed from their sight. He reached the thick willows where he had been attacked and where he had broken his unknown assailant's arm. He doubted if he would be attacked again, but he could feel a new tension coming over him.

He pushed through the willows to the next rifle pit. He looked down into it, recognizing Manuel Vega as the scout at the bottom of the pit. Automatically he said, "Wounds?"

The man glanced up, at first startled, then turning almost sullen. His face was grayish and he winced every time he moved. Sessions slid down into the pit. Vega reached for his gun with his left hand but Sessions kicked it out of his reach.

The muzzle of his rifle was now only inches from Vega's face. Sessions said softly, "Leave the gun where it is. Stand up."

Vega got sullenly to his feet. He showed no inclination to attack. He winced visibly with pain and sweat sprang out in beads on his forehead. Sessions asked harshly, "Where are you hurt?"

"I took a bullet in my arm."

Sessions stared at the arm. "How come no blood?"

"I bandaged it. It wasn't bad but it sure hurts like hell."

Sessions shifted the rifle into the crook of his arm, still leaving his index finger through the trigger guard. With his left hand he seized Vega's wrist, pulling the arm up and toward him.

Vega drew in his breath with the sharpness of the pain. Sessions released his wrist, and immediately grasped the man's shirt at the shoulder. He yanked savagely and heard the cloth tear as the sleeve tore loose. It stripped away, leaving Vega's right arm bare.

Vega hunched his shoulders and whimpered like a wounded dog. Sessions stared at his arm. It was black and blue, bruised from above the elbow to four inches below it. There was a sizeable lump below the elbow showing where the bone was trying to break through the skin. The arm was oddly twisted.

Sessions gave the man a vicious shove. Vega went backward, tripped and fell on his back. The cry he uttered just missed being a scream. Sessions said, "So you're the third."

"I don't know what the hell you're talking about."

"You know."

"You're crazy. What the hell's the idea coming up here and pushing me around like this. You've got to be crazy or something."

"Maybe I am crazy. Crazy for not killing you right now."

"Get out of here. Get out of here and let me alone."

Sessions nodded. "I'm going. But you think about it while I'm gone. It's not going to be easy, the way you die. It's not going to be any easier than it was for my wife and boys."

"I didn't . . . You can't prove . . ."

"I don't have to prove. I've already tried you and found you guilty. And I've sentenced you to die."

He climbed out of the rifle pit. He stood there looking down. Deliberately he wrote on the notebook page, "Vega. Broken arm." He backed away until he could no longer see the man in the bottom of the pit.

He discovered that both his hands were shaking violently. But there was a savage kind of exhilaration in him too. He now knew all three of the murderers. Nor would he have to go after them. He had taunted them enough to make them come after him.

THIRTEEN

━━━━━━━━━━

Sessions finished his tally of the dead and wounded and took it to Forsyth at the island's lower end. The sun continued to beat down mercilessly. Forsyth glanced up at him questioningly, but Sessions did not volunteer any information. Forsyth scanned the list. When he came to the name of Manuel Vega, he looked up again.

"Is Vega the man whose arm you broke?"

"Yes sir."

"And he is the one who attacked you with a knife?"

Sessions nodded.

"I could put him under arrest."

Sessions shook his head.

"So you can kill him?"

Sessions felt weak and dizzy and irritable. He said, "Colonel, you keep saying that but so far I haven't done a damn thing to them. Krebs shot *me,* remember? And Vega tried to kill me with a knife."

Forsyth studied him. "Tell me what happened just now when you ran into Jouett and Krebs."

Sessions grinned faintly. "I told Krebs he'd have to shoot straighter if he figured on getting rid of me."

"What did he say?"

"He promised to try."

"Then he admitted shooting you?"

"Sure. But he didn't have to admit it to me. I saw him do it."

"What about Vega?"

"He claimed his arm had been broken by a bullet. I ripped off his sleeve and there wasn't a scratch on it."

Forsyth smiled wryly. "Then all you really accomplished

302

was to taunt them enough to make sure they'd come after you. They know you know who they are and now they figure they have to kill you to shut you up."

Sessions grinned faintly again. "Colonel, they got in the first licks. They're strong and I'm getting weaker all the time. If they come after me at least I won't be using my strength going after them."

"And you think I can't blame you for defending yourself."

Sessions' grin widened. "Colonel, that's about right."

"I need those three men, Sessions. I need you too."

Sessions shook his head. "Huh uh, Colonel. Not the way you needed us yesterday. The Indians aren't going to attack the island any more. They're going to lay back and snipe at us but they're not going to attack."

Forsyth nodded. "You may be right. But those three men ought to be turned over to the law. If they're proven guilty, they'll hang."

"Knowing they're guilty and proving it are two different things. It's my word against theirs. They've got the money they took from my root cellar but it isn't marked. I can't prove it's mine."

"Didn't you trail them to Fort Hays?"

"Sure, but there were fifty sets of tracks going into Fort Hays and by the time I got there, all three of their horses had been shod. Huh uh, Colonel. I'm not going to depend on the law. The law didn't help my wife and kids."

Forsyth shrugged. His face was white and drawn and his eyes were narrowed with pain. His skin was flushed and Sessions knew he had a fever. He said, "That bullet ought to come out of your leg."

"I know it. But I don't dare let anyone try taking it out for fear I'll lose consciousness. I can't afford to do that, Mr. Sessions. Not while my command is threatened by the Indians."

Sessions slid down into his own rifle pit. The sun made it a well of stagnant heat. Weakness kept washing over him in waves, each wave worse than the last.

He closed his eyes. The whole world seemed to whirl dizzily. He opened them again but he couldn't keep them open. He was too weak. The bullet gouge across his ribs was like a red-hot iron. His whole arm ached from the deep cut in his palm. His back burned almost as badly as did his side.

Moreover, he had a fever from his wounds. His face burned and his body felt hot. At intervals a chill would take him and he would shiver uncontrollably until it passed.

Green-bodied flies still buzzed around in his rifle pit. And from the pit where the wounded were came groans and occasionally a wordless shout as the pain, for someone, became intolerable.

Sessions slept for a time, tossing uneasily in his sleep. His dreams were terrible things, in which time after time he came upon his murdered family. Occasionally the pain of his wounds would awaken him and he would stare briefly up into the flawless sky before dropping off to sleep again.

He finally awoke for good in midafternoon after a particularly horrible dream. He sat up, soaked with sweat from head to foot. He had the feeling that he had been shouting because his throat felt hoarse.

He glanced toward Forsyth's rifle pit. The colonel was looking at him, frowning worriedly. Sessions looked the other way and saw McCall staring at him in much the same way Forsyth had.

He grinned faintly. "Nightmare."

"It sure must have been a dandy. You were yelling like somebody was killing you."

Sessions managed a rueful grin. He glanced toward the riverbank. "They're trying."

"They haven't got us yet. I figure Trudeau and Stillwell got through or the Cheyennes would have let us know they'd caught them by sending their bodies back tied across a horse."

"Trudeau and Stillwell can't get to Fort Wallace in less than four days no matter how they try. And it'll take at least two more for help to get back to us. You think we're likely to last that long?"

"It's not likely but it's possible."

Sessions smelled the sweetish, gagging odor of rotting flesh. "That putrid smell is going to get worse."

McCall nodded.

Sessions said, "And the colonel ought to have that bullet taken out of his leg."

"I know it, but he won't hear of it. Not until the danger from the Indians is gone."

"He can't wait that long. If he doesn't get it out pretty soon he's going to lose his leg."

"I'll talk to him." McCall crawled along the trench connecting the rifle pits. He edged past Sessions and went on to Forsyth's pit. Sessions could hear him talking to the colonel in lowered tones. After a while he came crawling back, shaking his head. "He won't listen. He's afraid he'll faint."

The wound in Sessions' side had become uncovered and he discovered a fly crawling on it. He brushed the fly away irritably and covered the wound again, hoping the fly had not had time to lay any eggs.

Once more he closed his eyes. Desperately he prayed for strength.

The remainder of the afternoon dragged endlessly. Occasionally an Indian sniper would shoot at someone on the island, but no one was hit. Even though the Indians seemed to have lost their enthusiasm for the fight, they had not gone away. They were waiting—until the scouts either died of starvation and wounds, or until they could stand the smell of rotting flesh no longer and tried to break through the Indians surrounding them.

Dusk brought relief from the searing heat of the sun, which for those who were feverish had seemed so unbearable. But the same feverish wounded who had suffered so during the day, now suffered equally in the cooler air of evening because they were repeatedly wracked by chills.

Sessions clutched his blankets around him and clenched his jaws to keep his teeth from chattering. He hoped Jouett, Krebs, and Vega didn't know how weak he was, how helpless when having one of his frequent chills.

Soon after it got dark, Forsyth again called for volunteers to try and make it back to Fort Wallace, in case the others had not gotten through the Indians' lines.

Sessions heard men passing through his rifle pit. He heard Forsyth talking to them but he could not make out his words. Again he marveled at Forsyth's stamina. The man was more seriously wounded than he, but he had not once lost consciousness. Nor had he once lost his ability to command.

Sessions kept his revolver in his hand. His finger was through the trigger guard, his thumb on the hammer. In spite of his weakness, in spite of his chills, he watched every man who passed until he was sure it wasn't Jouett, Vega, or Krebs.

Two men were selected from among the volunteers and the

others returned to their rifle pits. Forsyth talked in lowered tones to the two he had picked to go. Each took some of the putrid meat. Each took a canteen and ammunition for both his rifle and revolver. Then, walking backward in stocking feet as had Trudeau and Stillwell, they crossed the seventy yards of bare sand to the riverbank.

Sessions raised up enough so that he could watch. He saw them disappear in the darker shadows along the riverbank. He listened intently for an outcry, but heard nothing. For more than an hour every man on the island waited in tense silence, listening.

Sessions lay awake, fearing now to sleep. He listened to the sounds of the night, to the soft murmur of the river running past less than a dozen feet away, to the stirring of wind in the lone cottonwood at the foot of the island, to the distant barking of coyotes on a hill.

No one came past his rifle pit. Midnight passed and the hours dragged. They knew how weak he was, he thought. They had seen his weakness when he tallied the wounded earlier. They might be figuring that if they waited and did nothing he would die.

He judged it must have been two or three in the morning when he heard splashing in the river not far from his rifle pit. Puzzled, he raised his head.

He heard a soft voice call, "Don't shoot, boys, it's only us. We couldn't get through them damn Indians. They're everywhere out there."

They splashed on through the river and climbed out on the island. They located Forsyth's rifle pit and reported to him. "We hid in the grass right over there for more'n an hour, Colonel, with Indians all around. Finally we went on and tried to get through, but every way we turned, we ran into more Indians. They're watching for anyone leavin',' sir. They figure that's what we're going to do."

Forsyth said, "All right. Return to your rifle pits. We'll try again tomorrow night."

Sessions tried to stay awake. It was possible that the three killers were not going to attempt killing him tonight. He might be right in believing they were waiting for him to die of wounds.

But he couldn't count on it. He didn't dare close his heavy-lidded eyes.

FOURTEEN

It still was dark, and would remain dark for a couple or three hours more. Sessions closed his eyes for an instant but forced them open again immediately. His head whirled. He felt that if he let his eyes stay closed for a couple of seconds he'd go to sleep and sleep forever.

He said, "McCall?"

From the next rifle pit a voice answered that was not McCall's. "He ain't here. He went up to the head of the island to see somebody."

Sessions said, "I've got to have some sleep. Will you keep an eye on me?"

It sounded silly the minute the words were out. The man said, "Hell man, Injuns never attack at night."

Sessions said, "I know that."

"Well then, what the hell are you worried about?"

Sessions hadn't the strength to give the man a complete explanation. He grunted, "Forget it," and closed his eyes again. He suddenly didn't care if they came after him or not. All he cared about was closing his eyes and dropping off to sleep.

He was whirling and falling, and then blackness descended over his mind and he slept in the bottom of his rifle pit, lying on his back, his hand on his revolver grips.

Once more his dreams were tormented. He relived the discovery of his murdered family. He relived the screaming cavalry charge of the Cheyennes the first morning here. He watched Krebs shoot him from behind and he fought desperately with Manuel Vega for the knife.

But there was something wrong about his dreams. They began to take on the feel of reality. He felt pain in his ribs and in the knife slash across his back. He dreamed he was fighting but he was pinned down and helpless and for some reason or other he couldn't seem to breathe.

Choking, gasping, he began to fight more furiously. And suddenly he realized that this was no dream. This was reality.

A stinking, hair covered saddle blanket was pressed down over his face. There was weight on the saddle blanket and there were weights on both his arms and legs.

Desperately he tried to turn his head, to gulp fresh air into his lungs. He failed because the weight holding the saddle blanket over his mouth and nose was too great. He fought to turn his body, to free one arm or one leg, and he also failed in this.

A sudden and horrifying realization came to him. He was not going to save himself this time. He was going to die, suffocated by this stinking saddle blanket, held down by the men who had murdered his family. They were going to win against him because he had not the strength to throw them off.

Frantically, Sessions arched his body, but one of the men was sitting on his belly and his maximum effort was no more effective than a muscle spasm would have been.

He had heard once when he was a boy that drowning is not an unpleasant way to die after the first few moments of terror. Now he discovered that suffocation and drowning were alike in that respect. He had, at first, been overcome with terror because he couldn't move, because he couldn't draw air into his lungs.

Now, a lassitude began to steal over him. His struggles became less agonized. The starvation of his lungs ceased to trouble him.

One of the men muttered softly, "Won't be long now." The words came to Sessions' ears through the saddle blanket, muffled but decipherable. And suddenly he understood why they had chosen to kill him like this.

A blow on the head or a stab wound would have pointed the finger straight at the three of them. They were fully cognizant of the fact that his rifle pit and that of Colonel Forsyth were next to each other. They must know, or at least believe, that he had confided in the colonel, that he possibly had even told the colonel their names.

But if he died of suffocation it would be assumed that he had died from his wounds, probably from loss of blood. The matter would be closed. Colonel Forsyth might suspect what they had done, but he'd be unable to prove a thing. And if they survived this island siege they'd be free—to spend the money they'd stolen from Sessions and from Dow Perrault in any way they pleased. The brutal murderers would go unpunished.

That realization was, for some reason, harder for Sessions to bear than the thought of death. There had to be something he could do. There had to be!

Once more, with the last of his waning strength, he tried to turn his head, to gulp one clean breath of air. And perhaps because they were so sure it was nearly over, perhaps because the one holding the saddle blanket against his face had relaxed, he succeeded.

Suddenly, unbelievably, he felt cold, clean air flowing into his lungs. And with it came the most maddening pain he had ever experienced.

It was a pain both physical and of the mind. Physical because the sudden inrush of air into his starved lungs actually hurt. Of the mind because even while it was hurting, that fresh, sweetly cold night air was a renewed promise of life when death had seemed so inevitable.

Swiftly the man above him jammed the saddle blanket down again. Angrily he cursed and angrily dug a savage knee into Sessions' belly. But that single breath of air had given Sessions the will to resist again. Once more he arched his body trying to throw them off. Once more he failed. Someone said, "Hold the son-of-a-bitch! Hold him!"

He tried to turn over and also failed in that. He wondered how they dared talk so close to Forsyth's rifle pit and realized that Forsyth must have gone to sleep.

He hadn't the strength to save himself. But he still had a mind. Was there anything he had overlooked? Where was his gun? He had gone to sleep with it in his hand.

They might have taken it from him when they jumped on him. But it was possible that they had overlooked it in the dark. His hand was empty now. But might not the gun be within his reach?

Still pretending to struggle, he groped with his right hand. The arm was held against the sand by one of his assailants. He knew that even if he found the gun, he could probably not direct it against any of them. But he could fire it and a gunshot would bring help. A gunshot would drive his attackers away.

His groping hand encountered only damp sand. He was choking again now, choking and gasping for air and his head had begun to whirl once more. Frantically, knowing this was his only chance, he groped a little farther than before.

His hand touched something, and at first he couldn't tell for sure what it was. There was sand on it—it was half buried in the sand. And now his head was reeling more wildly than before. His consciousness was slipping ever more swiftly away from him.

Putting forth an effort nothing short of superhuman, he arched his body, at the same time driving his hand farther toward that elusive object that he had, so far, managed only to touch but not to grasp.

His hand closed over something . . . Suddenly he realized it was the barrel of his gun. He drew his hand back, released the gun and got another grip on it.

He seemed to be floating now. Unconsciousness was very close. His mind wanted to wander but he forced it desperately to concentrate on the task at hand. Somehow he had to reverse the gun. Somehow he had to get his hand around the grips instead of the barrel. And then, somehow, he had to find the strength to thumb the hammer back and pull the trigger.

Even then it might be too late. Even if they left him almost immediately, it might be too late. But if he feigned death now . . .

He let himself go limp. He couldn't breathe anyway, so he held his chest still. But his questing fingers didn't stop. He released the barrel of the gun and groped for the grips again.

He touched them but he couldn't make his hand close over them. Once more he stretched, reached, groped, and at last felt his thumb and forefinger on the walnut grips.

Now it was only a matter of holding on, of fighting the curtain of darkness that was descending over his mind. His hand was now around the grips. He willed his mind to return from the dark places where it was wandering. His thumb felt the hammer, and slowly, agonizingly, drew it back.

He never heard the hammer click. But he tightened his finger on the trigger and he heard the muffled blast of the gun as it discharged with its muzzle half buried in the sand.

The weapon literally exploded in his hand because of the sand that had closed the muzzle opening. One of the men holding him said, "God damn it, who did that?"

He heard other voices and he heard Forsyth shout, "What's going on over there? McCall! What's going on in Sessions' rifle pit?"

McCall did not reply. The weight on Sessions' arms and legs relaxed. The saddle blanket over his face was snatched away. Sand was kicked over him as his assailants scrambled to get out of the rifle pit and away.

Once more now the sweetly chill night air flooded Sessions' lungs. He choked on it, but it was like a drink of cold water to a man who had been near death from thirst. Unable to move, unable to speak, he lay gasping, fighting to retain his fading consciousness.

He lost the battle to remain conscious but his lungs went on gulping the pure night air greedily. When Sessions did regain consciousness, McCall was bending over him saying, "Hey! Wake up! What the hell's going on? Who fired that goddamn gun?"

Sessions fought to a sitting position and slid back enough so he could put his back to the side of the rifle pit. He still couldn't seem to get enough of the pure, sweet air blowing across the island from the east. McCall asked, "You all right? Was it you that fired the gun? What the hell were you doing, having another nightmare? That's the first time I ever heard of a man firing a gun in his sleep."

Sessions said, "Hell, I don't know what happened."

"Well, by God, you'd better be careful how you sleep. Maybe you'd better put your guns out of reach. Them Injuns is bad enough without me havin' to worry about the man in the rifle pit next to me." He groped around until he found Sessions' gun. He felt of it in the darkness. "It's a wonder you didn't kill yourself. This gun was full of sand and blew apart. It ain't worth a damn any more."

Sessions took the gun from him. He felt it, then tossed it over his shoulder into the river. It had saved his life but it was of no further use to him. It would never fire again.

He said, "I'm sorry, McCall." His voice was hoarse and his chest hurt when he spoke.

McCall said, "Hell, that's all right. Them wounds you got have made you delirious. Why don't you try and get some more sleep? I'll wake you if you start havin' them dreams again."

Sessions nodded. "Thanks."

McCall got up and moved away, a shadow in the darkness. Sessions could feel his wounds bleeding again. He felt a lot weaker than he had before the attack.

Of one thing he was very sure. If he did not soon kill Jouett, Krebs, and Vega they would kill him. Time was on their side.

FIFTEEN

Dawn came grayly out of the east, accompanied by a breeze that was both cool and damp. No sun shone through the heavy, moisture-laden overcast and the men on the island in the Arickaree breathed a collective sigh of relief. Today would not be hot, as yesterday had been. Today the wounded would not, at least, suffer from heat, or from the blistering rays of the sun.

Sessions slept fitfully through the morning, his lungs seeming to absorb the sweetish, gagging odor of decaying flesh. The breeze died and the stink hung over the island like a pall. The only sounds were the sour curses of the men, the groans of the wounded, the buzzing of the flies and an occasional, probing shot from an Indian sniper hidden on the riverbank. But the men were keeping down and no one was hit.

It was stalemate now, and every man on the island was aware of it. They knew their only chance of survival lay with the relief force that Trudeau and Stillwell were to bring from Fort Wallace. There wasn't a man on the island who did not wonder if Trudeau and Stillwell had actually gotten through. If they had not, then every man here was doomed.

At midday, Grover called out to Forsyth. "Colonel, them women an' kids is leavin' the bluff. You reckon they've decided the show's over?"

Sessions shifted his position so that he could see the bluff. Grover had been right. A general exodus had begun. The Indian women and children, who had come to the bluff to watch the defeat and annihilation of the hated whites, were now leaving dispiritedly, saddened by the heavy losses their own men had sustained.

Since he no longer had a revolver, Sessions lay with his rifle resting on his chest. His finger was through the trigger guard. His attention was directed toward the island's upper end, from which direction the killers would come when they came again. He didn't think they would attack by day but he intended to take no risks.

He admitted that they might now do anything at any time. They were getting desperate. He had survived the wound Krebs had inflicted on him and the wounds inflicted on him by Vega during the fight for possession of the knife. He had survived their attempt to suffocate him last night. They might not be willing to sit back and hope he would die from wounds. They had to take action soon. They had to be sure he was dead before the relief force arrived.

Not long after he had observed the Indian women and children leaving the bluff, Grover once more called to Forsyth. "Colonel, looks like them redskins would like a little palaver with us."

Sessions glanced toward the riverbank. Several Cheyenne braves were approaching cautiously, waving a white cloth on a stick back and forth above their heads.

Forsyth stared at them several moments before he asked, "What do you suppose they want?"

"Likely to get on the island and see how bad we're hurt. Maybe they figure they can find out enough to know whether they should give it one last try or whether they should just get the hell out of here an' leave us be."

"Then you don't think there's any point in talking with them?"

"With a redskin? Huh uh, General."

"Then warn them off."

Several of the men jumped out of their rifle pits and began to yell and wave at the approaching Cheyennes. Their gestures were plain and the Cheyennes must have understood. But they kept coming on.

Forsyth asked, "Grover, you understand their language, don't you?"

"Sure, General. I've lived with 'em."

"Then tell them to back off or we're going to shoot."

Grover stood up and began to yell at the oncoming Cheyennes in their own tongue. They stopped once, hesitated, but then came on again. Forsyth said wearily, "All right, put a few rounds into the ground in front of them."

Immediately half a dozen of the scouts fired. Bullets kicked up dust in front of the advancing braves. They stopped. All but one seemed inclined to retreat out of rifle range immediately. The single warrior stood fast, motionless, defiant.

Forsyth said, "That one looks different. Do you suppose that is young Charles Bent?"

Grover grunted a reply that might have been either yes or no. Sessions stared at the Indian. At this distance, which was more than three hundred yards, it would have been difficult to positively identify any man. And when that man's face is covered with war paint . . .

Forsyth said, "Lay a few more shots at their feet. Get a little closer if you can."

Again a ragged volley rang out. All but the one defiant warrior retreated hastily. He looked after them, then back toward the island. At last, with a fatalistic shrug visible even at this distance, he turned and followed, walking slowly and defiantly.

The scouts watched him go almost reluctantly. The approach of the group of braves with their white flag had been a diversion. Now the diversion was gone. All that remained was the deadly inactivity, the stink of rotting flesh, the flies.

The afternoon dragged away and Sessions slept in snatches, waking often, never releasing the rifle, never withdrawing his finger from the trigger guard.

McCall glanced toward him occasionally, raising his head so that he could see. Sessions thought that as long as McCall remained in the pit next to him and stayed awake, none of the killers could get past. But he also knew there always was a chance McCall would leave his pit as he had last night. There was a chance McCall would go to sleep.

Some of the men assembled in the pit where the meat had been cooked the first night on the island. They started a game of cards and their cries of triumph or disappointment began to ring out occasionally from the pit.

Forsyth made no attempt to stop their game and Sessions understood that the colonel believed the diversion was good for the morale of the men as well as being demoralizing to the Indians, who could not help but hear their shouts. The Indians, who themselves loved gambling, would know what was going on. They would, Forsyth undoubtedly hoped, believe the island's defenders were in pretty good shape if they could while away the time gambling and enjoying themselves.

Eventually the game wore itself out and the men in the big pit built another fire upon which to cook some meat. But the smell that rose from it now was a rotten, putrid smell, anything but appetizing. Smelling it, Sessions did not want any for himself.

McCall left his pit to cook some meat. Grover called to Forsyth that he would cook some for him. Sessions grew tense, knowing now was the best chance the killers had had all day.

But none of the three appeared. And after a little while McCall came back with a piece of blackened, smelly meat on a stick. He said, "Sprinkle a little gunpowder on it, Sessions. It kills the putrid taste."

Sessions tried it but it didn't kill the rotten taste of the meat any more than the blackened, charred outside did. Still, he knew he needed the strength the meat would give to him. He also knew that spoiled meat wouldn't hurt him if he could get it down.

Determinedly he bit off a chunk and determinedly chewed it as long as he could. He swallowed and gagged afterward.

He fumbled around until he found his canteen. Afterward, taking bites of meat alternately with long drinks of water, he managed to finish eating the chunk of meat. And surprisingly, after the putrid taste went out of his mouth, he felt better for having eaten it.

Darkness descended and another night began. The fire in the pit was allowed to die because it silhouetted the men passing it for the Indian snipers on the bank. Meat was still being cooked over the coals for the wounded. And men were still eating, who had not eaten earlier.

Now, again, a night-long vigil began. Sessions was determined that he would not again let himself be surprised. He forced himself to stay awake. Whenever he felt himself drowsy, he would pour water over his head from the canteen.

Mercifully, the flies had disappeared when darkness fell,

and the stink of rotting flesh had diminished, perhaps because it was cooler, perhaps because there was a light breeze blowing across the island from the east.

In the next rifle pit, Forsyth composed a letter to be taken to Fort Wallace. He had selected Donovan and Pliley to carry the letter to the fort. The two waited in Forsyth's rifle pit, one holding a torch to give him light by which to write.

Having finished it, Forsyth signed and gave it to them. The two disappeared into the darkness. Sessions heard them wading through the water and saw their dim shapes against the white sand beyond.

Then they were gone, and once more the men on the island all but held their breaths waiting for sounds of commotion on the riverbank which would tell them Donovan and Pliley had been caught by the Indians.

But no sounds came. The night dragged on and this time the two did not return in the early morning hours as had the pair sent the night before.

Sessions had managed to stay awake all night but the effort was wasted. Dawn came and none of the three murderers had put in an appearance to try and dispose of him. He couldn't help feeling irritated at their failure to show up. He had lost a whole night's sleep.

But he understood their strategy. They knew they still had plenty of time. Even if Trudeau and Stillwell made it to the fort in three days, there were still at least three nights in which to get rid of him. They must also know that he would have stayed awake all night waiting for them and that he would be very tired today as a result.

The sky was clear on the fourth day and the sun came up bright and hot. Scarcely had the first rays touched the island than the flies rose into the air in clouds.

Forsyth seemed to be in great pain this morning and several times Sessions heard him groan. At last he called Grover, McCall, and another man into his rifle pit and asked if one of them would volunteer to cut the bullet out of his leg.

Grover examined the wound. Straightening he said, "Not me, General. It's layin' right next to an artery. If a man's hand was to slip or if you was to flinch, the knife would break through into that artery, an' then you'd die."

"It's got to come out, Grover. I'm willing to take the chance."

"But I ain't, General."

"Then I'll have to cut it out myself. Get me my saddle-bags."

Grover brought the colonel his saddlebags. Sessions saw him take a razor out of it.

Sessions had known many officers during the war but he had never known one quite like Forsyth before. The man's fortitude was tremendous. Sessions would have said it was impossible for any man to cut a bullet out of his own thigh. With Forsyth . . . he was equally sure that for this man it was possible.

Forsyth settled himself more comfortably in his rifle pit. He ripped his trousers away to expose the wound, and removed the cloth that had been tied around it.

Sessions wanted to turn his head and look away. He wanted to slide deeper into his rifle pit so that he wouldn't have to watch. But he seemed unable to force himself to move. In fascination he watched as Forsyth ordered two of the scouts with him to pull the flesh back away from the bullet hole as he cut into it. The third was to hold his foot so that he wouldn't flinch as the razor bit into his flesh.

He heard Forsyth's sharp intake of breath as the razor cut deep into his yielding flesh. He saw the colonel's face turn gray. Grover said, "Easy, General. Take it easy. We got lots of time."

Forsyth did not reply. He rested a moment, then bent and cut into his leg again.

Sessions couldn't see the wound. One of the scouts' bodies was in the way. But he could see Forsyth's face. He could see the beads of sweat that sprang out on the colonel's forehead. He could see the compressed lips and the hard-clenched jaw. He could see the eyes, narrowed with pain.

Grover said, "I can see the bullet now, General. Only a little more, but watch that artery. The bullet's layin' right next to it."

For another agonizing minute, the colonel worked. Then, suddenly, he lay back against the sand bulwark of his rifle pit with closed eyes and a long, slow sigh.

Grover retrieved the bullet from the sand where it had fallen and held it up between thumb and forefinger. His hands were bloody and so was the bullet, but there was a wide grin on his dirty, unshaven face.

Forsyth lay with closed eyes, breathing audibly. McCall asked, "You all right, Colonel?"

"I'm all right, gentlemen. You may return to your rifle pits."

SIXTEEN

On one of his trips between his own rifle pit and Forsyth's, McCall gave Sessions a revolver taken from one of the dead men to replace his own. Sessions was glad to get it because it was easier to use at close quarters than a rifle.

Having laid awake all night, Sessions now slept. With no clouds in the sky and no breeze, the heat in the rifle pits became intense during the afternoon. Flies buzzed around in clouds, alighting on every exposed wound, blackening the carcasses of the dead horses, particularly in places where meat had been cut from them. The stench increased as the heat increased.

Firing from the riverbank had been desultory all day. Now it ceased entirely. Few Indians were visible. In mid-afternoon, Sessions heard Forsyth say, "Grover, I think they're giving up."

"Don't count on it, General. Give 'em something to shoot at and they'll soon let you know they're there."

"I believe I'll do just that. Get me four men, Grover, and get a blanket. I want them to lift me so that I can see."

Grover called out several names and the men came from their rifle pits. They eased Forsyth onto a blanket, then, one at each corner of the blanket, lifted him carefully and carried him out of his rifle pit.

Forsyth stared out across the dry-baked sand. The bluff was empty. All the Indian women and children had disappeared. The riverbank was equally bare.

Half a dozen scouts, besides those holding Forsyth, were now standing erect, staring across the empty plain.

A few Indians and horses were visible on the nearby hills. Otherwise the landscape was completely bare.

Forsyth said, "By heaven, I believe we're going to make it, gentlemen."

"Provided someone gets through to Fort Wallace," a man reminded sourly.

"They'll get through," Forsyth said confidently. "They've got to get through."

Rifle fire crackled suddenly on the riverbank. Puffs of powdersmoke lifted into the still air from a dozen or more hidden locations in the heavy grass and brush.

Those of the scouts who were standing, dived for their rifle pits. Before Forsyth could say anything, the man holding the corner of the blanket that supported his broken leg, dropped it and scuttled into the nearest rifle pit.

Forsyth slid off the blanket. He struck the ground first with his broken leg. The bone separated and a jagged end of it broke through the flesh. Forsyth uttered a wordless cry of pain. The other three men, who had held onto the blanket, now helped him into his rifle pit, ignoring the bullets cutting through the grass and brush nearby.

Forsyth was cursing steadily at the man who had dumped him so unceremoniously. Sessions had never seen him so angry and he had never before heard him curse.

The shooting from the riverbank ceased as suddenly as it had begun. Then, well out of rifle range, a completely naked Indian jumped up and began to shout insults at the scouts on the island, making obscene gestures as he did.

The insults were not understandable because of the distance, but the obscene gestures were unmistakable. Several of the scouts began firing, their bullets falling short.

Sessions stared at the naked Indian, grinning in spite of himself. Most of the other men failed to find him humorous. At last Forsyth, still bathed with sweat from the pain he had so recently endured, raised up and called, "Some of you men have Springfields. Let's see if one of you can't bring him down. Raise your leaf sights to their limit because the range is close to 1200 yards."

Three men on the island had breech-loading Springfields, which had a range several hundred yards farther than the repeating Spencers with which most of the men were equipped. Forsyth called, "Take aim and fire on command."

The three eased themselves up against the sand bulwarks in front of them. They rested their Springfields on the sand to steady them, taking careful aim. Forsyth called, "Take a deep breath."

An instant later he said, "Release half of it. Hold it. Fire!"

The three shots racketed, sounding almost like a single shot. For an instant, the men on the island held their breaths, waiting for the three bullets to reach their target. Sessions had almost decided that all three had missed when the naked savage suddenly jumped into the air and fell. He struck the ground and did not move again.

A ragged cheer rose from the men on the island, particularly when the Indians who had fired the volley at the island only a few minutes before began to retreat from their positions on the riverbank. Several shots were fired at them, none with any apparent effect.

All afternoon there was not an Indian in sight save for the half dozen or so stationed on high points where they could observe the scouts. The sun sank slowly toward the horizon in the west.

Sessions was thinking that it was possible Trudeau and Stillwell had already reached the fort. If they had, a relief force might even now be starting out.

He slept again, and did not awake until dusk. He lay still after awakening, listening to the sounds of the men, listening to the breeze that had sprung up stirring the grass and brush. Forsyth's pit was quiet. So was McCall's.

Jouett, Krebs, and Vega would be coming for him again tonight, he thought. They would be as aware as he of the possibility that Trudeau and Stillwell had, by now, made it to the fort. They would have to assume the relief force might reach the island within the next day or two.

Light faded gradually from the sky. And now, Sessions didn't dare to close his eyes. He held the revolver McCall had given him, resting it on his chest.

Forsyth was stirring in his rifle pit. So was McCall on the other side. Sessions wished McCall would leave or that he would settle down to sleep. Tonight he wanted the three to come for him. He had slept fairly well off and on all day. He was rested and as ready for them as he would ever be.

But for a while there was too much activity on the island to expect the three to come. Men who had lain still in their rifle pits all day now got up. They stretched and walked briskly back and forth. Some were in the river, washing, or drinking, or just splashing around. Some were cooking meat, although fewer seemed interested in eating the rotten stuff than yesterday. One man slipped away from the island to try and find some food that the wounded men could eat.

If there still were Indians in the vicinity, they were neither visible nor audible. No fires winked against the black night sky. No singing or chanting drifted in on the evening breeze. From a nearby hill a coyote barked, to be answered by a chorus of barks and yelps. The coyote cries might have been made by Indians, but Sessions didn't think they had. They sounded much too real.

With the passing minutes, the tension increased in him until, by ten o'clock, it was almost intolerable. McCall's rifle pit was silent now. From the direction of Forsyth's pit, Sessions could hear only an occasional snore.

They might risk using a knife tonight, he thought. They would certainly not try to suffocate him again. A knife wound could be blamed on a skulking Indian. No one would be able to prove that one had not sneaked onto the island in the dark.

He thought he saw a shadow against the sky and shifted the revolver into a more comfortable position. Muffling the sound with one hand, he drew back the hammer with the other.

There was a sudden flurry of movement where the shadow had been earlier. Sessions raised the gun to take aim . . .

Something thudded viciously into the sand beside him and Sessions knew it had been a knife. One of them had thrown at the sound he'd made thumbing back the hammer of his gun.

He froze, holding himself motionless. If they thought they had killed him, they'd be coming into the pit to retrieve the knife. They wouldn't want it found in him since it would be clearly identifiable as a white man's knife.

There was now no movement where he had seen movement earlier. But suddenly, behind him, he heard the scuff of a boot in sand.

He rolled frantically, raising the gun as he did to cover the area in back of him. They had maneuvered behind him so stealthily that he hadn't even heard.

Their shadows, two of them, were silhouetted faintly against the starlit sky. Once more something thudded into the sand beside him, so close that it went through the loose cloth of his sleeve.

But he didn't fire because he was once more facing them, once more able to defend himself. Let them come into the rifle pit to retrieve their knives. Let them come close enough so that he would be sure of his target when he shot.

They could see him no better than he could see them. They were, at least, vaguely silhouetted against the stars. He lay in a black rifle pit and was virtually invisible to them as long as he did not move.

He could hear them whispering now but he could not make out their words. Sand shifted as one of them started to slide into the rifle pit.

Sessions tightened his finger on the trigger. But suddenly he heard Forsyth's voice, "Who's that? Sessions? McCall?"

The shadowy figures froze. They remained motionless for a moment until Forsyth's voice came again, more sharply than before. "Who is it there? Identify yourself or I'll fire!"

There was a sudden scuffling in the sand. Two figures swiftly faded past and disappeared toward the island's upper end. Forsyth's voice came again, now filled with alarm. "Mr. Sessions? Are you all right?"

"I'm all right, Colonel." Sessions' voice was soft but it was heavy with relief. "I'm all right."

"Who was that?"

"The three I told you about, or at least two of them. They threw two knives at me but both of them missed."

"I'm going to arrest those men and put them under guard. This has got to stop."

"Tomorrow, Colonel. Plenty of time for that tomorrow. They won't be coming back tonight."

He'd give them time to get to their own rifle pits. He'd give Forsyth time to go back to sleep. Then he was going to do a little hunting on his own. He'd been resting long enough to regain at least part of his strength. And now, tonight, he'd have the advantage of surprise.

SEVENTEEN

Sessions waited until he heard Colonel Forsyth snoring in his rifle pit. Turning his head, he softly called, "McCall?"

When no answer came from McCall's rifle pit, he got stiffly and carefully to his feet. He climbed out of the rifle pit and stood for a moment on the level ground in the middle of the island. The grass and brush had been trampled by the scouts walking back and forth but it still made a crackling sound beneath his feet. Carefully, one step at a time, he headed for the island's upper end.

The stench of death still hung cloyingly in the air. The wounded still moaned in their pit. Sessions eased the hammer of his revolver back, muffling the metallic click with his other hand. He knew the risk he took in going after the three. If he succeeded in killing them, he would be arrested by Forsyth. Once back in civilization, he would be brought to trial. He might be convicted and he might be hanged.

He discovered that he didn't care. Being tried and convicted of the murder of Jouett, Vega, and Krebs was better than having them escape. And escape they would if they were brought to trial or if they succeeded in killing him before he could kill them.

Slowly, testing each step before he put his weight down, he moved up the island. It wasn't very far but tonight it seemed like a mile from his pit to the upper end, where Jouett and Krebs had dug in earlier. He had no idea where he would find Vega, but he knew it was possible the three were together now.

He heard whispering voices while he was still ten or fifteen yards away. He slowed his pace. When he was close enough to make out the words he knelt in the darkness, listening.

It was impossible to recognize any of the voices because the men were whispering. But he didn't have to recognize each individual voice to know that all three belonged to the men he had come to kill.

There was an argument going on. One of the whispering voices said, "I don't care what you say. I'm going. Trudeau and Stillwell must have got through and so must Pliley and Donovan or we'd sure as hell have heard about it by this time. And if they can get through the Indians, then so can I."

The voice had an accent and Sessions recognized it as Vega's voice. One of the other voices whispered urgently, "You damn fool, why run away? What the hell's the point? Even if we went to trial, Sessions couldn't prove a thing. And we ain't going to go to trial. We're going to kill that son-of-a-bitch tonight."

"How do you know? You've tried twice and you've failed both times."

"We'll get him."

"I'm not going to wait. I can get through the Indians. I can head for Mexico."

"You'll *have* to go to Mexico. Because Forsyth will list you as a deserter and you'll be a wanted man."

The third whispered voice now broke in. "Don't be stupid, Manuel. All we got to do is just sit tight. We'll get Sessions, but even if we don't, what can he do? He can accuse us but he can't prove a thing."

"We got the money. That's evidence enough."

"Why is it evidence? It ain't marked. It ain't got his name on it."

"How do you know? Maybe there's some way he can prove it's his."

"There isn't."

There was a scraping sound in the sand ahead of the place where Sessions crouched. A shadow loomed against the starlit sky.

"The hell with it. I'm going anyhow."

One of the other voices growled, "The hell you are. You'll get caught by the Indians and all that money will get scattered around and go to waste. You may be stupid enough to run away, but we ain't stupid enough to let you take your share of the money along with you. How about it, Krebs?"

"That's right. You can go if you want, Manuel, but you ain't taking them saddlebags."

There was the sound of a scuffle up ahead. Sessions got to his feet and stood in a crouch, trying to penetrate the darkness with his glance. He could see three shadowy forms struggling and he heard the sharp intake of breath, the sudden whimper of pain from the man who had first stood up.

Vega's arm was broken and the others must have grabbed and wrenched it, probably deliberately. The struggle continued, more noisily, and from a rifle pit nearby a voice complained, "What the hell's going on over there?"

Vega suddenly stopped struggling. He stood completely still. Sessions had no idea where the saddlebags were now. Vega whispered, "Jouett, come along with me. You come too, Krebs."

"Huh uh. If we run now that damn Sessions will be on our trail just as long as we live. If we get rid of him here, we can forget about him."

Vega's shadowy figure seemed to slump. "All right. Maybe you two are right."

The others stepped away. "Now you're making sense."

Sessions eased closer. He didn't know exactly what he was going to do but he was suddenly unable to stand idly by while the murderers of his family, the confessed murderers were this close to him. He stepped on a twig and it snapped and the three figures tensed. "What's that?"

Vega took advantage of the diversion and broke away from the other two. Scrambling, clawing frantically, he climbed out of the rifle pit. The other two dived for him. Vega went down, still trying to scramble out. There was a soft curse as one of his feet kicked solidly into the face of one of the other two.

Released, Vega succeeded in scrambling out of the pit. Sessions was close enough to see that he now carried the saddlebags over one shoulder, that he carried a rifle in his left hand. He plunged off the edge of the island into the water with a splash. He was instantly up again, wallowing noisily through the water toward the riverbank.

Jouett's voice said, "Come back, you stupid bastard! You can't . . ."

Krebs said fatalistically, "It's too late now."

Vega came out of the water onto the bare stretch of dry white sand, more visible now as an indistinct black shape. He was running, awkwardly shambling, trying to steady his broken arm with his other hand.

He reached the bank and sprawled on it. Voices were rising on the island, demanding to know what was going on. One man called, "Who the hell is that over there? Should we shoot?"

Jouett said, "Yeah. Shoot the son-of-a-bitch. He's tryin' to desert."

Instantly a rifle roared. The figure on the riverbank got up and ran and the rifle roared again. The figure didn't stop. It disappeared into the darkness.

All the scouts on the island were, by now, awake. Sessions stood frozen, not six feet from the rifle pit occupied by Jouett and Krebs.

They seemed to have forgotten the noise that they had heard earlier. They were staring at the place where Vega had disappeared. Jouett growled, "If the Injuns don't get him after all that racket then there just ain't any Injuns there."

Sessions realized he had been holding his breath. He was in the grip of conflicting emotions. He was disappointed that Vega had escaped. If Vega got through the Indians, he might lose himself forever and escape Sessions' vengeance. But Vega's death at the hands of the Indians would be worse than anything Sessions could do to him.

Everybody on the island was silent, waiting for the commotion on the riverbank that would tell them Vega had been caught. Sessions shifted his position slightly, keeping his revolver ready in his hand.

Suddenly, faintly, a not altogether unexpected sound drifted to the island on the breeze. It was a sound to make chills run along a man's spine, to make the hair follicles stir on the back of his neck.

It was a scream issuing from the throat of a grown man and more terrible than any woman's scream could be. It was a sound of terror and of pain, and of the knowledge of a gamble lost, the loss irretrievable.

Sessions knew the Cheyennes seldom tortured prisoners but he believed they might make an exception in Vega's case. They had lost heavily in the battle with Forsyth's scouts. They had lost Roman Nose and they had lost prestige because so many had been defeated by so few.

Once more that terrible sound drifted along the breeze. And then came a lower, more continuous sound that was equally terrible because it seemed to be more the sound of an animal in pain than that capable of being made by man.

Jouett whispered, "And the son-of-a-bitch took all that money along with him."

"Maybe we can pick it up later. The Indians sure as hell have no use for it."

Sessions said softly, "If you're alive. But I don't think you're going to be."

EIGHTEEN

Instantly both men whirled. Jouett snatched his rifle and swung the muzzle toward Sessions, trying to bring it to bear. Krebs batted it aside. "No! Shoot him and you'll hang for it."

Sessions' revolver was in his hand, its muzzle bearing on Jouett's chest. All he had to do was pull the trigger and Jouett would be dead.

But suddenly that seemed too easy a way for the man to die. It seemed too quick. His finger failed to tighten sufficiently to make the gun discharge.

Confused and angered by his own confusion, Sessions stood there staring toward the two. The only light came from the stars but it was enough to clearly see their shapes, if not their faces. Desperately he wanted to kill them but even more than that he wanted them to suffer before they died, to suffer as they had made him suffer when they killed his family. He hesitated a fraction of a second and in that length of time, Jouett scrambled clumsily toward him up the side of the rifle pit, swinging the rifle barrel as he came.

The gun barrel struck Sessions' knee, instantly numbing it. He grabbed the gun in his free hand and pulled it toward him to throw Jouett off balance.

Jouett kept coming and Sessions kicked him squarely in the face. Jouett went down on both knees, still holding onto his rifle, silent and stunned and for that instant out of the fight.

Krebs came scrambling out of the rifle pit and dived at Sessions' knees. They were knocked violently out from under him and he was brought down in the loose, damp sand. He released Jouett's rifle barrel, at the same time swinging at Krebs with his own revolver.

It struck Krebs in the face, a raking blow that cut and hurt but did not stun the man. Krebs continued to claw along the sandy ground.

Jouett now re-entered the fight, closing with Sessions and wrenching the revolver violently from his hand. Jouett said between clenched teeth, "All right, kill him. But no marks. Just choke the son-of-a-bitch to death."

Krebs groped for and found Sessions' throat. Sessions' wounds had been re-opened by the fight. They now were bleeding heavily once more. He had been a fool. He should have killed Jouett and Krebs when he'd had the chance.

He fought with all his waning strength but it was not enough. Krebs' powerful hands closed off the air flow into and out of his lungs. His head began whirling crazily . . .

But, suddenly and plainly, there was a shout that seemed to come from right above his head. "Hey! What the hell's going on here! What is this, a fight?"

The fingers around his throat tightened with frantic desperation at the sound of that unexpected voice. Once more it came, this time as an angry roar, "Get offa him, you two! Get off, goddamn it, before I bust your heads!"

He was near unconsciousness now, nearly gone. Another half minute, a minute at most, and he would be beyond return. But above there was a sudden flurry of violence and the hands closing his throat were torn away. Krebs was sent rolling by a savage, angry kick.

Choking, gasping greedily the life-giving air, he lay helpless for what seemed a long, long time. Above him, the man stood spread-legged, glaring angrily at Krebs and Jouett. "Jouett and Krebs, ain't it? What the hell are you doing, and who the hell is he?"

Neither answered him. The man said, "I think the colonel ought to know about this. Get on your feet, the three of you, and we'll go see what he's got to say."

Jouett and Krebs struggled to their feet. Sessions didn't think he could make it, but he tried. He got to one knee and then the man reached down and helped him up.

Jouett and Krebs stumbled along ahead. Sessions let himself be helped, feeling blood running from his wounds, still gasping and choking, still trying to completely fill his lungs.

They reached the colonel's rifle pit. The man, still not recognized by Sessions, said, "Colonel, these three were fighting near the upper end of the island. Two of them had the third one down and were chokin' him."

"Who are they?"

"Jouett and Krebs are two of them. I don't know the other one. It's too dark to see his face."

Forsyth said, "Sessions?"

"Yes sir."

"What happened?"

Jouett broke in, "Colonel, he attacked us. He threatened to kill us and then he attacked us first. All we did was to defend ourselves."

"Is that right, Sessions?"

"No sir. I didn't fire any gun."

Forsyth asked, "What did he attack you with, Mr. Jouett? I know he's wounded and I know you're not. Neither one of you."

"He had a gun. He was pointin' it at us and he said he was goin' to shoot. I swear to God . . ."

"Who was the man that deserted?"

"Manuel Vega, Colonel."

"Why did he desert? And why did you yell at the men to shoot?"

"Ain't that what you're supposed to do with deserters, Colonel? What would you have done if you'd seen him leave?"

"Mr. Sessions says the three of you attacked his ranch and killed his family for some money he had hidden there. What have you to say to that?"

"He's crazy. That's what I've got to say."

"How much money have you got?"

"I don't know what the hell that's got to do with anything."

"Maybe a lot, Mr. Jouett. A man with several thousand dollars in his saddlebags wouldn't be joining up to fight the Indians. Not for seventy-five a month, unless he had a mighty powerful reason for doing it."

Neither Jouett nor Krebs said anything. Sessions said, "Vega took his saddlebags when he deserted, Colonel. He had his share of the money in them."

Forsyth's voice seemed to come from a black and empty rifle pit. He said, "Morgan, go back to the rifle pit where these two men were and get their saddlebags. Bring them here to me."

The man who had stopped the fight turned and disappeared. Jouett and Krebs fidgeted uneasily. Morgan was gone several minutes. When he returned, he said, "I've got them, Colonel. Want me to look inside?"

"Yes, Morgan. Look inside and tell me what is there."

Morgan knelt on the ground and opened the saddlebags. He fumbled for a moment and then he said, "Feels like money, Colonel. Feels like a hell of a lot of it."

Forsyth asked, "How much is there, Mr. Jouett? In each set of saddlebags?"

"Colonel, I . . ."

"How much, Jouett? I can have it counted as soon as it gets light."

"That ain't necessary, Colonel. There's just under fifteen hundred dollars in each set of saddlebags."

"An exactly equal amount in each?"

"Pretty close, I guess."

"How do you explain that, Mr. Jouett? Even to an old Army officer that adds up to a split of some kind of illegal enterprise."

"Well it ain't. We sold a herd of cattle in Abilene. We each owned a third of the herd, Krebs an' Vega an' me. We split the money three ways."

Forsyth asked, "Mr. Sessions, how much money did you lose?"

"Three thousand, Colonel. My neighbor, who was also burned out and who was killed along with his mother, had fifteen hundred."

Forsyth murmured, "A strange coincidence, isn't it, Mr. Jouett? That the money the three of you have is exactly the amount Mr. Sessions and his neighbor lost?"

Jouett said sullenly, "It don't prove anything. We got it for a herd of cattle we sold in Abilene."

Sessions said, "That's a lie. Krebs told me he signed on because he was broke."

"That can be verified," Forsyth said.

"What are you going to do with us?" Jouett asked.

There was a moment's silence in Forsyth's rifle pit. Sessions heard a bird chirp over on the riverbank. The bird was answered by another. Sessions glanced at the eastern horizon, not surprised to see a graying line.

"I can't arrest you because I can't spare men to keep you under guard. I suppose the best way to make sure you don't try deserting as Vega did is to impound your saddlebags. Later, if you can establish that the money is honestly yours, it will be returned to you."

Neither man spoke. The line of gray in the east was wider now. Forsyth said, "Mr. Sessions, I warned you against trying to kill these men. I'll warn you again. Leave it in my hands. I will see that they are turned over to the proper authorities when we return to civilization. If they are guilty, they will pay for their crimes."

"Yes sir." But there was no conviction in Sessions' voice.

"In the meantime, I believe we can assume that Manuel Vega is dead. Or that he will shortly be."

"Yes sir."

Forsyth looked toward Jouett and Krebs. It was now light enough to see their faces. "Return to your positions. And I warn you, if Mr. Sessions turns up dead I intend to determine the cause of death and fix responsibility. Is that clear?"

Both men grumbled something that Sessions did not make out. They turned and shuffled away into the graying dawn. Morgan, after a puzzled look at Sessions, followed them.

Forsyth said, "So one of them is dead. Did you have anything to do with his running away?"

Sessions shook his head.

"If he did what you say he did, then he probably deserved to die that way."

"Do you think the Cheyennes tortured him?"

"I doubt it. Cheyennes aren't supposed to torture prisoners. But I also doubt if they dispatched him as quickly as he might have wished."

Sessions suddenly felt weakness flooding over him. He staggered and Forsyth quickly said, "Get into your rifle pit, Mr. Sessions, and see if you can't get some rest."

Sessions nodded. He slid down into his rifle pit and lay against its sloping side. Forsyth's voice followed him. "I wish you hadn't gone to Jouett's rifle pit. Now if they kill you they can claim you were trying to kill them and they can probably get away with it. And if they can find someone who will confirm their story of selling cattle in

Abilene, there's little or no chance of getting them convicted of killing your family."

Sessions had been thinking the same thing. He also knew that before the relief column arrived Jouett and Krebs would have to try killing him one more time.

NINETEEN

This day, the fifth, began with a cloudless sky and a blazing sun. Sessions was weaker than he had ever been before. Lack of food had weakened him. So had loss of blood. There were times when he was feverish and delirious. There were times when he slept as though he were already dead.

The stench of decaying flesh hung over the island like a pall. The Indians must have gone, Sessions thought during one of his more lucid intervals, because the wolves were moving in. They sat on their haunches just out of rifle range, tongues lolling out, staring and waiting patiently. Some of the men fired at them, willing to eat even wolves, but none were hit.

Flies, large, green-bodied flies, crawled on everything. Whenever a man moved, flies would rise from him in a cloud. Maggots had already hatched from eggs laid the first day in the carcasses of the dead horses and soon they would begin to hatch in the open wounds of the men.

Some of the wounded already had gangrene. Angry red streaks ran upward from leg wounds that were festering. And today, for the first time, the island was in the grip of despair. Help might come, summoned from Fort Wallace by Trudeau and Stillwell, Pliley and Donovan. But it would come too late. Men who should not have died would be dead from the neglect of their wounds. Others would die from starvation because the putrid meat was no longer edible. Still others might die from madness brought on by the heat and the smell and the hopelessness.

Sessions slept as much as he could, his hat tilted over his eyes to shade them from the sun. Once he awoke for no reason he could name. He felt someone watching him and when he removed the hat from his eyes he saw Jouett and Krebs standing at the edge of his rifle pit looking down. Both were smiling unpleasantly. When he saw that Sessions was awake, Jouett said softly, "Looks like he's about done for, Floyd. Maybe we won't have to do a thing."

Sessions stared unblinkingly at them. He didn't speak and after a moment the taunting grins faded from the faces of the two. They seemed to have difficulty meeting his eyes. They had started to turn as Sessions said, "I'm not dead yet."

The pair disappeared and Sessions put his hat back over his eyes. They might try to kill him but they wouldn't do it in broad daylight except as a last resort.

Toward evening, two of the men, risking being seen by Indians who might still be lurking in the area, set off downstream to see if they could shoot some game and thus supply desperately needed food for the wounded.

They were gone for a long time, and had just about been given up for lost when someone shouted that they were coming back.

Neither carried any game but they had found some bushes upon which wild plums grew and both men had filled their hats. Immediately driftwood that had been deposited on the island by floods was gathered and a fire built. The wild plums were put on to boil and, when they had been cooked into a thick stew, were distributed among the wounded.

Ketterer woke Sessions and handed him a tin cup in the bottom of which was some of the wild plum stew. Sessions ate it hungrily. It was sour, but it tasted more delicious than any food he had ever eaten. When he had finished, he filled the cup with water and drank it in order to get the last bit of juice that remained in it.

Shortly afterward, as the flaming clouds in the west were turning gray, Forsyth edged himself along the trench that separated his rifle pit and that of Sessions. He asked, "Did you get some of the plums?"

Sessions nodded. "Best damn food I ever tasted, too."

"Feel any stronger?"

"Some. Food helps. And I've been sleeping most of the day."

"Tell me about yourself. Were you in the war?"

Sessions nodded.

"Confederates?"

"Uh huh. I'm from Texas originally."

"I thought you talked like a Texas man. What unit were you with?"

"Army of Northern Virginia. Fourth Texas, under Colonel Bane."

"Then you were surrendered by General Lee at Appomattox."

"Yes sir."

"What rank did you hold?"

"Captain."

"What made you come north and settle in Kansas?"

Sessions was silent a moment. "Bluebelly troops and carpetbaggers, I suppose. I figured if I didn't get out of Texas soon I was going to tangle with some of them. I gathered up what cattle I had and bought some more, and drove them north."

"What will you do when this is over with?"

"I guess that depends on Jouett and Krebs. One way or another I'm going to see them dead. Then I suppose I'll go back home." The word "home" conjured up memories and his eyes hardened.

Forsyth said, "I'm sorry. I was just trying to make the time pass for both of us."

"I know, Colonel. It's all right. I'm going to have to live with it."

"How much land do you have?"

"Two homestead claims, one on each side of the creek. But my cattle roam for miles."

"All this land will be taken up and settled before many more years have passed."

"The Indians will have to go first."

"They're going. The buffalo are being slaughtered and once the buffalo are gone the Indians will have no alternative but to capitulate."

Sessions said, "These Indians may have pinned us down, but we whipped the hell out of them. They lost close to a hundred men killed and they had twice that many wounded, at least."

Forsyth remained where he was in companionable silence until the sky was wholly dark. Then he crawled painfully back to his own rifle pit.

Sessions now remained awake, knowing he did not dare go to sleep. From time to time he drank from his canteen, having discovered that an occasional drink of water helped to keep him awake. Twice during the night he splashed water into his face.

Dawn came at last, the dawn of the sixth day. Jouett and Krebs had not put in an appearance during the night. As soon as the sun came up, Sessions pulled his hat over his eyes and went to sleep.

He was awakened in midmorning by Ketterer. The man had a tin cup which he handed him. It was half filled with a thin broth and had two or three chunks of meat in it. Sessions stared up at Ketterer questioningly and the man said, "Someone shot a coyote and this is coyote soup. Go ahead and eat it. The first boiling is for the wounded. The second boiling will be for the other men."

Sessions ate the soup ravenously and once more rinsed the cup out with water, which he drank. He handed it back to Ketterer with a nod of thanks.

Once more the day passed, with Sessions sleeping every chance he got. There was little noise to disturb him except for the groans of the wounded, except for the endless buzzing of the flies. His hat helped to keep them off his face but there was nothing to keep them off his neck and ears, or off his hands and arms.

At sundown, Forsyth asked Donovan to summon all the unwounded men. He said he wanted to talk to them.

Grover stood up and shouted for all the unwounded men to assemble at the colonel's rifle pit.

A cooling breeze now blew across the island from the east, bringing blessed relief both from the stench and from the flies. No one had seen an Indian all day.

The unwounded men, more than twenty-five of them, gathered at the foot of Forsyth's rifle pit. He waited until they quieted, then said in a voice grown weak from pain and loss of blood, "I have summoned you here to give you the opportunity to make a choice. It appears that all the Indians have gone. At most, there are a few stragglers in the area.

"As you know, Trudeau and Stillwell tried to make it to Fort Wallace and probably got through. If they did not, it is likely that Pliley and Donovan did. So the chances are very good that relief will reach us in the next couple of days."

He drew in a long breath and let it slowly out. "However, if none of the four managed to reach the fort, then our condition is critical. I would therefore like to give all of you an opportunity to decide for yourselves whether you wish to go or stay. If you go, you can leave us ammunition and we will defend ourselves until you can return."

There were several moments' silence. Over on the riverbank, the ring of wolves sat on their haunches, waiting patiently. One of them lifted his muzzle to the sky unexpectedly and howled. The other wolves also began to howl, as if in answer to the first.

The sound sent a chill traveling down Sessions' spine. It was as if this was what the wolves had been waiting for. As soon as the sound men left, the wolves would move in to finish off the wounded ones.

Forsyth said, "It is a decision you will have to make among yourselves. Walk away someplace and talk it over. There will be no criticism if you choose to try making it back to Fort Wallace. But you all understand that to move the wounded now would be the same as killing them. I for one do not even want to try traveling. And besides, with the wounded to slow you down, your chances of making it safely back would be very much reduced."

The silence among the members of the group lasted only a few seconds. Then a shout came from the rear, "Nothing doing, General! We ain't going to leave you and the rest of the boys alone!"

And McCall, standing in the front, said, "We've fought together, Colonel, and by heaven if need be we'll die together!"

Forsyth nodded and turned his head but not before Sessions had seen moisture in his eyes. The men dispersed. A couple headed downriver to try and find another coyote before it got too dark to shoot.

McCall slid down into Sessions' rifle pit. He deepened the hole at the foot of it so that water would be easier to dip out. He glanced at Sessions. "Mind if I sit here with you a while?"

Sessions grinned at him. "In case I have visitors?"

McCall grinned back. "In case of that. Somebody ought to be around to welcome them when they come."

Sessions said, "Thanks, McCall."

"Forget it." McCall settled himself comfortably. The sky flamed from the setting sun, then grayed with dusk.

The men who had gone off to hunt coyotes returned emptyhanded.

Sessions was weak, and tired, and had little hope of surviving until the relief column arrived. But he discovered to his astonishment that he was no longer as hungry to kill Jouett and Krebs as he once had been.

Perhaps he had seen too much death and suffering in the last few days.

He forced himself to think of Sally and his sons. He thought of the way they had been killed, of how the boys had been tortured to make Sally tell where the money was.

The old anger, the old thirst for vengeance returned. But it was somehow different. No longer did he want to shoot Jouett and Krebs. He was thinking in terms of a scaffold. He was thinking what it would be like for Jouett and Krebs to sit in a jail cell somewhere waiting for the day to come when the trapdoor would be sprung.

That might be what he would now prefer, he thought. But the decision as to how it was going to be was probably not his to make. Jouett and Krebs were free. They both were armed. All they had to do to remain free was to kill him and thus keep him from charging them with the murder of his family.

TWENTY

Sessions got through the sixth night with no visit from either Jouett or Krebs, probably because of McCall's presence in his rifle pit.

He slept fitfully and awakened often, bothered by pain in his wounds. His hand ached constantly. His back was extremely painful, so much so that he couldn't sleep on it. His side was also much too sore to sleep on. Which left him but two positions in which he could sleep—on the unwounded side and on his stomach.

The seventh day passed and all through this day the men kept watching the horizons toward the east for the movement of troops or the sight of a guidon, and straining their ears for the sound of a distant trumpeter.

Forsyth stayed conscious, though he slept in snatches both day and night. The unwounded men paced back and forth, up and down the length of the island. Some ventured onto the riverbank, but they found no game. Several times they started a game of cards, but no one had any enthusiasm and none of the games lasted long.

Fort Wallace was a hundred and ten miles away but, as far as these men were concerned, it might have been a thousand. There were no horses. Even the unwounded men were too weak from hunger to travel far.

On the eighth day, discouragement began to turn into despair. Most of the men just sat listlessly, staring into space. There was little conversation. Sessions couldn't remember when he had last heard a laugh.

He had again expected Jouett and Krebs to try getting to him last night but neither man had appeared. He wondered briefly if they had deserted, and called to Colonel

Forsyth to ask if Forsyth still had their saddlebags. Forsyth replied that he did.

Sessions asked, "Have you looked inside them lately?"

Forsyth was silent and Sessions could hear him dragging the impounded saddlebags toward him. A few moments later Forsyth called, "The money's here. Why do you ask?"

"I haven't seen either Jouett or Krebs for two days now. I was beginning to wonder if they had deserted. But if the money's here, then I guess they're still here too."

"Do you think they might try recovering their saddlebags?"

"I think they might."

"Then I'll give them to someone for safekeeping."

Sessions heard him call to Grover but he did not hear the instructions he gave Grover regarding the saddlebags.

Sundown was a blessed relief from the relentless heat of day. With it came a cooling breeze out of the east, a breeze that temporarily blew the stench of death away. And as night fell, the flies once more disappeared.

Surely, tomorrow, the relief force will arrive, Sessions thought. If it did not arrive tomorrow, then the scouts would be forced to the conclusion that neither Donovan and Pliley, nor Stillwell and Trudeau, had gotten through and reached the fort. A decision would then have to be made. It would be foolish for wounded and unwounded alike to stay here and die when some of the unwounded had a chance, however slim, of getting to the fort.

He couldn't help thinking that both Jouett and Krebs were among those unwounded in the fight. If the decision was made to send them to Fort Wallace, what could he do to prevent them from getting away from him?

He told himself that he'd shoot them both before he'd let them get away. But he wasn't sure he would, even if he could.

As soon as it was dark, he tried to rise. Jouett and Krebs had let two nights go by without trying to murder him and that was puzzling. He wanted to go to the upper end of the island and see if they still were there.

But he couldn't make it to his feet. He was too weak. He sank back and lay in his rifle pit listlessly, panting softly from the exertion of trying to get up. He realized for the first time how near the end was for him. His strength was almost gone.

Somewhere on the island a voice began to sing, a deep voice but one that trembled with weakness. "Rock of ages, cleft for me . . ."

The song died out and for a while the silence was complete. On the riverbank, a wolf began to howl. He was answered by several others. A man growled, "The bastards! They know they ain't got long to wait."

Forsyth said, "Tomorrow. The relief will come tomorrow. It *has* to come tomorrow."

Grover muttered, "It sure does, General, because tomorrow is just about the last day for us."

Sessions tried to force himself to stay awake. He held his revolver in his hand, hammer back, weapon and hand lying on his chest. But in spite of his efforts not to, he dozed frequently.

Jouett and Krebs did not come. And at last, dawn grayed the eastern sky and birds began to sing. The sun came up and the morning began to grow hot. Once more the men scanned the eastern plain anxiously, knowing that today had to be the day. If the relief did not come today, then something would have to be done to salvage at least some of the men who remained alive.

A man yelled suddenly, "Hey by God! I saw something move!"

Sessions pulled himself laboriously to the edge of his rifle pit. He stared at the hills lying to the east.

In a voice filled with awe, a man near him breathed, "By the God above us, it's an ambulance!"

And he saw it then, an Army ambulance rocking along behind two teams of mules, its canvas top flapping in the breeze.

Several of the men began to sob unashamedly. Others cheered hoarsely. All who were able splashed through the river and ran across the bare, dry sand to the riverbank. They stood there, staring at the approaching ambulance and at the trotting cavalrymen who followed it.

Forsyth himself had crawled to the edge of his rifle pit. He stared at the approaching troop of cavalry, tears spilling out of his eyes and running across his dirty, unshaven cheeks.

Sessions felt tears in his own eyes. Suddenly, behind him, he heard the scuff of a boot in sand.

And he knew that this was the opportunity for which

Jouett and Krebs had waited and planned. They had known that, when the relief arrived, every eye, every mind, every thought would be with the approaching force. They had known that all who were able would leave the island, would run to meet the approaching cavalry.

As indeed they were. And Jouett and Krebs had come.

In the excitement of seeing the approaching ambulance, Sessions had laid aside his gun. He reached for it now but Jouett dived for it. Sessions touched it at the same instant that Jouett's hand closed over it.

Jouett flung it away. In his other hand he had the same, stinking saddle blanket with which he had tried to suffocate Sessions once before. Neither he nor Krebs had made a sound. Sessions opened his mouth to yell at Forsyth but Jouett's hand clamped over his mouth and nose and immediately afterward his face was covered with the saddle blanket so that he couldn't yell.

He struggled, but he had no strength. Last night he had only tried to rise and he had failed. He was no match now for these two, neither of whom had even sustained a wound.

How long did a man take to die of suffocation, he asked himself. How long before he became unconscious for lack of air?

Not long, he knew. Not long and there was no use struggling. He would only waste his strength.

His hand fumbled for his gun even though he knew Jouett had flung it out of his reach. He clawed sand futilely with his fingers while the darkness descended like a curtain over his mind.

His hand was digging now, digging with its last spasmodic, dying twitch. And suddenly, surprisingly, his fingers touched something hard and cold.

Even though his mind was floating in darkness, he knew exactly what it was. It was one of the knives Jouett, Krebs, and Vega had flung at him several nights before. It had become buried by his movements in the rifle pit.

His hand closed on the handle, and his hand came up holding it. With all the remaining strength in his arm he drove it up and in toward the body of the man straddling him. He felt it enter flesh, felt it penetrate, felt the flesh it penetrated recoil away from it. For an instant the pressure on his face was less, the weight pinning him down released. He put the last strength he could summon into driving the knife home all the way to the hilt. It encountered bone, slipped on past and stopped.

Sessions had not the strength to draw it out. He heard, through the saddle blanket, a cry of agony. The weight on him was gone, but a foot stepped squarely on his belly and drove a painful gust of air from him.

He found the strength somewhere to pull the saddle blanket away from his face. The sun momentarily blinded him. Then he saw Jouett, both hands clutching his belly, staggering up out of the rifle pit. The knife hilt still protruded. As Sessions watched, he yanked it out and blood spilled sluggishly from the hole in his abdomen.

Krebs was nowhere to be seen. Sessions rolled, and clawed laboriously up the side of his rifle pit. He could see the men on the riverbank staring at the approaching troop of cavalry. And suddenly he saw Krebs.

The man was running across the dry-baked sand. He reached the riverbank.

None of the other men paid any attention to him. Sessions opened his mouth and croaked, "Stop him!"

No one seemed to hear except Forsyth in the next rifle pit. Forsyth's, "Stop that man!" reached the men on the bank but it came too late. Krebs had passed through the waiting line of men and was now running straight toward the approaching cavalry. Forsyth yelled, "Shoot him!" but either the command was not heard or it was not understood. Krebs continued to run and, once out of rifle range, turned away from the approaching rescuers.

Sessions swung his head to see where Jouett was. The man was now down on his knees. His face was gray with pain, his eyes narrowed, his lips compressed. He met Session's glance and Sessions stared back, his own eyes implacable and fiercely grim.

Jouett had killed, and tortured, and burned for the money in the impounded saddlebags. Now the money was lost to him and his life was rapidly leaking out. His eyes said he knew he was facing death but there was no forgiveness for him in Sessions' face. He watched coldly as Jouett swayed, and tottered, and finally fell forward to bury his face in the island's sand.

The Indians had killed one, and now he himself had killed a second one. He turned his head and followed Krebs' progress with his eyes.

The man was now nearly a quarter mile away, running, stumbling and falling, getting up and running once again. He kept looking back over his shoulder, face white, terror visible in every line of his body despite the distance between him and the other men.

Two cavalrymen detached themselves from the trotting, advancing column and headed after him. They loped their horses and the distance between them and the fugitive closed rapidly.

Krebs stopped and dropped to one knee. He raised the rifle he carried. Bluish powdersmoke billowed from its muzzle. The two cavalrymen dismounted and took cover behind their mounts.

Krebs continued firing until his rifle was empty. He flung it away from him and began firing with his revolver. When it was also empty, he turned to run again.

The two troopers, who had not once returned his fire, now mounted and cantered after him. Reaching him, they dismounted. They seemed to talk with him. Shortly thereafter one of them boosted him onto his own horse, then mounted behind the other trooper. Leading Krebs' horse, the two returned.

Sessions turned his head and saw Forsyth watching him. There was the faintest of smiles on Forsyth's face. He said, "He'll hang, Mr. Sessions. There is little doubt of that."

Sessions nodded wearily. It was over at last and the knowledge that it was seemed to drain off what little was left of his strength. Yet despite his weakness, there was a strong feeling of satisfaction in him. He thought of Sally and the boys and because he had caught their murderers he now could remember them with a little less pain than before.

From what seemed like a distance, he heard Forsyth's voice. "Mr. Grover, didn't you have an old novel in your saddlebags?"

"Yes sir."

"Well, bring it to me, man. Someone in this command has got to act a little unconcerned."

Colonel Carpenter, commanding a troop of the 10th Cavalry, splashed across the narrow river and climbed his horse out on the island near its lower end. He looked down at Colonel Forsyth, laying half buried by sand in his rifle pit. He saluted and said, "Lieutenant Colonel Carpenter, sir." He stared unbelievingly at the novel in Forsyth's hands. He grinned suddenly and swung down from his horse. He said softly, "Well, I'll be damned."

Lewis B. Patten wrote more than ninety Western novels in thirty years and three of them won Golden Spur Awards from the Western Writers of America and the author himself the Golden Saddleman Award. Indeed, this points up the most remarkable aspect of his work: not that there is so much of it, but that so much of it is so fine. Patten was born in Denver, Colorado, and served in the U.S. Navy from 1933-1937. He was educated at the University of Denver during the war years and became an auditor for the Colorado Department of Revenue during the 1940s. It was in this period that he began writing Western fiction that was from the beginning fresh and unique and revealed Patten's life-long concern with the sociological and psychological affects of group psychology on the frontier. He became a professional writer at the time of his first novel, *Massacre At White River* (1952). The dominant theme in much of his fiction is the notion of justice and its opposite, injustice. In his first novel it has to do with exploitation of the Ute Indians, but as he matured as a writer he explored this theme with significant and poignant detail in small towns throughout the early West. Crimes, such as rape or lynching, were often at the center of his stories. When the values embodied in these small towns are examined closely, they are found to be wanting. Conformity is always easier than taking a stand. Yet, in Patten's view of the American West, there is usually a man or a woman who refuses to conform. Among his finest titles, always a difficult choice, surely are *A Killing At Kiowa* (1972), *Ride A Crooked Trail* (1976), and his many fine contributions to Doubleday's Double D series, including *Villa's Rifles* (1977), *The Law At Cottonwood* (1978), and *Death Rides A Black Horse* (1978).

THE WORLD'S MOST CELEBRATED WESTERN WRITER

MAX BRAND

Author of more than 100 straight shootin', fast-action Westerns!

'Good and gripping...plenty of punch!"
—*New York Times*

THE RETURN OF THE RANCHER

Accused, tried, and convicted of robbery and murder, Jim Seton rotted in jail for five long years. Although the townspeople say he was lucky not to hang, that isn't how Jim see it. He doesn't take kindly to being railroaded—especially not by a bunch of yellowbellies who call themselves his friends.

Finally free, Seton figures the last place he should go is back to Claymore. He figures right. It doesn't take the gutless desperadoes long to come after him with bloody murder in their eyes and blazing Colts in their hands. But Jim is ready. He is an innocent man who's been sent to hell—and he is ready, willing, and able to return the favor.

___3574-X $3.99 US/$4.99 CAN